"In this tender
coming-of-age novel, McNeal
brings to life a place, an era, and
an amazing cast of strong, larger-than-life
characters. Heartrending, captivating,
and ultimately, triumphant." —**Cassandra King**,
New York Times bestselling author of *Moonrise*

"Deeply southern and evocative, McNeal's beautifully
written debut takes us back to a not-so-long-ago time when
we were learning to look through different eyes at the fabric
of our society, race, youth and family." —**Susan Crandall**,
author of *Whistling Past the Graveyard*

"A touching coming-of-age story that is sincere and poignant."
—*Booklist*

"An amazing novel in the vein of *The Secret Life of Bees*.
Laura McNeal's prose is poetic and hypnotic. Her characters are
so alive you wish you could walk down the magnolia-lined streets
of New Orleans with them....Definitely worth reading."
—**Historical Novel Society**

"*Dollbaby* is an absolutely spellbinding debut that
is written with intelligence, warmth, humor and reverie;
though comparisons to *The Help* and *The Secret Life of Bees*
are inevitable, Laura Lane McNeal has captured
something entirely her own. A love letter to the
indomitable spirit of New Orleans, *Dollbaby*
marks the celebratory arrival of an
unforgettable new voice in fiction."
—*The Hartford Examiner*

Praise for *Dollbaby*

"McNeal's *Dollbaby* is such an impressive debut—a powerful roux of family drama, long-simmering secrets and resentments, and ultimately, forgiveness and redemption. Deeply evocative, with memorable characters, *Dollbaby* belongs on the keeper shelf along with *The Help* and *The Secret Life of Bees*."
—Mary Kay Andrews, *New York Times* bestselling author of *Beach Town*

"Brilliantly captures New Orleans during the civil rights era . . . A deeply personal tale about growing up and searching for family as well as a provocative exploration of race and kinship."
—Walter Isaacson, *New York Times* bestselling author of *Steve Jobs*

"Don't be surprised if you see McNeal's book in a lot of beach totes along the Gulf Coast this summer."   —*New Orleans Times-Picayune*

"A vivid portrayal of postwar New Orleans, lush and evocative in its descriptions. Fans of Pat Conroy and Sue Monk Kidd will enjoy this new Southern talent."   —*Library Journal* (starred review)

"In the vein of *Saving CeeCee Honeycutt* and *The Help*, McNeal's touching coming-of-age tale brings to life civil rights–era New Orleans. . . . A lovely read."   —*Kirkus Reviews*

"McNeal's witty prose and expertise on all things New Orleans will enrapture readers of *The Help* and *Divine Secrets of the Ya Ya Sisterhood*."
—*BookPage*

"Beautifully rendered and perfectly paced, *Dollbaby* is one novel this year not to be missed, with just the right amount of mystery mixed with coming-of-age drama."   —*Book Reporter*

"When someone asks you for a great book . . . every now and then there's a book you tell everyone to read, because it is that good. *Dollbaby* is that book."   —*Durham Herald-Sun*

Dollbaby

Laura Lane McNeal

Penguin Books

PENGUIN BOOKS
Published by the Penguin Group
Penguin Group (USA) LLC
375 Hudson Street
New York, New York 10014

USA | Canada | UK | Ireland | Australia | New Zealand | India | South Africa | China
penguin.com
A Penguin Random House Company

First published in the United States of America by Viking Penguin,
a member of Penguin Group (USA) LLC, 2014
Published in Penguin Books 2015

A Pamela Dorman / Penguin Book

THE LIBRARY OF CONGRESS HAS CATALOGED THE HARDCOVER EDITION AS FOLLOWS:
McNeal, Laura Lane.
Dollbaby : a novel / Laura Lane McNeal.
pages cm
ISBN 978-0-670-01473-6 (hc.)
ISBN 978-0-14-312749-9 (pbk.)
1. Families—Fiction. 2. Redemption—Fiction. 3. New Orleans (La.)—History—20th century—
Fiction. 4. Louisiana—Race relations—Fiction. I. Title.
PS3613.C585937D65 2014
813'.6—dc23 2013048523

Printed in the United States of America
1 3 5 7 9 10 8 6 4 2

Designed by Nancy Resnick
Map copyright © 2014 by Virginia Norey

In loving memory of Fannie and Louise,
the grandmothers who shaped my life
in more ways than they could ever have imagined

Author's Note

The sit-in at Woolworth's on July 1, 1964, is fictitious, although several sit-ins had occurred at this location previously. The mood surrounding the impending passage of the Civil Rights Act was contentious, and while most of the civil-rights protests had taken the form of picketing businesses that wouldn't comply with desegregation, a few days prior to July 1, a young black man was beaten up at the state capitol building in Baton Rouge for sitting at the cafeteria lunch counter. The black man was carted off to jail for his actions; the white perpetrators were never charged. Based on this scenario, I felt a final sit-in on Canal Street would have been feasible.

The band The Moody Blues was formed in 1964 but did not become popular in the United States until the following year.

New Orleans sits between two large bends in the Mississippi river that form a large U that virtually surrounds the city on three sides, which is the reason it's often referred to as The Crescent City. The city conforms to these bends and curves, creating fan-shaped neighborhoods that often converge. Using compass points to indicate directions are confusing, so locals instead use the river as the main point of reference: Lakeside (away from the river toward Lake Pontchartrain to the north), Riverside (toward the river), Uptown (upriver from

Downtown, even though it lies a bit south due to the bend in the river) and Downtown (meaning downriver).

Sadly, many of the neighborhood markets and pharmacies mentioned in the novel no longer exist, falling victim to a new concept called the supermarket. A few notable exceptions include Plum Street Snowballs, the Prytania Theatre, as well as the venerable Antoine's Restaurant. The iconic Butterfly, which sat at the tip of Riverview Park overlooking the Mississippi, was hit by a barge one foggy morning in the 1980s and had to be bulldozed, although the park itself is still referred to as "The Fly" by the locals. Madame Doussan's moved to Royal Street and is now called Bourbon French Parfums. Fannie's house on Prytania is fictional, although you will find several examples of Queen Anne Victorians in the Uptown area. Likewise, Our Lady of the Celestial Realm Catholic School for Girls, the Starlight Jazz Club on Bourbon Street, the Ebony Lounge, and the True Love Baptist Church are fictional, although entities similar to the ones I describe in the novel exist throughout the city.

Acknowledgments

A special thanks to literary agents Marly Rusoff and Michael Radulescu for recognizing the potential in my writing, for taking me on, and for championing me along the way. For your continued support and dedication, I thank you from the bottom of my heart. To Clare Ferraro and Kathryn Court who have allowed me to become a member of the Viking/Penguin group, an honor I will always cherish. To my brilliant editor Pamela Dorman, whose insight and wisdom helped shape the novel, I am deeply grateful and thrilled to be published by Pamela Dorman Books. Thank you, Kiki Koroshetz, for your unwavering dedication to the project and for answering my every little question, and to Beena Kamlani, whose steadfast demeanor, lovely voice, and quiet perseverance helped polish and hone the final story. Thanks also to Carolyn Coleburn, Maureen Donnelly, Kristen Matzen, Patrick Nolan, and the dynamic Viking/Penguin marketing and sales force, including Nancy Sheppard, John Fagan, Dick Heffernan, and Norman Lidofsky for warmly embracing *Dollbaby* and me. To Roseanne Serra and Nancy Resnick for the beautiful cover and design of the book, and for all the wonderful people who took me under their wings at SIBA—Diana Van Vleck, Dave Kliegman, Kasey Pfaff, Mike McGroder, Diane Kierpa, and Michelle Malonzo.

I would also like to thank James Nolan and the members of his writing workshop who taught me not only the craft of fiction but how to laugh at myself, and in particular Aneela Shuja, whose friendship was key in helping me believe in myself. And to my family—Rob, Beattie, Will, Lou, Charlie, and Carol—who put up with me and supported me from the beginning, I love you all.

And to the people of New Orleans, without whom there never would have been a story.

Dollbaby

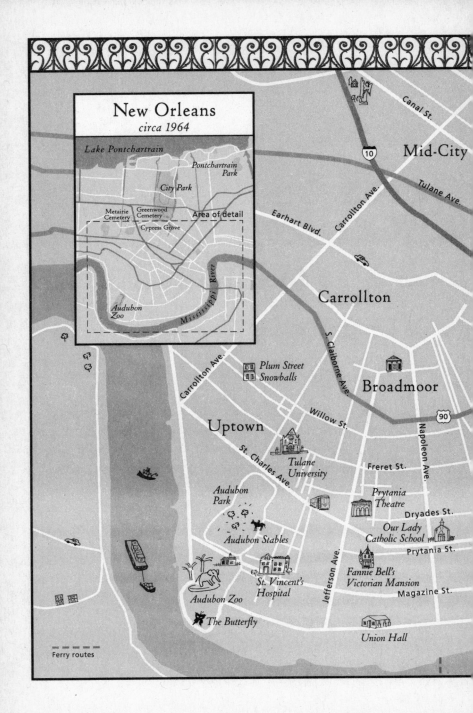

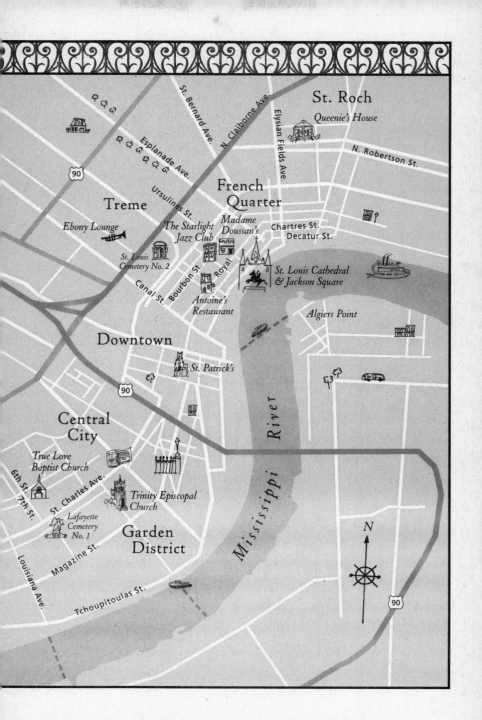

Part One

1964

Chapter One

There are times you wish you could change things, take things back, pretend they never existed. This was one of those times, Ibby Bell was thinking as she stared bug-eyed out the car window. Amid the double-galleried homes and brightly painted cottages on Prytania Street, there was one house that didn't belong.

"Ibby?" Her mother turned down the radio and began drumming her fingers on the steering wheel.

Ibby ignored her, letting her mother's words mingle with the buzz of the air conditioning and the drone of the idling car engine as she craned her neck, trying to get a better look at the house that was stubbornly obscured by the sprawling branches of a giant oak tree and the glare of the midmorning sun. She cupped her hands over her eyes and glanced up to find a weathervane shaped like a racehorse jutting high above the tallest branches of the tree. It was flapping to and fro in the tepid air, unable to quite make the total spin around the rusted stake, giving the poor horse the appearance of being tethered there against its will.

I know that feeling, Ibby thought.

The weathervane was perched atop a long spire attached to a cupola. Ibby's eyes traveled to the second-floor balcony, then down to the front porch, where a pair of rocking chairs and a porch swing swayed gently beside mahogany doors inlaid with glass. Surrounded on all sides by a low iron fence, the house looked like an animal that had outgrown its cage.

Her mother had described it as a Queen Anne Victorian monstrosity that should have been bulldozed years ago. Ibby now understood what she meant. The old mansion was suffering from years of neglect. A thick layer of dirt muddied the blue paint, windows were boarded up, and the front yard was so overgrown with wild azaleas and unruly boxwoods that Ibby could barely make out the brick walkway that led up to the house.

"Liberty, are you listening to me?"

It was the way Vidrine Bell said Ibby's real name, the way she said *Li-bar-tee* with a clear Southern drawl that she usually went to great lengths to hide, that got her attention.

Vidrine's face was glistening with sweat despite the air conditioning tousling her well-lacquered hair. She patted the side of her mouth with her finger, trying to salvage the orange lipstick that was seeping into the creases and filling the car with the smell of melted wax.

"Damn humidity," Vidrine huffed. "No one should have to live in a place hot enough to fry an egg on the sidewalk."

The heat, her mother claimed, was one of the reasons she and Ibby's father had moved away from New Orleans just after they married. Far, far away. To a little town called Olympia, in the state of Washington. Where no one had a Southern accent. Except, on occasion, the Bell family.

"Whatever you do, Liberty Bell, don't forget this." Vidrine patted the double-handled brass urn sitting like a sentinel between them on the front seat. Her mouth curled up at the edges. "Be sure and tell your grandmother it's a present from me."

Ibby glanced down at the urn her mother was pushing her way. A week ago that urn didn't exist. Now she was being told to give it to a grandmother she'd never met. Ibby turned and looked at the house again. She didn't know which was worse, the sneer on her mother's face, or the thought of having to go into that big ugly house to meet her grandmother for the first time.

She eyed her mother, wondering why no one had bothered to mention that she even *had* a grandmother until a few months ago. She'd learned about it by chance, when on a clear day in March, as her father went to pay for ice cream at the school fair, a faded photograph fell from his wallet and floated wearily to the ground. Ibby picked it up and studied the stone-faced woman in the picture for a moment before her daddy took it from her.

"Who is that?" Ibby asked.

"Oh, that's your grandmother," he said, hastily stuffing the photo back into his wallet in a way that made it clear that he didn't want to talk about it anymore.

Later that week, while she and Vidrine were doing the dishes, Ibby got up enough gumption to ask her mother about the woman in the photograph. Vidrine glared at her with those big round eyes that looked like cue balls and threw the dish towel to the ground, slammed her fist on the counter, then launched into a lengthy tirade that made it clear that Frances Hadley Bell, otherwise known as Fannie, was the other reason they'd moved away from New Orleans right after she and Graham Bell were married.

And now here Ibby was, about to be dropped off at this woman's house without any fanfare, and her mother acting as if it were no big deal.

"Why are you leaving me here? Can't I come with you?" Ibby pleaded.

Her mother fell back against the seat, exasperated. "Now, Ibby, we've been through this a thousand times. Now that your father has passed away, I need some time away . . . to think."

"Why won't you tell me where you're going?"

"That's something you just don't need to know," Vidrine snapped.

"How long will you be gone?"

Vidrine frowned. "A few days. Maybe a week. It's hard to tell. Your grandmother was kind enough to offer to keep you until I figure this whole thing out."

Ibby's ears perked up. *Kind* was not one of the words her mother had used to describe Fannie Bell.

In the background, she could hear the radio.

"This is WTIX Radio New Orleans," the announcer said. "Up next, The Moody Blues . . ."

"Turn that up—that was one of Daddy's favorite new bands," Ibby said.

Vidrine turned off the radio. "Now go on. She won't bite." She poked Ibby in the ribs, causing the brass urn to teeter and fall over on the seat.

Ibby straightened it back up, letting her fingers linger on the cool brass handle. She swallowed hard, wondering why her mother was being so secretive. Now that her father was gone, she got the feeling that what her mother *really* wanted was to get away from *her.*

Vidrine leaned over and said in a soft voice, "Now listen, honey, I know it's hard to understand why God takes some people from this earth before their time. But he took your daddy in a silly bicycle accident. And now . . . well, we just have to move on somehow."

Ibby gave her mother a sideways glance. *God* was a word her mother had never uttered until her father died, and being left with someone she'd never met for an indefinite period of time wasn't exactly Ibby's idea of moving on. But she was just shy of twelve years old, and no one had bothered to ask her opinion on the matter.

She let her hand fall from the urn. "Aren't you at least going to come in with me?" Ibby asked.

Vidrine crossed her arms. "Liberty Alice Bell, quit your whining and get on out of this car right now. I've got to go."

"But Mom—"

"Now remember what I told you. Be a good girl. Don't give your grandmother any trouble. And one more thing." Her mother leaned in closer and wagged a finger. "Try not to pick up any of those awful expressions like *y'all* or *ain't*. It's just not ladylike. Understand me?"

Before Ibby could answer, Vidrine reached over, opened the door, and pushed her out of the car.

Chapter Two

"L awd," Doll declared as she scratched the top of her head with a long red fingernail and held back the lace curtains in the front window with the other hand.

She'd expected to see the milkman, or the egg man, or maybe even the fish man, but the sight of a young girl standing on the sidewalk in front of the house took her by surprise. She let the curtains fall back into place, wondering what she should do.

"Girl, what you going on about?" came her mother's voice behind her.

Doll turned to find Queenie standing in the doorway between the kitchen and the dining room, holding the swinging door open with her foot as she heaved her huge bosom up with her forearms.

"She here, Mama," Doll said as she brushed off her uniform with a nervous sweep of her hand.

"Who's here?" Queenie asked.

"Miss Fannie's grandbaby," Doll replied in a way that sounded as if she didn't believe it herself.

Queenie stormed headfirst through the dining room to where Doll was standing. "What day is it?"

"Ironing day, Mama."

Queenie shook her head. "No—the date, baby. What's today's date?"

"July fourth is this Saturday, so it must be coming up on the first of July. Why you want to know?"

Queenie huffed, "She can't be here. Weren't expecting her until tomorrow."

"Well, she's here, bright as day," Doll said as a white Ford Galaxie sped off down the street.

"Miss Fannie—she gone have a fit!" Queenie stomped her foot.

Doll and Queenie stared out the window in a moment of silent bewilderment as they examined the young girl standing just outside the gate dressed in shorts, a striped T-shirt, and red sneakers, gazing at the house with a pained expression on her face.

Queenie mashed up her mouth. "Her mama don't even know how to dress her proper for a plane ride."

"How you know, Mama? You ain't never been on a plane."

Queenie put her hands on her hips. "On account I read Miss Fannie's LIFE magazines. I know how them other folks live." Then she turned and peered out the window again. "What's she got in her hand?"

Doll leaned in to get a better look. "Looks like some kind of trophy. But bless her heart, she holding on to it for dear life."

"Strange looking," Queenie said.

"The girl?" Doll asked.

"No, baby." Queenie slapped Doll's arm. "That thing in her hand."

"She got the same haircut as Miss Fannie," Doll added.

"Sure enough." Queenie gazed out the window. "Like Captain Kangaroo."

Doll shook her head. "If everything else be like Miss Fannie, we gone have ourselves a heap of trouble."

Queenie wagged a finger. "Now, don't you go judging that poor child just yet." Then she mumbled under her breath, "God Almighty, pray for a miracle."

"I believe that little girl gone stand there all day, lessen we go out and fetch her," Doll went on.

"Well, what you doing, just standing there like you is waiting for a bus? Go on out and get her!"

Doll would have done just about anything rather than deal with the little problem standing by the front gate. There'd been no overnight visitors to the house on Prytania Street for more than twelve years, not since Miss Fannie's son, Graham, ran off with Miss Vidrine Crump from Dry Prong, Mississippi. Doll felt sure that bringing this little girl into the house was only going to stir things up. *Don't need no more trouble, got enough here already,* Doll was thinking.

"You scared of a little girl can't weigh more than ninety pounds?" Queenie squawked.

"No, Mama, I scared of what Miss Fannie gone do when she finds out her grandbaby already here. I overheard what Miss Vidrine say on the phone when she called to say Mr. Graham had passed. Miss Vidrine, she didn't exactly *ask* Miss Fannie if it be all right for her daughter to come visit. She *told* Miss Fannie that she'd be dropping her off, without knowing when she'd be back to fetch her. Never seen such a look on Miss Fannie's face, like she don't know what to say. And you know Miss Fannie." Doll shook her head. "She always knows what to say."

Queenie crossed her arms and rocked back onto her heels. "You listen here. We ain't got no choice. She's here, and we got to deal with it. Miss Fannie ain't in a good humor this morning. Be best if I break the news to her. You go and bring the little missy inside."

"What's all that fussing about out there?" Fannie's voice ripped through the air.

Doll and Queenie gave each other a knowing glance. It wasn't going to be an ordinary day in the Bell household.

Then again, as Doll knew all too well, no day in the Bell household was ever ordinary.

Chapter Three

Ibby wasn't sure what to make of the tall slender woman standing on the porch by the front door with her hair piled high on her head in a beehive hairdo. Her big eyes were all aflutter, and she was swinging her hips from side to side as she talked. Ibby couldn't make out a word the woman was saying, but one thing she did know for sure. There was something peculiar about her.

She came down from the porch and started walking toward Ibby, waving her hand. "Come on now."

The woman made her way to the gate and opened it, then bent over until she was eye level with Ibby. That's when Ibby noticed she had one eye as dark as obsidian, and another as light as a washed-out sky, a combination that made her pretty face seem off-balance somehow. Ibby stared unabashedly. The woman didn't seem to notice, or if she did, she didn't seem to mind.

"You Miss Fannie's granddaughter?" The woman blinked several times, then smiled a big smile.

Ibby kept staring, not quite sure what to make of her.

"Girl, you deaf? What you got there?" she asked.

The woman tugged at the urn in Ibby's arms. Ibby took a step back and shook her head. Her mother had given her strict instructions to hand the urn over to her grandmother and not some fast-talking woman waving her arms all over the place.

"Okay then." The woman tapped her foot as if she were thinking. "You hungry?"

Ibby had barely eaten in over a week, not since her daddy died. Suddenly, she felt as if fire ants were trying to eat their way out of her stomach.

The cockeyed woman stood up. "Well, come on."

Before Ibby knew it, she'd grabbed her hand and was pulling her along as if she were a small child. Ibby tried to yank her hand away, but the woman held on tight. The warmth of her hand somehow made Ibby feel at ease. Ibby let go a smile without really meaning to.

"Well, that's what I like to see," the woman said as they picked their way past the gnarly branches of the boxwoods and walked up the brick walkway toward the house. "My name's Dollbaby, by the way. But you can call me Doll."

Ibby tried to hide the expression on her face at the funny-sounding name.

"Got a daughter about your age. Call her Birdelia," Doll went on.

Another name Ibby had never heard before.

Doll stopped short. "You got a birthday coming up, from what Miss Fannie tells me. That right?"

Ibby drew her hand away. Birthdays weren't celebrated in the Bell household. No use making a fuss over something everybody has, Vidrine reminded Ibby every year on her birthday.

"How old you gonna be?"

"Twelve."

"I knew it!"

Ibby looked up, startled.

"I knew you could talk." Doll took Ibby by the shoulders and guided her up the front steps onto the porch.

When they got just inside the front door, Doll started up the wide staircase with a heavily carved banister. Ibby held back, her attention drawn to the front parlor, where dark Victorian furniture and red velvet curtains made the room feel heavy despite the soaring fourteen-foot ceiling. There was an empty ashtray on the marble-topped coffee table. Ibby noticed the house smelled of stale smoke.

Pocket doors led to a second parlor where a wood-consoled television left just enough room for a lumpy, moth-eaten couch. Just beyond that, a crystal chandelier hovered over a walnut table in the dining room, where a massive china cabinet on the far wall was brimming with silver serving pieces. Ibby got a weird feeling about this fusty old house that looked as if time had stopped a century ago.

"Well, what you waiting on? Christmas?" Doll tapped her fingers on the banister impatiently.

When Ibby didn't budge, Doll came back down the stairs and motioned for her to hand over the urn.

Ibby reluctantly gave it to her.

"Why you keep looking at me like that? Don't they have maids where you come from?" Doll took the urn from Ibby and placed it on the hall table next to a vase filled with wilted lilies.

Ibby scrunched up her shoulders, wondering how Doll seemed to know what she was thinking. "We never had one."

Doll cocked her head to one side. "Who clean the house then?"

"Nobody," Ibby replied.

"Nobody? That something." Doll twisted her mouth to one side. "Well, let me tell you how it is around here. I'm the keeper of the house. I do the cleaning, the tidying up, and a bit of sewing here and there. My mama, Queenie, she do all the cooking, a little ironing, and is the keeper of the peace, which you gone find is a mighty big job around this here house. You understand?"

Ibby looked up at Doll, not really understanding at all.

"What now?" Doll scratched her scalp with the tip of her red fingernail. "Why you keep looking at me like I got two heads?"

Ibby blinked a few times, but no words would come out.

"Don't they have colored folks where you come from?" Doll finally asked.

Ibby shook her head. "I never talked to one before."

Doll rolled her eyes. " 'Colored folks.' You can say it. That's what we are. And you better get used to it on account there's lots of us colored folks down here in New Orleans. Now we got that out of the way, I'll show you your room, then we can come down and get you introduced to your grandmother right proper and all." She started up the stairs and spoke to Ibby over her shoulder. "Hope that ain't all you got to wear, Miss Ibby. Might want to change into something more suitable to meet your grandmother."

Ibby followed Doll up the stairs, wondering what was wrong with her T-shirt and shorts.

The second floor opened onto a spacious hallway lit by two bronze chandeliers. At the far end, a mosaic of sunlight sprinkled onto the Oriental carpet through a stained-glass window. Ibby went over and touched the window lightly with her fingers, following the design of the large white flowers.

"They got them stained-glass windows in all these old houses around here," Doll explained. "That one there is of magnolias. Not my favorite. They kind of smell like sour laundry to me."

As Ibby backed away, her arm knocked against a stone object perched upon a pedestal in front of the window.

Doll hurried over. "Be careful, child." She put her hand on top of the sculpture to steady it. "This here is a bust of Miss Fannie. Your grandfather, Mr. Norwood, he gave it to her as a wedding present, but Miss Fannie never liked it much. That's why it's up here, 'cause she don't want nobody to see it."

The perfectly chiseled features left no indication whether the bust was of a man or a woman. The eyes had no pupils and were flat but nonetheless gave Ibby the feeling she was being watched.

"The person made that thing, he sure knew your grandmother.

You'll see what I mean when you meet her." Doll chuckled. "You got plenty of time to poke around up here later. Don't want to keep Miss Fannie waiting." Doll set her foot squarely on a smaller set of stairs nestled in the corner of the hall near the bust.

Ibby pointed to the four doors on the second floor. "Is one of these rooms for me?"

"No, baby. This floor's all booked up, especially now that your daddy's passed. Now follow me."

They started up another set of stairs that got narrower and steeper as they went along. "I've never been in a house with a third floor," Ibby remarked.

"Used to be the servants' quarters, back in the day, when the house was built," Doll said over her shoulder.

The third floor was tiny, consisting of a boxy hallway with one door, whose rusted hinges seemed reluctant to open no matter how hard Doll tugged. Doll kicked the door with the bottom of her foot. It finally opened with a creak to reveal a room just large enough for two twin beds and a diminutive chest of drawers. Doll switched on the overhead light, a single bulb hanging from the ceiling that sprayed a paltry glow on the faded yellow wallpaper peeling away from the wall in places.

"Didn't expect you until tomorrow. Hadn't had a chance to tidy up yet. Some animal been up here leaving droppings all over the floor. Never did find it. You run across it, you be sure and let me know." Doll pointed toward a sliver of a door at the far end of the room. "That there's the toilet. It only got a shower. You want to take a bath, you come down to the second floor and use the one in my sewing room. And there ain't no closet. You can hang your clothes there." She pointed to a wire suspended from the ceiling like a U.

Ibby looked disappointed.

"What?" Doll put her hands on her hips.

"Mama didn't let me bring my radio. I was hoping the room might have a radio but I don't see one."

"You like music? Well, you come to the right place. New Orleans is known for good music. I'll see what we can do about getting you a radio. Now then, Miss Ibby, you got a dress you can put on?"

Ibby made a face. She'd worn a dress only once in her life, and that was to a wedding a few years back.

"I take it that be a no." Doll put her hand up to her face and tapped her cheek with her finger. "You bring anything with you, like a suitcase, for instance?"

"Oh no!" Ibby's knees almost gave way. She'd been concentrating so hard on bringing the urn that she'd forgotten her suitcase. "It must still be in the car," she said in a small voice.

"Not to worry." Doll put a hand on her shoulder.

Ibby gave her a funny look. Doll seemed to be reading her mind again. At this point, she wasn't sure if that was a good thing.

"You make yourself at home. I'll be right back."

She turned and bounded down the stairs, leaving Ibby alone in the room with a decrepit oscillating fan on the dresser that was making noises like a jet engine. She sat down on the bed and began to twiddle a strand of hair with her finger, the way she did when she was nervous. She pulled aside the faded gingham curtains on the window, only to find it loosely boarded up. She let the curtains fall back, noticing the thick layer of dust on the bedside table. She ran her finger across it, leaving a thin line. Then, with one clean swoop of her hands, she wiped the table clean, sending dust scattering into the air.

Ibby leaned over and put her head on the pillow that had lost most of its stuffing and watched the dust particles sifting sideways about the room. If Doll hadn't brought up her birthday a few minutes ago, she might have completely forgotten about it. Her daddy always made her birthday special. He'd come into her room in the wee hours of the morning to sneak a homemade birthday card under her pillow. She'd pretend to be asleep as he kissed her on the cheek, the soapy smell of his Burma-Shave tickling her nose. She scrunched her eyes tight. There would be no more birthdays with her daddy. When she pulled her knees to her chest, she felt her heart beating. Why had she been relegated to this tiny room in the attic when there were plenty of bedrooms on the second floor? She got the feeling that perhaps her grandmother didn't want her here.

The next thing she knew, Doll was shaking her awake.

"You must be tuckered out from your trip. Gone five minutes, and you fall asleep. Here, slip this dress on." Doll held out a perfectly starched blue cotton dress with a Peter Pan collar and puffy banded short sleeves, then shook her head. "Can't do anything about them red sneakers you got on."

"That's a baby dress," Ibby protested. "I'm not putting that on."

"You a debutante or something? It'll have to do until I can make you something more to your liking."

"Whose dress is it anyway?"

"That don't matter none," Doll said. "Now put it on and be done with it."

Ibby slipped the dress over her head. It was so starched, it puffed out like an open umbrella. Ibby felt silly.

Doll stood back and crossed her arms. "What's wrong, baby?"

"I feel like Dorothy in *The Wizard of Oz*," Ibby said, pointing down at her red sneakers. "I hate Dorothy."

"Now listen here. From the way I see it, that ain't such a bad thing. Dorothy got what she wanted in the end, didn't she?" Doll gave an impatient tap of her foot. "Your grandmother is waiting. And one thing you never want to do is keep Miss Fannie waiting."

Ibby put her hands on her hips and mashed her lips together. She didn't want to go anywhere looking like this.

Doll said in a low voice, "Calm yourself. She ain't gone bite."

She ain't gone bite. It was the second time in an hour Ibby had heard that, first from her mother, and now from Doll. Ibby reluctantly started toward the door.

Doll caught Ibby by the arm. "It'll be all right, just you wait and see."

Ibby didn't believe a word of it.

And by the way Doll was grinning, Ibby could tell Doll didn't believe a word of it either.

Chapter Four

When they got to the bottom of the stairs, Ibby heard voices coming from the dining room.

Doll put her arm out for Ibby to stop. "Wait one second, child. Miss Fannie and Queenie having some words."

Ibby could just make out an old heavyset black woman standing beside a disheveled lady in a faded housedress seated at the head of the dining room table.

"Is that your mama?" Ibby asked Doll.

Doll put her finger up to her mouth. "Yes. That's Queenie," she whispered. "Don't want them to know we standing here just yet."

"Miss Fannie, don't you remember?" Queenie was saying. "You been expecting her. Her name's Liberty Alice."

"I know my own granddaughter's name," Fannie sighed. "That dimwit of a woman that married my son—oh, what's the damn woman's name . . ."

"Vidrine," Queenie said.

"Vidrine. How could I forget? She named her Liberty Bell because she was born on the Fourth of July. What kind of stupid person does that?"

"Someone with a name like Vidrine, that's who," Queenie said, trying to make light of the situation. "Now calm down. Could be worse."

"How so?" Fannie asked.

"Miss Vidrine, she could of named the child after herself. Then we'd have another little Vidrine running around this here house. Now, wouldn't that be something?"

Fannie waved her hand. "Perish the thought."

"She's coming down right now to meet you," Queenie said.

"Who?"

"Your granddaughter, that's who."

"What?" Fannie sat up. "She's here?"

"That's what I been trying to tell you, Miss Fannie. Miss Vidrine, she done dropped her off not an hour ago."

With that, Doll nudged Ibby ahead of her into the dining room.

"I do believe she look just like you, Miss Fannie," Queenie rattled on. "And lookey there. She even got that little mole on the side of her cheek, same as you."

"That's a beauty mark," Fannie snapped. "Not a mole."

Ibby looked around, then ran out into the hall as Fannie stared after her, flabbergasted.

Queenie piped up. "Not five minutes, you done scared that child half to death, Miss Fannie."

"Ain't that something," Doll marveled. "Second time this week, Miss Fannie gone speechless."

❧❧❧

Ibby caught her reflection in the gold-leaf mirror above the marble fireplace, keenly aware of three sets of eyes watching her when she came back into the room carrying the urn she'd retrieved from the hall table.

"Come here, child." Fannie beckoned. "I didn't mean to scare you."

Fannie pulled Ibby so close, their noses almost touched. Ibby had no choice but to stare straight back into Fannie's face. Doll had been right. The artist who made the bust on the upstairs landing had captured the essence of this strange woman—her hard gray-blue eyes and silvery hair, her long Roman nose, the thin lips set in one straight line.

"Yep, she the spitting image of you, Miss Fannie. Sure is," Queenie said.

As far as Ibby was concerned, the only thing she remotely had in common with this woman was their pageboy hairdo, a cut Vidrine had given Ibby after she'd seen a picture of Jackie Kennedy's daughter in a fashion magazine. Ibby reached up and tucked her hair behind her ears, the way she used to do when it was long. It fell back into her face.

"What do they call you, young lady?" Fannie sat back and took a long drag from her cigarette.

Ibby put the urn on the dining room table, then pulled out her dress and curtsied. "Liberty Alice Bell, ma'am."

"I know your name, for God's sake, but what do you want me to *call* you? Certainly not Liberty Bell. I'd feel like I'd have to say 'ding-dong' every time I said your name."

Ibby scrunched up her shoulders, not knowing how to answer.

"Speak up, or I'll make up a name. How about—"

"She say her name's Ibby," Doll piped up.

"Ibby? What kind of name is that?" Fannie snorted.

Ibby kicked the ground with her tennis shoe. "When I was little, I couldn't say Liberty. It came out sounding like Ibby."

"What she gone call you, Miss Fannie? Grandma? Mee-maw? Too-tie?" Queenie chuckled. "How about Granny Fannie? That one got a certain ring to it."

Fannie waved her hand dismissively. "Just plain Fannie will do." She leaned in toward Ibby. "Now tell me, dear, what happened to my boy Graham?"

Ibby glanced down at her red sneakers, the same shoes she'd had on the day it happened. She felt her chest tighten.

Queenie gave her a reassuring smile. "Take your time, child."

It had been less than two weeks since the accident. Ibby had just sort of wandered around in a quiet daze since that day, secretly harboring the idea that if she never spoke of it, maybe the whole thing would just go away and her daddy would come back and say, "Morning, pumpkin," like he always did and they would go on with their lives as if nothing had happened. Ibby wasn't sure she was ready to talk about it, but Fannie's eyes were set on her like a dog set to attack. It took another moment before she felt the courage to speak. Her words came out haltingly at first.

"Every Saturday morning . . . Daddy . . . he would take me for a bike ride down the hill and over to the bakery to get a doughnut. It was our little secret. Mama doesn't like . . . for me to eat sweets. She would have killed Daddy if she'd known." Ibby clamped her hand to her mouth, realizing her choice of words.

"It's all right, child. Go on," Fannie said.

"When we started back, it was drizzling. The road was slippery. Daddy turned his head to tell me to hurry up and bumped into one of the boulders on the side of the road. His bike slid out from under him. When I pedaled over, there was blood all over the side of his head." Ibby stopped for a moment. It was all coming back to her now.

"Then what happened?" Fannie asked.

Ibby took in a deep breath. "Daddy managed to get up, so we rode our bikes back up the hill to the house. Mama was mad when she saw Daddy's face."

"Did you call a doctor?" Fannie asked.

Ibby shook her head. "Mama wanted to, but Daddy said no, he was fine."

"Should of called a doctor," Queenie said.

"Let her speak," Fannie said.

"Daddy said he wasn't feeling well, so he went to lie down. When I went to check on him later, he was asleep." Ibby looked up. "He never woke up. They came and got him the next morning, and I never saw him again."

"Bless her heart," Queenie said.

"Weren't your fault," Doll said.

Ibby glanced over her shoulder at Doll. She didn't tell them the rest of the story—that her mother had pointed a finger at her the next morning and told her it was indeed her fault, that if they hadn't been sneaking around behind her back for a stupid doughnut, none of it would have ever happened.

Fannie pursed her lips. "Was there a funeral?"

"No, ma'am."

Fannie slammed her fist down on the chair. "Then we need to bring Graham back here and give him a proper burial."

"Daddy *is* here, Grandma Fannie."

"What do you mean, he *is* here? Where?"

Ibby tilted her head toward the double-handled brass urn. "My mama told me to make sure and give him to you."

There were three succinct gasps before Fannie grabbed her chest and her head plunked facedown onto the table.

"Lawd, now you done it," Doll said as she came over and lifted Fannie's head.

Fannie's eyes were open but unseeing. Ghastly. Dead. Empty. Just like the eyes on the bust on the upstairs landing.

Doll motioned for Queenie to help her get Fannie out of the chair. Queenie placed Fannie's arm around Doll's neck, and Doll lifted her up. As they carried her down the hall toward the bedroom at the back of the house, Ibby remembered the sneer on Vidrine's face when she'd reminded Ibby to give Fannie the urn.

Then it dawned on Ibby.

This is exactly the way Vidrine had planned for it to turn out all along.

Chapter Five

Doll threw back the covers and settled Fannie onto the four-poster canopied bed. Fannie's eyes were closed, her chest rising in shallow breaths. Doll placed the back of her hand on Fannie's forehead. It was cold and clammy.

Doll reached up and tugged on the cord to the ceiling fan. The fan began to whir over the canopy, ruffling some papers on the rolltop desk across the room. Doll tugged on the cord once more to slow it down, then went into the bathroom and ran a washcloth under the faucet in the sink. As she was wringing it out, she heard Fannie groan.

"Be right there, Miss Fannie," Doll said, giving the cloth a final twist.

When she came back into the room, Fannie's eyes were open, and she was staring straight up at the canopy above her head.

"Why, after all these years, have I never noticed that the fabric on the canopy has a little pattern to it? I thought it was just plain blue damask. Now I see it has a tiny waffle pattern."

Doll placed the washcloth on Fannie's forehead and glanced up at the canopy. "Could be you look at something for so long, you see what you want to see, and not what's really there."

Fannie grabbed Doll's hand and squeezed it. "You trying to tell me something?"

"No, Miss Fannie, just telling it the way I see it," Doll said flatly.

"Maybe I should look more closely at the things around me."

Doll nudged her hand away. "Maybe you should."

Fannie peeled the washcloth away from her face and held it up for Doll. "I don't need this anymore."

Doll took it from her. "Whatever you say, Miss Fannie." She was about to leave when she heard Fannie calling after her.

"Doll, come back over here. I want to ask you something."

Doll crossed her arms and jutted her hip to one side. "What you want?"

"Something wrong?" Fannie asked.

"No."

"Then why are you standing there like you have better things to do?"

Doll let her arms drop to her side. "What you want to ask me?"

"What do you think of Ibby?"

Doll didn't really want to have this conversation. She glanced around, trying to figure a way out of answering.

"Do you like her?" Fannie asked.

"'Course I do. Why wouldn't I?" she said a bit more defensively than she'd intended.

"She reminds me a lot of myself when I was her age. I remember how scared I was when my mother died," Fannie said reflectively. "I was only—"

Doll cut her off. She'd heard the same story at least a dozen times over the years. "Yes, Miss Fannie. I believe I know about how you lost your mama."

"It's just . . . I don't want that little girl to have to go through what I did."

Doll shook her head. "That were a long time ago. Times different now."

Fannie fixed her eyes on the canopy above her head. "Feeling un-wanted doesn't have a timeline attached to it."

"Don't I know," Doll said under her breath.

Fannie kept talking. "Now that Graham's gone, I wonder if Ibby would be happy living with Vidrine. Vidrine's not exactly a loving person."

"Like you is?" Doll interjected.

Fannie made a face. "You just don't know me."

"After all these years working in this house, I believe I do."

When Fannie closed her eyes, Doll took that to be the end of the conversation and started toward the door.

"What if I kept her?" Fannie blurted.

Doll turned. "What you mean, Miss Fannie?"

"Well, what if I ask Vidrine if Ibby can stay here and live with me?"

That was the last thing Doll expected to come out of Fannie's mouth. "Live here? With you? For good?"

"Is that such a dumb idea? She reminds me so much of myself. It would be nice to have a child in the house again."

Doll wanted to say yes, that was the dumbest idea she'd ever heard. Miss Fannie couldn't take care of herself, much less a child. Doll was about to say as much, but Fannie kept rambling.

"Then we could all be together, all of us, in this house." Fannie smiled up at the canopy as if she had just solved the problems of the world.

Doll was silent for a moment. "Don't want to burst your bubble, Miss Fannie, but you and Miss Vidrine don't exactly get along."

"I don't think Vidrine ever really wanted that child. I think she had that baby just to keep Graham from running off." Fannie reached over and picked up an empty perfume bottle on the bedside table. She pulled the stopper out and ran the bottle under her nose. "I'm out of perfume. When did I run out?"

Doll took the bottle from her and put it back down on the table. "You been out for a good number of years, Miss Fannie. Can't remember the last time you had an occasion to wear none. Now back to Miss Vidrine. What makes you think she don't want Ibby no more? Miss Vidrine just say she needed some time away. She didn't say nothing about leaving Miss Ibby here for good."

Fannie waved her hand. "Anyway, I don't think Vidrine has once stopped to consider what Ibby must be going through. The poor child witnessed her father's death, and instead of taking Ibby with her, she leaves her here with strangers. She doesn't give a rat's ass about anyone but herself."

"You ain't a stranger, you her kin."

Fannie sighed. "Lord knows what kind of nonsense her mother has filled her head with. You saw the way she looked at me just now."

"Everybody looks at you that way, Miss Fannie. You could scare the stripe off a skunk. Why, just last week you ran that Fuller Brush man out of here. Left his case full of brushes on the dining room floor. Never did come back for them."

Fannie went on. "Now Vidrine's off on some mission to find herself. If that's not selfish, I don't know what is."

"You got a point, Miss Fannie, but what makes you think she'd give up her only daughter? That's the one hold she has on you, now that Mr. Graham has passed."

Doll took in a deep breath. What Miss Fannie was saying got her to thinking. What if Miss Vidrine planned to move herself into this here house once Miss Fannie passed? Maybe she wouldn't even wait that long. . . . Miss Vidrine knew Miss Fannie'd been to the nuthouse on occasion over the years. What if she tried to have Miss Fannie committed? What if she knew the truth about Miss Fannie? The thought of Miss Vidrine becoming mistress of the house made Doll sick to her stomach.

"Miss Fannie, you just had a shock, and I can see a bump coming out on your head where you hit the table. You ain't thinking too clearly right now. Why don't you take a little rest?"

"Yes, let me think on it some more." Fannie closed her eyes. "Let me think on it."

Doll glanced down at Fannie. She had a Cheshire smile spread wide across her face, the kind Doll had seen many times before.

Just pray it passes, Doll thought as she shut the door.

Chapter Six

The cane-seat stool squeaked across the linoleum floor as Ibby pulled it toward the kitchen table. Queenie was up at the sink humming to herself, her sturdy legs, with the stockings rolled down to just below her fat knees, swaying beneath her gray uniform. From the back, her head looked like a bowling ball, save for the tiny bun the size of a quarter set squarely in the middle of it.

The counter where Queenie was working was cluttered with tins of flour and sugar, a grease-filled coffee can, a ceramic container full of spoons and whisks, a cookie jar, a bread box, several wooden cutting boards stacked against each other, and a small transistor radio. She glided back and forth across the counter like a trolley on wheels—cutting, dicing, rinsing; pulling things from the shelves; stirring the big pot on the heavy relic of a stove; checking the oven and intermittently dabbing her forehead with a dish towel.

"Queenie?" Ibby asked after a while.

"Yes, baby?" Queenie answered without turning around.

"My grandma—is she going to be all right?"

Queenie tapped the spoon on the side of the pot, wiped her hands on her apron, then glanced over her shoulder and gave Ibby a motherly look. "Miss Fannie been mighty worked up ever since she got the news that Graham passed. And that urn you just set on the table in front of her about did her in. Doll took her into the bedroom for a little rest. She'll be just fine. Just give her some time."

Queenie must have noticed the sweat running down the side of Ibby's face. She took a rag from the drawer and ran it under the faucet.

"Hold this up against your cheek. It'll cool you off. Ain't no air conditioning in this old house. You'll get used to it after a while." Queenie grabbed a bottle from the icebox and tapped the metal top on the edge of the blue Formica counter until it popped off. She stuck a straw into the bottle and handed it to Ibby. "Here, drink this. Maybe something cool will help."

Ibby couldn't decide if she liked the almond soda, called Dr. Nut, but it was cold, and that was all that mattered. She glanced out the back window, where, beyond the reach of the tall pecan tree, several sets of sheets flapped from a clothesline. Just off the back of the house was a screened porch with a picnic table. Above the table, six or eight plastic bags filled with water dangled from the rafters, glistening in the sun like uncut diamonds. Queenie saw her staring at them.

"Those called penny bags. Each of them got a brand-new penny on the bottom. The light reflecting off the penny supposed to confuse the flies, so they don't come around and bother the food, although every time I see a fly, they confused enough already. Know what I mean?" Queenie chuckled.

The smell from the cast-iron pot filled the air.

"What are you cooking?" Ibby asked.

"This here's redfish courtbouillon." The word came out of Queenie's mouth sounding like *koo-bee-yon*. "Kind a like a fish stew. It got to cook a good while, know itself first, before it be done. Just waiting on the redfish that Mr. Pierce the fish man gone bring by the house later." She began dicing up some vegetables and tossing them into a bowl. When she finished, she tilted the bowl so Ibby could see what was inside. "This here is the Holy Trinity. Onion, celery, and *poivron*, or what some folks call bell pepper. Along with a touch of garlic and a smidgen of cayenne pepper, the Holy Trinity goes into just about everything I cook. Can't use too much pepper, though. Miss Fannie gets indigestion, and believe you me, you don't want to be around when that happens." She tossed the contents of the bowl into the pot, stirred it a few more times, then put the lid on.

Doll came into the kitchen and tugged at her hair. Ibby was aghast when Doll pulled it completely off her head.

"Miss Ibby, you gone catch one of them flies in that mouth if you don't close it," Queenie said.

Doll laughed when she saw the look on Ibby's face. "You thought that was my real hair? No, baby, just a wig." Doll tossed the hairpiece onto the counter by the back window.

"How's Miss Fannie? Should we call the doctor?" Queenie asked.

"She got a mighty fine bump on her head, but she'll be all right."

"You sure we don't need to call the doctor?"

"No, Mama, she just needs a little rest, that's all." Doll sat on a stool near the back window and stared out into the backyard.

Ibby could tell something was on her mind.

Queenie placed a bowl in front of Ibby. "Go on, eat up, baby. You must be hungry after your trip."

Ibby poked at the white blob in the bowl with the spoon. "What is it?"

"Taste it first, then I'll tell you," Queenie said.

Ibby didn't like that answer. That was the kind of answer her mother used to give her when she was trying to get her to eat cauliflower, and the one thing she hated more than anything was cauliflower. She gingerly pinched off a minuscule portion and examined it before letting the tip of her tongue linger on the spoon, trying to decide if it was to her liking. To her surprise, the stuff was pleasantly sweet. She noticed Queenie watching her.

"You never had clabber before, I can tell," Queenie said.

Ibby shook her head. "What is clabber, exactly?"

"You let the milk sit out for a day or two until it sours and the top part congeals. I sprinkled a little nutmeg and cinnamon on top to give it some punch."

Ibby pushed her empty bowl away. "Glad you didn't tell me what it was before I ate it."

"Doll here tells me you like music," Queenie said. "What kind you like?"

"Moody Blues," Ibby said.

"Blues? We got plenty of blues in New Orleans," Queenie said.

Doll gave a little laugh. "No, Mama, The Moody Blues, they a new band from England."

"England? You don't need no band from England when we got the likes of Allen Toussaint, Dr. John, and Irma Thomas right here. Ain't that so, Doll?"

"I guess." Doll shrugged.

"Girl, what's wrong with you this morning?" Queenie waved the dishrag in Doll's direction. "You love Miss Irma."

Doll began plucking at her hairpiece as if she had a vendetta against it.

"I think maybe Doll's upset that I'm here," Ibby interjected.

"Now, Miss Ibby," Doll said. "Where'd you get such an idea?"

"Because I know Fannie didn't invite me to visit. My mama just dropped me off here because she didn't have anywhere else for me to go."

"You take that sorry look off your face and listen to me, little girl," Queenie said as she pulled up a chair and sat next to Ibby. "Miss Fannie, she was beside herself when she found out you were coming."

Ibby shook her head. "Fannie doesn't *seem* to be very happy that I'm here."

"That's just Miss Fannie." Queenie reached over and grabbed a brown egg from the counter, then placed it on the table in front of Ibby. She gave it a slight twirl. "Look at it this way. Your grandmother, she's kind a like this here egg. If the egg wobbles, means it's raw, so I throw it into the batter and make a cake. If it spins kind of even, like this one here, means it's cooked, so I make egg salad instead."

"Maybe you should get a cracked egg, Mama. Be more to the point," Doll quipped.

Queenie glared at Doll. "Point is, you got to know whether the egg is cooked or raw before you know what to do with it."

"Was she always like that egg?" Ibby asked.

Queenie got up and went over to the counter. "No, Miss Ibby. She didn't start out that way. She start out fresh and new, like we all do. Did you see that big tree out in the front yard?"

"Yeah," Ibby said. "Why?"

"Well, you see how big the trunk is and how those limbs kind of fall down all over the place? That tree didn't start out that big. It grew over the years until it got so tall that it start to lean. Sometimes we got to prop it back up so it don't topple over. Same as we do with Miss Fannie." She put her hand on her back and winced.

"What's wrong, Mama?" Doll asked.

"Got ninety-five-year-old legs on a sixty-year-old body," Queenie said as she leaned back against the counter and nodded over at Ibby. "See what I'm telling you? Kind of like that tree in the front yard. My legs, they just don't want to hold me up no more."

"Now your mama, *she* another story," Doll said to Ibby. "Put Miss Fannie and Miss Vidrine in the same room, be hard to tell which one come out standing."

Queenie frowned at Doll. "Now why'd you go and bring that up? Miss Fannie wouldn't like it if she knew we were talking about her. It ain't our place."

"Okay then, if you won't tell me, I'll just have to ask her myself," Ibby said.

Queenie and Doll looked at each other.

"No, baby, don't do that." Queenie sat down at the table next to Ibby. She pointed a finger. "Rule Number One in this house. Don't *ever* go asking Miss Fannie about her past. Gets her all emotional. Rule Number Two. She starts talking about her past, let her talk but don't go asking no questions. Rule Number Three. You see her hand start twitching, you better change the subject or she gone have one of her spells. Rule Number Four. You got something you want to know, you come ask one of us."

"But you said it wasn't your place to say anything," Ibby said.

"You did just say that, Mama," Doll added.

"So I changed my mind. Just remember them rules, and we won't have no trouble."

"Then tell me. Why do they hate each other?" Ibby said.

"All right, I'll tell you what I know, but don't *never* let on to Miss Fannie that I said nothing. That's Rule Number Six."

"That's Rule Number Five, Mama. There ain't no Rule Number Six," Doll said.

"Doll, shut your mouth. Miss Ibby knows what I'm getting at."

Doll rolled her eyes. "Maybe Rule Number Six should be, don't argue with Mama."

"That's an unwritten rule. Don't need no number." Queenie paused for a moment. "You want to know about your mama and your daddy? I'll tell you. Miss Fannie had Mr. Graham's life all planned out for him. She figured as soon as he finished law school at Tulane, he'd take a job in town, get married, and move into this here house and start a family. Miss Fannie always wanted this house to be full of life, full of children running around. That all changed the night Mr. Graham went out with some of his law school buddies over to a restaurant on Carrollton Avenue, where he met a waitress named Vidrine Crump. Miss Fannie thought it was just a passing crush. There were plenty of other girls chasing after Mr. Graham. But somehow Miss Vidrine caught his eye. She weren't the kind of girl . . ." Queenie cast her eyes down.

"Not the kind of girl Mr. Graham was used to going with. That's what Mama's trying to say," Doll interjected.

Queenie narrowed her eyes at Doll before turning back to Ibby. "Fannie weren't too happy about Mr. Graham seeing Miss Vidrine, and she made her feelings known. She wanted Mr. Graham to marry someone, someone—"

"Someone better," Doll chimed in. "Miss Fannie used to call her that good-for-nothing, big-busted, loudmouthed redneck from Dry Prong, Mississippi. Remember?"

Queenie pinched up her face. "Girl, hush your mouth. That's her mama we talking about." She put her hands on her knees and let out a big sigh. "Your daddy, he comes home one day and announces that he gone marry Miss Vidrine whether Miss Fannie likes it or not. Miss Fannie told Mr. Graham that if he did that, he weren't to step foot in this house again. So what does Mr. Graham do? He elopes with your mama. Now, whose idea it was to move so far away? I think that was your mama's doing on account I think your daddy loved living here, thorns and all. Been a good twelve years, and Miss Fannie ain't seen Mr. Graham since. Miss Fannie didn't even know she had a grandbaby until your daddy broke down and sent a picture few years back."

All three looked up when the screened door off the back porch creaked open and a dark-skinned man dressed in overalls and a white T-shirt came into the kitchen. He took off his hat, scrunched it up in his weathered hands.

He nodded his gray head toward the ladies. "How do, Queenie? How do, Doll?"

"How do, Mr. Pierce," Queenie said as she pushed herself away from the table.

"Got some mighty fine redfish for you today." He looked over in Ibby's direction. "Who've we got here?"

"This here's Miss Fannie's grandbaby, Ibby. She's gone be visiting for a while." Queenie nodded. "Mr. Graham's daughter. Can't you see the resemblance?"

"Sure enough." He tipped his head. "She got his same eyes. Your daddy, he were a good man, Miss Ibby. Smart as a whip, too."

"You knew him?" Ibby asked.

"I been coming around this here house ever since your daddy were a little boy," Mr. Pierce said. "Sorry to hear he's passed on."

Queenie followed him out the back door to a battered pickup truck, parked in the driveway, where blocks of ice held fish spread out evenly in rows. She inspected the fish by running her finger down the scales. Mr. Pierce wrapped the three she'd chosen in newspaper, then followed her back into the house with a red mesh sack flung over his shoulder.

"Thank you kindly, Mr. Pierce," Queenie said.

He set the sack of oysters down onto the picnic table on the back porch, tilted his hat, and left.

Queenie placed a wooden cutting board on the table and unwrapped the fish. "Lookey here. Mr. Pierce done thrown in a little lagniappe, gave me four fish instead of three. Mighty fine of him to do that." She took a meat cleaver from the drawer and, with a thump, chopped the head off one of the fish. She held the severed head up in front of Ibby. "See the eye of this here fish, it's clear. That means it's fresh. My mama had a saying: 'Dead fish rot from the head.' You can see it in the eyes, before you can smell it gone bad." She gouged the eye out with the tip of the knife and popped it into her mouth. "That's for good luck."

"Better get used to Mama's ways, Miss Ibby." Doll pointed a fork in her mother's direction as Queenie filleted the fish. "She could have got Mr. Pierce to fillet that fish for her, but Mama's way too picky. She likes to get every scrap a meat off them bones."

"No use wasting." Queenie wrapped the fish fillets in a milk-soaked cloth and put them in the icebox. Then she placed all the bones, including the head, into another piece of cheesecloth and tied the four corners up into a knot. "This here is what gives the stew its flavor." She tossed the bag into the pot and put the lid on. Then she tilted her head and looked over at Ibby. "Miss Ibby, now you brought it up, I'm curious. Your mama, she say anything else?"

Vidrine had been full of all sorts of directives this morning: *Give the urn to your grandmother. Don't say y'all. Be a good girl and don't give your grandmother any trouble.*

She'd said something else, too, when they got into the car at the airport, but Ibby hadn't quite understood what she meant. Now she repeated it, just the way her mother had said it: "She said not to listen to anything those two wily niggas tell you about me."

Queenie and Doll looked at each other. Queenie made a face like she'd eaten something sour, then the meat cleaver came down so hard, Ibby thought the table might split in two.

"How dare that redneck call us wily! Just who she think she is!" Queenie hissed.

"I'm sorry. I didn't mean to say anything wrong. I was just repeating what my mama told me," Ibby said.

"Ain't nothing we ain't heard before," Doll said, shaking her head, trying not to laugh.

Queenie looked over at Ibby. "Miss Ibby, why don't you go upstairs for a while, take a little rest? Been a long morning."

◈

After Ibby left the room, she turned to Doll. "Just curious, after the way you been acting all funny this morning. Miss Fannie, she say anything to you when you were in the room with her earlier?"

Doll shrugged. "Miss Fannie picked up an empty perfume bottle and talked about how she needed to get some more."

"No, I mean about Miss Ibby. She say anything about her?"

"Well, yeah. She say she want Miss Ibby to come and live with her."

"You mean for good?"

"Yeah, Mama. That's what she say."

"I'd hate to know what Miss Vidrine might think about that."

A loud voice in the hall startled them. "Yoo-hoo, anybody home?"

"Oh, Lawd." Doll's head jerked around. There was no mistaking that voice.

"What she doing here?" Queenie said under her breath.

Doll peeked through the kitchen door to find Vidrine standing in the hall holding a small suitcase.

Doll whispered to her mother, "Miss Ibby forgot her suitcase in the car this morning. Looks like Miss Vidrine done come back to give it to her. I thought she had a plane to catch. Why she still here?"

"You ever know Miss Vidrine to tell the truth?" Queenie said. "Maybe she planning to drive off into the sunset and join a cult. I don't know. Never can tell with her. Don't matter now. She's here, and you got to go out and get her before Miss Fannie comes out of her room and have a heart attack at the sight of that woman."

"No, unh-unh. I ain't going out there. You go."

Queenie went over to where Doll was standing and peered through the door under Doll's arm.

"Liberty?" Vidrine yelled up the stairs.

Queenie winced and put her hands to her ears.

Vidrine surveyed her surroundings as if she were taking inventory, bending over to a painting on the wall, rubbing her hand along the hall table.

"Look at her," Queenie muttered. "She still got those awful eyes that are way too big for her head. Make her look like she stuck her finger in an electric socket."

Doll never did understand Mr. Graham's attraction to the woman. Besides the manic eyes, Vidrine had the habit of looking sideways over her nose as if she were constantly smelling poop. Thank goodness Miss Ibby looked more like her father, Doll was thinking.

Queenie nudged her. "Go on out there and get Miss Ibby's suitcase like I told you."

"Maybe Miss Vidrine will just leave it in the hall and go," Doll said, not budging.

Queenie craned her neck. "Don't look like she going nowhere to me."

"Liberty Bell, come and get your damn suitcase!" Vidrine screamed.

The door to Miss Fannie's room opened, and there were footsteps in the hall.

"Now look what you done," Queenie said. "Miss Fannie's coming out. Hurry. Go out there and see if you can stop her."

But it was too late. Fannie was already making her way down the hall toward Vidrine. To Doll's surprise, Fannie was dressed and had on a bit of makeup.

"Why Miss Fannie smiling? She hates that woman," Queenie said.

"Oh no," Doll said.

"What?" Queenie nudged Doll. "What now?"

"Remember what we was just talking about? I believe Miss Fannie's getting ready to ask Miss Vidrine about Ibby living in this here house with her. Why else would she have a smile on her face? Miss Fannie only smiles real big like that when she wants something from somebody. And she must want it awful bad, from the look of that big grin."

"Well, Fannie, how long has it been?" Vidrine asked icily.

Doll was expecting Fannie to say something like *not long enough.*

"A pleasure to see you again, Vidrine," Fannie said cordially, extending her hand.

Vidrine lurched back and raised her hand in the air as if Fannie had just pointed a gun at her. "I just came to drop off Ibby's suitcase, not to make amends. She forgot it in the car. I have to go." She started toward the door.

Fannie hurried after her. "Wait a minute. Please. There's something I'd like to talk to you about."

"I don't have time." Vidrine opened the front door, the suitcase still in her hand.

Fannie grabbed her arm. "Where are you going, anyway?"

Vidrine yanked it away. "None of your business."

Fannie grabbed her arm again, this time harder. Vidrine struggled against her grip.

"Ohhhh . . . we gone have a catfight," Queenie said excitedly to Doll.

Fannie let go. "Just hold on a minute. I'm not asking because I care where you're running off to. You can go to India as far as I'm concerned. I'm asking because I wondered if you would let Ibby stay here with me."

Vidrine rubbed her arm. A bruise was beginning to form where Fannie had grabbed it. "Now look what you've done!"

"I'm sorry."

"Sorry? You're sorry all right. What are you prattling on about anyway? Ibby is staying with you, like we agreed. Now, if you don't mind, I've got to go." Vidrine opened the door wider.

Fannie closed it with her foot.

Vidrine turned toward her. "What are you doing? Are you crazy?"

"I mean for good. I want Ibby to come live here."

Vidrine put her hand on her hip. "I asked if Ibby could stay with you for a while. I didn't mean forever."

"I know," Fannie said. "But I think she might be better off here. With me."

"With you? And just what the hell do you mean by that, better off with you? I'll be the judge of who Ibby's better off with, thank you very much. And if you hurl any more insults like that, we're leaving and Ibby is coming with me."

"I just thought you might like your freedom now that you're a widow," Fannie said. "I can take care of Ibby. You can visit whenever you like."

"Are you out of your mind? Look at you. What's that bump on your head? You fall down drunk again? You been drinking this morning? Is that it? Is that where all this is coming from? You think that's the sort of environment to raise a child?"

"No, I haven't been drinking. I'm perfectly sober."

"Then that just proves you're even crazier than I thought," Vidrine said. "Graham always said so, you know. He hated you from the time you sent him away to boarding school. Why do you think he moved so far away after we were married?"

"That was your doing," Fannie said. "Not Graham's. He was perfectly happy to stay here in New Orleans."

"Then why did he never come back to visit?" Vidrine put her hand on her hip. "He hated you. You think he'd want his daughter to live with a mother he hated? I don't think so."

"Why don't we let Ibby decide?"

Vidrine glared at her. "This was a mistake. I should never have brought Ibby here in the first place. Liberty Bell, come on down here! We're leaving!" Vidrine screamed so loudly, the chandelier tinkled above her head.

Ibby appeared at the top of the steps. "What is it, Mama?"

"Oh, no. Miss Ibby's coming down," Doll said to her mother.

"How long you think she been listening? Poor thing," Queenie said. "We got to do something."

Doll shook her head. "Nothing we can do now but watch and see what happens."

"Come on. We're leaving." Vidrine picked up Ibby's suitcase from the floor.

"But I just got here," Ibby protested.

"I'm sorry, Vidrine," Fannie pleaded. "We can talk about this later. Let Ibby stay."

"Did you hear me, Ibby? Get down here. Now!" Vidrine yanked at the doorknob and kicked the door open with her foot.

Ibby came bounding down the steps.

Fannie grabbed Ibby and pulled her toward her. "Let her stay."

Vidrine looked from Fannie to Ibby, then at her watch. She threw the suitcase at them. It landed just in front of Ibby's feet. Then the front door slammed. Doll could see Vidrine rushing toward the car. She never looked back once.

Queenie came away from the kitchen door. "I hope that's the last time I ever see that woman."

"I wouldn't bet on it," Doll said.

After Vidrine left, Fannie grabbed Ibby's arm. "Come on. We're going for a ride."

Chapter Seven

Doll and Queenie stood by the back window and watched Fannie back the car out of the driveway.

"Now where in the heck you think they going? Miss Fannie ain't driven that car in years. Think they gone be okay?" Queenie fretted.

Doll put her arm around her mother's shoulders. "How I know? Besides, it wouldn't do no good to try and stop her on account she never listens to what two wily niggers have to say."

Queenie swatted Doll's arm. "I ain't laughing. Had enough of that joke for one day."

Queenie went over to the counter and turned the radio to the gospel station. She swung her head from side to side as she washed some dishes. After a while, Doll reached over and turned the dial to a different station.

Queenie looked at her. "Now why you go and do that? You know I like to listen to my gospel music while I do the dishes."

A deep voice resonated from the radio. "This is WBOK, the one and only rhythm and blues station in New Orleans, and I'm Chubby Buddy, bringing you the sound of our very own queen of soul, Irma Thomas. Her new song, 'Wish Someone Would Care,' is making it up the charts. And the rest, they say, is history. Come on down to La Ray's Village Room on Dryades Street to hear Miss Irma tonight."

Doll turned up the volume just as Irma Thomas let out a soulful cry.

Queenie reached over and turned the volume back down. "Don't know why all you young folks think you got to turn the music up so loud. Give me a headache."

Doll ignored her mother's comment and began dancing around, waving her arms in the air and swinging her hips to the beat of the music. "Be all right if I leave a little early?"

"Now listen here. You got plenty a time to go hear Irma later. What you got up your sleeve?"

Doll went over to the counter near the back window, picked up a fork, and started singing into it as if it were a microphone. She paused to answer her mother. "Oh, nothing."

"Don't you 'oh nothing' me." Queenie switched the radio back to the gospel station. "What you not telling me?"

Doll leaned against the counter. "Me and some folks, we might head on down to the five-and-dime on Canal Street in a little while."

"Who? What folks you talking about?"

"You know, Doretha, Slim, maybe Lola Mae . . ."

"What for?" Queenie crossed her arms and gave Doll her oh-no-you're-not-doing-that look.

"Just, you know, to hang out." Doll cast her eyes out the back window. She wished she hadn't said anything. She wasn't a very good liar and her mother could always see right through her.

"You not trying that lunch counter stuff again, is you?" Queenie picked up a knife from the sink and pointed it at her. "Last time your friends tried sitting at the counter down at the Woolworth's, they got arrested. Remember? Every one of them lost they jobs or got kicked out a school. Earline Murray had to make her son move out of their house 'cause they started getting bomb threats. And Jerome Smith? He almost got beat to death."

"That's 'cause Jerome went on one of them freedom rides, Mama, not 'cause he sat at the Woolworth counter."

Doll knew her mother was about to start in on the plight of all the poor folks who had gotten the short end of the stick, which according to her mother was just about everybody in the St. Roch neighborhood, where they lived. She slumped down on the stool, pretending to listen to her mother's little speech that she'd already heard a hundred times before.

"Why, just yesterday, Virgie Mae Jefferson's son was beaten up real bad, just for sitting at the counter at the state capitol cafeteria up in Baton Rouge. And who they haul off to jail? Not the white men that do the beating. What you think gone happen if you go down to the Woolworth's today?"

"Calm down, Mama."

Queenie came over and pounded her fist on the table. "Why can't you leave well enough alone?"

There was nothing Doll could do but let her mother ramble. Queenie was a strong believer in the status quo. Separate but equal was just fine with her as long as nobody gave her any trouble. But Doll had other ideas. Her daughter, Birdelia, wasn't much older than Ruby Bridges, the little colored girl who'd been escorted by armed guards to the Frantz Elementary School for Whites in the Ninth Ward in 1960 in an effort to integrate the school. It made national headlines, started white flight from the city, and riled up the Ku Klux Klan. Here it was four years later, and what good did it do? As far as Doll was concerned, nothing much had changed. She wanted something better for her daughter. She wanted Birdelia to be able to decide what she wanted out of life, not have it dictated to her, the way her own life had been. And she was willing to fight for it. She just wasn't sure how.

"That's the problem," Queenie muttered. "Most people living in fool's garden don't even know it."

"I heard that," Doll said.

"Well, it's true, baby. You a seeker."

"What you mean, a seeker?" Doll peered over at her mother. She'd never heard her use that word before. She wondered if it was a "word of the day" from Miss Fannie's newspaper.

Queenie jabbed the knife in Doll's direction. "A seeker, baby, a seeker. You looking for something you ain't never gone find."

"I ain't no seeker, Mama. You just ain't been paying attention to the world around you. Things are changing."

"Uh-huh. Ain't you heard nothing I just said? People going to jail, getting killed. That much ain't changed. Now you set on down here and help me shuck them oysters."

"I'm almost twenty-three years old. About time you quit telling me what to do."

"I'm your mama. I don't care how old you are. You're my daughter, and I'm gonna keep you out of trouble the best way I know how."

"Like how you kept Ewell out of trouble?" Doll said.

Queenie put her hand to her chest and let her eyes fall to the floor. Doll's brother Ewell had died from a gunshot wound to the chest several years ago in a senseless shooting that left four young black men dead and the neighborhood paralyzed with fear.

"I'm sorry, Mama. I shouldn't have said that." Doll touched her mother's shoulder, knowing she'd gone too far, had brought up the one thing that could bring her mother down—the fear she carried inside, wondering which one of her children might be next. The only reason Doll hadn't been hauled off to jail or been beaten like her other friends at the last sit-in was because Lieutenant Kennedy, a longtime police officer friend of Miss Fannie's, recognized her and sent her on home before all the trouble started. She might not be so lucky the next time. That's what all the fussing was about. But Doll couldn't help the way she felt, like a seed buried in the wrong kind of soil. Maybe her mother was right. But that seed inside her was ripe, and it was ready to burst open any minute, no matter what her mother said.

Queenie raised her eyes. "I see you over there thinking, like I don't know what I'm talking about. But you're wrong, baby. I'm just trying to save you all the trouble. Now go on and fetch that sack of oysters Mr. Pierce left out on the back porch."

Doll came back in and plunked the sack of oysters down on the kitchen table. "Your arthritis acting up again?" she asked when she saw her mother rubbing mustard powder on her elbows.

Queenie nodded. "Shucking oysters do a number on me."

"Why'd you get oysters anyhow?" Doll slit the small sack open with a knife. "You know oysters best only in months with an *r* in them. They gone be mighty puny this time a year."

"Thought Miss Ibby might like to get her first taste of an oyster while she here," Queenie said. "Can't help that she's here in the middle of summer."

Queenie stuck the tip of the knife in the joint in the back of the oyster. With a few twists, the shell popped open. She held the oyster up with the tip and examined it before tossing it into the bowl she'd set on the table.

"Let me tell you something else I noticed," she went on. "You acting like you scared a that little girl."

"What you mean scared? Why would I be scared a Miss Ibby?" Doll balked.

"I hear the way you been talking to that child. You afraid Miss Ibby gone march right in and take Miss Fannie's attention for herself."

Doll threw a shucked oyster into the bowl and pointed her knife at her mother. "What you mean, the way I been talking? I talk to Miss Ibby just the same way I talk to you."

"That's what I mean. Don't go shooting your mouth off like you do with Miss Fannie. You can't talk to Miss Ibby that way. She ain't used to it."

Doll sat back, exasperated. "Mama, why you pounding on me like I'm some of your bread dough?"

"Don't mean to, baby. It's just . . . I can't ever seem to make you understand how lucky you are, to be here in this house." She twisted the knife into another oyster shell, then looked over at Doll. "How many times I got to tell you, baby? You can't change the way things are. It were God's choice you here. And ain't nobody or nothing can change that."

That was her mother's answer to everything. Doll tightened her mouth but said nothing. What her mother didn't understand was that no matter how much she tried to douse Doll with common sense, her unrest just kept smoldering.

They sat quietly for a few minutes, each in her own thoughts, until Queenie shook her head and said, "I shouldn't have told that child the truth about her mama. She too young."

"You didn't say nothing that weren't true."

"Yeah, but God help me, I didn't tell her the whole truth neither." Queenie flicked an oyster into the bowl. "You remember Miss Vidrine. Can't imagine she's changed a lick in the last ten years."

Doll had been around twelve years old when Mr. Graham brought Miss Vidrine to have dinner at the house. She'd never forget that first visit. It still made her seethe. During dinner, Miss Vidrine had called Doll over. She told Doll how much she hated liver and told her never to serve it when she came to visit. Then, in front of everyone, she proceeded to spit the chewed-up liver out into Doll's hand. She did it right there in front of Miss Fannie and Mr. Graham. Everybody saw it. And nobody did anything about it.

"Sure I remember, Mama, but why does it matter?"

"I'll tell you why. That Vidrine, she saw this big house, thought Mr. Graham was rich. Then she come around, put some kind a spell on Mr. Graham, the only way I know how to explain it."

"It weren't no spell. Way I remember it, she announced to Miss Fannie over dinner one night that she was having Mr. Graham's baby."

Queenie wiped the sweat from her forehead with the back of her hand and gave Doll an intent stare. "We got bigger problems, now that Mr. Graham's gone. All Vidrine got to do now is wait for Miss Fannie to pass on. Then she can move in here and take over, become mistress of this here house."

Doll dropped an oyster onto the table and looked up. "I know, Mama. I been thinking the same thing."

"Don't you go running your mouth to Miss Ibby about all this.

Don't want her to get no wrong ideas, think we meddling. You understand? Not a word." She shucked a few more oysters, then looked up at Doll. "Where you think Miss Vidrine go off to anyway?"

Doll shrugged. "Don't think she had the right mind to tell nobody."

Queenie was silent for a moment. "We got to come up with a plan to make sure she never gets her hands on any a Miss Fannie's money. And we got to come up with something right quick."

Her mama had a fierce, determined look on her face. Doll knew that look. It meant by the time that sack of oysters was empty, Queenie was going to have a plan all hatched and ready to go.

Chapter Eight

Queenie was so riled up trying to come up with a plan to keep Miss Vidrine out of the house that it only took about twenty minutes to finish the oyster shucking. All the while, Doll was conjuring her own plan so she could join her friends on Canal Street. She decided to use the same ploy she often did, by pretending to be upstairs in her sewing room working on a new dress for Miss Fannie. Her mother never came upstairs anyway, so if she planned it right, she could sneak away while her mother was watching her stories on the television as she did the ironing.

"My, look a the time," Queenie said as she wiped her hands on her apron. "Almost eleven-thirty. Better hurry up so I can watch my stories."

Queenie pulled the ironing board from the utility closet in the kitchen and dragged it into the parlor. Doll hurried down the hall toward the stairs.

"I'll be upstairs if you need me," Doll said.

Queenie didn't answer. She was too busy tuning into *Search for Tomorrow* to care. Once her stories came on, she was in a different world. That's one thing Doll could count on. Doll stood at the top of the stairs, waiting for her moment. When she heard Queenie talking back to the television, she knew her chance had come. She tiptoed down the hall past her. Not that it really mattered. Queenie had the volume on the TV turned up so loud the whole neighborhood could probably hear, even with the windows closed.

Doll made her way out the back door and to the garage, where she'd stashed a set of clothes for such occasions when she wanted to get away from the house. She changed out of her maid's uniform into a pair of slacks, a white cotton shirt, and some loafers. When she got to the front of the house, she peeked through the window, where she could see her mother leaning on the ironing board with her chin in her hands, staring at the television. She hurried down the street toward the bus stop, aware that she was garnering suspicious stares from some of Miss Fannie's neighbors because to them, a black person out of uniform scurrying down the street only meant trouble.

When she reached the corner, she found a few maids in uniform huddled together at the bus stop on their way to run errands for the mistresses of the house. She checked her watch. It was eleven-forty. She was supposed to meet her friends at the corner of Canal Street and St. Charles at noon. She felt a sense of relief when she spotted the bus only a few blocks away.

She paid her fare and followed the rest of the maids toward the rear of the bus, nodding at a few people she knew. She wasn't much in the mood to talk so she found an empty seat next to a window and gazed out. Every couple of blocks, the bus stopped to pick up a few more colored women in uniforms who shuffled wearily down the aisle and slumped into a seat near Doll with exhausted expressions on their faces, all of them wishing they were somewhere else, doing something different. Just as she did.

About thirty blocks later, the bus line ended at Canal Street near the Mississippi River. Doll started toward the five-and-dime where she was supposed to meet her friends. She passed an empty storefront with a "For Lease" sign, in a small redbrick building with plate-glass windows that used to be a shoe repair. Doll thought it would be the perfect spot to open a dress shop.

She cupped her hands over her eyes and looked in. She pictured herself with a sewing room in the back, designing gowns for all the Negro balls, displaying one or two of her favorites in the front window. She reached into her pocketbook to jot down the information when she noticed some writing beneath the phone number on the sign.

"No Negroes Need Apply."

Doll stood there blinking hard, the "For Lease" sign reflecting back against her chest, leaving a dark rectangular shadow. She felt her blood boiling up inside her, and at that moment, all she wanted to do was punch the window until it shattered into small pieces. Instead, she walked away, her head hung low with disappointment.

It wasn't until a few blocks down, when she spotted her friends near the corner of St. Charles Avenue, that she brightened up, remembering why she'd come in the first place.

"Where you been, Dollbaby?" a young man in a cloth hat rimmed with blue ribbon called out as she approached. "We thought you might be bagging us."

"Sorry, Slim," she said. "Got caught up. Where's Lola Mae?"

"I'm right here," a young woman in a checkered shift said as she walked up behind Doll.

"Where's everybody else at?" Doll asked.

Slim nodded toward the other side of the street, where a few of their friends were milling around, trying hard not to look as if they were up to anything.

"Don't want too many of us hanging together," he said. "Might draw attention."

Doll stole a glance across the street, trying to figure out how many of them had shown up for the sit-in. "Doretha here?"

"Yeah. She standing behind Jerome on the other side of Canal Street," Slim said. "Now that you showed up, we all here. Follow me, and remember what I told you."

When Slim tipped his hat to Jerome, Jerome did the same. It was the signal for them to begin their approach to the store. They followed one another, keeping a good distance, going into the Woolworth in five-minute intervals. Doll stood on the corner, pretending to wait for a bus. One came and left. Then another. She was beginning to get a little uneasy as the third bus approached, but then Jerome gave her the signal. She opened the door to Woolworth and looked around the store with the pretense of searching for hairspray. After a few minutes, she made it up to the lunch counter, where five other colored folks, including Jerome, Doretha, and Lola Mae, were already seated.

The soda jerk behind the lunch counter came up to Jerome and pointed to a sign on the wall. "Jerome, what in the hell do you think y'all are doing? Can't you read? This counter is for white folks. No coloreds. You know the rules. How many times I got to tell you?"

The soda jerk knew him because this was about the fourth time he'd staged such an event.

Jerome ignored him and said in his most sophisticated voice, "I'd like a nectar soda, if you please."

The young man behind the counter crossed his arms and rolled his eyes. Then he walked away, untying his apron. Doll knew he was probably on his way to get the manager. By the time he returned, the lunch counter was filled with colored folks. The store had become unusually quiet as all the white folks, seeing what was happening, slipped out of the store. The only sound was the ticking of the clock on the wall in front of them. Twelve-fifteen. Had they been there only fifteen minutes? It seemed like an eternity.

"What do we do now?" Doll whispered to Doretha, who was seated next to her, wearing a nervous face.

"Remember what Jerome told us. We need to wait for the reporters to show up so they can get our picture," she said. "Hope the reporters get here first, before the cops, otherwise we gone get beat up for nothing."

A short man in a starched white coat with "Mr. Balducci, Manager" stitched in red on the front pocket came up behind them. "I'm going to have to ask you folks to leave."

No one at the counter moved.

"All right then. You leave me no choice but to call the police," Mr. Balducci said.

Still no one moved, but Doll could hear Lola Mae breathing heavily at her side. *Where are the damn reporters?* Doll wondered.

The front door burst open, and a man with a camera raced in and began taking pictures.

Mr. Balducci rushed up to him and put his hand up. "No pictures. Not in my store."

He tried to grab the long lens of the camera, but the reporter ducked and ran behind the lunch counter, snapping away at a dozen somber black faces.

Doll noticed a paddy wagon pulling up to the front of the store. Before she could nudge Lola Mae, six policemen barged in the front door pulling handcuffs from their belts. One of them came over to Doll.

"Come on, baby, don't give me no trouble," he said as he held up the cuffs.

When Doll glanced at his nametag, her heart sank. She'd been warned about Gormley. He was fat and pink-skinned with small beady eyes, and he was snarling at her in a way that made Doll catch her breath. Gormley grabbed her wrist and pulled her until her face was even with his.

"What's this?" he said, pointing at her face. "Hey, Frank. Come take a look at this one. She's got one nigger eye and one blue eye. Your mama been fucking a white man, honey?" he said loud enough for everyone to hear. Then he whispered in Doll's ear as he slapped the cuffs down hard on her wrist. "You like to fuck white guys, too? You want to fuck a white cop? That's the only way I'm going to let you go."

Gormley tried to pull Doll up out of her seat by the handcuffs. She resisted. She gave Doretha a pleading look, but Doretha pretended not to notice what was going on. Something worse than fear gripped Doll, a feeling of pure helplessness. She tightened her lips, determined never to feel this way ever again. Never. Not if she could help it.

"Come on now, don't give me no trouble." Gormley grabbed the billy club from his belt and was about to backhand Doll when Lola Mae jumped up from her seat.

"No!" she screamed.

From the corner of her eye, Doll saw Lola Mae stick out her arm just as the billy club came down. Lola Mae fell to the floor, writhing in pain.

Another officer, a tall, thin man with jet-black hair came running over before Gormley could get in another blow. "What the hell you doing, Gormley? You had strict orders not to use any unnecessary force."

Doll recognized him. It was Lieutenant Kennedy. She began to breathe a little easier.

"The bitch wouldn't listen," Gormley said, giving Lola Mae a good kick as she lay on the floor.

Lola Mae let out a moan and began to cough.

"I'll take it from here," Lieutenant Kennedy said. He motioned for another officer to come over and assist. "From the look of that arm, you might want to call an ambulance."

The young officer helped Lola Mae up and escorted her outside.

Gormley grunted and followed them out the door, but not before he gave Doll a look of pure hatred.

"Come on, I'm taking you home." Kennedy uncuffed Doll and walked her out of the store and around the corner. He helped her into the backseat of his squad car. When he got in, he took off his cap and leaned over the seat. He spoke calmly, even though he was scolding her. "What in the hell were you doing here, Doll? You could have gotten yourself locked up, or worse."

Doll knew what he meant. Gormley was notorious for such behavior.

She fell back against the seat. As they drove off, she began to wonder what might have happened if Lieutenant Kennedy hadn't been there to help her, the truth of her mother's words ringing in her ears.

You may not be so lucky next time.

Doll was relieved to find that Fannie's car was still gone when they pulled up to the house.

"You won't say nothing?" Doll said to Lieutenant Kennedy.

He shook his head. "Go on. Before Fannie misses you."

Fannie wasn't the one she was worried about. Queenie was going to kill her if she found out she'd gone against her wishes. Doll hurried down the driveway, hoping no one had seen her getting out of the squad car, and went into the garage to change back into her uniform. She sneaked up to the back door, and when she didn't see Queenie in the kitchen, she went in, took a seat by the back window, and began polishing silver.

"Where you been?" Queenie asked as she came in the kitchen.

"What you mean?" Doll answered. "I been upstairs working on Miss Fannie's dress, like I told you. Why?" She felt a trickle of sweat drip down the side of her neck.

"I didn't hear the radio. You always play the radio when you sewing," Queenie said.

"I had the door shut. Didn't want to disturb you while you was watching your stories," Doll said.

Queenie gave her a hard look. "Really? Since when you so considerate?"

"I'm always considerate, Mama. You taught me that. You a good mama."

Queenie closed one eye. "Then why you sweatin'? You been up to something?"

Doll shook her head. "No, Mama, I been here the whole time. You just too busy with your stories to notice."

Chapter Nine

Ibby could tell that Fannie was upset from her altercation with Vidrine a few moments ago. She was driving with one hand, smoking a cigarette with the other, and barreling down the street as if there were an emergency somewhere. Ibby wondered if she should be driving at all, considering the bump on her head.

"Where are we going?" Ibby managed to ask.

"To see old Madame Doussan," Fannie said as her gray hair swirled around from the open car window. "In the French Quarter."

"Oh," Ibby replied.

No one had mentioned a Madame Doussan. She'd never heard anyone referred to as a Madame before. What kind of a place was Fannie taking her to?

Fannie drove through an older part of town called the Garden District, known for the canopies of oaks that lined the streets and the grand mansions hidden behind them. This soon gave way to the tall buildings of the downtown district. Once they crossed Canal Street, they were in the French Quarter, where the streets narrowed and the buildings were only two or three stories high. Most were of brick covered in plaster, with intricate ironwork balconies gracing the upper floors. With few exceptions, the ground floors had multiple sets of French doors, many of which were open onto the street this morning,

giving Ibby a glimpse of life in this grand old part of the city, where
the aroma of stewpots and wet cement left from the passing street
cleaners mingled together in a strange but pleasant way.

Fannie pulled the car up to a shop on Royal Street with a vast display of tin soldiers in the window. There must have been hundreds of
them, lined up three and four deep on glass shelves, as if on parade.
Ibby got out of the car to admire them.

Fannie came up beside Ibby. "Your father used to love this shop."

"Is this where Madame Doussan lives, above the tin soldier shop?"
Ibby asked.

"No, dear. Madame Doussan lives around the corner on Chartres
Street."

Ibby looked up at Fannie, not realizing until now how tall a woman
she was. She could see some of her daddy in Fannie, especially the way
she always seemed to be thinking about something she wanted to keep
to herself. But there was a difference. Based on their conversation in
the dining room this morning, Fannie was far more direct than her
father had ever been. That part scared her a little.

"For years, all Graham wanted were tin soldiers to add to his col-
lection," Fannie went on. "I bet they're still in his room. I'd forgotten
about this shop until now. Brings back memories."

Ibby could see Fannie's reflection in the window. She remembered
what Queenie told her to do when Fannie started talking about the past.

Rule Number Two. Fannie talks about her past, don't ask questions.

Fannie started down the street, swinging her pocketbook and tapping the large umbrella she was carrying on the sidewalk as if it were
a walking stick. They passed a handful of colored boys, no more than
eight or nine years old, who were tap-dancing and singing in the
street. When Ibby stopped to listen, one of the boys came over to her.

"I bet you a dollar I can tell you where you got them shoes," he said,
pointing at her red sneakers.

Fannie turned back around and grabbed Ibby's hand. "Come on,
dear. That's the oldest one in the book."

"I bet you a dollar," the boy repeated, still pointing.

"Where?" Ibby asked.

"On your feet, on Royal Street," he said as he stuck his hand out and grinned.

Fannie shook her head and handed the boy a dollar. She turned to Ibby. "If anyone else stops you, just keep walking, okay? Otherwise, we'll never get to Madame Doussan's."

On the way, they passed a man painted silver from head to toe. Fannie explained that the man was a pantomime who went from corner to corner, standing on a washbasin, pretending to be a statue.

"Why?" Ibby asked.

"For money, dear. They all do it for money."

Just up the street, Ibby spotted a heavyset man wearing a kilt talking to two women in bunny costumes. In the next block, a young boy carrying a tuba bigger than he was began playing near a food stand that looked like a giant hot dog. The man standing beside the stand yelled over to them.

"Lucky Dog for the little lady?"

"Not today." Fannie waved him off.

Ibby glanced up at the sky, which was covered in a blanket of white. New Orleans was certainly a different kind of place, she was thinking. The people, the food, even the sky was different. Where she was from, you barely noticed the clouds. They were thin and gauzy and high in the sky. Here, the clouds were everywhere. They rolled in from the river, jostling up against each other, hovering so low Ibby felt she might be able to reach up and touch them.

"Is it going to rain?" Ibby asked as she watched the clouds glide by, one after another.

"This time of year, you never know. It could rain this block and not the next. I always carry an umbrella just in case. Now come on, dear."

They turned the corner, went up another block, then stopped in front of a shop on Chartres Street with fancy gold letters stenciled on the window.

"Madame Doussan's French Perfumery"

Oh, Ibby thought. *It's a shop. Madame Doussan owns a perfume shop.* Her heart slowed down. In the back of her mind she'd harbored a notion that perhaps Fannie was going to drop her off at this Madame's house and leave her for good.

Fannie opened the door to the tinkling of a brass bell. As they stepped inside, a barrage of fragrances bombarded them. The tiny shop was long and narrow, crammed with glass-enclosed counters on the right side, and thin shelves holding a variety of perfume bottles, atomizers, and a splendid display of bath salts, powders, and lotions on the other.

An elderly woman in a long flowing silk gown burst out from behind a red velvet curtain at the rear of the store and came toward them with a grand wave of her hand.

"I'm Madame Doussan. May I help you?"

"Yes," Fannie said, pulling out a perfume bottle from her pocketbook.

The bottle was empty except for the dried residue at the bottom. Madame Doussan turned the bottle upside down, noted the handwritten inscription, then took the glass stopper from the bottle and sniffed it.

"This is Oriental Rose, a special blend for a client I once had. Where did you get it?" she asked.

"You made it for me," Fannie replied.

The woman studied Fannie's face. "Fannie? Is that you? We haven't seen you in quite some time. According to the date on the bottom of the bottle, it's been a good twelve years since you've been in the shop."

"Has it been that long?"

"Yes, my dear. I apologize for not recognizing you. You had such pretty auburn hair the last time I saw you. As for me, my hair has grown so thin that I've taken to wearing this scarf every day." She touched her head. "Please have a seat at the counter."

Fannie and Ibby settled themselves on the stools as Madame Doussan went behind the counter.

"Would you like a refill of this perfume?" She pulled a wooden box from under the counter and flipped through the file cards. "Oh, yes, here it is. A rose base with hints of amber, vanilla, and sandalwood, with a touch of musk and magnolia."

"I'd also like you to prepare a special perfume blend for my granddaughter. She has a birthday coming up."

Ibby, surprised and touched by Fannie's gesture, grinned widely. The day wasn't turning out at all as she had expected.

"Thank you, Grandma Fannie."

Fannie patted her hand. "Please, dear. Just call me Fannie, and we'll get along fine."

Madame Doussan placed a carton filled with small glass vials on the counter. "The younger girls seem to prefer a citrus blend—something lighter. Let's try a few out, why don't we?"

Madame Doussan opened the first vial. Ibby leaned in to smell it.

"If you don't like it, you just need to tell me. We'll move on until we find the ones you prefer. That was magnolia." She jotted some notes on a file card.

Doll had been right about magnolia—it smelled like sour laundry. Ibby shook her head.

"Try this one." The shopkeeper held a vial out for Ibby.

Ibby shook her head.

"Carnation is a no as well," she noted. "Try this."

Ibby leaned in. This one was more pleasing, soothing.

"Musk. The young ones always like musk. And this?"

"Oh yes, I really like that," Ibby said.

"Wild orchid. You have good taste, young lady," Madame Doussan said.

She went through at least twenty more vials until she announced that Ibby had chosen the perfect blend of wild orchid, citrus, musk, gardenia, and spice.

"Feel free to look around the shop while I go back to my workroom and prepare these for you," she said.

Ibby strolled over to examine the display in the front window. Fannie joined her.

"Madame Doussan's family has been making perfumes in this same shop for over a hundred years. Those were some of the original perfume decanters," Fannie said, pointing at the ancient-looking colored bottles.

"They're beautiful," Ibby said.

Ibby noticed an old woman skating back and forth in front of the window, making faces at them each time she passed.

"Lucy," Fannie said, as if to herself.

"You know her?" Ibby asked, astounded.

Ibby went over to the front door and peeped out. The woman, who must have been close to Fannie's age, had gray hair braided in a long plait down her back. She was roller-skating up and down the sidewalk in a tattered wedding dress and a big floppy hat as a small flock of ducks followed her. When Lucy turned one way, the ducks followed; when she turned the other way, the ducks scrambled to keep up, making low noises as if they were exasperated.

"Everyone knows Lucy the duck lady," Fannie said. "Story goes that she was jilted at the altar years ago and wanders around the French Quarter in her wedding dress looking for her fiancé. She's been here as long as I can remember."

"And the ducks?"

"She started feeding the ducks down by the river one day. They followed her home. They've been following her ever since."

"And the roller skates?" Ibby asked.

"I don't know about the roller skates, but I've never seen her without them."

To Ibby's surprise, Lucy stopped in front of the door and pointed a finger.

"Do I know you?"

Startled by her booming voice, Ibby jumped back.

"You look like somebody I used to know," Lucy said.

When Fannie stepped up behind Ibby, Lucy pointed at her. "You—I know you. Fannie. You're Fannie. I know you."

"That's right, Lucy dear. It's Fannie."

"Been a long time. You look like an old lady now," Lucy said.

"I guess we all do," Fannie replied.

"Not me." Lucy shook her head and started off down the street. "Not me."

"Why does she do it?" Ibby asked. "For money?"

"No, dear. She's just a little different," Fannie said, watching Lucy skate away and disappear around the corner.

"How do you know her again?" Ibby asked.

"I told you, sweetheart. Everyone knows Lucy."

"Yes, but how does Lucy know you?"

Fannie gave her a sideways glance. "I used to live in the French Quarter when I first came to New Orleans. It was a long time ago. She was around even back then."

Ibby noticed that Fannie's hand had begun to tremble. Ibby grabbed it and squeezed.

Fannie shook her hand free. "What is keeping Madame Doussan?"

"I'm right here." She came up and presented Fannie with a small box tied nicely with ribbon.

She handed Ibby a separate package. "This is for you, young lady. This is your own special scent that we are going to call Wild Orchid Number Seven. Anytime you need more, that's all you have to say. And I threw in some talc and body lotion as a little lagniappe."

Ibby took the package from her. "Thank you."

"Just make sure your grandmother comes back to see me soon. I'm not getting any younger." She winked.

When they were in the car, Ibby pulled the stopper out of the perfume bottle and sniffed.

"Wild Orchid Number Seven. I like the sound of that," Ibby said, and applied some to her neck, the way Madame Doussan had shown her.

"Don't overdo it. A little goes a long way," Fannie said. "We can always get more."

"Thank you for the perfume, Fannie. Daddy was the only one that used to give me presents. Mama says presents are a waste of money."

"Well, young lady, now that you're with me, things are going to be a little different. We'll see to that."

When they got to Canal Street, they saw that the police had put up a barricade in front of the Woolworth and were escorting a number of colored folks out in handcuffs. Instead of going around the mayhem, Fannie drove her car right up to one of the barricades. She flagged down an officer.

He leaned in and put his elbow on her door. "Why, Fannie. I haven't seen you out in a while."

"What's going on, Kennedy?" she asked.

"Another sit-in at the lunch counter."

Fannie shook her head. "Another one? Anyone I know in there?"

"Not at the moment," he said before he patted the door and walked off toward the commotion.

"Thank God," Fannie said.

As they drove off, Ibby wondered how Fannie knew so many people. Where she was from, everyone kept to themselves. It was true, Fannie had lived in New Orleans for a long time, but it still seemed curious how people like Lucy the duck lady knew Fannie. She was itching to ask Fannie about it, but she kept her mouth shut.

Rule Number One. Don't ask Fannie about her past.

Chapter Ten

Between arriving yesterday with her father in a jar, Fannie fainting, and her mother and Fannie having words, Ibby didn't know what to expect the next day when she went down for breakfast. She was pleasantly surprised to find Fannie sitting at the dining room table sipping a Coca-Cola from a bottle and reading the morning paper as if nothing had happened.

Queenie came out of the kitchen as Ibby took a seat at the table. "Yes, Miss Fannie?"

"Make Ibby some breakfast, will you please?"

"Sure enough. What you usually take for breakfast, Miss Ibby?"

"I usually have cereal," Ibby replied. "And maybe some Tang?"

Queenie scrunched up her face. "Tang? You ain't no astronaut, Miss Ibby. We gone feed you real people food. How about some *pain perdu* with syrup and fresh-squeezed orange juice?"

"Pan what?" Ibby said.

"You know. *Pain perdu.* It's like French toast," Queenie said.

Fannie cleared her throat. "Here's the word of the day, Queenie. *Oxymoron.*"

"Oxymoron. That's a right funny-sounding word. What it mean?" Queenie asked, looking over Fannie's shoulder.

"It means contradictory words that come together to form an

incongruous meaning. For example, 'a deafening silence' or 'even odds.' 'Pretty ugly,' how about that one?"

"Uh-huh. 'Pretty ugly,' I can relate to that one." Queenie winked, then disappeared back into the kitchen.

Fannie was now concentrating hard on something else in the newspaper. She squinted between drags of her cigarette. Finally, Fannie put the paper down and stubbed out her cigarette. "How'd you sleep?" Fannie asked.

"I could have sworn I heard a tiger." Ibby shrugged. "I must have been dreaming."

"No, dear, you weren't dreaming. The Audubon Zoo's only a couple of blocks from here." Fannie pointed behind her. "When the wind blows north toward the lake, you can hear the foghorns from the ships on the Mississippi River and smell the molasses coming from the plant next to Audubon Park." Fannie leaned in and said in a much lower voice, "And on still nights, over the din of the attic fan, you can sometimes hear the screams from the nuthouse over on Henry Clay Avenue." Fannie closed one eye as she lit another cigarette. "Found one walking up the street just the other day."

"A tiger?" Ibby asked.

"No, dear, a woman from the nuthouse."

"Did they catch her?"

"I'm not sure." Fannie smiled ruefully.

Ibby looked around for the urn she'd left on the table.

"Something wrong, dear?" Fannie asked.

"Uh, no ma'am," Ibby answered, not wanting to upset her. She fiddled with the napkin in her lap, praying that Doll hadn't disposed of the urn in her haste to calm Fannie down yesterday.

The kitchen door swung open, and Queenie set a large tray of food on the table. Ibby had never seen so much food—scrambled eggs and bacon, a plate of *pain perdu* drizzled with syrup and powdered sugar, and a bowl full of white mush with yellow liquid floating in the middle of it.

"What's that white stuff?" Ibby pointed.

"Grits, baby. Just stir the butter in with your spoon."

A few moments later Queenie appeared again. "Yes, Miss Fannie?"

"Can you bring me a pencil so I can mark today's horses?"

"Got one right here in my pocket."

A few minutes later Queenie was back again. "Yes, Miss Fannie?"

Ibby piped up. "Grandma Fannie, how does Queenie always seem to know when you want something?"

Queenie heaved up her bosom. "I guess I been working here so long, I just know."

"Look under the table." Fannie pointed at her foot. "There's a button in the floor. Every time I press it, a bell rings in the kitchen. Something left over from the olden days, when people had servants."

"Yeah, left over. When people had servants," Queenie said as she left the room.

Two seconds later she was back again. "What you want now?"

"You left before I could tell you," Fannie said.

"Oh, guess I did. What you want?"

"Look at this. The paper says there was a scuffle down at the Woolworth's, and there's a picture of a woman sprawled on the floor . . ."

Queenie peered over her shoulder, her eyes wide. She grabbed the paper from Fannie and hid it behind her back.

"What'd you do that for?" Fannie asked.

Queenie thought hard for an answer. "Got a recipe in there I wanted to try today."

"I didn't see a recipe."

"Oh, it's there all right," Queenie said.

"Let me see. Which one?" Fannie held her hand up.

"It's gone be a surprise." Queenie winked at Ibby.

Fannie turned to Ibby. "Queenie's full of surprises. So tell me, Queenie, what do we have planned for Ibby today?"

"We? Thought you might have some ideas of your own." Queenie put her hand on her hip as she shoved the newspaper into the pocket of her apron.

"Why don't you take her over to the swimming pool at Audubon Park? She might like that."

"Can't do that, Miss Fannie."

"Why not?" Fannie asked.

"You know why not." Queenie crossed her arms over her chest and tapped her foot.

"No, I don't."

"Yes, Miss Fannie, you do."

"Remind me."

"'Cause, Miss Fannie, you know darn well they closed the pool last summer."

"It was a nice pool," Fannie sighed.

Queenie narrowed her eyes. "Sure it was. I wouldn't know."

"Then why'd they close it, for God's sake?"

Queenie was beginning to look put out. "You don't remember, do you?"

"Just tell me, please. I'm getting a headache."

"The city closed it 'cause they didn't want colored folks in the water mixing with the white folks, dirtying it all up. So rather than integrate like they supposed to, they closed the pool."

Miss Fannie closed her eyes. "I guess I just haven't been paying attention."

"Guess you haven't," Queenie said as she went back to the kitchen.

Fannie turned to Ibby. "So what are we going to do with you today?"

Queenie came back into the dining room, looking a little exasperated. This time she just crossed her arms and waited.

"Why don't you take Ibby on down to Honey Friedrichs's house? She's got a daughter about Ibby's age, Annabelle, I think her name is."

"I'll have Doll walk her down soon as she finished the ironing." Queenie gave Ibby a nod and left the room.

About a minute later Queenie pushed the kitchen door open and looked into the dining room.

"I didn't call you," Fannie said.

"I know, Miss Fannie, but Mr. Henry already here with the groceries."

"Tell him I'll just be a minute." Fannie stubbed her cigarette out and left the table hurriedly.

"Run on up and put some clothes on, baby," Queenie said to Ibby as she picked up the empty plates. Then she mumbled to herself, "I sure hope Annabelle Friedrichs don't bite Miss Ibby's head off. She's about as stuck-up as they come."

When Ibby got to the second floor, she noticed the bedroom door to the left of the stairs was open a crack. There was an intermittent sound of a machine being turned on and off. She peered in to find sewing patterns and fabric strewn across the floor. Doll was sitting behind an old black Singer sewing machine, as the breeze from a ceiling fan riffled the edges of the pattern she was sewing. She stopped to inspect her work, then pressed the pedal on the floor as she guided the material through the machine. She didn't have her wig on today. Her hair was ironed flat against her head and hung straight down just below her chin. She was singing softly to the song on the radio, as if she were trying not to awaken anyone.

When Ibby opened the door a little wider, it let out a screech.

Doll looked up, startled. "What you doing in here?" She yanked her sewing from the machine and hid it behind her back.

"I'm sorry, I didn't mean . . ." Ibby didn't finish the sentence, wondering why Doll looked so nervous.

Doll got up from the sewing machine and gently guided her out of the room.

As she shut the door, Ibby asked, "What's in there that you don't want me to see?"

"Normally, you welcome in my sewing room anytime, but I'm working on a project for Miss Fannie. Something for you."

Ibby gave Doll a sideways glance, hoping it wasn't another Shirley Temple dress.

"Don't tell Miss Fannie you know, or she'll get right mad."

"Don't worry," Ibby said, looking past Doll.

"What's wrong, baby? You missing something?"

"My daddy's urn. Do you know where it is?"

"Oh, Miss Ibby, I had to move it. Miss Fannie's not able to get past the fact that Mr. Graham is just a bunch of ashes in a jar, so I brought the urn up to Mr. Graham's room for safekeeping." She put her hands on her hips.

"I was afraid you'd thrown him away," Ibby said.

Doll tapped the side of her face with her finger. "Come on, then—I'll let you have a peek. But don't tell no one I let you in there, understand? Not a word." She stuck a key in the door directly across the hall from her sewing room. "This was your daddy's room. He was a few years younger than you when he got sent away to boarding school over in Mississippi. Don't think it's changed much since then."

In the center of the blue linoleum floor was a beautiful compass rose with long spikes of white and silver marking north, east, south, and west. A four-poster bed with a patchwork quilt was pushed against the wall, and next to it, a bookcase held an army of tin soldiers, just as Fannie had said. On the far wall, a large armoire took up the wall between two windows covered with blue plaid curtains. A stack of comic books was piled neatly in a corner.

"I put the urn in the armoire." Doll pointed to the other side of the room. "If you want, I can leave the door unlocked—that way you can come visit whenever you want. But it'll be our little secret. Understand?"

To Ibby's surprise, the armoire was still full of her father's clothes—T-shirts neatly stacked on the shelf, a few jackets and collared shirts, and a green Tulane sweatshirt hanging from the rod. Several pairs of shoes lined the bottom of the armoire. Doll had placed the urn between a pair of worn tennis shoes and brown penny loafers.

"I'll leave you alone with your daddy." Doll closed the door softly.

Ibby sat on her knees and stared at the brass urn for a good long while. She tried to envision her daddy's eyes, the way they crinkled up at the edges when he told her how much he loved her. She missed hearing the sound of his voice. The cold linoleum floor only reminded her of how lonely she felt. She wondered if he had felt the same way when he lived here. She wanted to tell him how sorry she was for causing his bicycle to slip on the wet pavement that day. She tried to find the words, but none would come. She bent her head and closed her eyes. The room was so quiet she could hear herself breathing.

"I'll take care of you, I promise," she said.

She placed the urn back in the armoire, then went over to the bookshelf where the tin soldiers were lined up. She searched until she found one she thought would have been his favorite, a soldier mounted on a stallion with his sword raised high in the air. She stuck it in her pocket and closed the door behind her.

Chapter Eleven

Ibby changed her clothes and came back down to find a dozen women dressed in maids' uniforms buzzing around the picnic table on the back porch. Queenie was out there with them, standing off to the side, waving her hands around like a referee. Doll was leaning against the kitchen counter with her arms across her chest, watching them.

"Who are all those people?" Ibby asked.

Doll twisted her mouth to the side. "You know that newspaper Miss Fannie was looking at this morning? Sometimes she spends all day with her nose stuck in that paper, figuring the odds, working the numbers. This afternoon she'll be in her favorite chair in the front room, glued to the TV, just to make sure her team won."

"I don't understand."

"See all those women out there shoving their way toward the picnic table? Their employers wouldn't be caught dead coming down here themselves. The women who live in these big old houses on Prytania Street send their maids down here a couple of times a week just to place their bets with Mr. Henry." Doll pointed to the only man on the porch, who was busy scribbling on a notepad. "Mr. Henry works for Mr. Salvatore, who owns the little grocery over there on Garfield Street. Besides delivering the groceries, Mr. Henry brings line sheets with him every day so all the women in the neighborhood can place their bets. He's kind a like a bookie."

"Is that bad?" Ibby asked.

"No, baby. That's a good thing, especially where Miss Fannie is concerned. You see, Miss Fannie, she's got a good track record, she do her homework, knows what to bet on. She made a lot a money that way. People found out. Started coming around, asking Miss Fannie for advice."

"What do they bet on?"

"Lawd, child, all sorts of things. Horses. Dogs. Football. Who's gone win the next election. When the first hurricane's gone hit. Right now, they betting on horses, baseball, Wimbledon, the Olympic trials, and a few golf tournaments. Your grandmother, she can recite the odds right off the top of her head. So almost every morning, the second Mr. Henry shows up in our driveway on his red bicycle, it's like a stampede to the back door. That's why Miss Fannie jumped up and got dressed so quick-like. She knew what was coming."

Ibby pointed at the mob of women. "Fannie's out *there*?"

"Sure is. Smack dab in the middle, settin' at the picnic table yelling out her picks to Mr. Henry. It's a little game she like to play." Doll shook her head.

"Baltimore over New York, three to one," Fannie said.

"What she say?" one of the women asked.

"Philly," another one answered.

"No, Baltimore," another said.

"Miss Fannie won't write her picks down for nobody but Mr. Henry, so he don't get confused," Doll went on. "But the women, they have to listen close, see if they can figure out what she telling Mr. Henry. They get it wrong half the time, but still, they do pretty good."

Fannie let the women argue among themselves before she threw out another bet. "Emerson over Stolle, three sets to one in the finals."

"Who?" one of the women asked.

"Shhhh. I can't hear if you keep talking, Millie," another said.

Doll shook her head. "The ladies of the house, they happy with the extra money they make off betting, helps buy them pretty dresses or that extra pair of shoes they been wanting but their husbands won't pay for. And all those women out there in those maid uniforms? They like it 'cause they make a few extra bucks each week on account they get to place their own bets when they come. Makes everybody happy."

Ibby and Doll watched the women bickering with one another. Poor Mr. Henry was scribbling down what Fannie told him, but every once in a while, even he had to look up and ask her to repeat the bet.

"What was that you say?" Mr. Henry squinted.

"Broncos to pick up Billy Lott from the Patriots."

Mr. Henry nodded and scribbled some more.

Doll sighed. "Miss Fannie has made a pretty penny on her picks. Everyone knows about it. Shucks, a few days, we even get the police coming around, asking Miss Fannie for tips. Used to scare the living daylights out of me when them blue uniforms would show up and knock on the door, but now I'm used to it. Most a the time, anyhow."

Money was being shoved at Mr. Henry from all directions. He'd look around, trying to see who was doing the shoving, and each time he did, his head hit one of the plastic penny bags hanging from the rafters. It kept swinging around and hitting him in the face no matter how many times he swatted it away. Grab the money, swat, grab the money, swat the bag again. Ibby stifled a giggle.

Finally, Mr. Henry put his hand up in the air. "Please, ladies, one at a time. I'm not going anywhere."

Doll pointed out toward the porch. "Like flies on flypaper whenever Mr. Henry comes by. Got some mighty big flies out there, too." Doll chuckled. "Now come on. I'm supposed to take you over to Mrs. Friedrichs's house so you can play with her girl."

As they started down the sidewalk, Ibby asked, "How far is the Friedrichses' house?"

"Just up the block," Doll said, walking slowly, as if she were in no hurry to get there.

"You been working for my grandma a long time?" Ibby asked as they strolled along.

"Started coming by to do the ironing when I was about your age. Had to quit school. Mama said I didn't need no more schooling anyway. Said all I needed was right there in that house." Doll shook her head.

Ibby sensed regret in her voice.

"How long has Queenie been with Fannie?" Ibby asked.

Doll stopped and picked a flower from an azalea bush, studied it, then tossed it over the fence of the house they were standing in front of. "Long time, baby. She came with the house."

"What does that mean?"

"You know, like the furniture, the rugs, the silver. It all came with the house."

"And how long ago was that?" Ibby asked.

"The way Mama tells it, an old widow lady by the name of Miss Althea lived in that house before Miss Fannie. Miss Althea lost her husband when she was young. Never had any children. So when she died, the house went up for sale, lock, stock, and barrel. Mr. Norwood bought it for Miss Fannie right after they married. That first day when Miss Fannie and Mr. Norwood moved in, with nothing more than one little suitcase apiece, my mama was standing in the dining room like she did every morning. Mama say she remembers that day as if it were yesterday."

⚜⚜⚜

The new owners of the house had just arrived. Queenie could hear the man talking in the hall as she stood nervously beside the dining room chair where she had waited for instructions from Miss Althea every day for the past fifteen years. Queenie brushed off her uniform and straightened her starched cap as she peered into the hall, trying to get a glimpse of the young couple. *Gal can't be no more than eighteen,* Queenie thought.

The woman dropped her suitcase onto the ground. "We're living here, in this old house?"

"Don't you like it, Fannie darling?" her husband asked as he took off his hat and fingered it nervously.

"Norwood, it's just that . . . it's so big!" she cried. "Aren't we in a depression? How can we afford it?"

"Sweetie, you don't need to worry about that," he said. "I told you when I married you that I'd take good care of you."

Queenie didn't quite know what to make of the couple. The young woman was all dolled up, wearing a tight-fitting skirt and a silk blouse that barely hid her ample bosom.

"You'll get used to it, sugar," Norwood said as he started up the stairs. "Now come on. Let's check out the bedroom." He gave Fannie a quick wink.

Fannie stood in the hall as if trying to decide what to do. Instead of following Norwood, she went into the front parlor and looked around. She tugged on the red velvet curtains, ran her fingers along the white marble fireplace, rubbed the fabric on the settee, then turned and walked into the dining room and began tracing the lines of the dining room table with her fingertips.

"How do, ma'am?" Queenie said when Fannie got to the end of the table, where she was standing.

Fannie jumped back. "Who are you?"

Queenie stood calmly, trying to hide her apprehension despite the tiny specks of sweat that had formed on her forehead. It was clear this young woman was nothing like old Miss Althea, a very proper lady full of manners and grace. This new woman was so rough around the edges that Queenie thought it might be in her best interest to find another position. On the other hand, did she really want to go to all that trouble when she already knew the house, the neighborhood, and the weekly routine? She had to make a decision, and she had to make it quickly.

"Didn't you hear what I said? Get out!" Fannie ordered.

It took Queenie less than a second to figure out that this woman had never had a maid before. She was going to be a challenge, for sure. Queenie drew in a breath.

"I'm the maid, ma'am. My name's Saphronia Trout. I comes with the house," Queenie said, trying to sound as if she belonged.

"I never heard a no maid come with a house before," Fannie said.

Lawd, listen how she talks. Working class—Queenie was sure of it now. *And that accent, she ain't from the city. Probably country folk, the way she draws out her words like they is taking their time getting out of her mouth. But one thing's for sure. She gone live in this neighborhood, I'm gone have to teach her how to talk proper so she don't stick out like a sore thumb. Lawd, all I need is for the other help to make fun. Can't have none a that. Maybe start her on the word of the day in the newspaper, to improve her vocabulary. Gone try to make her more like Miss Althea. Now that lady, she had manners.*

"And what kind of highfalutin' name is Saphro . . . Saphro . . ."

"Saphronia, ma'am," Queenie interjected.

"What kind of name is that anyway? Just who do you think you are? Queen of the Nile? Huh, Queenie?" Fannie put her hands on her hips. "Now go on home, like I told you." She gave Queenie a dismissive wave of her hand.

"Yes, ma'am." Queenie left the dining room, grabbed her pocketbook from the kitchen drawer, and left.

The next morning, Queenie came back. And when Miss Fannie came down the stairs, Queenie was standing in the same spot as she had been the day before, beside the dining room chair.

"Queenie, what the hell you doing here?" Fannie huffed. "I thought I told you to go home and never come back."

Queenie was afraid to look at her on account she had on a see-through nightie. Instead, she peered at her sideways, trying not to flinch. "What can I get you for breakfast, ma'am?"

"You cook?" Fannie folded her arms across her body, suddenly conscious she was standing there half-naked.

"Yes, ma'am. I'm a mighty fine cook, according to Miss Althea."

"I don't need no cook," Fannie said, waving her hand at Queenie. "Now go on home, like I told you."

For the next week, Queenie came back to that house on Prytania Street every day. And each morning she asked Miss Fannie what she wanted for breakfast. Finally, on the seventh day, Miss Fannie gave Queenie a different answer.

"You know how to make eggs benedict?" she asked.

"Oh, yes, ma'am," Queenie answered.

A little while later Queenie came back into the dining room and placed the eggs in front of Miss Fannie along with a brandy milk punch, hoping the brandy might make her more palatable.

Fannie looked at the plate with wonder in her face. "I ain't never had eggs benedict before."

"Well," Queenie said, hoisting up her bosom, "now you can have them every morning, if that's what you want."

Fannie cut a portion of the eggs benedict and tasted it.

"Why, this is the best thing I've ever put in my mouth!" she declared.

"I got plenty more where that came from. Can make you gumbo, or grillades, or whatever else you like. I make me a mean crème brûlée."

Fannie turned her steely blue eyes up at Queenie. "Really? You'll stay? I'll call you Saphro . . . Saphro—you know, your name—if that's what you want."

Queenie wasn't quite sure what to make of her sentimentality. No employer had ever talked that way to her before, so intimate like. *Maybe she not so bad after all.*

"Queenie'll do just fine, Miss Fannie."

ʚ৩ঔৎ

"Your grandma, she been calling her Queenie ever since. Been a good thirty years now," Doll said.

"Did Fannie make up your name, too?" Ibby asked.

Doll shook her head. "No, child. The way Mama tells it, the day I came into this world, she said I looked like a little brown baby doll, the kind you find in a king cake. From that day on, she called me her little Dollbaby."

"What's a king cake?" Ibby asked.

Doll twisted her mouth. "I forget you ain't from around here. You heard of Mardi Gras, ain't you?"

"Yeah."

"King cakes are an oval-shaped strudel they serve during the Mardi Gras season. I don't really know why, but they stick a little naked doll the size of a half my pinkie in the middle of the cake. Sometimes it's porcelain, sometimes plastic, but they always look the same—they got their little arms and legs sticking up in the air like they getting ready to pee."

"Is Dollbaby your real name?"

"No. It's Viola, but nobody calls me that, lessen we at church."

Doll stopped in front of a large clapboard center-hall cottage painted the color of strawberry ice cream. A boxwood hedge led up to a raised front porch lined with columns. In the side yard, a towering pecan tree held a swing on its lower branches, the grass beneath it worn thin.

Doll bent over and whispered to Ibby, "Now, don't you let little Miss Annabelle get under your skin. You hear me? She thinks she's a real princess, just like her mama do. Don't be put off by no airs she puts on, that's all I'm saying."

With that, Doll led Ibby up the stairs and rang the doorbell. Through the etched-glass paneling in the front door, Ibby could see a long-legged woman in uniform approaching.

"Fine morning to you, Doll." The woman opened the door. "And who we got here?"

"Ernestine, this here is Miss Fannie's grandchild. She visiting for a while. Miss Fannie thought Miss Ibby might be good company for Miss Annabelle."

Ernestine waved them in. "Miss Annabelle's out in the kitchen do-ing her best to finish off the batch of chocolate lace cookies I just made."

"Miss Honey here?" Doll asked with a slight catch to her voice.

"She's out shopping."

Doll sighed with relief. In the kitchen, a little girl with beribboned pigtails was perched on a stool, eating a large lace cookie. Her kinky hair was the color of a brand-new penny, and her face was covered in freckles of almost the same hue.

"Cookies just came out of the oven. Want one?" Ernestine asked Ibby, picking up a plate of cookies.

"Yes, please," Ibby said politely as she placed a cookie on the napkin Ernestine held out for her.

Annabelle jumped down from the stool and looked at Ibby. She had chocolate smeared on the side of her face. Ibby took an instant dislike to her. And from the nasty look on Annabelle's face, the feeling was mutual.

"Who are you?" Annabelle demanded, her mouth falling open to reveal a gap in her front teeth large enough to fit a number-two pencil.

Ibby thought Annabelle looked like a cross between Howdy Doody and Raggedy Ann. It wasn't a good combination.

"Be nice, Miss Annabelle," Ernestine said. "This here is Miss Fannie down the street's granddaughter. She come to visit a spell."

Ibby took a bite of the cookie and watched Annabelle. Annabelle in turn cocked her head as if she smelled something awful.

"You two run on outside and busy yourself in the backyard," Ernestine said.

Annabelle licked the chocolate off her fingers and opened the back door. "You coming or not? I don't have all day."

Ibby looked up at Doll with pleading eyes.

"You go on now, Miss Ibby. It'll be all right." Doll nudged Ibby for-ward and whispered in her ear. "You just remember what I told you."

Chapter Twelve

Not an hour later, Doll peered out the back window to find Ernestine walking up the driveway wearing a nervous face, with Ibby trudging along beside her.

"Look like we got a little problem," Doll said, pinching her mouth to one side.

Queenie wiped her hands on her apron and went to the window just as Ernestine came to the back door.

"What happened?" Doll propped the screened door open with her foot.

"Ibby and Annabelle, they got into a fight. I'll let her tell you about it." Ernestine nodded at Ibby.

Queenie grabbed Ibby's chin as she came up the back steps. "God Almighty. What happened to you? You got one doozy of a black eye."

"Her knee, it's kind of scraped up, too." Ernestine looked up at Doll from the bottom of the steps. "Miss Honey says Miss Ibby ain't welcome at their house no more for beating up her Annabelle." She leaned closer to Doll and Queenie. "Been a long time coming, far as I'm concerned. Looked like a catfight in the backyard until I got the garden hose and sprayed 'em down. Just sorry Miss Ibby here got hurt."

"Thank you kindly for bringing her home," Queenie said as she closed the screened door.

Ernestine turned to go.

A second later Queenie opened the door and called after her. "If that be the case, might want to let Miss Honey know that Miss Fannie won't be able to help her out no more when Mr. Henry come around, if you know what I mean." Queenie smiled real big.

Ernestine's shoulders heaved with laughter. "I understand. Certainly do. I'll be sure and pass that on to Miss Honey."

Queenie pointed to a bush at the bottom of the steps next to where Ibby was standing. "Child, reach down and pick me a leaf off that bush."

Ibby picked a leaf and handed it to Queenie. Queenie crushed the leaf in her hands and handed it back to her.

"Here, press this up against your eye. Geranium leaf will calm it down a bit." She turned to Doll. "Where's Miss Fannie at?"

"She's taking a nap, resting up before the big game on the TV this afternoon," Doll answered.

"Good. Give me some time to think about how to handle this. Miss Ibby, come on over here and sit on this stool so I can get a better look." Queenie scoured the kitchen. "One around here somewhere. Just saw it."

"If you looking for that spiderweb, saw one out on the porch," Doll said. "Noticed it when Mr. Henry came by earlier."

Doll climbed onto the picnic table and removed a large web from the corner. She came back into the kitchen and handed it to Queenie, who gently folded it over several times and placed it on top of Ibby's skinned-up knee.

"No need to buy no gauze when we got spiderwebs do just as good." Queenie winked at Ibby. "Just hold it in place a spell. It'll get that knee to quit bleeding." She motioned toward the refrigerator. "Now, Doll, go fetch me one of them tallow candles, the ones I keep in the icebox in case Miss Fannie hurts herself."

Doll handed the candle to Queenie, who placed it against Ibby's eye, which was now a splotchy mess of purple and red where Annabelle had punched her.

Queenie's forehead crinkled up. "You want to tell me what happened?"

"Is it true?" Ibby asked.

"Is what true?" Queenie asked.

"That my grandma was a stripper on Bourbon Street?" Ibby said with eyes so wide they looked as if they might pop.

Doll shook her head. What had that devil child been telling Miss Ibby?

"Now, tell me, Miss Ibby, how on earth something like that ever come up?" Queenie asked.

"Annabelle said her mama told her that the lady who lived in the haunted house down the street was nothing but trash, a stripper from Bourbon Street."

"Miss Annabelle said that?" Queenie asked.

Ibby nodded. "I got mad, so I pushed the swing and it accidentally hit her in the head. She started screaming bloody murder."

"Bet she did," Doll said. "She's one big drama queen."

"Then Annabelle came over and raised her fist at me, said she was gonna beat me up until I saw stars coming out of my eyes."

Doll pulled up a stool next to Ibby and handed Queenie another cold candle.

"Bet that's not the first time Miss Annabelle been in a fight." Queenie changed out the candle and held the new one up against Ibby's eye.

"Then what happened?" Doll prodded, wondering how much Miss Annabelle had told Miss Ibby.

"Annabelle punched me, so I kicked her. Next thing I know she's pushed me down on the driveway, so I yanked her down by the ankle. We were rolling around on the ground when Ernestine came out and turned the hose on us." Ibby's words were coming out so fast she could barely catch her breath.

"Calm down, Miss Ibby. We ain't going nowhere," Queenie said.

Ibby began to hiccup.

Queenie patted her on the back. "Take a deep breath."

"Then what?" Doll asked.

"Well . . . when Annabelle's mother comes outside to see what was going on, Annabelle leaps up and tells her mama it's my fault, that I called her names. So her mama tells Ernestine to bring me home. Says I'm not welcome there anymore. Tells me not to come back."

"I knew it weren't a good idea when Miss Fannie suggested it," Queenie mumbled.

"What we gone do?" Doll asked. "Miss Fannie gone notice that eye for sure."

Queenie took the candle away and inspected Ibby's eye. "Just gone be one a those times we pretend there's nothing wrong, 'less she asks. Miss Ibby, you run on upstairs and change out of them wet clothes. Don't say nothing about your run-in with Miss Annabelle when you come back down for lunch, and whatever you do, child, don't let on what Miss Annabelle say about your grandma, you hear me?"

Ibby jumped down from the stool. "Don't worry, I won't."

After Ibby left the kitchen, Doll looked over at her mother. "So, Mama, just how long you think you can keep putting off Miss Ibby? Sooner or later she gone find out the truth about Miss Fannie."

Queenie glanced out the back window. She had on one of her thinking faces. She turned back around. "Rule Number Six."

"Since when we get a Rule Number Six?" Doll asked.

"Since just now."

"So what's Rule Number Six?"

"Whatever you do, you got to keep Miss Ibby away from Miss Annabelle."

Chapter Thirteen

Ibby inched sideways into her chair, trying to keep her eye turned away from Fannie, as she took her seat at the table for lunch.

"What's all this?" Fannie asked as Queenie placed a platter on the table.

"Thought Miss Ibby might like to try something different while she's here." Queenie put a bottle of hot sauce on the table. "Know how you like gazpacho during tomato season. And on the platter we got oysters three ways—on the half shell, oysters Rockefeller, and oysters Bienville. On the small plate is some cornbread, already buttered, just the way you like it."

Fannie leaned over and whispered to Ibby, "She's trying to impress you. She never makes all this just for me."

"Oh, and there ain't no hereafter today, Miss Fannie, just so you know." Queenie gave Ibby a brief smile before she went back into the kitchen.

It was one of those keep-your-mouth-shut kind of smiles.

Ibby reached for a piece of cornbread. "What's hereafter?"

Fannie stuck a spoon into the soup. "That's what Queenie calls dessert. Doesn't look like we're going to need it today anyway."

Ibby followed Fannie's lead and tried the soup. It was cold and had floating chunks of onion and green pepper. She put the spoon down, hoping the oysters might taste better, but from the looks of them, she wasn't so sure.

"I can tell by that look on your face that you've never had oysters." Fannie picked up a three-pronged fork. "Use this oyster fork, and kind of jab at the oysters. They're small this time of year, so just swallow them whole."

The oysters were gray and blobby, and the thought of eating one made Ibby get that salty taste in her mouth, the kind you get when you're about to throw up. Fannie was watching her with interest so she dropped a raw oyster into her mouth. When Fannie wasn't looking, she spat it into her napkin.

"What have you been up to this morning?" Fannie asked. "Did you have a nice visit with Annabelle Friedrichs?"

Before Ibby could answer, Queenie burst through the door.

"Miss Fannie, I just wanted to remind you that Miss Ibby's birthday is this coming Saturday. You made reservations at Antoine's for lunch."

"Did I?"

"Yes, ma'am. Eleven-thirty. Crow is coming by to wash the car on account he gone drive you to Antoine's, then you gone come back here and have cake."

"I see."

"Yes, ma'am, then Doll and me, we most likely gonna take the rest of the day off, considering Saturday is the Fourth of July and all. That is, if that be all right by you," Queenie added.

To everyone's surprise, the doorbell rang.

Queenie shuffled into the hall. When she opened the door, a woman with a red bouffant hairdo burst through.

"Miss Fannie here?"

The screechy voice gave her away. Ibby stiffened as Honey Friedrichs pushed her way past Queenie and into the dining room. She stood at the end of the table holding a plate of cookies in one hand while attempting to adjust her close-fitting blue shift with the other, leaving Queenie standing by the front door with her mouth gaping open.

"Soooo nice to see you, Fannie. It's been a while. I can see I'm interrupting your lunch so I won't keep you. I have to rush out to a Junior League meeting, but not before I brought by this tray of cookies that Ernestine made especially for Ibby, to welcome her to the neighborhood." Honey placed the tray on the table, then stood back with her hands on her hips, tapping her foot nervously.

Ibby noticed that Honey Friedrichs didn't look the same as she had this morning when she came out into the backyard wearing black trousers with her hair pulled back in a ponytail. Now her hair was so heavily teased and lacquered that it didn't move when she spoke.

"Annabelle and Ibby had so much fun playing together this morning, didn't you, dear?" Honey put on a thick smile, waiting for Ibby to agree. "Didn't you, dear?" She widened her eyes at Ibby.

Miss Honey was trying so hard not to let her smile slip that the sides of her mouth began to quiver. Ibby was afraid if she didn't answer soon, Miss Honey would burst and the truth about this morning would come spilling out.

"Yes, ma'am," Ibby replied, trying hard to sound as if she meant it.

"Well, good, that's all I wanted to say. I don't want to keep you from your lunch. Ibby is certainly welcome to come over and play with my little Annabelle anytime she likes. We're all good, right?" Miss Honey looked from one person to another, waiting for an answer. "Well, I'll be off then. Don't want to miss the baseball game I bet on this afternoon. Go, Cardinals!" She raised her hand in the air as if she were leading a cheer, then turned and trotted out the front door as fast as she'd come.

Queenie shut the door behind her and straightened her uniform.

"Mind telling me what that was all about?" Fannie asked.

"Beats me," Queenie said, then disappeared into the kitchen.

Fannie studied the plate of cookies on the table in front of her. "Well, lookey here. It appears we got our hereafter after all."

Chapter Fourteen

Doll looked up when her mother came back in the kitchen.

"Miss Honey gone?" Doll asked.

Queenie chuckled. "Yes, thank the Lawd. Never seen her like that before, falling all over herself."

"Good thing she didn't mention the eye in front of Miss Fannie. Miss Ibby looks like a prizefighter who done lost the fight. We gone have to come up with some story, like maybe she tripped and fell in the backyard."

"I know. I been thinking on it," Queenie said.

Doll picked up a pecan from the bowl in the middle of the kitchen table and inspected it. "Maybe I'll make me a pecan pie to take to the Fourth of July party out by the lake."

Queenie crossed her arms. "What you mean, a party out by the lake? We got the church picnic that day. The Reverend Jeremiah, he gone be expecting you to help serve."

"The party ain't until later on. But there's no way I'm gone miss it. It's the last day Lincoln Beach gone be open."

"Why they close the beach so early this year? Thought they waited until end of the summer."

"They closing Lincoln Beach for good, now that Pontchartrain Beach, where the white folks swim, is integrated. The city says they is no use having two public beaches no more, so what they do? They close the Negro beach."

Queenie sat down at the table and leaned on her elbow. "You see what I'm telling you? If the government would have left well enough alone, they wouldn't be closing the Negro beach. And by the way, did you see the front page of the paper today? There's a big picture of your friend Lola Mae sprawled all over the floor at that sit-in on Canal Street. Could have been you."

"But it wasn't, Mama. You made sure of that."

Queenie held up the paper and pointed at the photo. "Really? Take a closer look."

Doll stared at the photo showing Lola Mae on the ground, a policeman standing beside her, and a bunch of wide-eyed Negroes looking on from their stools at the lunch counter.

"Look at the shoulder and the side of the head at the edge of the photo. Now, who you suppose that is?" Queenie narrowed her eyes.

"What you going on about? I don't see nothin'." But just then, Doll did see. In the corner of the photograph was her profile. There was no mistaking it.

"Don't you pretend you don't know what I'm talking about. That's you sitting there on that stool. Why'd you lie to me?"

"I'm sorry, Mama. I felt like it was something I needed to do."

"You need to start thinking more about Birdelia," Queenie said, "and less about yourself."

"And why you think I gone down there—for fun? I'm doing it *for* Birdelia and everyone like her," Doll said. "You just don't seem to understand that."

"Yeah, well, it ain't gone do no good if she don't have a mama around to take care of her no more. You got to be more careful. And don't you dare lie to me again like that." Queenie wagged her finger at Doll and threw the paper onto the kitchen table. "I'm telling you, ever since President Johnson said he might sign that new civil rights law into place, it got people mighty jittery. Don't want no trouble." Queenie got up from the table and peeked into the dining room.

"Mama, come sit back down. Last time I looked, Miss Fannie was already in front of the TV, waiting for the game to come on."

"It don't start for another hour—why she just sitting there? Gone miss my stories," Queenie fretted. "And where's Miss Ibby?"

"She's sitting right next to Fannie. I told her to sit with the bad eye toward the hall, but I don't think you need to worry about Miss Fannie noticing Miss Ibby's eye. She too busy watching the pregame show."

The screened door creaked open, and a man who barely filled his overalls came through the door walking slowly, in a sort of back-and-forth shuffle to accommodate his bowed legs. He was carrying a brown paper bag folded over at the top.

"Come on in and take a load off, Crow," Queenie said to him.

Crow set the bag on the table and pointed at it. "Queenie, wish you'd get Doll to run your errands. Them folks down at Haase's Children's Fashions gone think I'm some kind a queer, you keep sending me to buy things like that."

Doll opened the bag and pulled out a pair of black patent-leather Mary Janes. "Thank you, Daddy. These'll fit Miss Ibby just fine."

Queenie handed a glass of sweet tea to Crow, paying no mind to his comment. "Doll, you finished with Miss Fannie's dress you making for Ibby's birthday lunch?"

"Almost."

"Ibby's, too?"

"Be ready tomorrow, Mama."

Crow finished his tea and wiped his mouth with a red bandanna he'd pulled from the pocket of his overalls. "I can see you got other things on your mind. I'll be out in the back washing Miss Fannie's car if y'all need me."

Queenie grabbed two sodas from the icebox and went into the front room and set them on the coffee table in front of Fannie.

"You want to come help me in the kitchen?" Queenie nodded toward the kitchen.

Fannie was so busy talking back to the television that she didn't seem to notice that Ibby had followed Queenie out of the room.

As Ibby sat down at the kitchen table, Queenie asked, "What kind of cake you want for your birthday? You ever had *doberge?*"

"What's *doe-bash?*"

"They a specialty around here, a cake that's got about twelve paper-thin layers filled with pudding. They a favorite of Miss Fannie's."

"I guess so," Ibby said, then added, "Who's Crow?"

Doll was sitting on a stool over by the back window, eating her lunch. "Crow's my daddy. Matter a fact, he's out back shining up that old Cadillac of your grandmother's so he can drive you to your birthday lunch."

Ibby looked over at Doll. "Is Crow his real name?"

"No, baby," Queenie answered. "His real name is Cedric Cornelius Trout, bless his sorry soul." Queenie pointed toward the back window. "The way his mama used to tell it, he was so ugly when he came into this world that he scared all the crows out of the field, every single one of them. So she nicknamed him Scarecrow. Later on they just start calling him Crow."

"Mama's just kidding," Doll said.

"No, I ain't," Queenie shot back. "That's the Lawd's truth."

"You never told me that story about how Daddy really got his name."

"You never asked," Queenie said before turning to Ibby. "Now, Miss Ibby, why don't you run out back and help Crow wash that car? He's looking mighty lonely out there. Just don't go messing with my vegetable garden, you hear?"

After the screened door slammed shut, Doll turned to her mother. "You just trying to get Miss Ibby out of the house so Miss Fannie don't notice the eye, ain't you?"

"There's more than one way to skin a cat."

❧❧❧❧

Later that afternoon, Doll yelled through the screened door, "Daddy, get on in here!"

"What now?" He tossed his sponge into the bucket and turned off the hose.

"Just come on," she said urgently.

Doll held the door open for her father, then settled herself onto a stool by the window. Ibby came in a few minutes later.

"Why's everybody so quiet?" Ibby asked.

Doll put her finger up to her mouth. "Just listen." She tilted her head toward the radio. "The president's about to come on and give an address."

Queenie had her elbows on the kitchen counter with her head bent toward the transistor radio. Crow took a few steps closer to Queenie as she reached over to turn the volume up.

"The following announcement is broadcast from the East Room of the White House," came a voice on the radio. "I give you Lyndon B. Johnson, the president of the United States."

There was a ruffling noise, like papers being shuffled, and then another voice came on the radio. "My fellow Americans."

"Think he really did it?" Doll whispered to her mother as she fidgeted, barely able to control her excitement.

Queenie put her finger up to her mouth.

"I am about to sign into law the Civil Rights Act of 1964. I want to take this occasion to talk to you about what the law means to every American." President Johnson cleared his throat. "One hundred and eighty-eight years ago this week, a small band of valiant men began a long struggle for freedom. They pledged their lives, their fortunes, and their sacred honor not only to found a nation, but to forge an ideal of freedom—not only for political independence, but for personal liberty."

Doll noticed Ibby was swinging her feet back and forth as if she were bored. She had to fight the urge to go over and shake her. She wanted to say *Listen to what the president is saying! Listen!* She closed her eyes, the sound of her own breathing resonating in her ears.

"This is a proud triumph. . . . Now our generation of Americans has been called on to continue the unending search for justice within our own borders. We believe that all men are created equal. Yet many are denied equal treatment."

Doll opened her eyes and glanced over at Crow. There were tears in the corner of her father's eyes. *Poor Daddy,* she thought. *If anybody understands the meaning of what the president is saying, it's him. Lawd knows he's been through the wringer, knows firsthand what Jim Crow can do to a man, make him feel lower than a barn animal.*

"The purpose of this law is simple," the president said, emphasizing the word *simple.* "It does not restrict the freedom of any American, so long as he respects the rights of others. It does not give special treatment to any citizen. It does say the only limit to a man's hope for happiness, and for the future of his children, shall be his own ability. It does say," the president continued, "that those who are equal before God shall now also be equal in polling booths, in the classrooms, in the factories, and in hotels, restaurants, movie theaters, and other places that provide service to the public."

Crow was nodding with every word the president uttered, and Queenie was staring at the radio with ferocious intensity.

"Its purpose is to promote a more abiding commitment to freedom, a more constant pursuit of justice, and a deeper respect for human dignity. . . . This Civil Rights Act is a challenge to all of us to go to work in our communities and our states, in our homes and in our hearts, to eliminate the last vestiges of injustice in our beloved country. . . . My fellow citizens, we have come now to a time of testing. We must not fail. Let us close the springs of racial poison. . . . Thank you and good night." There was a loud noise as the microphone was pushed away.

Everyone sat quietly in their own thoughts as the president's words lingered in the room like an elephant, heavy and fat.

"That new law gone change everything," Doll said after a while.

"It ain't gone change nothing." Queenie spat out her words as if there were a bad taste in her mouth.

"We ain't what we want to be. We ain't what we gonna be. But thank God we ain't what we was," Crow said, his head bent toward the floor. "Still, far as I know, there ain't a white man ever been born that understood what the colored man's thinking, what he's feeling. Heck, half the time, that colored man don't know hisself."

"What you mumbling over there, old man?" Queenie snapped.

Crow just shook his head.

Doll tightened her arms across her chest. "For sure, the Reverend Jeremiah's gone have a few things to say about it this coming Sunday."

Queenie shook her head. "But I still say, you can't go mixing people up like they a bunch of eggs."

Crow took a bandanna out of his back pocket and wiped his eyes. He went out the back door just as a bellow came from the front room.

"How dare that good-for-nothing president interrupt my show!"

Queenie and Doll exchanged glances.

Queenie reached over and turned off the radio. "Ain't nothing ever gone change around this house. That's for sure." Queenie rolled her eyes. "And ain't nothing gone change for the black man neither, no matter what the president say on the radio."

Doll glanced out into the backyard, where her father was now bent over, scrubbing the car.

And she hoped, just this once, that her mother wasn't right.

Chapter Fifteen

Ibby noticed the door to Doll's sewing room was ajar the next morning as she made her way down to breakfast. When she peeked in, she was startled to find a set of dark eyes staring back at her.

"Get away from that door, like I told you!" Doll fussed at the dark-eyed girl.

"But, Mama," the girl said, "they is someone there!"

Flustered, Ibby ran across the hall to her father's room. She listened for a moment to make sure no one was coming after her before she took the urn from the armoire and placed it on the floor in front of her.

"Good morning, Daddy," she said.

"That your daddy in that jar?"

Ibby looked up to find a pair of spindly brown legs attached to a girl about her age in a sleeveless gingham dress. Her hair was braided all over her head. She was standing with one hand on her hip and staring down at Ibby.

"That your daddy?" the girl said again, pointing at the urn.

"Yes," Ibby answered, flustered by the girl's sudden appearance in her father's room.

The girl sat cross-legged beside her. "What were his name?"

"Graham," Ibby said.

"That's a nice name."

They studied each other a few moments. Ibby could see Doll in the girl. They had the same wide mouth, long thin face, expressive eyes, and beautiful almond skin.

"You Birdelia?" Ibby asked.

The girl nodded. They stared at each other a little while longer.

"Is that your real name?" Ibby asked.

"Yeah. Mama gave me that name on account of when I was born, I had my mouth open like this." Birdelia lifted her head, pushed her lips out, and began opening and closing her mouth. "Just like a baby bird do when they looking for food."

"My name's Ibby."

"That your real name?"

"No, it's Liberty, but the only person that calls me that is my mama when she gets mad," Ibby said, clenching the urn.

Birdelia leaned in and looked Ibby squarely in the eyes with an intensity she wasn't used to. "You miss your daddy, don't you?"

"He loved me," Ibby blurted. She had no idea why she said it, especially to a stranger.

"My daddy loved me, too. Least that's what my mama say."

"Did something happen to your daddy?" Ibby asked.

"Don't rightly know. Left before I was born." Birdelia cupped her chin in her hands, as if she were thinking about it some more.

"So . . . you never met your daddy?"

"Don't matter none." Birdelia shrugged. "Mama say he went back to Sorrowful Swamp, where he belonged."

"Where's Sorrowful Swamp?"

"Just a blot on the map, in the low country. Mama say no matter how hard you try and scratch it off the map, the stain of Sorrowful Swamp still shows through."

"You ever been there?"

Birdelia shook her head. "No. People shy away from the place, like it reeks, 'cause they say once you go there, you never come out."

"Is it haunted?"

Birdelia inched closer. "The way the story goes, there's a strange silence in Sorrowful Swamp. Once a person gets caught up in that silence, they can't live without it. And once they there, they can't leave anyway on account they believe every bush and every tree harbors Satan. And if it ain't Satan up in that tree, it's bound to be the boogeyman, or maybe one of them plat-eyes."

"Is that where your daddy is now?"

Birdelia nodded. "Mama say he went there before I was born, and no one ever seen him since."

Ibby felt sorry for Birdelia, never having met her father. "Your daddy, I know he loves you, in his own way."

"Yeah. That's what Mama say, too." Birdelia looked Ibby in the eye. "Your daddy, even though he's up there now"—Birdelia pointed up to the sky—"he'll always be with you as long as he's in here." She took Ibby's hand and placed it over her heart. "Every time you want to be with your daddy, that's all you got to do."

"Birdelia! I told you not to leave the sewing room. You not supposed to be in here." Doll stood by the door, tapping her foot.

Birdelia stood up and pointed at Ibby. "*She* in here."

"Don't you give your mama no sass. That's different, and you know it. Now, tell me, Birdelia Trout. What kind of stories you been telling Miss Ibby?" She squinted at Birdelia.

"Nothing, Mama. We just talking."

"Miss Ibby, don't believe a thing Birdelia tells you," Doll huffed.

The truth was, Birdelia's story had intrigued her. Ibby took a sort of newfound comfort in knowing that her daddy would always be with her, in her heart. She smiled to herself.

"Miss Ibby, you listening to me?" Doll asked.

Ibby looked up at her, realizing she had been lost in her own thoughts.

"Why don't you go on up and get dressed? Queenie got some biscuits and grits waiting for you in the kitchen. Miss Fannie's already taken her breakfast, so don't go disturbing her. She busy picking her horses before Mr. Henry gets here. Birdelia can keep you company today. Now, come on, Birdelia." Doll took her daughter by the hand and led her out of the room.

When Ibby got downstairs, Birdelia was sitting at the kitchen table with a pile of biscuits in front of her. She took a big swig of milk and smiled at Ibby.

"I see you two have met." Queenie wiped her hands on her apron.

Crow opened the back door and came in with a big box. "Here's the cake you asked me to pick up from the bakery. What you making today? Smells mighty fine." Crow moved things around in the icebox to make room for the cake.

Queenie stirred the pot. "Gumbo. Mr. Pierce gave me some extra shrimp to put in. I'll save some for you. Knows how much you like gumbo."

"Morning, Poppy," Birdelia said through a mouthful of biscuit.

"Birdelia, child, you know better than to talk with your mouth full." Queenie tapped the spoon on the side of the pot and placed it on the counter. "Now listen, young ladies, soon as Mr. Henry gets here, stay out of the way, understand?"

Crow rubbed the side of his face nervously, then whispered to Queenie, "Maybe they should stay in the backyard and not go wandering around the neighborhood after the president's announcement yesterday. The mayor called for peace, and as far as I know, there ain't been no trouble, but best be safe."

Queenie nodded, then looked at the two girls. "Poppy is right. You two stay in the backyard today. Don't go wandering off nowhere, you hear?"

"But Mee-maw, what we gonna do in the backyard?" Birdelia whined. "You said we could go over to Plum Street and get a snowball."

Crow shook his head and headed out the back door. "You women never listen to me anyway. Don't know why I waste my breath."

"Please?" Birdelia clasped her hands and smiled.

"Oh, all right," Queenie said after Crow was out of earshot. "But if you run into any trouble, you come on back home, you hear me?" Queenie squinted at Birdelia. "No trouble."

"Yes, ma'am, I promise." Birdelia jumped from the stool.

Queenie reached into the cookie jar and placed four dimes and two quarters in front of them. "No trouble," she repeated, and pointed at Birdelia.

Birdelia grabbed the money and stuck it into her pocket. "Well, come on, Miss Ibby."

As they walked up the street, a throng of uniformed maids passed them, heading for the Bell household to place their bets. As they got farther up the block, Ibby hesitated.

"What's wrong?" Birdelia asked.

Annabelle Friedrichs was sitting on the wooden swing hanging from the tree in her front yard, her back toward them.

"Let's cross the street," Ibby said.

"What for?"

"See the girl in the swing? That's Annabelle."

"Yeah, so?" Birdelia put her hand on her hip.

"She's the one that gave me this black eye." Ibby pointed at her face.

"Then we gonna walk right on past her. Don't do nothing until I give you the signal. She's behind a fence—what she gone do?"

Ibby thought about it for a moment. "Okay."

"She say anything to you, don't say nothing back. Understand? She wants to get under your skin—just act like you don't care. Now follow me." Birdelia started walking real slow, swinging her arms and whistling as if she didn't have a care in the world.

Ibby followed, imitating her.

Annabelle heard the whistling and turned around. Birdelia and Ibby kept on walking, swinging their arms. Annabelle jumped down from the swing and came over to the fence.

"See you still got that black eye," Annabelle said, following along behind the fence as they strolled by. "And I see you're a nigger lover, too."

Ibby wanted so badly to turn around and pull Annabelle's braids, but she remembered what Birdelia had told her.

"Now!" Birdelia said.

With that, Birdelia turned, pulled down her underpants and mooned Annabelle, then ran away as fast as she could. Ibby turned her head to see Annabelle Friedrichs standing with her hands on her hips and her mouth open.

Birdelia kept running. Three blocks later the girls stopped to catch their breath.

"I can't believe you just did that," Ibby said.

"She won't be bothering you no more," Birdelia giggled.

They took their time walking the rest of the way up to St. Charles Avenue. They crossed the street to the median, which Ibby discovered was called the neutral ground in New Orleans, and stood beside a yellow sign to wait for the streetcar. A few minutes later, a green streetcar with a red roof pulled up.

"Just give the money to the conductor." Birdelia handed Ibby a dime and stepped onto the streetcar.

They walked up to the front, handed the money to the driver, then went to the back of the streetcar and found a seat.

A woman sitting behind them tapped Ibby on the shoulder. "You go on and sit up by the driver, like you supposed to."

Ibby looked around. There were plenty of empty seats, both in the back and up front by the driver.

"Go on now." The woman waved her hand.

Ibby got up, waiting for Birdelia to follow.

"You stay put." The woman pushed Birdelia down by the shoulder.

Birdelia jutted her chin out, nodding to Ibby to do as the woman said, then looked the other way.

The streetcar traveled a good ways down St. Charles Avenue before making a turn at the bend of the river. About six blocks later, Birdelia jumped up and pulled a white cord over the window. She tilted her head toward Ibby.

"Why'd she make me go sit somewhere else?" Ibby asked when they got off the streetcar.

"That was the section for colored folks. I thought you knew that white folks supposed to sit up front."

"Why?"

Birdelia shrugged. "Always been that way, far as I can remember. Mee-maw say, a long time ago, when she was just starting to work for Miss Althea, they used to have streetcars marked with yellow stars for just colored people. Problem was, they didn't come around too often, and when they did, they was always full, so Mee-maw ended up walking to Miss Althea's most days. She say she was happy when they got rid of the streetcars for colored folks 'cause at least she could always find a seat on the back of the regular streetcars."

As they crossed the street, Ibby thought about what Birdelia said. She couldn't imagine being treated so differently.

They walked a few blocks down Plum Street until they came upon people milling about a purple clapboard building on the corner.

"You go and wait in that line out front." Birdelia pointed to the people standing just outside the front door of the building. "I got to go to the side window around back, where all the other colored folks are." She handed Ibby a quarter and disappeared down the street.

Ibby opened the screened door to the snowball stand. A sign over the counter advertised about a hundred different flavors of snowballs. A man in a white apron and funny paper hat held a Chinese takeout container under the opening of a large machine. Fine bits of shaved ice fell into the container and piled up over the rim. It took about twenty minutes for Ibby to reach the front of the line.

"What flavor?" the man in the paper hat asked.

Ibby pointed to a little girl in the next line over. "I'll have what she's having."

"That's wedding cake with whipped cream and sweetened condensed milk. That what you want?"

"Can I get it for a quarter? That's all I got," Ibby said.

"No problem, little lady."

After she got her snowball, Ibby walked out to look for Birdelia, who was waiting for her out front.

"What did you get?" Birdelia asked.

"Something called wedding cake." Ibby followed Birdelia to a bench near the sidewalk.

"I get the same every time. Cherry." Birdelia licked the red syrup off the side of the container, where it was dripping.

The girls sat on the bench, enjoying the warm sun on their backs and the coolness of the snowballs on their throats. As Ibby sipped her snowball through a straw, she noticed Birdelia fiddling with the gold chain around her neck.

Birdelia held it out for Ibby to see. "Miss Fannie gave me this necklace for my eleventh birthday this year. See? Got a letter B on it, for Birdelia."

"It's a mighty handsome necklace," Ibby said. "But I can't see Fannie out shopping for jewelry."

"She don't have to go shopping," Birdelia said. "They come to her."

"Who do you mean, they come to her?"

"If Miss Fannie needs a necklace, she calls up Mr. Norman, and he brings a case over from his shop. She needs some shoes, Miss Odille from Gus Mayer brings over a dozen pairs to choose from. If she wants something and they don't deliver, then Crow goes and picks it up for her."

"Oh," Ibby said. "Things don't work that way in Olympia, where I'm from."

As they slurped their snowballs, a policeman in a blue uniform came up to Ibby and bent down.

"Do you know this colored girl?" He pointed at Birdelia.

"Yes, officer," Ibby answered, puzzled by his question.

"Where'd you get that black eye?" he asked.

"A neighbor girl did that to me," Ibby said.

"Mind stepping over here a minute?" He pointed toward a tree up the street and smiled.

Ibby didn't understand why he wanted to talk to her, but she did as she was told. Birdelia stopped eating her snowball and watched them.

When they got to the tree, the policeman bent down to talk to Ibby. "Did that girl you were sitting with give you that black eye?"

He had a kind face, but the question was making her nervous. Why would he think Birdelia punched her?

"No, sir. Like I told you. Another girl did that. And my knee, too." Ibby pointed down at her skinned-up knee.

"Who is the little colored girl you're sitting with?" He pointed at Birdelia, who was craning her neck in their direction.

"Birdelia."

"And how do you know her?" the policeman asked as he stood up.

"Her mama works for my grandmother."

"Who is your grandmother, if I may ask?"

"Her name is Fannie Bell."

"Why didn't you say so?"

"You know her?" Ibby looked at him, surprised.

"Sure do. I've known your grandmother for a long, long time. My name's Lieutenant Kennedy. And Birdelia is Dollbaby's daughter. I just didn't put two and two together."

Ibby recognized him now. It was the same officer who'd come over to the car the other day when they were downtown buying perfume.

"Why don't you let me take you on home?" He pointed toward his squad car.

"I'd get in trouble if I didn't show up with Birdelia," Ibby said.

Lieutenant Kennedy adjusted the peaked cap on his head. "She can come, too."

Ibby and the policeman walked back over to where Birdelia was sitting.

"Why don't you come along with me?" he said to Birdelia.

"I didn't do nothing," Birdelia protested as she stood up.

"I'm going to take you home, as a favor to Miss Fannie," Lieutenant Kennedy said. "That's all."

Birdelia eyed him suspiciously before tossing her container in the trash can. On the way home, they passed the Friedrichses' house. Annabelle was still sitting on the swing in the front yard. When she saw the squad car pass and the two people looking out the back window, she jumped up and shouted for her mother. Ibby slumped down in her seat, just imagining what Annabelle was going to tell her mother this time.

Lieutenant Kennedy pulled up to Fannie's house and walked the girls to the door. When he rang the doorbell, Doll answered.

"Good day, Dollbaby," Lieutenant Kennedy said, tipping his hat. "How are you?"

"I'm fine, thank you."

"Good, glad to hear it. Fannie home?"

"Miss Fannie's taking a rest. Something I can help you with?"

"It's just that some ladies down at the snowball stand, when they saw the black eye on Fannie's granddaughter here, they thought there might have been some trouble. We're being extra vigilant this weekend, given the announcement by the president yesterday. Thought I'd bring the girls home, just to be on the safe side. Might want to keep them around the house today."

"Thank you, Lieutenant Kennedy," Doll said, ushering the girls inside.

"You got a right fine daughter there, Dollbaby. Take good care of her. And please give Fannie my best." He tipped his hat again.

"Sure will."

As soon as Doll shut the door, Birdelia piped up. "I didn't do nothing, I promise."

"I know, child." Doll put her arm around Birdelia's shoulder and squeezed it. "I know."

Chapter Sixteen

Ibby yawned as Queenie held up the Saturday paper and pointed at the front page, where there was a sketch of the American flag with LIBERTY written in bold letters beneath it.

"Lookey here, Miss Ibby. They got your name right on the front page of the paper today. They must have known it was your birthday!"

"Gosh, I completely forgot." Ibby took the paper from Queenie and looked at the front-page headline.

"How could you forget your own birthday?" Queenie asked.

"I don't know. So much going on, I guess. Has my mama called?"

It had been four days and not a word from her mother. Ibby thought the least Vidrine could do was call to wish her a happy birthday. But Vidrine was Vidrine. Sometimes she wondered if her mother cared about anyone other than herself. But it didn't stop Ibby from hoping.

"No, baby. Day still young, though." Queenie stirred the batter. "Oh, and one more thing. Don't go mentioning to Miss Fannie that Lieutenant Kennedy brought you home yesterday. Okay? That's something she just don't need to know."

Through the open door, a crack of thunder snapped in the distance as a gust of wind swept through the backyard, stirring up the dust and rustling the leaves on the pecan tree.

Queenie glanced out into the yard. "I hope the skies don't go spitting down on us today, or it'll spoil our church picnic. Be a shame, all that good food going to waste."

Doll darted into the kitchen, grabbed some scissors from a drawer, then swooped out without saying a word.

Queenie nodded toward Fannie's bedroom. "Doll's in there trying to get Miss Fannie ready for your birthday lunch, but your grandma, she ain't cooperating. All she wants to do is watch some of the baseball game on the television this morning. She bettin' on the Twins over the Yankees. Lawd, hope her team wins, 'cause she hates them Yankees."

After breakfast, Ibby went back up to her room. After a while, Doll came up to find her.

"What you doing sitting up here all alone?" Doll laid the dress she'd made for her on the bed.

Ibby picked it up and ran her fingers over the material—a sleeveless cobalt blue sheath with a contrasting white band at the hem and neck.

"It's very nice," Ibby said.

"So what's the matter?" Doll asked. "Why the long face?"

Ibby shrugged.

"What you normally do for your birthday?"

"Daddy gives me a card scribbled with some silly rhyme he made up, then takes me to do something special. Just me and him. No Vidrine."

"And now your daddy ain't here no more. I understand." Doll put her finger to her cheek. "Listen, baby. I know you gone have a good time today at Antoine's. Supposed to be one of the finest restaurants in town."

"Have you ever been?"

Doll gave Ibby a sideways glance. "No, baby. Never been myself. Now come over here so I can slip this on, see how it fits." She put the dress over Ibby's head and zipped it up, then handed her a pair of white lace socks and patent-leather shoes. "Go and take a look in the mirror on the back of the bathroom door."

Ibby turned from side to side, admiring herself in the mirror.

"Well?" Doll flicked one of her long fingernails.

"It's perfect. Thank you."

"I still don't see no smile on your face. What's wrong?"

"No, I like it. Really, it's lovely. It's just that I'm not used to wearing dresses, that's all."

"You look fine. Now come on over here so I can comb your hair," Doll said.

Doll combed Ibby's short hair over to the side and stuck a bobby pin with a striped bow in it. Ibby looked in the mirror again.

"I look like a baby," Ibby protested.

"You got to quit being a tomboy one of these days, Miss Ibby." Doll yanked the bow, pulled a headband from her pocket, and slid it on her head. "How about that?"

Ibby looked in the mirror. "Better I guess."

"Now put these on." Doll handed her a pair of white cotton gloves.

Ibby made a face. "Gloves? I thought only old ladies wore gloves."

"Down here all proper ladies, young or old, wear gloves to go out," Doll said.

Ibby wiggled her fingers to get them on. "Out where?"

"Everywhere, baby. To a restaurant, to church, even shopping on Canal Street. Oh. One more thing." She took a small jar of makeup from her pocket. "Let me see if I can do something about that eye."

Doll dabbed her finger in the jar and rubbed the creamy beige cover-up on the bruises, which had turned from a bluish purple to a sickly yellow green.

"Good. Now let's go on downstairs and see if we can get a smile on Miss Fannie's face, too."

"Wait a minute." Ibby ran over to the bedside table and dabbed a bit of perfume on her neck.

"Well," Doll said, "maybe you not such a tomboy after all."

When they got to the kitchen, they found Crow leaning against the doorjamb to the back porch, wearing black pants, a black dress shirt, and polished leather shoes. He was holding a chauffeur's cap in his hand.

"Happy birthday, Miss Ibby," he said.

Queenie turned from the stove. "My, what we got here? Future beauty queen, for sure. You remind me of Miss Fannie when she was young—such a perfect long neck, that pointy little nose, those beautiful blue eyes."

"And a stupid pageboy haircut," Ibby added.

"Hair will grow, Miss Ibby," Doll said, then turned to her mother. "Mama, I got to finish with Miss Fannie. She sitting in her room waiting for me to do her hair."

A little while later Doll held the kitchen door open, looking exhausted. Fannie appeared behind her, fiddling with a beige alligator handbag as she patted down the skirt to a green silk shantung dress. Doll had applied mascara, rouge, and red lipstick, lending a radiant glow to Fannie's normally sallow complexion, and Fannie had evidently doused herself with a good bit of her Oriental Rose perfume, because Ibby could smell it all the way across the room. What astounded Ibby was Fannie's perfectly coiffed hair, which was now a soft chestnut brown. If Ibby didn't know better, she would have sworn the woman standing in the kitchen was a stranger.

"Well, what's everyone staring at?" Fannie pulled on a pair of white leather gloves.

She said it with a grunt, but Ibby could tell there was a smile hiding behind her blue eyes.

Crow escorted Fannie to the car and opened the back door for her. Ibby got in and sat next to her. Crow drove leisurely down St. Charles Avenue as Fannie smoked a cigarette. Ibby rolled the window down, trying to get some fresh air. When they approached Lee Circle, a huge clap rang out overhead. From the heavy storm clouds lumbering across the sky, Ibby thought it was thunder, but then she heard another clap, then another.

Crow looked at his watch. "Close to noontime. Must be the fifty-gun salute over at the Armory on Dauphine Street."

"Someone die?" Fannie waved the cigarette smoke away from her face.

"No, Miss Fannie." Crow glanced at them through the rearview mirror. "Don't you recall? Today is Independence Day."

"I know what day it is, for God's sake," Fannie said.

"It's for the Fourth of July celebration," Crow added.

A few minutes later Crow pulled up to a building on Rue St. Louis with a sign hanging from a chain painted with the words: "Antoine's Restaurant, since 1840." A man in a black tuxedo came over and opened the car door for them.

"Good afternoon, Mrs. Bell. Numa has your table waiting for you."

"Thank you, Alciatore," Fannie said, taking the man's hand.

Ibby followed her grandmother into a brightly lit room. Most of the tables were empty, save for a lone couple sitting in the far corner next to one of the French doors.

"Right this way," the maître d' said, leading them through the room into a small hallway to the left.

Fannie urged Ibby forward. "Only the tourists eat in the front room, dear," she whispered.

The hall opened into a large airy back dining room bustling with waiters who were darting about like ferrets. The maître d' ushered them to the only empty table and pulled out a wooden bistro chair for Fannie.

"Numa will be right with you," he said as he placed paper menus on the table in front of them.

When Ibby sat down, she noticed the walls were covered with dozens of framed photographs of famous people. Fannie saw her looking at them.

"Every dignitary or celebrity who's ever been to Antoine's has their picture tacked up on the wall," Fannie said. "That adds up to a lot of people after a hundred years."

The picture beside Ibby on the wall was of a swarthy-looking man with slicked-back hair who was staring down at her with a flirtatious grin. She tried to make out the signature on the bottom of the photo.

"'Frankly, my dear, I don't give a damn,'" Fannie said.

Ibby looked at Fannie, puzzled. Had she said something to offend her?

Fannie pointed at the photograph on the wall. "Haven't you seen *Gone With the Wind*? That was Clark Gable's most famous line in the movie. He's the man in the photograph you're staring at."

"No, my mom doesn't let me watch movies about the South," Ibby said.

"Why? Is she afraid you might get some ridiculous ideas like we have alligators in our backyard and we don't pay our help?"

Ibby was too embarrassed to answer. "Something like that."

"Then she's teaching you that ignorance is bliss," Fannie remarked.

A portly waiter approached the table. "Mrs. Bell, we haven't had the pleasure of your company in quite a while."

His accent was so strange, Ibby had to struggle to understand what he was saying.

"I haven't had a reason to come, Numa." Fannie pulled a cigarette from her pocketbook. "But today I do have a reason. It's my granddaughter's twelfth birthday. So let's celebrate."

Numa bent over to light her cigarette, patting his brow with a white cloth as he did so. He looked over at Ibby. "Happy birthday, young lady."

"Would you be so kind as to bring me a cocktail? An old-fashioned. Ibby here will have a Shirley Temple."

"Right away." He gave a slight bow and left.

"Why does he sound so funny?" Ibby whispered to Fannie across the table.

"He's a Cajun, honey. They come from the bayou country, where they speak a mangled sort of French as their first language."

Ibby picked up the menu, turning it upside down, then right side up again.

"Unless you can read French, don't bother trying to understand it," Fannie said as she slipped off her gloves.

"You speak French?"

"No, dear, but most people in New Orleans can at least read a French menu. I'll order for you. I practically know it by heart anyway."

As Fannie was making up her mind about what to order, Ibby took the opportunity to ask a question that had been on her mind ever since her conversation with Birdelia the day before. "Grandma Fannie, where is Sorrowful Swamp? Is it in the bayou where the Cajuns live?"

Fannie peered over the top of the menu with a puzzled look. "Ibby dear, please just call me 'Fannie.' I'm barely fifty-two. 'Grandma Fannie' makes me sound so old. As for Sorrowful Swamp, I've never heard of such a place. Why do you ask?"

"Birdelia told me that's where her daddy lives."

Fannie frowned. "Listen, honey, that's probably just a story Dollbaby made up to satisfy Birdelia's curiosity. Birdelia was a boo-boo baby." Fannie cleared her throat. "There was an unfortunate incident. As a result, Dollbaby got pregnant. She was just a child. It never should have happened, but it did, and now we have Birdelia. There never was a daddy in the picture. Dollbaby doesn't like to talk about it, so don't bring it up. And don't go bursting Birdelia's bubble. Let Birdelia believe what she wants."

Ibby thought about it for a moment. "Was I a boo-boo baby, too?"

Fannie squinted one eye. "Why, no dear. Get that silly notion right out of your head."

When Numa returned, he stood at the table with his pencil and pad, waiting for Fannie to order. Fannie took her time, sipping her cocktail.

"Ibby will start with the shrimp rémoulade, then for an entrée she'll have the pompano *en papillote*. I'll have the turtle soup and trout meunière. And please bring a platter of soufflé potatoes." Fannie handed the menu to Numa. "And another drink please."

"Right away." Numa took away the empty glass.

"Did you used to come here a lot?" Ibby asked.

Fannie squinted. "Yes dear, once upon a time. This was your grand-father's favorite restaurant. He proposed to me at this very table."

"Really?"

"Really." Fannie glanced up at the ceiling. "I used to bring Graham and Balfour here on special occasions, too. I ordered you the same thing I used to order for your daddy."

After a few seconds, Ibby asked, "Who's Balfour?"

Fannie rubbed her bottom lip with her finger, as if she were trying to decide how to answer the question. "Didn't your daddy ever men-tion that he had a brother?"

"No, ma'am," Ibby said.

Numa returned with the potatoes and appetizers. *"Bon appétit."*

Ibby took a bite of the shrimp as she waited for Fannie to answer.

"He didn't tell you much about your family, did he? Perhaps that's for the best." She took a long drag from her cigarette. "Balfour was your father's younger brother."

"Where is he now?"

"There was an accident." Fannie's voice drifted off, and she began staring off into the distance.

Rule Number Two. If she talks about her past, don't ask questions.

Fannie turned to Ibby and looked her squarely in the eye. "Why don't we talk about something else? Like how you got that black eye, for instance."

"Oh." Ibby touched her eye lightly.

"Think I hadn't noticed?" Fannie said. "That makeup Doll smeared on your face isn't exactly helping."

They ate in silence, but Ibby could tell Fannie was thinking hard about something. Her eyes had become glassy and distant.

Numa came over to the table and placed a plate topped with a brown paper bag in front of Ibby. Ibby was wondering what on earth Fannie had ordered for her when Numa brought out a knife and slit the bag open. Steam filled the air as he cut away the bag and slid the fish out onto the plate, butter and crabmeat tumbling out with it. He placed a plate of fish in front of Fannie.

Numa turned to Fannie. "Would Madame like some wine with dinner?"

Fannie stubbed out her cigarette in the ashtray, never having touched her soup. "Why ever not?"

Just as Ibby picked up her fork, Fannie asked, "So, dear, tell me how you came about that eye."

Ibby put her fork down, wondering if she should make up a story or just tell the truth. She decided it was time for the truth. "Annabelle punched me."

"And why did she do that?"

"I accidentally hit her with the swing. She got mad and whacked me in the eye with her fist."

"And did you fight back?"

Ibby looked down at the fish on her plate. "Yes, ma'am." She said it quickly, hoping maybe Fannie wouldn't catch what she said, but the crooked grin on Fannie's face told her she had.

"That explains Honey Friedrichs's presence at the house the other day," she said with a laugh. She patted Ibby's hand. "I would have done the same thing, dear. Guess we'll just have to find someone else for you to play with."

When they finished lunch, Numa cleared their plates and scraped bits of French bread off the tablecloth with a blunt knife. "Coffee for Madame?"

"Yes, lovely," Fannie said. When Numa was gone, she turned to Ibby. "Let me ask you something, Ibby dear. Your mother told me in no uncertain terms the other day that your father hated me, that I was the reason he moved away from New Orleans. Did he ever mention anything like that to you?"

"Why no, ma'am. I never heard him say that."

Fannie eyed her a moment. "Did he ever talk about me, or his father perhaps?"

Ibby looked down, trying to figure out how to answer without upsetting Fannie. "Well, no, not really."

"Whatever do you mean? Either he did or he didn't."

Ibby fiddled with her napkin, then looked over at Fannie. "I could tell how he felt about you by the way he looked at your picture."

"What picture?" Fannie tilted her head.

"The one he used to carry in his wallet."

"Oh," Fannie said. "And how was that?"

"In a loving sort of way." Ibby added, "I think he missed you."

"I'm glad to hear that, dear."

Their conversation was cut short when four waiters approached the table with a large silver platter.

"A Baked Alaska for Mademoiselle's birthday," one of the waiters said before waving his finger in the air like a baton. "A one, a two, and a three."

The waiters burst into a barbershop rendition of "Happy Birthday." All eyes in the restaurant were on Ibby.

"Happy birthday, dear," Fannie said, holding up her wineglass. In between two meringue doves perched on either end of the domed cake, *Happy Birthday* was sprawled in a swirly script. It was so pretty, it almost looked like a sculpture. Ibby was about to point that out when she noticed tears streaming down Fannie's face. Fannie was whispering to herself, making no attempt to wipe them away.

"Fannie, are you okay?" Ibby reached over and touched her hand.

Fannie glanced in her direction, but Ibby could tell she was in a place very far away.

Chapter Seventeen

Doll could see Crow staring out the car window as he pulled the car into the driveway. Doll knew that look. It meant Miss Fannie was in trouble.

Queenie came up beside Doll. "Think Crow's gone need some help getting Miss Fannie inside."

By the time Doll got to the car, Crow was trying to get Fannie to move, but Fannie just sat there staring straight ahead, stiff and motionless, as if she'd turned to stone. Ibby was sitting next to her in the backseat.

Crow touched Fannie's elbow. "Come on now, Miss Fannie. Time to go inside. I know you can hear me. Let's go on in the house."

"Time to have cake and give Miss Ibby her birthday present. Ain't that so, Miss Fannie?" Doll's eyes met Crow's.

Crow went around to the other side of the car and opened the door. "Let's go on inside, Miss Ibby. Miss Fannie'll be just a minute."

Crow escorted Ibby to the back steps, where Queenie was waiting.

She took Ibby inside. "Go have a seat at the dining room table. We got a surprise for you." Then she whispered to Crow, "What's going on?"

"No need to whisper, Mama. I can hear you all the way out here," Doll said. She had managed to get one of Fannie's legs out of the car. At this rate, Doll thought, it would be tomorrow before she got Fannie inside.

"All I know, the whole way back from the restaurant, Miss Fannie kept talking about getting Master Balfour a birthday present, like he was in the car with us," Crow said to Queenie.

"Balfour? Why she going on about Master Balfour? She hasn't mentioned his name in at least ten years," Queenie said.

Crow removed his cap and scratched his head. "Far as I can tell, Miss Fannie and Miss Ibby were talking about Master Balfour over lunch."

"Oh, dear Lawd." Queenie glanced over at Doll. "Better go on over there and help Doll get Miss Fannie into the house. Then we can decide what to do with her."

Crow and Doll tussled with Fannie a good fifteen minutes before they finally got her out of the car. They led her inside, each supporting an elbow.

"Afternoon, Miss Fannie," Queenie said as they came through the back door.

Fannie eyed the cake on the kitchen table. "Whose birthday is it?"

"Why, Miss Fannie, you remember. It's your granddaughter Ibby's birthday. She's sitting at the dining room table now. And Doll here is gone bring down the present she made for her. Was your idea, remember?"

Crow had Fannie trudging along in a slow shuffle toward the dining room. "We getting there, sure enough."

"I'll be right back." As Doll slipped past her daddy and up the stairs, she didn't have a good feeling.

When Doll returned, Fannie was in her chair, and the candles on the cake were lit.

"Come on now. Let's all sing 'Happy Birthday,'" Queenie said.

As soon as Ibby blew the candles out, Doll presented her with a life-size rag doll with brown yarn hair, a stitched-on face, and clothes that were an exact replica of the clothes Ibby had on, down to the Mary Jane shoes. Fannie, who had been sitting quietly, suddenly turned and pointed at Ibby. "That doll looks just like the little girl," she said.

"Supposed to, Miss Fannie," Queenie said.

Ibby stared at the doll with the oddest expression Doll had ever seen. After a few moments, Ibby leaned over and gave Fannie a kiss on the cheek.

"Thank you, Grandma."

Ibby put the doll on the chair next to her, sneaking furtive glances as she ate her cake.

Doll motioned for Crow and Queenie to follow her into the kitchen. As soon as the door swung closed, she said, "She don't like it, Mama. I can tell."

"You done a mighty fine job on that doll. Looks just like her," Crow said.

"Don't make no difference," Doll said. "Those weren't happy-to-see-my-new-doll sort of eyes."

"Oh, she gone like it," Queenie said. "She just don't know it yet."

No sooner had the door closed than they heard a crash. Queenie and Doll rushed back into the room to find Fannie sprawled on the floor, holding her stomach and laughing. One of the cut-crystal water glasses lay shattered next to her.

Queenie motioned to Crow. "Come help get her up, then go and fetch the broom."

"What happened?" Doll asked Ibby.

"Fannie knocked the glass over with her hand," Ibby said. "Then she just sort of rolled out of the chair onto the floor and started laughing."

Doll grabbed Fannie by the arm and tried to pull her up. "Come on, Miss Fannie. You've had a long day. We best get you to bed."

Queenie took Fannie's other arm, waving Crow and Doll away. "I'll do it."

"Need help getting her to her room?" Crow asked.

"We'll manage just fine, won't we, Miss Fannie?" Queenie said in a small voice, talking to Fannie as if she were a child.

Doll looked at her watch as her father went into the kitchen to get the broom. "Five o'clock. Lawd Almighty, how did it get so late?"

Crow returned with the broom and handed it to Doll. "That broom about worn out. Best pick up a new one soon 'cause you know it's bad luck to buy a broom in August."

Doll swept the glass into a dustpan. "This rate, Daddy, best buy two."

"So what you gone call her?" Doll asked Ibby, hoping to distract her from all the commotion in the bedroom.

"Who?" Ibby asked.

"Your new friend here." Doll nodded toward the doll in the chair.

"Oh, I don't know." Ibby shrugged, staring down at the remnants of the cake on her plate.

"Been a long day. Why don't you run on upstairs? I'll be up in a minute."

After Ibby left, Doll scraped up the last of the glass shards. When she got back to the kitchen, she found Crow digging into a piece of cake he'd cut for himself.

"She don't like it." Doll dumped the glass into the trash can.

"If I recall," Crow said, "you and your mama were going on the other day about how Miss Ibby say Miss Vidrine don't believe in birthdays. Could be no one ever gave her a doll before. Ever think of that?"

Doll said, "Maybe you right. Think I better go check on Miss Ibby."

She was making her way down the hall when she noticed the doll still sitting in the chair where Ibby had left it. As Doll tucked it under her arm, she could hear Queenie in the bedroom, trying to calm Miss Fannie down. After all these years, listening to Miss Fannie when she got this way hadn't gotten any easier. Doll wondered how a person could become so broken.

When she opened the door to Ibby's room, Ibby was sitting on her bed.

"You forgot this." Doll sat down next to her and handed her the doll.

"Oh, I guess I did," Ibby said, setting it off to the side.

"Don't you like it?" Doll said.

"It is supposed to look like me?"

"Yeah, supposed to."

"Do I really look like that, with stringy hair and eyes that never close?"

Doll laughed. "No, baby. Fannie thought you might like someone to keep you company up here, that's all. Don't worry what it looks like. Was a silly idea, I guess."

"Doll?"

"Yes, child?"

"I think I broke Rule Number Two at lunch today. I asked her who Balfour was when she brought up his name."

Doll stroked Ibby's hair. "Now listen, them rules just something my mama made up. You'll learn soon enough there ain't no rules as far as Fannie is concerned. Just got to roll with the punches. Now listen, before I go, did you find something?"

"What do you mean? Like what?"

"Look under your pillow."

Ibby reached under the pillow and pulled out a rectangular package wrapped in newspaper and tied with twine. She looked at Doll. "What's this?"

"Open it."

When Ibby slipped off the twine, the paper fell away to reveal a small transistor radio.

"That's from Queenie and me," Doll said. "I know how you like music. Music makes everything better, don't you think?"

Ibby stood up and hugged Doll around the neck. "Thank you. I don't know what to say. It's the best birthday present ever."

"Here, hand it to me. Let me see if I can find a station for you. Hard to get reception up here sometimes." She fiddled with the dial until she found one. "There you go." She set the radio down on the table next to the bed.

"Up next," the announcer said, "a hit song by Frankie Valli and the Four Seasons, one we all love to sing along with, called 'Rag Doll.'"

Doll grabbed the doll and started dancing around with it as the song played, then grabbed Ibby and got her up and dancing, too. When the song was over, they both collapsed onto the bed, giggling hysterically.

"See what I told you? Music makes everything better." She kissed Ibby on the forehead. "Now I got to go. I'm sure Queenie's downstairs waiting on me."

"Doll?"

Doll stopped on the threshold. "Yes, Miss Ibby?"

"Is Fannie going to be all right?"

Doll scratched her head with her fingernail, trying to figure out how to answer. "Sure she is. She gone be fine. Just one of those days."

Ibby was staring at Doll as if trying to decide whether to believe her. *She got the same eyes as Miss Fannie*, Doll was thinking.

"Now you get some rest, and I'll see you in the morning," Doll said.

As she went down the stairs, a thought occurred to Doll. *What if Miss Ibby is like her grandmother? What if she got that crazy gene, too? Like Mama say, you can pick a fight, but you can't pick your family.*

Sometimes that was the part that hurt the most.

 birds

When Doll and Queenie arrived at the house the next morning, there was a low whimpering coming from inside the house.

"What is it?" Queenie asked.

"Miss Fannie. I can hear her—she's in the bedroom," Doll said.

"I best go check on her."

Doll followed Queenie to Fannie's room. Queenie twisted the knob, but the door was locked. They could hear banging on the other side.

"Miss Fannie. It's Queenie. Open the door."

There was no answer. Queenie went to the kitchen and returned with a key. When she opened the door, Doll let out a gasp. It looked as if someone had taken a sledgehammer to the room. The dressing table was turned over and the mirror broken, pieces of glass were scattered over the floor, and the photos that had once stood on the dresser were ripped from their frames and strewn about. A white slip dangled from one of the arms of the ceiling fan and was swinging around in circles like a flag. Fannie had a mirror shard in her hand and was brandishing it like a knife as blood dripped onto the floor.

"Now calm yourself, Miss Fannie." Queenie held her hand out in a conciliatory fashion. "Why don't you drop that piece of glass and come in the bathroom and let me get you cleaned up?"

Fannie swung the shard around in the air as if she were looking for something to stab.

"Miss Fannie, ain't no use getting all worked up." Queenie took a step closer.

Fannie jabbed the glass in Queenie's direction. Then she began to laugh. A few short laughs at first. Then she threw her head back and began to spin around in circles, her nightgown billowing out around her, her whole body shaking as her laughter grew manic. The dagger of glass fell from her hand. Queenie rushed up and kicked it aside, then grabbed Fannie around the waist and pulled her away from the broken glass on the floor. Fannie collapsed into her arms as if all the life had been stolen from her.

Queenie cautioned Doll to stay back. "Go call Doc Hathaway. Tell him to come right away."

"You gone be all right in here with her?" Doll had never seen Miss Fannie this bad.

"Just go!"

A few minutes later Doll appeared at the bathroom door. "They coming now. Good thing Doc Hathaway's on call this morning."

"Thank the Lawd that hospital only a couple blocks away." Queenie tied a washcloth around Fannie's hand. "Help me get her up and dressed before they get here."

She spoke to Fannie in a low voice and stroked her hair as Doll helped her into her clothes. Just as Doll slipped a shoe on Fannie's foot, there was a knock at the door.

"Go answer it before Miss Ibby comes down," Queenie said.

Doll returned with three men in white coats.

"How is she?" the doctor asked.

"Take a look around, Doc. See for yourself," Queenie said.

Dr. Hathaway placed his bag on the floor next to the bed, took out a syringe, and gave Fannie a shot. Fannie didn't move.

"Doc," Queenie said, "this the worst one yet."

"What brought it on?" Dr. Hathaway asked as he checked Fannie's vital signs.

"Her son Graham passed," Doll said. "That started it. Then a few days ago her granddaughter shows up with Master Graham nothing but a bunch of ashes in a jar. If that weren't enough, somehow, over lunch, Master Balfour's name came up. Afraid it was all too much for Miss Fannie. Too much."

"I see," Dr. Hathaway said.

When he gave the signal, one of the attendants put Fannie's arm around his neck, grabbed her by the waist, and escorted her out of the room. These episodes happened frequently enough that Doll had a small bag for Miss Fannie packed and ready. She handed it to the other attendant.

"We'll take her in, see how she does," the doctor said.

What that meant was, Fannie would be taken to St. Vincent's Hospital, where she'd stay until the doctor felt she wasn't a danger to herself or anyone else. Could be a day or two, could be a couple weeks. Never could tell.

"Her hand might need a stitch or two," Queenie said. "I got it wrapped up tight."

"I'll take a look at it as soon as we get to the hospital," the doctor said. "Okay, boys, let's go."

"You be good now, Miss Fannie. Don't you worry none about Miss

Ibby. We'll take good care a her until you get back," Queenie said as the attendant escorted Fannie down the hall, with Dr. Hathaway following closely behind.

Queenie and Doll stood by the front door, gazing through the etched-glass panel as the attendants loaded Fannie into the ambulance. Ibby appeared at the top of the stairs.

"Where are they taking Fannie?" Ibby asked.

She ran down the stairs, pushed past them, and threw open the front door.

Doll put her hands on Ibby's shoulders and drew her back. "They just taking her to rest for a few days."

"But *where?* Where are they taking her?"

Ibby was waving at Fannie frantically, as though she might never see her again.

"They taking her to St. Vincent's, Miss Ibby."

"The crazy hospital?" Ibby asked.

Doll turned Ibby around to face her. "Now listen, baby. They got revolving doors for people like Fannie who need a place to go when the sadness gets to be too much. She'll be okay. Don't you worry. She be back soon enough. Now come on." She gently pulled the girl away from the door. "You gone come to church with us this morning."

Ibby's head shot around. "To church?"

Doll put her hands on her hips. "Ain't you never been to church before?"

"Never."

"Why's that?"

"Mama says church is a bunch of garbage."

"Well then," Doll said with a tight-lipped smile, "this morning you gonna see for yourself. Then you can make up your own mind about it."

When Crow pulled up in the driveway about an hour later, Queenie got into the front seat as Doll and Ibby slid into the back of the Chevy Malibu. Doll saw Crow peering at them through the rearview mirror.

"Anyone gone explain what's going on?" he asked.

"Miss Fannie, she gone off for a few days," Queenie said.

"I understand." Crow nodded as he backed out of the driveway. "Sure do."

After a while, he asked, "Miss Ibby, she going to church with us then?"

"Yes, Daddy. She can keep Birdelia company. We need to go by the house and change into our Sunday clothes first, though."

"I understand," Crow said again. A few minutes later he added, "You think that's such a good idea, bringing her to church, knowing what the Reverend Jeremiah gone be preaching about this morning after the president's speech and all?"

There was a long pause before Doll answered. "It'll be all right, Daddy."

Lawd, Doll was thinking, *Daddy's got a point. The reverend's gone be going on about civil rights and how the black man has been oppressed and how it's the white man that keeps him down. Just what is Miss Ibby gone think about all that? Not a good day to bring a little white girl to church. Hope nobody say nothing to her. Miss Ibby never been to church before. Maybe she won't know the difference.* She shook her head. She didn't want any more trouble this morning. She'd already had her fill for one day. But who was she kidding? Everyone at church was going to notice the white child sitting with Birdelia.

Crow drove through downtown and the French Quarter, passing through a section of town called the Faubourg Tremé, where the houses were stacked close together with no yards. Eventually he turned onto Elysian Fields, a broad boulevard lined with live oaks and modest one-story raised shotgun cottages that had once been brightly painted but were now dingy and guarded by heavy iron burglar bars across the windows and doors. The boulevard's neutral ground was strewn with folding chairs and empty food containers that were being scavenged by a few mangy dogs.

"I wish the neighbors would learn to pick up after themselves," Doll said under her breath as Crow pulled up in front of their double shotgun, a long narrow house with two front doors on opposite ends that led to mirror-image apartments on either side.

Birdelia jumped up from one of the plastic chairs on the front porch. She was wearing a puff-sleeved blue dress with a white satin sash that was so starched it stuck out like a bell, making Birdelia's skinny little legs look like Popsicle sticks.

She tore down the steps and pointed at Ibby. "What's she doing here?"

"That any way to talk to Miss Ibby?" Doll scolded. "Where your manners at?"

"Well, like I say before, what's she doing here?" Birdelia asked again, still pointing.

"She gone spend the day with us," Doll replied.

Birdelia looked at Ibby as if she didn't know quite what to make of that.

"Why don't you two visit out here a few minutes while we go inside?" Queenie said.

"Okay." Birdelia shrugged.

When she and Doll got inside, Queenie stopped and leaned on the wall.

Doll put a hand on her shoulder. "You okay, Mama?"

Queenie waved her away. "I'm fine. Just never seen Miss Fannie like that before. Scared me a little, that's all."

Doll watched her mother shuffle toward the back of the house. She hadn't wanted to say anything, but she'd been thinking the same thing. Fannie had always managed to return from St. Vincent's Hospital after a few days, but what if this time was different? What if Miss Fannie never came back?

Gone have to say an extra prayer at church today, Doll thought as she followed her mother into her bedroom.

Chapter Eighteen

Ibby stood on the porch with Birdelia, studying the small ornamental tree in the front yard that was haphazardly strewn with Mardi Gras beads. Empty blue bottles were stuck on the tips of each branch. She'd never seen anything quite like it.

"Why does that tree have all those blue bottles stuck on the branches like that?" she asked.

"It's Queenie's bottle tree," Birdelia said. "Every time she finishes a bottle of Milk of Magnesia, she sticks it on a branch of the tree. The bottles, they supposed to capture spirits that wander in the night. Mama says them spirits love blue glass, so they crawl up inside, and once they there, they can't get out. Then, when the sun rises, they burn all up until they no more."

"What are all the beads for?"

"Them just Mardi Gras beads."

"What do they do?"

"They just for show. We throw them up in the tree after the parades. Make the tree right pretty, don't you think?" Birdelia smiled a big toothy smile. "Threw most of them up there myself."

Birdelia grabbed Ibby's hand and pulled her inside the house. It smelled of potpourri and overstuffed furniture. Birdelia plopped down on a brown Naugahyde couch that had a crocheted afghan thrown over the back of it.

"This side of the house is where Queenie, Crow, and T-Bone live. Me and Mama live next door, on the other side of the shotgun."

"Who's T-Bone?" Ibby asked as she came over and sat next to Birdelia.

"T-Bone? Oh, he's my uncle. His real name is Thaddeus. They call him T-Bone 'cause he likes to play the trombone. Got a picture a him up there somewhere." She pointed to a gas fireplace with framed photos perched on the mantel. Birdelia went over and picked one up. "Right here."

The boy in the photo didn't look much older than Ibby. He was tall and skinny, with a long face, a broad smile, and close-cropped hair. His eyes held a certain sparkle, as if he'd been up to some mischief.

"He looks awfully young to be your uncle."

"He's sixteen. Might be at church this morning, but never can tell with T-Bone. He got a habit a not showing up like he supposed to."

"Who are the other people in the picture?"

"That one on the left, that were my uncle Ewell, and that one next to him were my uncle Malcolm. Never knew either one. They died before I was born."

"What happened to them?"

"Not sure about Malcolm. Don't think no one ever told me. And Ewell, he was shot in a fight right outside this house." She looked around at the other photos. "Don't see no pictures of my uncle Purnell. Mee-maw must have taken them all down."

"Why would she do that?" Ibby asked.

"He ain't exactly been in Mee-maw's good graces lately. Been hanging out with bad brothers. Mee-maw kicked him out of the house 'cause she didn't want him bringing them around no more." Birdelia put the picture back on the mantel and pointed at Ibby's dress. "My mama make that?"

"Yes," Ibby said. "For my birthday. And she made me a doll, too."

"I know," Birdelia said. "I laid on the floor, and she drew the pattern around me. She say she gone make me one, too, if she ever has the time. My mama, she say she gone go into business someday, sew clothes and stuff for folks. She'd be real good at it, don't you think?"

Doll emerged from the back room. "You two about ready?"

Birdelia stood up. "You look mighty fine, Mama."

A white patent-leather pocketbook hung from Doll's arm and she was wearing a silk shantung dress similar to the one Fannie had worn to lunch at Antoine's yesterday.

"Thank you, baby," Doll said as she adjusted her hairpiece.

Queenie came up behind Doll.

"Come on—don't want to be late." Queenie shuffled her large frame toward the front door.

Ibby had never seen Queenie in anything but her gray uniform with the white apron. Today she had on a dark purple cotton dress with a lace collar and had somehow managed to puff her hair up into a short bob that peeked out from under a large purple hat. She was carrying a black leather pocketbook in one hand, and white cotton gloves in the other.

"Where's the old man?" Queenie looked around the room.

"I'm right here, woman." Crow came into the room wearing a dark pinstripe suit and two-toned shoes.

"Grab the deviled eggs from the icebox." Queenie pointed toward the kitchen. "And don't be forgetting the cornbread and collard greens."

"Already in the car," Crow said.

"Well, come on then. What you waiting on?" Queenie waved her gloves.

Ibby slid into the car next to Birdelia, who was balancing a tray of deviled eggs on her knees in the backseat. Doll came around the other side and got in as she fastened a scarf around her hair and put on a pair of sunglasses. Queenie rolled the front window down, holding on tight to her hat so it wouldn't blow off as Crow drove away.

About fifteen minutes later, Crow pulled up in front of the True Love Baptist Church on Dryades Street in Central City, a section of town near the interstate. The area had once been prosperous, catering to small minority-owned businesses, until the addition of a housing project in the 1940s caused the area to dwindle, leaving most of the buildings empty, save a few bars that dotted the corners and an auto repair shop. Streams of people in their Sunday best were making their way toward the church. Crow pulled up to the curb, then came around and opened the door for Queenie.

"Y'all go on in. I'll find a place to park," he said.

The sun shone brightly, reflecting off the metal cross perched high above the gabled roof of the small white clapboard church. The red doors to the church were open and two men in white robes greeted the congregation. Several women were accepting food donations in the empty lot next to the church, where dozens of folding tables had been set up under a tent.

"Good morning, Sister Saphronia, Sister Viola," a man with sparkly eyes said to Queenie and Doll.

"Blessed day to you, Reverend Jeremiah." Queenie accepted a program and a paper fan from him.

"And who have we here?" he asked.

"This here is Miss Ibby," Birdelia chimed in.

The man shook Ibby's hand. "Welcome, welcome." Doll and the reverend exchanged glances. "Take a fan, young lady. You and Birdelia can go on up to the front of the church with the other children."

Ibby took the fan from him, noting how the Reverend Jeremiah had a way of putting people at ease, even white girls who'd never been to church before.

Doll jerked her head toward the door. "Go on in, girls. I got to go with Queenie around back and make sure everything is ready for the picnic after the service."

Birdelia pulled Ibby inside and marched her down the center aisle. The windows were closed, making it so unbearably hot that Ibby had trouble catching her breath. When they got to the front of the church, just beneath the platform, they settled cross-legged on the ground.

The church was painted completely white on the inside and was unadorned, save for a large painted canvas hanging from the ceiling above the stage, a bucolic scene of a lake surrounded by snow-tipped mountains. Ibby wondered if it was Reverend Jeremiah's idea of heaven. Just beneath the canvas, a man in a robe was standing behind the pulpit, his head bowed as he flipped through the pages of a large Bible.

Several children of various ages joined Ibby and Birdelia on the floor, as infants were being left with two women in knee-length white robes. The girls sat fanning themselves as the rest of the congregation strolled in. After a while, the church took on a kind of low buzz as women in the pews began to sway from side to side, making a sound somewhere between a hum and a moan.

"What are they doing?" Ibby whispered to Birdelia.

Birdelia didn't bother to turn around to look. "They communing with the spirit."

Several of the children sitting with them began to do the same thing, swaying back and forth with their eyes closed, humming in a low monotone. As the congregation continued to file in and the pews filled up, the noise in the church grew louder, not just from people talking among themselves but from people talking *to* themselves. Ibby turned to ask Birdelia what was happening, but Birdelia's eyes were closed as she fanned herself. Every so often, a random shout rang out from somewhere behind them.

"So glad!" A woman near the back of the church rose from her seat and cried out, then closed her eyes and sat back down.

"Glory!" another woman shouted.

Near the front, a different woman hollered, "Sweet Jesus!"

"Amen!" another woman declared as she stood up, raised her hand in the air, then sat down again.

This continued on for a good half hour, gaining momentum. The longer it went on, the faster Ibby's heart raced. She felt as if she'd been deposited in some foreign land where people were speaking a different language. She wondered if it would be all right if she waited outside until it was all over. She tapped Birdelia on the leg, but Birdelia was too wrapped up in the frenzy to pay her any mind.

A woman with a large fabric flower attached to the bun on the back of her head stood up and proclaimed, "So glad!" But instead of sitting down, as the other women had done, she proclaimed in a booming voice: "I'm here to give praise to God's blessed name and to thank him for the gladness that's a-working in my heart." The woman grabbed her chest with both hands. "I'm here to tell about the peace that come to my soul, when Jesus took me from my sinful ways, and called me to stand with His Christian saints. . . . Amen! So glad!"

A heavyset woman who was perspiring heavily got up and held her fan in the air. "I seen the light leading my feet to the righteous path before it was too late," she cried. "For many years, the only thing that held my mind was wickedness and condemnation. But the spirit spoke through and Jesus stooped down low and sanctified my soul. Amen! So glad!"

Men, women, and even some of the children stood and declared their trust in Him. At times they spoke in whispers. Some ranted incoherently, twitching as if possessed. Then unexpectedly, and to Ibby's great relief, the hysteria subsided and the congregation lapsed into a sort of spent calmness, the only sound now a low humming.

Ibby fanned herself furiously, wondering what was going to happen next.

Reverend Jeremiah, who had remained stoic throughout, walked to the edge of the platform and raised his hands. "Thank you, brothers and sisters, for your praise of Him. Thank you, Sister Clementine, for your words. Thank you, Brother Joseph. Thank you all."

He paused, as if waiting for something.

Then there were shouts from the audience.

"Amen!"

"Praise God!"

Reverend Jeremiah held out his hands, calling for quiet. "It pleases me to see so many Christians coming together, putting aside the sins of the world, to turn your mind on the kind of pleasure recommended by God himself. Blessed be His name! None of the people outside this church know what the feeling of gladness is until they done laid aside their worldly ways and let the religion commence to working in their heart. . . . Ain't that true?" His voice was soothing, melodious.

"Amen!"

"Bless God!"

"Religion," he continued, "is a mighty breastplate to help you overcome the wicked ways of the world. Why, just this week, we overcame bigotry and hatred from those so low as to be prejudiced against people of color when our mighty president saw the wisdom to sign into law a bill that gave civil rights to all people. *All* people, you understand what I'm saying? If you listen closely, you can hear the dying groans from the Old South as she bites the dust of ignominious defeat in its futile but furious fight against the onward march of civil rights!"

"Amen!"

"Praise God!"

Reverend Jeremiah's voice was becoming louder with each passage. "Many of you sitting here can remember your parents talking about what it was like on the plantations when the wealthy plantation owner died. Brother Leroy, Brother Willie, you remember what they said? You remember?"

"I remember!" An elderly man near the front thumped his cane on the ground.

"Then you know, Brother Leroy, what a community-stirring occasion it was." Reverend Jeremiah paused for effect. "The poor, they came and went, and nobody cared. But when a plantation master died, whites and colored folks alike went about the business of mourning. Even those who were glad to see the deceased take his flight mourned. You know what I'm talking about!"

The room fell silent as the reverend paced back and forth across the platform in front of the podium. Ibby was mesmerized. She didn't understand half of what he was saying, but she liked the sound of his voice.

"There was a custom in those days, a custom to keep the passing plantation master alive as long as possible. They did this by propping him up in bed with many pillows. I remember hearing of a plantation owner who was dying for a whole two weeks, because of all the pillows propped around him. After all hope for survival was gone, the family held a caucus. You know why?"

"Why?" the congregation shouted.

Ibby glanced over at Birdelia, who was staring at the pastor as if he had cast a spell over her.

"They were debating *when* to pull the pillows out, and who should have the solemn task of doing it. You see, brothers and sisters, pulling the pillows out became a serious question! I tell you this because the remembrance of former times was forced upon us during the filibuster in Washington. When President Johnson decided that there would be a civil rights bill, it just became a matter of time before a decision had to be made about when to pull the pillow out from under the Old South. When the Senate voted for cloture to end the debate, that was the signal, brothers and sisters, *that* was the signal that the pillows had been pulled *out*, and with cloture came the demise of the Old South, which has been to the Negro such a grievous affliction. The filibuster had been an angel with a flaming sword, trying her best to keep the colored man from the gates of paradise of full citizenship. But led by our president, the Old South was beaten to its knees and had to surrender to shame!"

When Reverend Jeremiah stopped to wipe his brow, Ibby felt her face growing warm. She flicked the paper fan back and forth, but the heat in her face was rising. As it was, women were falling out into the aisle and collapsing, rolling around on the ground until male ushers picked them up and carried them out the front door like pieces of timber.

The rest of the congregation rose up and declared, "Free at last! Free at last!"

Reverend Jeremiah let this go on a few minutes before he raised his hand and called for calm. "That great man, Lyndon B. Johnson, who will go down in history as one of the men who could match and master Harry Flood Byrd, defeating his tactics designed to hold the Negro down. The Old South hath met its Waterloo, and may her dying groans be heard around the world to warn oppressors that God still lives and still moves in mysterious ways. The pillow has been pulled. Let it die! Let it die!"

The congregation jumped to their feet again. "Let it die, let it die!"

This time the reverend let them shout, and he yelled over them, "All the king's horses and all the king's men cannot make the oppressive and segregation-ridden Old South live again. Who would have believed that men of this generation would have lived to see the Old South on the run, beaten to its knees? Let it die! The pillow has been pulled out. Lady Liberty has shown her face. Give me liberty!"

"Give me liberty! Give me liberty!"

Ibby looked up when she heard her name, heard them calling for her to rise up and stand among them. Without giving it another thought, she got up and calmly walked over to where the reverend was standing. The congregation hushed.

The reverend bent over. "Yes, child?"

"I'm Liberty," she declared, raising her hands in the air the way she'd seen other women in the church do.

A lone scream rang out. Ibby turned to find a flurry of horrified faces staring back at her as a handful of women fell into the aisle like toppled bowling pins. Ibby glanced back at the Reverend Jeremiah. He was trying to say something to her, but his voice was faint and garbled and seemed to float above her like a dream. That was the last thing she remembered before her eyes fell back into her head and she crumpled to the ground.

Chapter Nineteen

The True Love Baptist Church was evidently prepared for the throngs of women who succumbed to the spirit set forth by the mighty Reverend Jeremiah each Sunday, given the number of fainting cots set up under a large tent outside the church. When Ibby awoke, that's where she found herself, surrounded by Queenie, Doll, Birdelia, and Reverend Jeremiah himself. Queenie and the reverend seemed to be in the middle of a conversation when Ibby opened her eyes.

"She's Miss Fannie's granddaughter. Miss Fannie got taken ill this morning, so I brought her along. Didn't think she'd be no trouble." Queenie was wringing her white gloves in her hands.

"Why didn't you say so?" he said. "Any granddaughter of Miss Fannie's is always welcome, you know that. But I'm confused as to her inclination to address me in the middle of my sermon."

"She ain't never been to church," Doll piped up, "much less a colored church, Reverend. But I think the poor child was confused. You see, her name is Liberty—Liberty Bell. When she heard her name, she done thought you was calling her up there to the stage, that's all."

He gave a slight chuckle. "Well, ain't that something."

"That something," Doll said. "One sermon the folks ain't likely soon to forget."

He nodded in agreement. "You can count on that, Sister Viola. Time heals all wounds. Including those festering on the inside, the ones only the Lord can see."

"So they say," Doll said, giving him a sideways glance. "So they say."

Ibby closed her eyes, wondering what they were talking about. Even though there was a slight breeze, she was still perspiring heavily and felt kind of woozy. When she cracked open an eye, she found a boy's face so close to hers that she could feel his breath on her face.

"Thaddeus Trout, what do you think you're doing?" Doll scolded. "Get away from Miss Ibby, and go and fetch some lemonade."

"Who is she? Why she here?"

"This here is Miss Fannie's granddaughter. I told you about her. Where you been, anyway? You at the service, or you just now showing up for the vittles?" Queenie pointed her finger at him.

"No, Mama, I been here."

"Where? I didn't see you?"

"I was standing in the back with Shorty."

"Uh-huh." Queenie heaved up her bosom, a sure sign she wasn't buying it. "Well, go on, fetch some lemonade, like Doll asked you to."

After Thaddeus ran off, the reverend looked around. "Where is Sister Etta Mae? Perhaps the laying of the hands will free this child of her affliction. Sister Etta Mae, we need you over here."

A short, fat woman in a white robe appeared by his side. "Yes sir, Reverend sir?"

"This child here is in need of your assistance." He nodded toward Ibby.

"I can see that." Etta Mae came and stood at the head of the cot. She closed her eyes and turned her head up toward the sky before placing the palms of her hands on either side of Ibby's temples.

The sudden shock of the woman's warm hands on Ibby's face made her bolt upright.

"I dare say, Sister Etta Mae, you work fast," the reverend declared. "Mighty fast, indeed."

By this time Thaddeus had returned with a paper cup. Birdelia tried to grab it from him. "Give me that, T-Bone."

T-Bone yanked it away. "No, I want to give it to her."

"Come on now—you all stop that," Doll snapped.

T-Bone made a triumphant face at Birdelia and handed the cup to Ibby, then disappeared into the crowd.

"What you gonna do?" Queenie sighed and rolled her eyes at the reverend.

"Keep them close, keep them close," he repeated, then turned toward Ibby. "I'm Reverend Jeremiah, but I do believe we already met in the church a little while ago."

Ibby blushed as she shook his hand. "I'm sorry."

"No need for sorry, child. Take your time, sip some lemonade, then come on over and enjoy the rest of the day." He patted her knee.

"Thank you, Reverend," Queenie said.

"Come on." Birdelia tugged on Ibby's arm.

Ibby looked timidly over at Doll.

"It's okay, baby. Go on with Birdelia," Doll said, jerking her head toward the crowd of people buzzing around several tables in the side yard of the church.

As they made their way through the crowd, to Ibby's relief, no one seemed to be paying her any mind. Birdelia walked over to one of the tables and handed Ibby a paper plate, a napkin, and a plastic fork. She moved along the edge of the table, pointing at the various bowls and casserole dishes.

"That there is poke salad, hoecake, black-eyed peas, collard greens, and fried okra. Oh, and Mee-maw's famous deviled eggs. Over there we got pickled pigs' feet, barbecue chicken, ribs, and hog's head cheese." Birdelia stopped to examine a big pot. "Not quite sure what that is."

T-Bone came up behind her, holding a plate full of food. "That's possum stew, dimwit."

"Don't need your help." Birdelia gave him a put-out look.

"Appears you do," he said, not budging. "I'm T-Bone."

Ibby was a little disquieted at the way T-Bone was smiling at her.

Birdelia pushed him. "Go away."

T-Bone gave Ibby a half-wink. "Catch you later." Then he ran off to sit with some teenagers hovering under a large oak tree near the edge of the churchyard.

Birdelia continued down the table. "That there's fatback, cabbage, jambalaya. Over yonder, on that other table, that's all the sweets. Bread pudding, that sort of thing."

As they sat on the ground under a tree clear on the other side of the churchyard, Birdelia warned Ibby about T-Bone. "Don't mind him. He thinks he God's gift to women. Got a way with him."

The whole time Birdelia was talking, Ibby noticed that T-Bone kept glancing over at her. It was making her feel all tingly inside.

Only this time, she wished that feeling wouldn't go away.

Chapter Twenty

That evening Doll hung Ibby's dress up and came back and sat on the edge of her bed.

Ibby gazed up at her. "I'm sorry about today."

Doll smoothed her hair. "Now, don't you fret none, you hear? Besides, you gave all them folks at church something to talk about for a good long while."

Ibby propped herself up on her elbow. "You don't have to stay with me. I'll be fine."

"I ain't gone leave you here all by yourself. Besides, sometimes when Miss Fannie's feeling low, I'll come around and stay a night or two on the second floor, just to make sure she don't get lonely in the middle of the night. I got a cot in the sewing room, just for such occasions."

"Doll?"

"Yes, child."

"When will Fannie be back?"

Doll thought a moment. "Don't know for sure, baby. Expect we hear from the doctor in a few days."

"Why is Fannie so sad all the time?"

"Oh, baby. Ain't no simple answer for that. She just gets that way sometimes, when the sorrow comes bubbling up." Doll put a finger under her chin and drew her eyes to hers. "Listen, your grandmother going to the hospital got nothing to do with you. Later, when you all growed up and got a family of your own, you'll understand. It hurts to love sometimes. But that's just God's way, I reckon." Doll thought about her own words. She knew she was speaking for herself as much as for Ibby.

"Doll?"

"Yes, child?"

"What happened to Balfour?"

"I had a feeling you might be asking about him after his name came up at lunch yesterday." She glanced up at the ceiling and took in a deep breath. "There was an accident. After that, Miss Fannie, she ain't been the same since."

 birthday

Graham Bell ran up to the third floor and flung open the door to the attic room. His younger brother, Balfour, whom he called Balfy for short, ran in behind him, carrying a balsa wood airplane in each hand. It was a few weeks before Christmas, and the boys were excited. They'd just finished listening to President Roosevelt's radio address downstairs with their mother and father. The president said the war in Europe was raging and the United States needed to stay on alert. He was planning to send help to the British to stave off a possible German invasion. The Japanese had been waging war in China for a few years. It was 1940. Graham was almost ten. Balfy had just turned eight. And all the boys knew about war was how to play at it.

Graham opened the window overlooking the front yard and leaned out. A cool breeze swept in, blowing a few leaves from the oak tree into the room. Balfy came up beside him.

"Here, Graham." Balfy handed him a plane, then took a box of matches out of his pocket.

"You're going to be in trouble if Mama finds out you been playing with matches," Graham said.

"So don't tell her." Balfy put the plane on the windowsill and lit a match.

All Graham could see was the top of Balfy's head as he bent over to light the match, his wavy hair the color of straw. The breeze from the window blew the match out. He bent over further, trying to shelter the next match from the wind.

"Give me the matches. I'll do it." Graham held out his hand.

Balfy waved him away.

"Ouch!" Balfy screamed and blew out the match. "I just burned myself!" He rubbed his finger against his wool knickers.

"You're going to burn the whole house down, the rate you're going."

"Shut up, Graham," Balfy said. "I'll tell you when to throw the plane. I'll light mine on fire, and you can throw yours out at the same time and pretend you just shot me down."

"Jeez Louise, you're a bossy little brother!"

Balfy stuck his head out the window and held up his plane. "Are you ready?"

Graham did the same. "Ready."

"Wait a second, while I light the plane on fire." Balfy sat on the window ledge and tried to light the match. He struck once, then again, almost losing his balance.

"Watch yourself, Balfy. I'd hate to have to pick up the pieces on the sidewalk because you're too damned retarded to light a match."

"Shut up, Graham." Balfy held the tip of the plane up to the lit match. "Wow, look at that!" he said as the flames shot up.

"Hurry up!" Graham yelled.

"Now!" Balfy shrieked. "Throw your plane!"

Graham's plane brushed against a few branches in the oak tree, then glided down and settled onto the brick walkway below. Balfy's got caught up in one of the branches and dangled by a wing.

"Boogers!" Balfy cried as he crawled out the window and stood on the gutter that was just beneath the window. "I can get it!"

"Are you crazy? Mama's going to tan your hide if she sees you standing on the gutter like that. Come on back inside before you kill yourself! You can have my plane. I'll buy another one tomorrow!"

Balfy held on to the roof shingles and leaned out. "I can get it. It's only another inch or two."

"Did you hear what I said?" Graham shrieked. "Come back inside now! It's just a stupid toy plane, and it's burned up besides. It won't fly again."

Balfy's eyes grew wide as the gutter groaned and gave way. He tried to grab the roof, but the gutter was ripping from beneath him.

"Help me, Graham!" Balfy was reaching toward him with panic in his eyes.

Graham tried to grab Balfy's hand, but it was too late. All he could do was watch Balfy's face, frozen in fear, as he fell to the ground and landed facedown with a thud. Graham leaned out the window, staring down at his little brother as the airplane Balfy had been trying to rescue unfastened itself from the tree and spiraled to the ground like a wounded butterfly. It landed just beside Balfy.

"Balfy?" Graham leaned out farther, repeating his name again and again, hoping Balfy would turn over and start laughing, as if it had all been a joke. His brother had a habit of doing things like that just to scare the tar out of him.

Then Graham saw a pool of blood by Balfy's head, just as his mother and Queenie came running out the front door. When his mother turned his brother over, Graham thought he was going to heave. There was nothing left of his face. Then Graham heard a bloodcurdling scream. It wasn't until much later that he realized the scream had come from his own mouth.

Queenie looked up at him. "What happened, Master Graham?"

Graham stared down at her, not knowing how to answer without sounding guilty. "We were just playing airplanes. He—he fell from the window."

Fannie was holding Balfy's head, kissing his bloody face in such a frenzied way, it scared Graham. When she looked up at him, there was desperation in her eyes.

Fannie waved a frantic hand. "Quick! Somebody call an ambulance, Queenie!"

Norwood came running out of the house and bent down next to Fannie. "For the love of God, what happened?"

Fannie glanced up at the window again. Her eyes were cold this time, so cold they tore through Graham like an ice pick. He knew in that instant that his mother blamed him for the accident.

His father looked up at him. He must have seen how distraught Graham was.

"It's okay, son," he said. "Don't be scared. Come on down here."

Graham shook his head.

"Son," his father said in a calm voice, the one he used when he was trying to get Graham to do something he didn't want to do. "We need your help. Bring some towels."

Graham tore down the steps, grabbed towels from the bathroom on the second floor, and ran as fast as he could down the last set of stairs and out the door to where his parents were huddled over his little brother. When his father moved aside to take a towel from him, he saw Balfy's face. His eyes were still open, as if he were screaming, and his mouth was filled with blood. His wheat-colored hair was tinged in red. He wasn't moving.

"Balfy!" Graham jumped forward, trying to hug his brother.

"It's too late, son."

Graham could feel his father's hands shaking as he pulled him back.

"Don't say that!" Graham screamed. "He'll be okay. Balfy, wake up. Wake up!"

Fannie was holding Balfy close and whispering in his ear, rocking him back and forth. "I love you, son. I love you. Remember that. I love you. Don't leave me. I love you."

"Balfy, wake up!" Graham shouted.

Queenie came bounding down the front steps as the ambulance pulled up to the house. "How is he?"

Fannie shook her head.

Queenie started to moan. "No. Can't be. Can't be. Lawd no. Not Master Balfour. No, Lawd."

Norwood jumped up and whispered to Queenie, "Look after Graham. I think he's in shock." Then he headed to meet the medics who were coming up the walkway toward them.

"It's all my fault," Graham whispered.

Queenie pulled him close. "Weren't your fault, Master Graham. Were an accident. An accident, that's all."

Queenie hugged him so hard he couldn't breathe. She was steering him away from Balfy toward the house. He tried to break loose, but she was gripping him so hard that he couldn't move his head.

"Let me go," Graham said, trying to push her away.

"No, baby, you stay right here with me."

They fought for a few moments until Graham gave up. Queenie was still holding him in a bear hug, but he could see underneath her arm as a medic listened for a heartbeat and then shook his head. Graham started crying, heaving sobs of disbelief.

"Now, now, Master Graham, it'll be all right. Queenie's gone take care of you."

Graham watched his brother's body being placed on a gurney and covered with a sheet. The ambulance driver spoke with Norwood for a few minutes. Then the medics rolled the gurney toward the ambulance. As soon as they closed the door, Fannie sank to the ground.

"Mama!" Graham called after her. He reached his arms out, wanting to run to her, but Queenie held him back.

"She's in shock, boy, just like you. I'm gone take you inside now. Nothing else you can do out here. They'll take care of your mama."

Queenie guided him inside. He kept turning his head, looking to see if they were going to take his mother away, too. Norwood was trying to put Fannie's arm around his neck so he could lift her up. He finally grabbed her around the waist and hoisted her up over his shoulder. One of the medics followed him inside.

"Watch out, Queenie," Norwood said as they carried Fannie up the steps and into the house.

Graham didn't know which way to turn. He wanted to run toward his brother in the ambulance to say one last goodbye. He wanted to run to his mother to make sure she was all right.

And part of him wanted to run away and never come back.

When they got in the house, Graham could hear shuffling sounds coming from his parents' room. Then the door shut, and his father and one of the medics came back down the stairs.

Norwood leaned down and spoke to Graham. "Listen, son. I have to go to the hospital and take care of the paperwork for Balfour. They've sedated your mother. She should sleep all night, so don't disturb her, you hear?"

"Yes, sir," Graham said.

Norwood stood up and looked at Queenie. "Can you stay here tonight?"

"Yes sir, Mr. Norwood, sir. I'll tend to Graham. Don't you worry none."

Graham didn't remember anything about the rest of that night, but in the morning when he woke up, he heard banging on the third floor. He stood at the bottom of the steps, afraid to go up. He went downstairs instead and out to the front yard, where he could see Crow up on a ladder boarding up the windows to the attic room and the turret. Crow acknowledged Graham with a tilt of his head. Graham did the same. When he looked down, he noticed there was still blood on the path where Balfour had fallen. He stooped down to touch it. It had soaked into the soft brick. He tried to scrape it off with his shoe, but no matter how much he scraped, the bloodstain still showed. He rubbed harder and harder, trying to make the stain go away. Harder and harder, until his foot wouldn't go any faster.

"Master Graham, what are you doing?" Queenie picked him up and carried him over her shoulder into the house. She set him down just inside the door, then bent over, speaking softly. "Now listen, Master Graham, you feeling mighty lost right now, but we can't take back the way things are no matter how much we try, understand? We got to go on. You got to be strong for your mother. There ain't nothing gone bring Master Balfour back, you hear me?"

If only I had grabbed his hand, climbed out onto the gutter, maybe I could have saved him, Graham thought.

Queenie turned his chin toward her. "Master Graham, are you listening to me?"

He cut loose and started running up the stairs toward his mother's room. When he tried the handle, it was locked. He turned and yelled down at Queenie, "Let me in!"

She shook her head. "No, baby. Doctor says your mama needs her rest. We ain't to disturb her."

"Where's my father?"

"He's at the hospital. He went back early this morning to make arrangements. Now come on down here so I can make you some breakfast."

A week went by. They buried Balfour out at the Metairie Cemetery on a bitter cold day when the rain was spitting down on them. Fannie came out of her room to go to the funeral. She didn't speak a word the whole time. Not to Norwood. Not to Graham. Not even to Balfour as they buried him. It was as if she'd died herself. After the service, Norwood escorted Fannie back to her room. Graham waited for him outside the door.

"Is she ever going to say anything again?" Graham asked his father.

"I hope so, son," Norwood said. Then he stooped down and hugged Graham. He could hear his father crying softly.

❧❦❧

Christmas came and went. Queenie took the tree down the day after New Year's and put the unopened presents in the hall closet.

When it came time for school to start again, his father came to Graham's room to speak to him.

"Son, I need to talk to you about something."

Graham was on his bed reading a comic book. He put it down and sat up. "Is it about Mother?"

"In part." Norwood smoothed back Graham's dark hair. "You need a haircut."

"I know, but everybody's been busy."

"I know, son. That's the problem. I feel bad. I'm sorry I haven't been a very good father lately."

"It's okay."

Norwood kissed him on the forehead. "Listen."

Graham tensed up. Every time someone said *listen*, something bad usually came after it.

"The doctors told me this morning that your mother is going to have to go away for a little while."

"What's a little while?" Graham asked.

"They don't know for sure. Until she gets better."

"Can I see her before she goes?"

Norwood reached over and took Graham's hand in his. "They've already come to get her, while you were asleep."

Graham yanked his hand away. "What do you mean? Why didn't anyone wake me up?"

"Calm down. It was in the middle of the night. She started having some sort of seizure. But don't worry—the doctor says she'll be all right."

"When will she be back?"

"I hope by the summer, when you come back."

"When I come back? From where?"

Graham adored his father, had always looked up to him. Tanned and rugged from working out on the tugboat, he had strong arms from heaving towlines. He wore his dark hair parted on the side, just as Graham did, and his steady hazel eyes turned green in the sunlight.

Today those eyes didn't look steady. Instead, they looked as if they were saying one thing and meaning another.

"I have to go away on an extended job down the river. I don't want to leave you alone."

"Queenie can take care of me."

"Queenie has a family of her own, son. She can't be with you all the time. I've spoken with the headmaster at St. Stanislaus, a boarding school over on the Mississippi Gulf Coast. I'm bringing you there first thing tomorrow."

"What?" Graham sat up on his knees. "No!"

"Listen, son." Norwood pushed him back down on the bed against the headboard. "I don't have a choice. I'm sorry. But for the time being, this is the way it's going to be."

The next morning at daybreak, Queenie woke Graham. She helped him get dressed and packed a breakfast for him. She handed him a small suitcase and waved goodbye as Norwood backed the car out of the driveway.

Graham looked out the back window of the car, wondering if he would ever come back to the house on Prytania Street again. And if he did, would things ever be the same?

Would his mother ever love him the way she had before Balfy died?

He wasn't so sure.

✰✰✰✰

"Did it happen in this room?" Ibby asked.

Doll nodded. "That's why that window is all boarded up. Been that way since the accident."

"One of the locked rooms on the second floor—is one of them Balfour's?"

"Yes, Miss Ibby. Fannie had Queenie lock it up that night. No one been in there since."

"I wonder why Daddy never told me about his brother."

Doll shook her head. "'Cause, Miss Ibby, the day Master Balfour died, something in your daddy died, too. He thought his mother blamed him for the accident. He thought that was why his parents sent him away to boarding school. He never said as much, but I could always see it in his eyes. Think that may have been one reason he ran away with your mother. But Miss Fannie, she never blamed him. All she wanted was for him to stay here in this house with her, so they could be a family. She tried to talk to him, tried to show him how much she loved him, but after the accident, Master Graham, he kept pushing her away. I think he had so much hurt inside that he just didn't know how to let it go. Broke Miss Fannie's heart watching him suffer like that."

"I wish he'd told me about it. I could have tried to help."

That explained the sadness she saw in her daddy's eyes sometimes. Ibby used to think that she was the one that made him sad. She thought perhaps he wasn't proud of her, or maybe he wished she'd been a boy. Now she understood. He was hurting inside from something that had happened a long time ago. Still, she wished he would have told her about the accident. Maybe she could have made it better for him somehow.

Doll let out a big sigh. "Some things too broke to fix sometimes. All you can do is make the best of it."

"Doll?"

"Yes, baby?"

"Is Fannie too broke to fix?"

Doll flicked one of her fingernails several times before answering. "Just remember that she loves you, no matter what," Doll said. "Now try to get some rest." When she got to the door, she turned around. "Tell you what, Miss Ibby. Tomorrow, first thing, I'm gone get Crow to take them boards off that window. Make it a lot more comfortable once we get some air circulating. About time we got some life back in this room."

Chapter Twenty-One

The next morning Ibby stopped by her father's room and held the urn for a while. She'd stayed awake all night, thinking about him. There was so much she never knew about him, so much he'd never told her. She remembered the way he had looked at the photo of Fannie the day it fell out of his wallet at the school fair, as if he wanted to say something to her but couldn't. She hadn't understood the pain in his eyes then, but she did now. He had wanted to tell his mother that he loved her, just as she wished she could tell her father at this very moment how much she loved him.

As she closed the door to his room, she knew it was too late to help her father, but maybe it wasn't too late to help Fannie. Somehow.

Queenie was taking some biscuits out of the oven when she went into the kitchen. "You look all tuckered out, Miss Ibby. What's the matter? Didn't you get any sleep?"

"Not much," Ibby said.

"Doll, she say she up all night, too, listening to that tiger down at the zoo." Queenie nodded toward the backyard, where Doll was yanking some sheets off the clothesline. "Better stay out of her way today. She gets mighty cranky when she don't get her sleep."

Queenie put a plate of bacon in front of Ibby and said cheerily, "So, what we gone do today? Could go on down to the poultry market off

Carrollton Avenue and get a few fresh chickens. Know they fresh 'cause they wring those chicks' necks right in front of you, then pluck 'em clean and wrap 'em up right nice so you can tote 'em home."

Queenie was awfully talkative this morning, even for Queenie.

Ibby shook her head.

"No? Well then, we could go by the fish market over on Jefferson Highway, get some fresh she-crabs or some shrimp, and make us up some stuffed mirliton. I got some nice Creole tomatoes in the back, could make some more gazpacho."

"I'm not really hungry," Ibby said.

Queenie kept rambling. "Well, how about a game of *bourré*? I got some cards right here in the kitchen drawer. Or better yet, we can watch my stories on the TV while Doll irons the sheets." Queenie kind of laughed at that last suggestion.

"Has the doctor called?" Ibby asked.

"No, baby. Expect it be a few more days before we hear from him." Queenie turned to face the sink.

Ibby got the feeling there was something she wasn't telling her. "Is something wrong?"

Queenie sat down at the table. Her happy face had vanished. "Your mama called this morning, Miss Ibby."

"My mother? Did she wish me a happy birthday?"

"Ibby, baby, I don't know how to tell you this." Queenie set her eyes squarely on the floor, a sure sign she was getting ready to deliver some bad news.

Doll came in the back door and set the ironing basket on the counter. "What's going on?"

"Her mama called a little while ago," Queenie said.

Doll's eyes widened. "What Miss Vidrine gone say when she finds out Miss Fannie ain't here?"

"Don't matter no more." Queenie shook her head.

"What you mean?" Doll asked.

Queenie looked from Ibby to Doll and back again. "'Cause Miss Vidrine, she say she ain't coming back."

⣍⣏⣪⣏⣋

One morning almost two weeks later, Ibby, Queenie, and Doll were in the kitchen when they heard the front door open and close.

Fannie had returned from the hospital. She dropped her suitcase in the hall and walked into the dining room, took her usual spot at the table, and began reading the newspaper.

"I'd like some coffee!" she bellowed.

"You go on in there and take your seat at the table, pretend like nothing has happened," Queenie said to Ibby. "You hear me? Don't say nothing about her being in that hospital. Just go on about your business like it's any other morning."

"How am I supposed to do that?" Ibby asked as Queenie pushed her through the door into the dining room.

"Just do what you do every morning—say hello and give her a kiss on the cheek."

"Then what? What am I supposed to talk about?" Ibby said.

"You just follow my lead." Queenie nudged Ibby toward Fannie.

Ibby went over to Fannie and kissed her on the cheek, then took a seat at the table. "Good morning, Fannie."

"Good morning, young lady. How'd you sleep?" Fannie didn't look up from the newspaper.

Before Ibby could answer, Queenie came over to serve Fannie some coffee. "What you feel like for breakfast this morning, Miss Fannie?"

"Maybe some bacon," she said. "They make terrible bacon in that place."

Ibby looked over at Queenie, hoping she was going to change the subject.

"Sure enough—got plenty of bacon I can fry up," Queenie said, making eyes at Ibby.

Ibby couldn't tell what Queenie was trying to get her to do.

"Miss Ibby, what you want?"

"Same as Fannie, I guess," Ibby said, making eyes back.

Queenie left the room for a second, then came back in. "You want something else, Miss Fannie?"

"I have a hankering for clabber. Could you bring me some of that, too?"

"Sure thing, Miss Fannie."

"Anything happen while I was gone?" Fannie asked to no one in particular while she was reading the paper.

Ibby looked over at Queenie.

Queenie nodded. "Might as well go on and tell her, Miss Ibby."

Ibby glowered at her. She'd hoped she could wait a few days, until she was sure Fannie was back to her old self, before bringing up Vidrine's phone call.

"Tell me about what?" Fannie asked.

"Miss Vidrine called," Queenie said. "About two weeks ago."

Fannie put the newspaper down. "What'd she want?"

"She say it be okay if Miss Ibby stay with you awhile," Queenie said.

Ibby tightened her lips. That wasn't exactly what her mother had said, and Queenie knew it.

Fannie's face brightened. "How long is awhile?"

"She don't say," Queenie said, making her way back to the kitchen. "Just thought you'd want to know."

Fannie jumped up from the table. Ibby could hear her dialing the phone in the hall.

Queenie came back into the room to refill Fannie's coffee cup.

"Why'd you go and bring that up?" Ibby whispered to her.

"She got to know sooner or later," Queenie said.

"Later would have been better," Ibby said.

"No time for later around this house," Queenie said.

"Who's she calling?" Ibby said. "I hope it's not Vidrine."

"Oh." Queenie sat back on her heels. "Never thought about that."
When Fannie came back into the room, she was smiling.

Queenie said to Ibby, low enough so Fannie couldn't hear, "Couldn't have been Vidrine. Not the way she's grinning."

"It's all settled," Fannie said.

"What you going on about, Miss Fannie?" Queenie asked. "What's all settled?"

"I just enrolled Ibby at Our Lady of the Celestial Realm Catholic School for Girls. She starts in a couple of weeks."

Ibby fell back against her chair.

Queenie shook her head. "Miss Ibby gone be a Catholic schoolgirl. Now, ain't that something."

Part Two

1968

Chapter Twenty-Two

Most of the girls at Our Lady of the Celestial Realm had known each other since preschool and were from good Catholic families, a phrase that tumbled from their lips like one long word, *good-Catholic-families*. There were few exceptions. In Ibby's sophomore class of twenty-five girls, there was only one non-Catholic—Ibby Bell. As far as Ibby could tell, the only reason she'd been accepted at Our Lady of the Celestial Realm was because Fannie knew the head nun, Sister Gertrude, although Fannie never would explain the connection. That was four years ago.

Today was the last day of school, and the girls were lined up like dominoes, in identical uniforms of green plaid skirts and white poplin blouses with initials monogrammed on their collars, as they made their way toward the chapel for the final prayer service. Ibby kept her head down in an effort to avoid being noticed by Sister Gertrude, who was trudging up and down the line like a drill sergeant, her rubber-soled shoes squeaking against the waxed-wood floor. Close to six feet tall, with piercing green eyes and thin lips that were forever pursed, Sister Gertrude could scare away the devil himself.

"Girls, girls, quiet!" she huffed.

The sound of Sister Gertrude's booming voice was usually enough to make the girls stand at attention, but not today, with only an hour before school let out for the summer. Our Lady of the Celestial Realm wasn't air-conditioned, and the open windows along the hallway leading into the chapel offered no respite, serving only to let in the stifling May heat and a few hungry flies. The girls were getting punchy and restless.

"Silence! If I have to say it again, detentions for each and every one of you."

Ibby held her breath as Sister Gertrude stopped beside her and tapped a ruler against her habit. The nun put out her hand to the girl in line in front of Ibby.

"Janice Jumonville, spit out that gum."

The startled schoolgirl leaned over and let a gob of pink bubblegum drop into Sister Gertrude's open palm. Sister Gertrude slipped the gum into the pocket of her habit and moved on. Ibby wondered how many wads of chewing gum she had in there, collecting lint.

The girl behind Ibby pushed her.

"Stop that, Annabelle," Ibby said. "You're going to get me in trouble."

Puberty had not been kind to Annabelle. Her unruly red hair had taken on a brassy tone, the gap in her front teeth had grown wider, and her freckles had multiplied and run together, making her look like she had some sort of skin disorder. Even so, she still carried herself as if the whole world owed her a favor.

Annabelle pushed Ibby again, this time harder, and the yearbook Ibby had been holding fell to the floor with a thud. As Ibby bent down to pick it up, her eye caught the small wooden plaque over the chapel door:

THE GOLDEN RULE

Do unto others
As you would have them
Do unto you.

She wanted to point the sign out to Annabelle, but she knew it wouldn't do any good. Annabelle would be forever stuck on the second line—*Do unto others.*

Sister Gertrude must have been watching the antics because she came over and yanked Annabelle out of line and marched her down to her office at the end of the hall without so much as a word.

"Serves her right," Marcelle whispered when Sister Gertrude was out of earshot.

Ibby hated chapel because she was relegated to sitting in the back while all her classmates lined up in the aisle to take communion, something Ibby wasn't allowed to do because she wasn't Catholic. After four years of enduring this, it still made her feel like an outcast.

When chapel was over, Ibby walked with her friend Winnie Waguespack to the streetcar stop on St. Charles Avenue. As they were waiting, Annabelle drove by in a shiny blue Mustang convertible and shot the finger at them.

"I think that was meant for me." Ibby kicked the ground with her saddle oxford shoe as the streetcar pulled up. "I don't know what her problem is."

"Don't let her get to you, Ibby," Winnie said in the syrupy Mississippi accent she'd inherited from her mother even though she'd grown up in New Orleans. "No one likes Annabelle. I don't know who she thinks she is."

Ibby handed a dime to the streetcar conductor and found a seat next to a window. Winnie slid in next to her.

"You know, Annabelle's daddy gave her that blue Mustang for her birthday last year," Winnie said, unleashing a mop of curly brown hair from a clip.

Ibby muttered, "I don't even have my driver's license yet."

"Why not?" Winnie asked. "I got mine a year ago, when I turned fifteen."

Ibby shrugged. "Fannie won't let me. I guess she figures I'll stay out of trouble that way."

"Well, it's not all that great really," Winnie said. "I think Mama got me my license so I could run all her errands for her after school, so don't feel so bad. By the way," she added, "I hear Annabelle got a horse for her sixteenth birthday, a few weeks ago."

Ibby looked at Winnie. "A horse? Really?"

"That's what I hear," Winnie giggled. "Can you imagine? I don't know how her father affords it, being an accountant and all. Still"— she sighed—"it must be nice, being an only child. I can't imagine what it's like not having to share a bedroom with three sisters and a bathroom with four brothers. And I'd give anything not to have to change my little sister's diapers."

"It's not all it's cut out to be, being an only child," Ibby remarked.

Winnie smiled a little too sweetly. "Bless your heart, I forgot."

They were good friends, but the one thing that bugged Ibby about Winnie was that she had a way of saying things that sounded like one thing but meant something totally different. Ibby was pretty sure Winnie was trying to be nice, but it still came out sounding condescending.

"Must be hard not having any parents." Winnie patted her hand.

Ibby pulled her hand away. "I have a grandmother . . . and a mother . . . somewhere."

"I'm sorry, I didn't mean . . ." Winnie shook her head and turned away.

Ibby let the awkward silence pass by staring out the open window. It had begun to drizzle, a warm rain that left the sidewalks steaming and the air sticky. She reached through the window and let the raindrops pool in her hand, wondering what it must be like to have a big family like the Waguespacks.

When she turned back around, she noticed the young hippie couple sitting just across the way. The man's long hair draped over the shoulders of his loose-fitting shirt, where a peace sign dangled from a leather necklace. He had his arm around a young woman in a halter top and batik skirt who was leaning casually against his chest.

It must be nice to be so free, Ibby thought as she watched them.

By the time the streetcar reached Jefferson Avenue, the rain had all but evaporated into a thin mist rising from the street.

"Here's my stop," Ibby said.

Winnie tugged on her skirt as she got up. "I didn't mean to hurt your feelings."

"It's all right."

Winnie tugged on her skirt again. "Listen. My parents are throwing a birthday party for me in a couple of weeks. You'll get an invitation in the mail. Want to come shopping with me to pick out a dress?" Winnie went on. "We can go down to Canal Street, to D. H. Holmes and maybe Maison Blanche, too, if we have time."

Most of Ibby's friends went shopping together on Saturdays, but they'd never asked Ibby because they knew Doll made most of her clothes.

"Sure," Ibby said. "Thanks for asking."

Ibby got off the streetcar and headed down Jefferson Avenue toward Prytania Street. Clouds left over from the earlier rain blanketed the sky, trapping the humidity beneath them. Ibby heard a low rumble in the distance. She glanced up at the sky. Thunder in New Orleans was sneaky. Just when you thought it was gone, it came up behind you and let out a big clap that resonated through your whole body. She'd never heard thunder like that before she came to New Orleans. It used to scare her. Not anymore. A lot had changed in the last four years. For one, she wasn't a shy twelve-year-old anymore.

Ibby put her hand on the gate to Fannie's house and wiped the sweat from her forehead. She remembered when her mother had dropped her off for the first time. The house had seemed so ominous and uninviting. It gave her a much different feeling now, like that of an old tattered blanket: it wasn't much to look at, but it made you feel safe just the same.

The branches of the oak tree in the front yard were waving, as if welcoming her home. The poor tree had begun to lean considerably, ever since Hurricane Betsy swept through the city in the fall of 1965. Ibby thought back to those hot days, when the power had been out and school was closed. Crow, Queenie, Doll, and Birdelia had moved in, fearing flooding in their neighborhood. She remembered eating cold food out of cans, barbequing in the backyard, playing card games to while away the time, and the never-ending search for ice to cool off. They had all complained, but looking back on it, it was the first time Ibby felt as if she were a real part of the family.

Every year after that, the tree had begun to lean a little more, so much that now it resembled the leaning Tower of Pisa. The neighbors had been on Fannie to cut the tree down, saying it was a hazard, but Fannie had resisted the idea. It was as if the tree meant something to her. In a way, that old tree reminded Ibby of Fannie—slightly off balance but clinging stubbornly to life.

Fannie had survived her trip to the hospital four years earlier, and many more after that. Ibby soon realized that Fannie needed an occasional escape from life. She had gotten used to Fannie's ways, and everyone carried on as if it were all perfectly normal.

New Orleans was like that. A live-and-let-live attitude was ingrained into the fabric of the city; no one cared who you were or what you looked like—you had a place, and everyone respected that. There were a few exceptions, of course, most notably Annabelle Friedrichs, who had continued to be a nuisance to Ibby. Ibby had grown used to her taunts and ignored her as much as possible, but Ibby's missing mother had become the butt of Annabelle's jokes over the years—and that was something Ibby couldn't tolerate.

No one wants you, not even your own mother. You're an outcast. Why don't you go back where you came from?

Ibby hadn't heard from her mother since Vidrine dropped her off four years ago. And except for Annabelle's occasional reminders, Ibby went on about her days as if her mother didn't exist. It was just easier that way.

Fannie had tried to explain Vidrine's disappearance as a simple case of wanderlust, but Ibby had a different word for a mother who would abandon her daughter and not even take the time to put in a call to say hello. As far as her mother was concerned, Ibby was never sure of anything, not even of what she might say to Vidrine if she ever did come back.

Ibby opened the gate and started up the driveway where two cars were parked—a very official-looking black Lincoln Town Car, and a brand-new red Lincoln Continental convertible with white leather seats. Ibby noticed Fannie's old blue convertible wasn't in the garage.

As she opened the back door, she found Queenie perched on a stool, cleaning softshell crabs at the kitchen table. As much as Ibby loved eating softshells, she could barely stomach watching Queenie clean them, the way their legs writhed as Queenie cut through the shell with a pair of utility scissors, then reached under and scooped out the white spongy lungs.

Queenie had slowed down a bit over the last couple of years. Her hair was now a salt-and-pepper gray, and she had taken to sitting at the table to do her cooking rather than standing at the counter, claiming her legs just didn't want to hold her up anymore.

"Lawd, look at you. Your face, it's as red as one of them Creole tomatoes," Queenie said.

Ibby set her books on the table and wiped the sweat from her face. "That's because New Orleans only has one season. Hot."

Queenie tossed a crab into a tub of milk batter and wiped her hands on her apron. "No, baby, we got seasons. We got oyster season, crawfish season, shrimp season, crab season. Come to think of it, we got alligator season, hurricane season, Mardi Gras season. We got a whole mess of seasons around these parts. And baby, it's only the end of May. Come September, even I begin to sweat." Queenie tilted her head toward Ibby's books. "Show me your picture in that there yearbook."

As Ibby opened it to the page that showed her class, Queenie leaned in to get a better look. "Who drew that big black mustache on your face, Miss Ibby?"

Ibby rolled her eyes. "Who do you think?"

Just then Doll came into the kitchen, humming. Doll hadn't changed much. She still had a penchant for red nail polish and liked to wear her hair piled high on her head, although today she'd straightened her hair with Morgan's Hair Refining Cream and rolled it under neatly at the bottom. Ibby thought the hairstyle made her look much younger than her twenty-seven years.

Doll leaned over to get a glimpse. "Miss Ibby, why you let that Annabelle do stuff like that to you?"

"I don't *let* her. She's just mean."

"Girl, I'd knock her upside the head if I was you," Doll said. "I wouldn't take none of that from nobody."

Queenie patted Ibby's hand. "You still the prettiest gal in the class. Even with that big mustache."

Ibby put her head down on the table. "No, I'm not. Y'all are just trying to make me feel better."

"Did you hear that, Doll? She said y'all! Miss Ibby, you is one of us now!" Queenie ran her fingers through Ibby's long brown hair. "You know, people would give their eyeteeth for hair like yours. You got a right nice figure with good-size titties for a girl your age. Got those from your grandmother."

"Mama, don't talk that way to Miss Ibby," Doll scolded.

"Well, it's true." Queenie laughed. "You all growed up, Miss Ibby. Could pass for a young woman of twenty, not a young girl about to turn sixteen."

Ibby waved her hand. "Not according to Fannie. I don't think she'll ever let me grow up."

"That's 'cause if you grow up, Miss Fannie thinks she gone grow old, and she don't like being old. Could be the reason she done gone out and bought herself that new car this morning."

Ibby stole a glance out the back window. "That big red convertible? That's Fannie's?"

"And that's not all," Doll chimed in. "Wait until you see the TV she done bought for herself on the way back from buying the car."

"A brand new *color* TV," Queenie gushed. "Come with a little clicker device so she can change the channels from where she sitting on the couch. She say she paid almost as much for the TV as she did for that new car, just so that she could get that channel changer that come with it."

"I wonder why?" Ibby said.

"You do things like that when you're old, just to make yourself feel young again. Ain't that so, Doll?"

"How would I know?" she said. "But Mama, you what—close to sixty-five? When you gone get a new car?"

"Didn't I tell you? Miss Fannie done give Crow her old blue Cadillac this morning. He already come over and picked it up. Bet he's driving all over town right now showing it off."

"How old is Miss Fannie? She old as you?" Doll asked.

"No, no. Miss Fannie, she a bit younger, maybe fifty-six last time I took a count."

"That gone make her an old fart in a red Cadillac," Doll chuckled.

"I wouldn't say nothing like that around Miss Fannie." Queenie pointed a finger at Doll. "No woman likes to be reminded about her age."

"Queenie, is Ibby home yet?" Fannie called out from the dining room.

"She just got here!" Queenie yelled back. "I'll send her right in."

Queenie came over and gave Ibby a squeeze around the shoulders. "Now, you better get on in there, Miss Ibby. Mr. Rainold and Miss Fannie, they got something they want to tell you."

"Why is Mr. Rainold here?" Ibby asked as Queenie guided her toward the door.

Emile Rainold was Fannie's longtime attorney who came over once or twice a year to go over business matters. Ibby should have recognized his black Town Car in the driveway.

"Never you mind," Queenie said.

But Ibby could tell by the way Queenie was averting her eyes that there was something she wasn't telling her.

Chapter Twenty-Three

Doll opened the door a smidgen so she could listen in on Fannie's conversation with Mr. Rainold.

Queenie motioned for Doll to get away from the door. "Come back over here."

She put her finger up to her mouth. "Hush, Mama. I want to hear what Mr. Rainold's got to say. You know what it's about?"

Queenie took in a deep breath. "Miss Fannie, she's afraid her worst nightmare is about to come true."

"What you mean?" Doll whispered.

"Just listen, baby," Queenie said without looking up from the crab she was cleaning.

Doll could see Mr. Rainold sitting at the table in a blue pin-striped seersucker suit with a red paisley bow tie and a rumpled white cotton button-down shirt. She often wondered if that was his only suit, or if he owned a closet full of identical suits so he wouldn't have to decide which one to put on each day. The only thing that ever seemed to change about Emile Rainold was his shoes—white bucks in the spring and summer, and brown suede bucks in the fall and winter. His straw fedora lay on the table next to his briefcase as he flipped through some papers, his cheeks billowing in and out like a puffer fish as he sucked on his pipe. Every so often he would push his gold wire-rimmed glasses up the bridge of his nose and smooth back his wavy gray hair with the palm of his other hand. He and Fannie were still arguing as Ibby took a seat across the table from him.

"That Mr. Rainold, he sure looks like he could use a good bath," Doll whispered.

"He's always been like that," Queenie said. "Most of the time, his face is glistening like he done stuck his head in the oven."

"He's getting up in age. He looks older than Miss Fannie. Why you suppose he never married?"

Queenie dropped her hands and looked over at Doll. "Girl, why you think? He ain't interested in no ladies."

Doll couldn't help but let out a laugh. Mr. Rainold must have heard her because he glanced her way. Doll eased the door closed an inch or two, not wanting to be seen.

"Nothing has changed, Fannie. The law is the law," Mr. Rainold said.

"Emile, are you sure?" Fannie squinted one eye.

"Miss Fannie looks like she wants to jump right up out of her chair and wring Mr. Rainold's neck. I wonder why?" Doll said to Queenie.

"On account she don't like it when he tells her no." Queenie shrugged. "They been in there a good two hours before Miss Ibby got home from school, arguing about something. What's Miss Ibby doing?"

"She's just sitting in her chair, listening," Doll said.

Fannie spoke to him in a stern voice. "Vidrine left Ibby here and never came back. She hasn't once corresponded with her daughter in four years. Can't we do *something*?"

Emile Rainold peered over his glasses. "The only way to gain legal custody is to petition the court and ask it to declare Vidrine an unfit mother by proving she poses a threat to Ibby."

"Well, she *did* abandon Ibby," Fannie said.

"That's not the issue. The issue is whether Vidrine poses a threat. She hasn't been around her daughter in years. The only way to claim she might be a threat is to say she left her daughter *with* someone who might be a threat."

"You mean me?" Fannie balked.

"I'm just telling you the way the courts might see it, should you try to pursue it." Mr. Rainold tapped his pipe in the ashtray and filled it with more tobacco. "The court wouldn't view leaving Ibby with her grandmother as abandonment, in light of the fact that you agreed to take her for an unspecified amount of time. We just had no idea it would be indefinitely."

"Why don't we file a petition anyway and see what happens?" Fannie asked.

"The problem is, I have to know where Vidrine is living in order to serve the papers."

Mr. Rainold's empty coffee cup clicked against the saucer.

"Mama," Doll whispered. "Mr. Rainold needs more coffee."

She grabbed the silver coffeepot and brushed past Doll into the dining room.

"It appears Vidrine has gone peripatetic," Mr. Rainold said.

"Yeah, pathetic," Queenie said as she refilled his cup.

Mr. Rainold grinned. "Perhaps *pathetic* is right, Queenie, but what I said was *peripatetic*. It means Vidrine doesn't appear to have a permanent address."

Queenie turned to go, stopping just short of the kitchen door. "That's what I said. Pathetic."

Fannie crossed her arms and sat back. "So what you're telling me is that Vidrine could walk in that door any minute and take Ibby away."

"I'm afraid so. The law remains on the side of the mother."

"So if I died tomorrow and left this house to Ibby, it would fall into the hands of her legal guardian until she's eighteen, and as of right now, that's Vidrine."

"Yes, Fannie, that's true, but . . ." He tapped his pencil on the table as if he were about to make a point.

"Then I better not die anytime soon."

He puffed on his pipe. "Not for at least two years, Fannie."

Doll stifled a laugh and whispered to her mother, "Mr. Rainold's trying to make a joke, but Fannie's not laughing."

Mr. Rainold looked over at Ibby. "There's something your grandmother and I were discussing before you got here, something I think you should know."

"Please, Emile. Is this really necessary?" Fannie asked.

"I feel I have an obligation to tell her," he said to Fannie before turning his attention back to Ibby. "One of my detectives thinks he may have spotted your mother recently."

Ibby's hand flew to her mouth. Her elbow accidentally hit a pedestal, sending a vase crashing to the floor.

"Lawd," Doll whispered.

"What was that?" Queenie asked.

"That ugly old Chinese vase," Doll said. "Done broke into a thousand pieces when Mr. Rainold told Ibby about her mama."

"Don't matter," Queenie said. "Miss Fannie always hated that vase. It came with the house."

"I wish you wouldn't have said anything, Emile," Fannie said.

"Ibby, I want you to take a look at this." Mr. Rainold slid a photograph across the table. "One of my detectives took it a few days ago. We're not a hundred percent positive it's your mother. Could be someone who just looks like her."

"You mean my mother is here, in New Orleans?" she asked.

Mr. Rainold said, "That photo was taken on Ursulines Street in the French Quarter, in front of a building owned by a middle-aged woman named Maude Hopper, who calls herself Avi. She's well known around the French Quarter, a flamboyant nutcase who runs a sort of free-wheeling boardinghouse for transients."

Ibby was studying the photo hard. Doll could see her hands were shaking.

"It's obvious I've upset you, Ibby. I'm sorry. I only mentioned it in case Vidrine shows up unannounced. As I said, we're not even sure if the woman in the photo is Vidrine." He looked at his watch. "Oh gosh, look at the time. I'm sorry to have to rush off, but I'm late for another appointment."

Fannie saw Mr. Rainold to the door.

Doll turned toward her mother. "You don't think Miss Vidrine's planning on showing up here, do you, Mama?"

"It'll break Miss Fannie's heart if Miss Vidrine comes back and take Miss Ibby away." Queenie put her face in her hands, then looked over at Doll. "She come back here, she asking for trouble."

Chapter Twenty-Four

After Emile Rainold left, Fannie came back into the dining room and grabbed Ibby's hand.

"Come on," she said. "We're going for a ride."

When they got in the car, Fannie tied a scarf around her hair and backed out of the driveway, sending oyster-shell gravel flying in all directions. She turned onto St. Charles Avenue, puffing furiously on a cigarette. Ibby looked over at Fannie, wondering where they were going in such a hurry.

Fannie had kept her hair dyed a soft auburn ever since that day they went to Antoine's for Ibby's twelfth birthday, and she'd made a concerted effort to keep up her appearance, wearing smartly tailored dresses that Doll made for her. Today she had on rouge and lipstick. Ibby could tell she was thinking hard about something.

It wasn't until they got to the river bend, where St. Charles Avenue meets Carrollton, that Fannie finally spoke: "I know you're probably a little unnerved, hearing your mother might be in town."

The truth was, Ibby wasn't sure how she felt about her mother, but she didn't want to upset Fannie by giving a wrong answer. "I don't know."

"Do you like living with me?"

Fannie's question made Ibby pause. "Of course I do, but . . . wouldn't I have to go with my mother if she said I had to?"

Fannie flicked her cigarette out onto the street. After a while, she handed Ibby an envelope. "Here. This came for you today."

Ibby noticed the envelope had been opened.

"I know I had no right to open it, but I was afraid after what Mr. Rainold told me this morning that it might have been from your mother. It's not."

Ibby slid the card from the envelope, admiring the blue linen paper with the white embossed lettering. "Oh. It's an invitation to Winnie Waguespack's sweet sixteen party. She told me about it on the ride home from school today."

"You have a birthday coming up, too. That invitation gave me an idea. I'm going to throw you your own sweet sixteen party."

"A party? For me?"

"Yes, dear. I've already arranged for T-Bone to start painting the house."

T-Bone had just gotten back from Vietnam a few weeks ago and was looking for work. Ibby hadn't seen him since that day at the True Love Baptist Church all those years ago. She wondered what he looked like now.

"Ibby darling, did you hear what I just said? We need to make a list," Fannie went on. "I will invite your classmates, of course. And Sister Gertrude."

Ibby's head shot around. "Sister Gertrude? Why on earth would we invite Sister Gertrude? She'll ruin the whole party. No one will come if they know she's invited."

"Don't be silly," Fannie said.

"It's true, Fannie. Everyone hates Sister Gertrude." Ibby crossed her arms and let out a harrumph.

"Now, dear, Sister Gertrude was one of the first people I met when I came to New Orleans. She went out of her way to be nice to me when I didn't know anybody. It would be rude of me not to invite her."

"How exactly do you know Sister Gertrude anyway?"

"She taught me how to dance."

Ibby balked. "Sister Gertrude knows how to dance?"

"She's quite good at it, or at least she used to be. A lot of things about Sister Gertrude might surprise you. She wasn't always a nun, you know." Fannie glanced her way. "Now, how about boys? Do you know any boys?"

"Not really," Ibby said.

Fannie tapped the steering wheel with her thumb. "That just won't do."

"Well, you *did* send me to an all-girls school. How am I supposed to meet boys?"

"How indeed." Fannie appeared to be thinking on it. "We'll have to come up with a list. Winnie Waguespack has a couple of brothers, doesn't she? I'll get Doll to see if she can borrow the De La Salle school directory without Winnie's mother knowing about it."

"How are you going to manage that?"

"Her maid Bertha comes to the house every morning to place Myrtis Waguespack's bets. I'm sure we can work something out."

Ibby fingered the dashboard. It was full of fancy new features, such as automatic temperature control and an eight-track tape player. "What made you go out and buy a new car?"

Fannie gave out a sigh. "When I got off the train from Mamou all those years ago, just a starry-eyed young girl with no money in her pocket, the first thing that caught my eye was a beautiful red Packard convertible. I promised myself that one day I'd buy myself a big red convertible just like that one. When I woke up this morning, I knew this was the day."

"Why today?"

Fannie shrugged. "I don't know. I probably should have done it a long time ago."

"Will I ever get to drive it?"

"All in due time, dear," Fannie said, flicking her cigarette out of the car.

They were passing through Mid-City, where the Victorian houses and Arts and Crafts bungalows soon gave way to dozens of cemeteries.

"They call these cemeteries 'cities of the dead' because the raised tombs resemble miniature houses from a distance." Fannie turned in to one of the cemeteries lined by an old iron fence. "When the Spanish first settled in the city soon after the French, they found that when they buried the dead, the water table pushed the bodies back up from the graves. Burying the dead above ground seemed the only way. Look at that one there, with the pillars. Isn't it lovely?"

They meandered through the cemetery on a narrow lane and eventually parked in front of a small gray marble tomb with a domed top, the entrance flanked by two columns. On either side of the steps leading up to the tomb were copper vases that had faded to a pleasing green patina. Ibby noticed there were fresh flowers in the urns, white lilies, Fannie's favorite. Above the entrance to the tomb, Ibby could make out two names—Balfour and Norwood. Queenie had told her never to ask Fannie about her grandfather Norwood. And the last time Balfour's name was mentioned, the day hadn't ended so well.

Fannie wandered over to a stone bench nestled beneath an oak tree.

"Come sit by me." Fannie undid her scarf. "Isn't it nice here? I planted this tree when Balfour died. It must be almost thirty years old now."

Ibby waited to see if Fannie's hand would shake at the mention of Balfour's name, the way it often did when she was thinking about someone she loved who'd died, but Fannie seemed calm, almost at peace in the cemetery.

"Do you come here often?" Ibby asked.

"Whenever I can," Fannie said. "See those pelicans circling overhead? They're always here when I come. I often wonder if they followed Norwood from the river." She was quiet as she watched the birds glide across the sky. "He was a tugboat captain, you know."

"No, Fannie. You've never told me much about Grandfather Norwood."

"He knew the river like the back of his hand." She looked away, as if gathering the strength to talk. "Your grandfather had names for all the pelicans on the Mississippi River. Oh, how he loved those pelicans. Sometimes I used to think he loved those pelicans more than he loved me."

୧୧୭⊙୬

A few days after they were married, Norwood took Fannie down to the river, to see his tugboat. They stood on the pier, admiring it together.

"Isn't she a beauty?" He waved his hand at the boat, the *Pelican II*.

Fannie had seen the tugs only from a distance, on the river, where they were mere specks behind the massive barges they pushed. She'd never been on one and was surprised at how big it was and how low it sat in the river, only three or four feet above the water.

"Over a hundred feet long and thirty feet wide. The wheelhouse sits way up high like that so you can navigate the river. You feel like you're in a crow's nest when you're up there. Come on. I'll take you for a ride." He jumped into the boat and dangled his hands over the side. "Give me your hand, and I'll pull you up."

He lifted her up as the breeze from the river tousled her hair. The wake from a passing ocean liner jostled Fannie. She reached behind her, looking for something to hold on to.

"Be careful, honey." He grabbed her elbow to steady her. "I'd sure hate to lose my bride the first week we were married."

She followed him across the deck to the wheelhouse, then up the steep metal steps. He held open the wheelhouse door for her as she stepped inside.

"This is my home away from home," Norwood said as he plucked his captain's hat from a shelf and placed it on Fannie's head. He took her hand and pulled her over to the podium where the wheel was mounted. "You want to drive, honey?"

"Oh, no. I'm not even good at driving a car," she said, fingering the pearls around her neck, the ones Norwood had given her as a wedding present. She took the captain's hat and placed it on Norwood's head. "You show me how."

A few seconds later one of the deckhands appeared at the wheel-house door.

"Captain Woody, I brought you them bucket of fish you asked me to. Left it up against the side of the wheelhouse in the front of the boat."

Fannie smiled at Norwood. She'd never heard anyone call him Woody before.

"Listen, Chappy, I want to take my new bride out for a spin, show her the river. You got some time?"

"Sure, Cap," he said.

"Once I get the boat out, think you could handle her while I go on deck for a few minutes?"

The young man's eyes lit up.

"All right then." Norwood pressed a button and moved a lever forward.

The engine revved, sending muddy water gurgling from beneath the boat. Norwood guided the boat out onto the river. After a few minutes, he gave a signal to Chappy to come over and take the wheel. "Bring her just beyond the bend at Algiers Point, then turn her around."

Chappy took the wheel. "No problem, Cap."

Norwood slipped a life jacket over Fannie's head. "Here, put this on and tie it up tight."

"Aren't you going to put one on?" she asked as she slid the ropes through the metal fasteners on the life jacket.

He shook his head. "You don't want to make me out to be a sissy in front of Chappy, do you? Now come on."

She followed him down the steps. He motioned for her to go toward the bow. The boat was so low in the water that the waves were lapping over the edge. She hesitated.

"Hold on," Norwood instructed, pointing to the small metal railing that ran the length of the wheelhouse.

Fannie held on with both hands, stepping sideways along the wheelhouse wall as he steadied her. When they got to the front, water was splashing over the sides of the boat. She was scared out of her wits but didn't want to let on.

"Hold on to the back of my belt," he said as he picked up the bucket of mullet Chappy had left for him.

She followed him out onto the bow, holding on tight. Norwood grabbed her arms and pulled them around his waist.

Between the roar of the engine and the sounds of the river raging by, he had to holler for her to hear. "Don't let go!"

"Don't worry," she said, leaning her head against his back, glad now for the life jacket.

After a few moments, Norwood gave Chappy the sign to cut the engine. The boat leveled off, traveling close to the far bank of the river at a steady cruising pace. As the engine died down, Fannie was able to let go and stand on her own. She gazed at the river, how it seemed to swirl about instead of flowing by, crashing up against the side of the boat from all directions.

"The river is amazing, isn't it?" he said as he came up beside her. "The Army Corps of Engineers has tried to tame her, but she's got a mind of her own. She's never at rest."

A flock of brown pelicans swooped overhead and surrounded the boat. They were graceful, gliding through the air with outstretched wings, their heads held back on their shoulders and their bills resting on their necks. They flew so low, Fannie felt as if she could reach up and touch them. Norwood grabbed a fish from the bucket and held it up in the air as one of the birds snatched it and tipped it into its bill.

"That one there is Whitey," he said. "Call him that on account he's got white tips on the end of his wings. Got names for all the birds." He held up another fish. "That one there is Sandy. She's got tan streaks on her underbelly—looks like sand."

She watched as the birds came in, one by one, as if in some pecking order. When he ran out of fish, a few of the birds nose-dived into the water looking for more, disappearing completely beneath the surface, while the others bobbed up and down like buoys.

"I always wished I could float like that," Norwood said, pointing at one of the birds. "They got hollow bones that make it so they can float. You or me go in that water, that would be the last anyone would see of us."

He pointed upriver. "The river doesn't flow smooth. It snakes around, sometimes at one-eighty-degree angles, and when the water hits the bank at one of the bends, it roils, driving the current straight to the bottom of the river. The diving current creates holes, some hundreds of feet deep, and eddies that jump up from nowhere. Can swallow a person down."

He was staring straight out into the river with his hands in his pockets.

"The river's like an uncoiling rope. It can snap like a whip. Anytime. Anyplace. Just when you least expect it." He paused. "You can't tame the river. But it can tame you."

ℰↃℰↃ

Fannie dropped her head for a moment. "One day your grandfather left for a stint on the river," she told Ibby. "He never came back. I don't think he really meant for it to happen that way. I think he went out with the pelicans." She gazed sideways at her granddaughter. "Life goes by so fast. Remember that, Ibby. Turn around one day, and life as you know it . . . is gone."

"Fannie?"

Fannie glanced her way.

"Did you bring me here because you think I'm going to leave you, too?"

"Listen, honey." Fannie's eyes grew dim. "I've come to realize that you must be willing to live the life that is waiting for you. That life may not be the one you planned. You have to learn to let go."

Ibby wasn't sure if Fannie was talking about her own life or was trying to prepare Ibby for what lay ahead.

"Fannie?"

"Yes, dear?"

"Does that mean you think Mama's come back for me?"

Fannie took her hand and stroked it. "I have no idea. But whatever happens, I want you to know I love you, just as I have loved all my children." She looked away. "All of them."

Workmen began hammering on a scaffolding surrounding a tomb under construction nearby.

"Come on, dear. I can't think with all that racket." She got up and started toward the car.

Ibby followed her, admiring the magnificent tomb that was being built with Palladian columns and a stained-glass window. It was so large, it looked as if a dozen people could be buried inside. Ibby was just able to make out the name on the tomb. She stopped in her tracks.

"Fannie, that tomb over there—the one they're building. The name on it. It says Bell."

Fannie waved her hand. "Don't worry, Ibby darling. I'm not going anywhere. Just planning ahead, for a time when we can all be together."

"What do you mean, 'all be together'?" Ibby asked.

"One day we might all be buried there together, in that tomb," Fannie said, then added, "It's better than being buried out in the woods like some wild animal, don't you think?"

Chapter Twenty-Five

W here's Miss Fannie off to this morning?" Doll watched Fannie back the car out of the driveway.

"I don't know," Queenie answered from the kitchen table where she was reading the *Louisiana Weekly,* the local Negro newspaper. "Ever since she got that new car, she's been joyriding all over town. Never do say where she going or where she been. But she's up to something. She had Mr. Henry bring her a poster board and some felt-tip markers this morning. Been in her room ever since, coloring like a child, then came in the kitchen and snatched the broom from the closet. If I didn't already think she was tetched in the head, I'd say she was tetched in the head."

Doll came over to the table and took a seat next to her mother.

"Lookey here." Queenie pointed to the headline. "It says three slain in fifty-hour period."

"No sense worrying about things you can't change." Doll tried to snatch the paper from her.

Queenie slapped her hand away. "Still worry. Worry about T-Bone. Worry about Birdelia. Worry about . . ."

"You thinking about Purnell, ain't you?" Doll said.

Queenie blinked a few times, as if the question had drained all the life out of her.

Doll wagged a finger at her mother. "When's the last time you seen Purnell? A year ago, maybe? And why did he come by?"

Queenie drew her lips in tight and began to rock back and forth in her chair. Doll hated when her mother got this way, all sentimental and sad over a lost cause like her older brother, Purnell.

"You know why he ain't been around, Mama. He only comes by when he needs money. Otherwise, he's out there running the streets. That's why Daddy kicked him out of the house in the first place, remember?"

Doll was trying to get her mother to react, but Queenie just kept staring out into space.

"You know I'm right, Mama."

"He's still my boy," Queenie said in a low voice. "I'm his mama. Can't help it. Still worry about him."

"That newspaper, it's got you all stirred up." Doll grabbed the paper and threw it into the trash can. "Why don't you drink some bush tea, make you feel better."

"I don't want no bush tea."

"Well, let me tell you something, Mama. Fretting about Purnell ain't gone change nothing."

Queenie quit rocking and set unblinking eyes on Doll.

Doll knew that look. "What?"

"There is something I ain't told you," Queenie said softly. She crossed her arms over her belly and began rocking again. "Last week I ran into Rosie Washington over at the Piggly Wiggly. She pulled me aside and told me about what happened over at the public pool on the West Bank."

"What happened? I ain't heard nothing about it."

Queenie stopped rocking. "If you shut your mouth, I'll tell you."

Doll rolled her eyes. "Go on."

"Her grandson was swimming over at the pool. There was a nice young white fella lifeguarding over there, teaching all the young ones how to swim. Rosie say her grandson really liked this fella 'cause he treat all them real nice, liked to play with the kids in the pool."

"Yeah. So?"

"One day, a week or so ago, a bunch of black boys wearing Black Panther T-shirts break into the pool while they there. They go up to this fella, the lifeguard, and ask for money. All the lifeguard got on him is ten dollars. This group, they ain't happy. They talk about killing this fella right in front of all the kids in the pool. The kids, they all jump out, yelling and screaming, thinking these young men gone kill them, too. Finally, the young men decide there ain't nothing else for them there, so they go to leave. Right then Rosie shows up to pick up her grandson. She saw the group leaving. Didn't think nothing of it at the time, not until later, when her grandson told her what happened."

There was fear in her mother's eyes as she spoke.

"So what's this got to do with anything except we got some angry brothers running around scaring little kids at a pool?"

Queenie sighed. "Because Rosie, she tell me, she could have sworn one of the young men she saw leaving the pool that day was Purnell."

Doll sat back. Now she, too, had a worried look on her face.

A few minutes later Birdelia came in the back door in her school marching uniform made of stretchy white satiny material, with silver sequins sewn all over it. She had on short white marching boots with tassels and was holding a baton.

"Somebody die?" she asked.

"No, baby," Doll said.

"Then why you all so quiet?"

Queenie's mood brightened at the sight of Birdelia. "Come on over here and give your grandma some sugar."

Birdelia propped the baton by the back door and went over and gave her grandmother a kiss. "What's going on, Mee-maw? Why you so sad?"

"She ain't sad. She just being Queenie. Don't your mama deserve some sugar, too?"

Birdelia gave Doll a kiss and sat down at the table. "Band practice done tuckered me out."

Queenie pushed herself away from the table. "I know what that means—you hungry. You always hungry. Growing like a weed. You as tall as your mother, and if I didn't know any better, I'd think you two were sisters you look so much alike, except for the way you wear your hair up in that braided ponytail all the time."

Ibby came into the kitchen, carrying a magazine. "Where's Fannie?"

"I don't know, and she don't say." Queenie placed a bowl of clabber in front of Birdelia.

Ibby sat down at the table. "She took me out to the cemetery the other day. She evidently goes there a lot."

"That so? Maybe she gone have her own little parade out at the cemetery."

"What do you mean?" Ibby asked.

"Miss Fannie, she made some sort of sign this morning and taped it to a broom handle," Doll said. "That's what Mama's going on about."

"Why?" Ibby asked.

"You been here four years now, and you still ask why Fannie does what she does?" Birdelia interjected.

"Miss Ibby, you got Miss Winnie's party in a few days. What kind of dress you want me to make?" Doll asked.

"I've got one all picked out." Ibby flipped the magazine on the table to a page she'd earmarked. "One like this."

Doll picked up the magazine and shook her head. "You want a Nehru-collared dress? That paisley print won't do, Miss Ibby—not dressy enough."

"What about if we take off the sleeves and make it in another fabric?" Ibby suggested.

"Okay. If that's what you want." Doll tore the page from the magazine and tucked it into the pocket of her uniform. "Got some nice blue silk left over from one of Fannie's dresses ought to do just fine."

Birdelia pushed the empty bowl away and stood up. "I'm going."

"Where you off to?" Doll asked. "Could use your help."

"Miss Fannie asked me to pick her up some lipstick from the pharmacy."

"That so?" Queenie put her hands on her hips.

"Yes'm, she sure did."

"When she do that," Doll said, eyeing Birdelia, "when you ain't even been around all morning?"

"She asked me yesterday, before we left to go home. I told her I'd pick it up on my way back from marching practice this morning. I plumb forgot."

"Miss Ibby, why don't you go along with Birdelia? A little fresh air do you some good," Queenie said as she tried to shoo the girls out the back door.

"You don't mind, do you, Birdelia?" Ibby asked.

Birdelia hesitated a moment before waving her hand. "Come on."

As soon as they left, Queenie sat down at the table and picked up the paper again. After a few moments, she lowered it and looked over at Doll.

"Mama, you ain't gone to start that again, are you?"

"No, baby, I just thought of something."

"What?"

"You don't think Miss Fannie is driving around looking for Miss Vidrine, do you?"

Doll sat back in her chair and made wide eyes. "I hope not. What she think she gone do if she finds her?"

Queenie shook her head. "That's what I'm afraid of."

Chapter Twenty-Six

I bby watched Birdelia's skinny legs move with purpose beneath her marching uniform, the tassels on her boots flapping as she walked. She was intent on going somewhere, but it wasn't the corner pharmacy.

"Where are you going?" Ibby asked. "Mozer's is the other way."

Birdelia gave her a sharp look. "You'll see. Now come on, we don't want to be late."

On the way, they passed Annabelle Friedrichs's house. It seemed unusually quiet. There were no cars in the driveway, and newspapers were stacked up on the front steps.

Birdelia cocked her head toward the house. "They gone."

"Gone? Where?" Ibby asked as they hurried past.

"Heard my mama say that Miss Honey done took up with that neighbor fella, Mr. Jeffreys. Miss Honey's husband found out, kicked her out. She and Miss Annabelle moved to an apartment down on Magazine Street last week."

"Oh," Ibby said. "I guess that's not the kind of thing you hear about at school. Annabelle certainly didn't mention it."

"Bet not," Birdelia said. "She the kind of person that pretends like her life is so perfect. She ain't gone tell nobody that kind of thing."

Ibby followed Birdelia up Jefferson Avenue, then up St. Charles

Avenue. When they reached Audubon Park, they crossed the street toward Tulane University and walked briskly through the campus until they reached Freret Street, where hordes of students were milling about in front of the ROTC building.

"What's going on?" Ibby asked.

"They protesting the Vietnam War," Birdelia said. "Mama told me to stay away. She don't want no trouble, so don't say nothing to her. You understand?"

Ibby and Birdelia fell in with the crowd that was heading down McAlister Drive. Ibby kept looking over her shoulder.

"You looking for somebody?" Birdelia asked.

"No," Ibby replied.

Birdelia glanced over at Ibby as they made their way toward an open field just past the student union building. "She ain't here."

"Who?"

"Your mama, that's who," Birdelia said.

"How'd you know about my mother?" Ibby asked.

"My mama told me how Mr. Rainold came by and gave you a picture. He shouldn't have said nothing. Now you got your hopes up, and I'm telling you, she ain't here."

"I don't care if she is or not," Ibby said defensively. "Besides, how do you know she's not here?"

Birdelia stopped and put her hands on her hips. "Because I just do. And you do care, otherwise you wouldn't be giving every person that passes us the once-over."

Ibby shook her head. Birdelia was getting as bossy as her grandmother.

The edge of the field was crowded with students. Near the center, dozens of students wearing "Tulane Liberation Front" T-shirts were bantering around posters scribbled with antiwar sentiments like "Hell, No, We Won't Go," "I Want a Better America," and "Whose War Is It?"

Birdelia waved her hand. "Stay with me, and whatever you do, don't talk to none of the cops. They mean."

Out of nowhere, one of the women began shouting, "Hey, hey, LBJ, how many babies have you killed today?"

Ibby glanced over at the student union building, where, on the second-floor balcony, onlookers gawked and cheered as campus security ordered the protesters to cease and desist. When they refused, kicking and spitting at the campus security, the New Orleans police charged in and began throwing them to the ground. People started running in every direction. In all the commotion, Birdelia somehow disappeared into the crowd.

"Here," a young man said, shoving a copy of an underground newspaper into Ibby's hand.

She was about to toss it onto the ground when a cartoon of a naked man on the front page caught her eye. She became so engrossed in the drawing that she didn't notice a paddy wagon pull up nearby until a police whistle made her look up. She stuffed the newspaper into her back pocket and began searching for Birdelia as police handcuffed protesters and escorted them into the back of the wagon.

She finally spotted Birdelia standing on one of the metal benches that lined the perimeter of the field. The one black face in the all-white crowd, wearing a white sequined uniform, she stood out like a beacon, especially given the way she was waving her hands around. *Look behind you*, Birdelia mouthed to Ibby.

Ibby turned to find a woman in a scarf and sunglasses cruising down McAlister Drive in a red convertible, honking the horn and waving a "Bless Our Boys" poster. She was stealing the show from the protesters. Even the police turned to look. Birdelia was now running toward Ibby at full speed, shoving people out of the way to get to her.

"Look who it is!" Birdelia said, out of breath.

"Did you know Fannie was coming to the protest?" Ibby asked as she watched Fannie waving to the crowd.

Fannie put two fingers up to her mouth and gave out a sharp whistle.

"No—are you kidding?" Birdelia replied. "Didn't know she could whistle like that neither."

The students up on the balcony of the student union began to clap. When Fannie stopped the car and got out, the crowd fell silent.

"Birdelia!" Fannie's voice echoed across the field.

Birdelia hid behind Ibby. "What we gone do?"

Fannie gave out another earsplitting whistle. "Ibby Bell! Come on over here!"

The whole crowd turned to look their way.

"Just smile real casual and follow me," Ibby said.

"But everybody is staring at us," Birdelia whispered as they made their way to the car.

"Get in." Fannie opened the door. "Birdelia, you stand up on the backseat and hold the sign. Ibby, wave your hands in the air and look proud."

Ibby and Birdelia looked at each other as Fannie started down McAlister Drive, honking the horn. The crowd whistled and cheered as Birdelia waved the sign around like a flag.

Birdelia shouted at the top of her lungs, "My uncle T-Bone just got back from Vietnam! We mighty proud of him! You should be, too!"

When they turned off McAlister onto a side street, Birdelia fell down onto the seat, giggling hysterically.

"That was the funnest I had in a long time," she said.

"Mind me asking what you two were doing there?" Fannie asked.

Ibby couldn't tell by her tone if it was a question or an inquisition, so she let Birdelia do the talking.

Birdelia gave Fannie a wide grin. "We could ask you the same thing, Miss Fannie."

"Fair enough," Fannie said.

"We just happened to see people all going the same direction, so we followed them," Birdelia said.

"Uh-huh," Fannie said.

Ibby could tell she wasn't buying it.

"What about you?" Birdelia asked. "Why you go?"

"We should support the boys that fight for this country, like T-Bone for instance," Fannie said.

"Mama say not everybody thinks that way, especially about colored boys. Some say they don't matter."

"Exactly why I went," Fannie said.

Birdelia tapped Fannie on the shoulder. "Miss Fannie, you can't tell my mama. She gone tan my backside if she finds out I was at that protest. She told me not to go near it, afraid I might get arrested or something."

Fannie patted Birdelia's hand. "It'll be our little secret."

When they got home, Doll was standing at the back door, on the top step, with her hands on her hips. She peered down at Birdelia. "Where you all been?"

"Mozer's," Birdelia replied nonchalantly.

"For two hours?" Doll narrowed her eyes.

"Took our time."

"Uh-huh." Doll tapped her foot. "Where's Miss Fannie's lipstick, the one you were supposed to get for her?"

Birdelia's eyes opened wide.

Without missing a beat, Fannie pulled a tube of lipstick from her purse and showed it to Doll. "She already gave it to me. I happened to see them walking from Mozer's and gave them a ride home."

"I see," Doll said. "You girls better not be up to any mischief."

"No, ma'am, we ain't." Birdelia brushed past Doll and went into the house.

"Where you think you're going, Birdelia Trout? You march on upstairs and help me with the ironing," Doll said. "And Miss Fannie, Wimbledon about to come on in about twenty minutes, the match you been wanting to see, the one between Margaret Smith Court and that woman who look like a man."

Fannie glanced at her watch. "Where does the time go?" she said as she walked through the kitchen.

Ibby hurried behind Fannie into the front parlor. Queenie came in a few minutes later with two plates.

"It's lunchtime, Miss Fannie. Made you a softshell po-boy, dressed the way you like."

As she was putting the sandwiches on the coffee table, the midday news came on the television.

"There was a demonstration today on the Tulane campus. Hundreds of students protesting the war were led away in handcuffs," the reporter said.

"Where is that thing?" Fannie began searching the folds of the couch.

The camera cut to a red convertible driving down McAlister Drive. Ibby held her breath as Queenie stepped closer to the TV.

"That Birdelia standing in the back of that car?" she asked.

By now, Fannie had found the clicker but was having trouble with the buttons.

Queenie leaned in. "Miss Fannie, that you driving that car?"

"What would I be doing at a protest?" Fannie said flatly as she pointed the clicker at the TV. The channel finally changed.

Ibby had to stifle a laugh.

Queenie gave Fannie a sideways glance. "I'm gone pretend I didn't just see that." As she turned to go, she called out over her shoulder, "By the way, Miss Fannie, guess you missed the word of the day."

"Yeah, what's that?" Fannie asked.

"*Eccentric*. It means 'unconventional and slightly strange.' Might be a good word for me to know," Queenie said, going back into the kitchen.

"Ha-ha." Fannie changed the channel to the tennis match.

After the match was over, Ibby sneaked up to her room. She opened the window, turned on the fan, and sat on her bed among the dolls she'd gotten for each birthday since she'd been living with Fannie. She shoved them aside, wondering why Fannie gave her such a silly gift every year. She took the newspaper from her back pocket, carefully unfolded it, and laid it on the bed. The poorly mimeographed paper was called *The Express*, an underground rag put out by a radical group on campus that was anti everything except drugs. Whenever she went anywhere near the Tulane campus, someone shoved a copy of *The Express* in her hands. She usually crumpled it up and threw it away without reading it. Not this time.

Ibby couldn't take her eyes off the cartoon of the naked man with long hair and a scruffy beard. He had a peace sign tattooed on his rear end and a penis that stuck out farther than his feet. He was holding up a newspaper in one hand and little round glasses in the other. The caption read, "What kind of man reads *The Express?*" Ibby had never seen a naked man. The image was stirring up something in her. She turned the fan on her face, then went back to studying the cartoon.

She became vaguely aware of a noise just outside her window, but she was too absorbed in the newspaper to bother finding out what it was. It sounded like the branches of the oak tree scraping against the side of the house, so she paid it no mind. Then a banging on the other side of the wall caused clouds of dust to fall from the ceiling. She jumped up and was about to run from the room in a panic when she heard a voice.

"Miss Ibby, that you?" A young black man peered through the doorway. "T-Bone. Remember me?"

Ibby didn't quite know what to think as T-Bone stepped lightly into the room. She never would have recognized him. She remembered him as a wiry teenager of sixteen full of bravado. He was now a man with a strong, sure face. Birdelia had told her that Vietnam had changed T-Bone, made him different, more serious.

"What are you doing up here?" Ibby stuffed the newspaper into her pocket.

"Didn't mean to scare you, Miss Ibby. I was sanding down the house to prep it for painting when I ran across a window hidden under the turret roof. When I crawled in, I found an empty room and a door with no handle. So I pried the door open with a crowbar." He looked down at his feet. "Didn't think nobody was up here."

"There's another room up here?"

T-Bone pointed behind him. "Just on the other side of this wall. Nothing to it. See for yourself."

Ibby followed T-Bone into the adjoining room. It was octagonal, no larger than her own room, with one small window facing the front of the house. Her eyes inadvertently landed on T-Bone, who was standing over in the far corner. She was surprised at how tall he was, well over six feet, and how muscular his arms and shoulders were. His hair was cropped close to his head.

"You grown right pretty," T-Bone said.

She was sure he was just being polite, his way of getting rid of the awkwardness that filled the tiny room. She changed the subject. "They must have shut this room off for a reason. I wonder why."

He scratched his head. "Don't rightly know."

Next to his feet was a small door, no more than two feet wide. She walked over and opened it. When he crouched down next to her, his thigh brushed hers.

He reached in. "Looks like somebody was trying mighty hard to hide this box, all tucked away in the corner like it was."

Ibby plopped down cross-legged on the floor and opened the box as T-Bone came and sat next to her. Inside, she discovered a photo album covered in a faded pink taffeta, the lace edging hanging off the side in places where it had come unglued. She gently lifted the album from the box.

There was an inscription on the inside of the front cover. "Look. It says 'To Pearl, the most beautiful woman in the world, from the luckiest man in the world.'"

"Who's Woody?" T-Bone asked, pointing to the signature below the inscription.

"My grandfather's name was Norwood. Maybe that was his nickname. But why would it say 'To Pearl'?"

Ibby flipped through the yellowed pages of the album, pretending not to notice the sound of T-Bone's breath and the smell of his musky cologne.

He leaned in closer. "What's that?"

Ibby picked up the newspaper clipping stuck in the creases of the album and examined it. It was an ad for the Starlight Jazz Club on Bourbon Street and contained a photograph of two women—one sitting provocatively inside a giant oyster shell in a satin bathing suit, the other, scantily clad, standing with her foot atop a papier-mâché alligator.

"Looks like an ad promoting a couple of dance acts. One for Miss Pearl the Oyster Girl and one for Gertie the Gator Girl."

T-Bone pointed to the picture. "I believe that there is Miss Fannie sitting in that oyster shell."

The woman in the photo couldn't have been more than about seventeen years old. Ibby gazed at the long legs and the ample bosom. It was the beauty mark on the side of her face that gave it away. Ibby let out a gasp.

"She sure was something," T-Bone said after a while.

Ibby couldn't take her eyes off Fannie. "She sure was" was all she could manage.

Chapter Twenty-Seven

Doll's words ripped through the air. "What are you two doing in here!"

T-Bone scrambled to his feet. "Nothing."

Doll waved a finger at him. "How'd you get in here, boy?"

"I run across a window. Pried the shingles off. Found this here empty room. I didn't know . . . I mean, I thought . . ." T-Bone was talking so fast his words ran together like one long sentence.

"And what? You thought what?" Doll snapped. "How long you been up here?"

"Just a minute or two."

"You better not be lying to me, Thaddeus Trout."

"I ain't lying," T-Bone said as he cast his eyes down.

"Get on out a here." Doll jerked her head toward the open window. "And don't let me catch you up here again. You hear?"

"I'm going," T-Bone said, one leg already out the window.

As Ibby stood up, Doll noticed she was trying to hide something behind her back.

"Now, missy, what you got there?" She motioned for Ibby to hand it over.

"I found it hidden in the little closet in the corner."

Doll turned the album over in her hand. "Anyone else know about this?"

"Just T-Bone," Ibby replied.

"Come on out of this room," Doll said.

Ibby slid past Doll and went over and sat on her bed. Doll came and sat next to her and opened the album.

As Doll was looking through it, Ibby asked, "Have you ever seen this before?"

"No, baby, never laid eyes on it until just now. I suspect it been locked away for a good long while. That turret room's been locked up ever since Master Balfour fell out the window."

"That *is* Fannie in that photo, isn't it?" Ibby asked after a while.

"Yes, baby, believe it is."

"Was Fannie really a stripper, like Annabelle Friedrichs said she was?"

Doll glanced over at her. "Wouldn't exactly call her a stripper. More like an exotic dancer."

"Did my mama know about Fannie?" Ibby asked.

"No, baby. I don't even think your daddy knew."

"How'd you find out?"

"Well, baby. It's like this. Back when Queenie first started working for Miss Fannie, and Mr. Norwood would go off on one of his stints on the river, Miss Fannie would often take to drinking to keep the loneliness away. Sometimes she let her lips flap." Doll turned and looked at Ibby. "Now I know what you're thinking, but don't go judging too harshly. Things was different back then. Them fools in Washington went and passed a law called Prohibition, making it illegal for people to buy liquor. Then the stock market crashed—people lost their homes, their jobs. Nobody had two wooden nickels to rub together. Your grandmother, she come from a family of sharecroppers. Her daddy had to give up his land, had no money coming in. So Miss Fannie, she had no choice really. She left home at sixteen, all on her own. Now, Miss Ibby, try to imagine how hard that was for a young girl."

Fannie marched off into the night, away from the sharecroppers' shack, made of hobbled logs and a rusty metal roof, down a long dirt road cloaked in darkness from the towering pine trees. She'd done it many times before, making her way sleepily toward the sugarcane fields before sunrise. Most mornings she could hear the shuffling of the other field workers and the occasional cough from one of the children trudging solemnly beside their parents. She remembered the first time she'd made this trip, at the ripe age of five. From sunup to sunset, her job was to gather the cut cane and load it onto the waiting donkey carts at the end of the row, weaving and ducking as she went along to avoid the sharp edges of the cane knives being wielded by the field hands.

On this late September morning, Fannie's muted footsteps were barely distinguishable from the whispering of the pine needles high above her head. She was making an extra effort to be quiet. She didn't want her father to catch her sneaking away in the middle of the night.

She walked nearly an hour before she reached the deserted highway. The sun was just peeking over the horizon marked with miles of green sugarcane fields. It was harvesting season, and white smoke from the burning of the cane before the harvest, something they did to make the cane cutting easier, billowed up from the fields, leaving a pungent scent of burnt sugar in the air. Fannie hated that smell.

When she reached the train station, a good five miles down the road, the front door was padlocked. She went around the back, climbed the steps to the train platform, and sat on the wooden bench by the back door to wait for the ticket master to arrive. She had no idea where she was going, but she prayed she had enough money to go far enough away that her father wouldn't come looking for her.

As soon as she heard the rattle of the door being unlocked, she jumped up.

"My, ain't we in a hurry this morning," the stationmaster said as he opened the door.

She gave him a minute to settle himself behind the ticket window. "Where's the first train out going this morning?"

"New Orleans." The bleary-eyed man peered over the ticket counter. "Say, I know you. You're Jake Hadley's daughter, ain't ya?"

"Yes sir." She had hoped he wouldn't recognize her.

The man behind the counter, O. D. Landry, also ran the only grocery in town. She was feeling a little guilty standing there in front of him, given that she had stolen an orange out of his store just last week.

"How much is a one-way ticket?" she asked.

He tilted his black visor back on his head. "One way, you say? Cost you about . . . well, let me see . . . how much you got?"

Fannie counted the coins in her hand. All she'd been able to scrape up for her journey was seven dollars and some change.

"Sorry about your mama," Mr. Landry said.

"Thank you kindly." She counted the money in her hand for the second time, trying hard not to think about her mama.

Fannie's mother, Clara, had taken ill a few weeks ago, after she developed an infection and then a fever from a cut on the back of her leg she'd received from a cane knife while out in the fields. It festered, no matter how much Mercurochrome Fannie swathed on it. The Hadleys were too poor to afford a doctor, and within a few days, her mother was dead. With no money for a proper burial, her father covered Clara in a blanket and carried her out to the woods, where he buried her next to a tree with nothing more than two twigs tied together as a grave marker. When Fannie went to look for it the next day, the grave was covered in leaves, the twig marker gone, probably carried away by squirrels. She never forgave her father for burying her mother out in the woods like a wild animal, and that very day she swore on her life that she'd never suffer the same fate.

After he buried Clara, her daddy took to chasing Fannie around the cabin at night. At first, Fannie thought the wildness in his eyes was from the liquor, but then he caught her and tried to force himself on her. That same night she packed her little bag, scraped up what money she could find in his pants pockets, and left.

"Tell ya what, sweetheart. Just give me a few dollars, and we'll call it a day." Mr. Landry gave her a friendly wink.

Fannie nervously handed over the coins.

"You ain't changing your mind. 'Cause if you is, you can go on back home, and I won't say nothing to nobody." Mr. Landry set his eyes on her as if he understood her predicament.

She shook her head. "I ain't changing my mind."

"Okay then. You take care now, you hear?" Mr. Landry nodded.

The train was pulling up just as Fannie went out onto the platform. She hurried over to the door at the rear of the first car. She found an empty seat by the window and let her head fall back against the headrest as the train engine sputtered and the wheels squealed against the tracks. She pulled her worn brown leather satchel up on her lap. It held everything she possessed in the world—a pair of breeches, a few cotton panties, her Sunday church dress, a poplin shirt, a few undershirts, a nightie, and a small tattered prayer book that had been her mother's.

Fannie rested her forehead on the window, watching the cane fields flash past—first green fields, then the burned fields dotted with the salt-and-pepper faces of the weathered field hands who would stop briefly from the cane cutting and look up with hollow glances, the same look she used to give the train as it passed, wishing one day that it would carry her away from all the misery. She turned away from the window and fingered the small gold cross around her neck, hoping that Mr. Landry would keep his promise not to let on where she'd gone. The last thing she wanted was for her father to come looking for her.

The swaying of the train soon sent Fannie into a deep slumber. She awoke with a start to a loud whistle as the conductor made his way down the aisle toward her.

"New Orleans!" the conductor called out. "The Crescent City. The City that Care Forgot. Last stop. All out. *Laissez les bon temps rouler.*"

Fannie grabbed her satchel and hastily followed the other sleepy-eyed people out of the train. When she emerged from the train station, she found herself on a wide boulevard called Loyola Avenue. Fannie had never seen so many cars puttering along in either direction, honking at the train passengers who were trying to cross the street. She'd only ridden inside one automobile, a rusted relic of a pickup truck that her father had owned ever since she could remember that had a hole in the floor the size of a tire.

Fannie's eye landed on a shiny red Packard. It was the most beautiful thing she'd ever seen: long and lean, with a black leather top that was rolled down in the back. The passengers, a man and a woman, were chatting gaily as they drove by. Fannie took in a deep breath. Perhaps one day she'd own a car just like that one.

She followed some of the other train passengers a few blocks to Canal Street, which was bustling. Noise seemed to come at her from every direction—the clanging of the streetcars gliding past in the middle of the boulevard, the honking of the passing autos, the whistles bellowing from the ships on the river, the bells from nearby churches ringing in the noon hour, and the street vendors hawking waffles, pralines, and lemon ice. She walked past restaurants, cafés, and movie houses clustered between department stores.

Dozens of people hurried past her, bumping and pushing her along, every once in a while hurling a comment in her direction to watch where she was going. She paused on a corner to let a trolley go by. Intrigued by the name on the front of the streetcar, Desire, Fannie decided to follow it down Bourbon Street.

Many of the buildings on Bourbon Street were tightly shuttered and appeared derelict, yet there was a feeling of old worldliness about the French Quarter that made Fannie want to linger, a certain splendidness that somehow made up for the squalor of the crumbling buildings and the stench of day-old trash piled waist-high in the alleyways. She clutched her satchel against her chest and smoothed down her ragged hopsack shift, suddenly feeling self-conscious as well-heeled people brushed past her.

She wandered aimlessly down Bourbon Street, wondering how she was going to get along with no money. The run-down bed-and-breakfast she just passed advertised rooms for three dollars a night. She only had enough for one night's stay. Then what?

Fannie found herself across the street from the Starlight Jazz Club, where a man was lingering against the doorframe. His eyes fell upon her, where they remained long enough for her to become uneasy. She turned to go.

"Hey there, you got a name?" he called out.

Fannie gripped the handle of her bag with both hands and peeked out from under her tattered cloche hat. "You talking to me, mister?"

The man waved her over. Fannie hesitated, unsure if she should talk to a strange man. Then again, what other choice did she have? She crossed the street and went over to where he was standing.

The toothpick in his mouth fluttered up and down as he studied her face; then he took the opportunity to study the rest of her. "You need a job?" he asked after a while.

"Um, well . . . yes sir," she said meekly.

The man motioned for her to follow him inside. He leaned his elbow on the massive carved oak bar. "How old?"

"What?" she asked, distracted by the heavy stench of pine oil and stale alcohol.

"How old are you?" he repeated.

"How old you got to be?"

The man let out a slight laugh. He came up to her and cupped her breast in his hand. Fannie jumped back.

"Not from around these parts, I take it?" His accent was sharp and clipped, as if he were too impatient to finish his words.

Fannie held her satchel up over her chest. "No, sir. I'm from Evangeline Parish."

"Whereabouts?"

Fannie hesitated. "Near Mamou."

"Mamou? Where in the hell is that?" The man scratched his head under his hat.

"Up the road from Ville Platte."

"You one of them Cajuns?" he asked, wrinkling up his nose.

"No, sir."

He fingered the gold cross around her neck, turning it over in his hand. "You a Catholic?"

"No, sir."

"Then why you got that cross around your neck?"

Fannie shrugged. "My mama, she give it me when I was a baby. Worn it ever since."

He let the necklace drop and stepped back. "Don't matter none. Lots of Catholics around these parts. Know anyone in New Orleans?"

"No, sir," Fannie said.

"You a drinker?"

"No, sir."

A half smile slid up one side of the man's face. "Well, you will be soon. No doubt about that. Got a name?"

"Frances Hadley." She drew in a breath, wishing she'd made up a name.

"Now listen here, Frances Hadley from near Mamou, this is a legit establishment. You got other ideas, you can go on down to Norma's place over on Burgundy Street."

Fannie would later find out that Norma was a notorious madam who owned one of the brothels around the corner. She would also learn that legit businesses in the French Quarter in 1929 were few and far between. And this wasn't one of them.

"Tell you what. I'll pay you ten dollars a week, plus tips. You can bunk with one of the girls up on the third floor. No cavorting with the clientele, unless it's your day off. Then I don't give a rat's ass what you do." He chewed on the toothpick, waiting for an answer.

"What exactly I got to do for ten dollars a week?" Fannie asked.

"There's a nightly show. The guys in the band come in and play a few rounds of jazz. Once they get the crowd going, the gals come out and just kind of pose in front of their props. See that there oyster shell?" He nodded toward a papier-mâché prop in the corner.

Fannie glanced over. "Yes, sir."

"The good-for-nothing girl that used it in her act just ran off to New York. Now it's yours. Your stage name is Miss Pearl. All you got to do is swing your ass a little and toss that papier-mâché pearl around like you're in love with it. One of the other gals can show you how it's done. Just keep the crowd happy. Keep them coming in. That's all you got to do. Now go try this on, let me see if you got what it takes." He tossed a satin brassiere, some panties, and a cape her way.

Fannie let the brassiere dangle from her finger, unsure of what she might be getting herself into.

"You change your mind, I got plenty of other gals that would jump at the chance for a paying job," the man said.

"No, no," Fannie said, brushing past him.

The man grabbed her arm. "My name's Tony Becnel, by the way. I'm the manager. And one more thing." He yanked the gold cross from her neck and handed it back to her. "Don't let me catch you wearing that cross around here. It'll scare off the customers."

The next night, after much coaching, a new haircut, and a cosmetics lesson from Gertie the Gator Girl, who shared the room on the third floor, Fannie appeared as Miss Pearl the Oyster Girl. She was timid at first, just kind of sat in the oyster and stared back at the audience as the jazz band played above her on a platform and waiters meandered through the crowd pouring drinks from bottles of liquor stashed in their apron pockets. The audience booed.

The following night Fannie watched Gertie to get a few pointers: the way she swung her hips about and raised her arms high above her head with her hands limp at the wrists, the way she pranced around the alligator with her eyes closed and her head back, as if she were in a trance. Sitting under the canopy of the papier-mâché oyster shell, Fannie closed her eyes and tried to mimic Gertie. She wasn't very successful at first, but after a few days, instead of boos, she was getting whistles.

And after a few weeks, when customers started flocking in to see her act, Tony changed the sign out front to read "Home of Miss Pearl the Oyster Girl." They were doing so well, the club hired a young cop named Peter Kennedy to watch the door. They were told his job was to make sure the girls weren't hassled by the patrons, but his real mission was to tip off the management when federal agents were in their midst.

Fannie had planned on staying on at the Starlight only until she could find a proper job, perhaps as a waitress or a clerk. But she'd become close with Gertie, who'd persuaded her to stay, if only a bit longer. She was surprised how quickly she'd become accustomed to her new life in New Orleans. The job wasn't so bad. In fact, she kind of liked all the attention she was getting with her Miss Pearl the Oyster Girl routine. For the first time in her life, she felt special. Besides, between the salary and the tips, she was making more money than she'd ever dreamed of.

One night a few weeks later, Fannie opened her eyes to find a dark-haired young man with a tanned face sitting quietly at a nearby table as she swayed to and fro inside the oyster shell. He smiled at her. She smiled back. The young man came over after she had finished her act.

"Can I buy you a drink?"

Fannie shrugged. "Sure."

"My name's Norwood. Norwood Bell. I'm a river pilot," he said proudly. "You about the prettiest gal I ever laid eyes on."

He stuck his elbow out, and Fannie slipped her hands through his arm. She knew the routine by now. Federal agents, whose job it was to enforce the law on Prohibition, warily eyed the clubs for lawbreakers. But the clubs had figured out a way to circumvent them by creating hidden back rooms, the only access through secret passageways. Norwood escorted Fannie through the ladies' dressing room into a closet, where he pushed on a coat rack. When he did that, a hidden door at the back of the closet opened up into a smoke-filled back room bustling with people. They stayed there most of the night, getting to know each other, sipping on fancy drinks like Sazeracs and Pimm's Cups.

Norwood came back to the club almost every night after that, except for the days he was on the river. Each night he came in, he asked Fannie to marry him. And each night Fannie demurely waved him off.

When this had gone on for a several months, Norwood took her aside one night and asked, "When you gonna come out with me, let me buy you dinner?"

"Only night off is Sunday," Fannie replied.

"I'm on the river all week, but I'll be by Sunday around six. Wear something special."

The following Sunday, after Gertie helped Fannie pick out a proper dress, Fannie and Norwood went to Antoine's Restaurant. She'd never been to such a fancy place, with cloth napkins, and waiters in tuxedos. They were seated at a table in the big room with soaring ceilings and dozens of fans whirring overhead.

When the waiter came over, Norwood leaned over and asked, "Say, where can a fella get some hooch?"

The waiter, his black hair oiled down against his head, winked at him and said in a thick Cajun accent, "If the gentleman would follow me."

The waiter escorted him toward the ladies' room, where he emerged a few minutes later carrying two large ceramic coffee cups.

"What's this?" Fannie asked as he placed a cup in front of her.

"Champagne for the lady," he said with a tight-lipped smile, as if he were keeping something from her.

"Champagne? What's the occasion?"

Norwood sat down, pulled a small box from his pocket, and opened it to reveal a gold ring set with a small round diamond. He held it out to Fannie. "Listen, baby, I make good money. I can take real good care of you. I promise never to lay a hand on you. And once we're married, you won't have to work at the Starlight. What do you say, Pearl? Will you do me the honor of becoming my wife?"

Fannie didn't quite know what to say. She thought he had been joking all this time about getting married. Now here he was with a ring.

Her head was swimming. He seemed nice enough. It was the first time in her life she'd ever felt wanted by someone. *Really* wanted. Besides, Norwood had a way of making her feel as if she really were a real lady. She put her hand in her lap and looked down, wondering if she'd fallen for him the way he seemed to have fallen for her.

"Well, what do you say, honey?" he asked anxiously, still holding the ring out in front of her.

Fannie gazed up at his handsome boyish face. "Of course, Norwood. I'd be honored." She put her hand over his. "But since we're going to be married, you should know my name's not Pearl. It's Frances Hadley. But you can call me Fannie."

❧❧❧❧

When Doll finished the story, Ibby pulled her legs up onto the bed and hugged them tight.

"So it was love at first sight?"

"That's one way of looking at it, I suppose," Doll said with a laugh.

"Now I understand Fannie's obsession with the cemetery. She hated the way her mother was buried out in the woods like an animal."

Doll nodded. "Was hard times back then. She don't like to talk about it much, particularly about her mama. Miss Fannie come a long way since she was Miss Pearl the Oyster Girl."

"Maybe that big red car is her way of proving it," Ibby said.

"I never thought of it that way, but maybe so." Doll scratched her head. "That Mr. Norwood—he adored your grandmother. You know them pearls Miss Fannie wears around her neck every day? He gave them to her as a wedding present. Ain't a day goes by she don't have them on. You know, when you think about it, Miss Fannie's like a pearl. Starts out rough, just a tiny piece of sand. Layer by layer, that piece of sand becomes round and smooth until one day you can't even tell that piece of sand is still buried in that pearl. Did you know that the more wear a pearl gets, the luster just grows finer? Just like your grandmother. She may not be high-and-mighty like other folks, but she a lady just the same. You remember that, no matter what other people might say." She patted Ibby's knee. "Now I got to go help Queenie in the kitchen." Before she left, she turned to Ibby and wagged her finger. "And one more thing. If I catch any boys up in this here room again, those boards are going right back up on the windows. Understand?"

Chapter Twenty-Eight

A few days later Ibby came in by the back door and set a package on the kitchen table.

"You go and buy yourself another record album?" Queenie asked.

"Yep." Ibby opened the icebox door and took out a pitcher of lemonade.

"I don't understand all that loud music you young folks listen to these days. But, you know, Miss Fannie, she used to do the same thing. She'd close the door, turn the phonograph up real loud, and dance around her room for hours on end, just like you do."

"She did?"

"She sure did. She was a good dancer, too." Queenie eyed Ibby as she took a glass from the cupboard. "You been drinking an awful lot of lemonade lately."

"It's hot in my room." Ibby grabbed the package from the table and started toward the dining room.

Queenie called out after her. "Miss Fannie says she needs to talk to you when she gets back. About your dress, the one Doll's gone make for your party."

When Ibby got up to her room, she put the lemonade on the bedside table. Now that there was an adjoining room to hers, she'd spent the last several days rearranging the furniture. The first thing she did was move one of the twin beds and all the birthday dolls into the turret room. She'd swiped a clothing rack from Doll's sewing room and moved all her clothes in there as well. She shoved the chest of drawers up against the wall where the twin bed had been, then moved her bed sideways up against the window. She looked around, pleased with the new arrangement.

She put her new album on the record player, one by The Moody Blues called *In Search of the Lost Chord,* and danced around the room, wishing her daddy could be here, singing the words along with her. She loved The Moody Blues, the way they spoke in a low monotone in some of their songs instead of singing the lyrics, making you feel ethereal and otherworldly. The band had become her connection to her father, a connection no one could take away. She'd listened to the album *Days of Future Passed* so many times she thought the walls of her room could repeat the lyrics to "Nights in White Satin" back to her.

When the album was over, she poured a glass of lemonade before reaching over and opening the window. She stuck her head out and watched T-Bone for a few minutes. He was wearing white overalls, a painter's cap, and dark sunglasses as he hummed and waved his paintbrush around.

"You thirsty?" she asked.

T-Bone's head swerved around.

"I'm sorry," she said, "I didn't mean to scare you."

He wiped his brow with a rag he pulled from the back pocket of his overalls. "No, no. Guess I was just lost in what I was doing."

"I brought you some lemonade," she said, holding the glass out to him.

"Right nice of you, to keep bringing me lemonade, Miss Ibby. A person gets mighty parched out here working in the sun all day." He downed the lemonade and handed the glass back to her.

"What were you humming just now?" she asked.

He shook his head. "Not anything you'd like."

"How do you know?"

He gave her a sideways glance. "Just a guess. What kind of music you like?"

She shrugged. "The Beatles, the Doors, the Supremes, Moody Blues. You like The Moody Blues?"

"Well, I really can't say," he said.

"That means no. So tell me, what kind of music do you like?"

He began painting again, then stopped and put the brush on the lip of the paint can. "Funk. I guess you could say I like funk."

"Funk?"

"It's kind of like soul music but with more beat to it."

"Is that what you were singing just now?"

"Yeah." He tipped his cap and scratched the top of his head. "You probably gone hear it on the radio anyway. It's gotten mighty popular. The song, it's called 'Say It Loud—I'm Black and I'm Proud.'"

"Oh," she said, feeling her face flush.

"By the godfather of funk, James Brown, also known as Mr. Dynamite or Soul Brother Number One. He's one cool brother, and he really knows how to dance."

"Show me," she prodded.

T-Bone looked down at the ladder, then back at Ibby. "Don't know if I can do it on this ladder." He tried to move his knees in a dance move but almost lost his balance. "Naw, can't do it on this ladder."

"Get off the ladder and come show me then," she said, pointing over her shoulder toward her room.

He looked at her and shook his head. "You heard Doll. She say she catch me in your room again, we all gone be in trouble."

"You scared of your big sister?" she teased.

"Well, no, not really, but she got a point."

"Aw, come on, please? Come show me how to dance." She held out her hand to him.

T-Bone looked around to make sure no one was watching. "Well, okay, maybe just for a minute. But don't tell nobody." He crawled in through the window. "Not much room in here. You're gone have to step aside so I can show you how it's done."

"Okay." She sat on the bed and pulled her knees to her chest. "Go ahead."

T-Bone took off his hat and sunglasses and placed them on the bedside table. He stood back and started shuffling his feet around as he bowed his knees and stuck his elbows out. The next thing she knew, he put his heel out and did a 360 in place, before jumping to the ground in a half split.

Ibby's jaw fell open. "Wow, you can really dance." She hopped up from the bed. "Teach me how to do it."

He jumped up from the floor. She was standing so close to him that the smell of his sweat mingled with paint was almost making her giddy.

"Okay, then, just follow me," he said.

Ibby tried to mimic him, but when she attempted the 360, she fell backward. T-Bone caught her by her arms. She let out a laugh as she looked up at him.

"You got a right nice laugh, Miss Ibby. You should laugh more often. Makes your face light up." He pulled her up until she was standing.

She turned to face him. "Mind if I ask you something?"

He put his hands in his pockets and shrugged. "Sure, what you want to know?"

"What was Vietnam like?"

T-Bone let his head drop until his chin almost touched his chest, then looked up at the ceiling. "Sure was an ugly time. Gone haunt me the rest of my life. That's all I can say about it."

"I'm sorry," she said.

He shook his head and glanced her way. "If there's one thing Mama taught me, it's that you got to dance even when there ain't no music. You know what I'm saying?"

Ibby nodded sympathetically. "Is that why you play the trombone? Is it your way of escaping the pain?"

T-Bone took in a deep breath. "I've always liked to play, but after I came back from Vietnam, it took on a whole new meaning. They say music is good for the soul. It's what saved me. When I play, I can just kind of crawl between the notes and forget."

They stood in silence for a few moments. Ibby fought back the urge to hug him.

He looked up and caught her eye. "Maybe you should come hear me play sometime."

"I'd like that." She took his hand in hers.

"By the way, Miss Fannie hired me to play at your party. Didn't she tell you?"

"No, she didn't mention it." Ibby shook her head. "I haven't exactly had any input as far as the party goes."

"Hope you don't mind."

"No. It's probably the only thing about the party I'm happy about so far."

Doll's voice rang out. "Miss Ibby, we need you downstairs!"

T-Bone and Ibby looked at each other.

"Gotta go," he whispered.

Before she could say goodbye, he'd scrambled out the window. A second later Doll opened the door to Ibby's room.

"What's going on in here? I thought I heard voices," Doll said.

"Oh . . . that was my new Moody Blues album I was playing. Some-times they talk instead of singing the songs." Ibby pointed at the stereo.

"Talk instead of singing—now ain't that something," Doll said as she followed Ibby out the door, giving one last glance at the window. "You get some new sunglasses, too?"

When they got downstairs, they found Fannie in the front parlor, flipping through a pattern book.

"We need to pick out your dress for your party so Doll can get started on it," Fannie said.

"Miss Ibby, come stand on this here coffee table," said Doll. "This is a long dress, not like the short one I made you for Winnie's party, and you growed so much I got to get all new measurements."

When Ibby stepped onto the table, Doll took the measuring tape and placed one end on her waist and let the other end drop. "So Miss Fannie, what you're telling me is that you want a full-length gown and not one, say, come up to here." Doll pointed to just below Ibby's knee.

"No, no," Fannie said. "To the floor. This is a formal party. She should have a formal dress."

"But Fannie," Ibby protested, "I don't think the other girls will be wearing long dresses."

"This is a proper party, and you will wear a proper dress."

Ibby picked up the *LIFE* magazine from the coffee table and flipped through it. "Look at all these women. They're wearing dresses above the knee. Mod dresses. It's the new style. Long dresses are so old-fashioned."

"If it were a tea party, maybe. This is a formal party. After seven o'clock, you wear formal dress. End of argument," Fannie said.

"Maybe fifty years ago," Ibby shot back.

As Fannie and Doll argued about the dress, Ibby saw that *The John Pela Show,* a local Saturday show where teenagers from across the city came to dance to the latest music, was on television. Ibby watched the young women in miniskirts and go-go boots swing their hips around to "Tighten Up" by Archie Bell and the Drells. Trying to imitate them, she swiveled her hips, then slid easily into the dance move T-Bone had just taught her.

Fannie and Doll both stopped their bickering and looked at her.

"Why, Miss Ibby, where'd you learn how to dance like that?" Doll asked.

Ibby pointed over at the television. "From *The John Pela Show.*"

Doll eyed her. "That don't look like no move I've seen on the Pela show."

The phone rang in the hall.

"I'll get it," Doll said.

"I'm going to look like an idiot in a long dress," Ibby complained to Fannie. "It's my party. Let me dress the way I want. Look at those girls on the TV. They all have on short skirts."

"Miss Ibby, it's for you," Doll said.

Ibby jumped down from the table and ran into the hall. She took the phone and placed her hand over the bottom of the receiver. "Go in there and reason with Fannie," she urged Doll.

A few minutes later Ibby came back into the room. "Well?"

Doll was flipping through the pattern book again. "What about this one?"

"Don't like the sleeves," Fannie said.

Doll flipped a few more pages and held the book up. "This one?"

"I like it. Simple yet elegant," Fannie said. "That's the one."

"Don't I even get to choose the style of dress I'm wearing?" Ibby came over and stood next to Doll.

"Miss Fannie likes this one." Doll pointed to a sleeveless empire dress with a sash.

"I told you. I don't want a long dress." Ibby stomped her foot on the floor.

"Then sort it out with your grandmother," Doll said, rolling her eyes.

Ibby and Fannie went back and forth about the dress for a good while until the doorbell rang.

Fannie craned her neck toward the front window. "Who could that be?"

Doll pulled aside the lace curtain. "It's your chubby friend with the frizzy hair."

"I don't have any chubby friends with frizzy hair," Fannie said.

"It's Miss Ibby's friend," Doll said.

"Winnie Waguespack and I are going downtown to shop for a party dress for her at D. H. Holmes Department Store. Why can't I just buy one there?" Ibby asked.

"Because Doll can make you a better one," Fannie snapped.

Ibby answered the door and came back into the front parlor with Winnie.

"How you, Miss Fannie?" Winnie said, smiling way too long.

"Why, just fine," Fannie said, mocking her. "How you?"

Winnie dropped her smile.

Ibby piped up, "Winnie, what are you wearing to *your* sweet sixteen party—a long dress, or a cocktail dress?"

Winnie looked from Ibby to Fannie, then back to Ibby. "Why, probably whatever my mother wants me to wear, I'm sure."

"I told you," Fannie said.

"Miss Fannie's always right." Doll picked up the pattern book and left the room.

"Please, Fannie, let me buy a new dress," Ibby said. "Just this once."

"Now, if you girls will excuse me, I have some things to attend to," Fannie said, making her way toward the hall.

When the girls got to Winnie's car, Ibby asked, "Why didn't you tell the truth, Winnie? You're not wearing a long dress to your party, are you?"

Winnie opened the car door and looked over at Ibby. "Why, Miss Ibby Bell. That *was* the truth. If Mama had her way, I'd be wearing her old debutante dress from the nineteen-forties. There was an old trunk up in the attic with all her old party dresses. I made sure that trunk disappeared. Now I get to pick out my own dress at D. H. Holmes. You just have to be smart about these things."

Ibby got into the car, thinking hard about what Winnie had just told her.

Winnie patted her on the knee. "It'll be fine. Just you wait and see. I'm sure Doll will make you a right pretty dress."

Ibby spent most of the afternoon watching Winnie wiggle into every dress at D. H. Holmes before she finally settled on five, all of which were to be sent to her house on approval.

"Mama's probably going to be disappointed I didn't bring home at least one formal gown," Winnie explained on the way to the car. "I'll just tell her they didn't have my size." She got into the driver's seat and checked her watch. "Oh Lord, I told Mama I'd be back by three. It's almost four."

Ibby leaned in the window. "You go ahead. I need to run an errand."

Winnie looked puzzled. "Why didn't you say something before? I wouldn't have dillydallied so long. Besides, it looks like rain. Don't you want a ride home?"

"I can take the bus. Don't worry about me."

Winnie gave out an exasperated sigh. "Alrighty. I'll see you at my party, if not before." She waved a hand out the window and disappeared down Canal Street.

All afternoon Ibby had been thinking of something other than shopping. The building on Ursulines Street where the photo of Vidrine had been taken was only a few blocks away, in the French Quarter. And even though Birdelia had tried on several occasions to convince Ibby that Mr. Rainold had been mistaken, she couldn't get the image of the woman in the photograph out of her mind.

Ibby hurried down Royal Street with the photo in her hand. The image was blurry, as if the woman had been fleeing from the photographer. Her head was turned to the side, leaving only a small portion of her face exposed to the camera, but something about the manic expression in the eyes reminded Ibby of her mother. Could it be her? And if it was, what exactly was Ibby going to say to her if she did find her?

Why did you leave me? Don't you love me?

Deep down, Ibby wasn't sure if she wanted to know the answer to that last question.

She passed a woman sitting huddled on a corner, her head covered by a scarf so that her face was concealed; the only thing showing was a bony hand holding out a tin cup. Ibby reached into her pocket and dropped a quarter. The woman let out a muffled thank-you but didn't look up. Ibby bent down, trying to see her face. The woman flinched and pulled the scarf down, but not before Ibby saw that the woman was toothless and gray-haired. Ibby dropped another coin into the cup and walked off.

Birdelia had been right. Ever since Mr. Rainold told her that her mother might be in town, she'd been eyeing every stranger. She just couldn't help herself.

Ibby noticed a woman coming out of a building up the street. She had her back to Ibby as she locked her door. She started off toward the back of the Quarter, in the direction Ibby was going. She had the same color hair as her mother and was about the same height. The woman glanced her way, then hurried on down the street. Ibby tried to catch up with her.

"Mama?" Ibby called out.

The woman kept going, then turned onto a side street.

"Vidrine, is that you?" Ibby yelled.

By the time Ibby reached the corner, there was no trace of her.

"Vidrine!" Ibby screamed in frustration.

What am I doing? Ibby thought as she stared down the empty sidewalk. *My mother isn't here. Why did Mr. Rainold lead me on like that? Why did he get my hopes up?* She was about to turn back when she noticed the tiles embedded in the sidewalk at the next corner—Rue Ursulines, the street where Mr. Rainold said the photo had been taken. Ibby crossed the street, toward a trio of musicians playing on the corner. The sky rumbled overhead as one of the young men, with wire-rimmed glasses, held out his hat, asking for a contribution. Ibby waved him off.

She didn't have to travel down Ursulines very far to find the building she was looking for. It was the second one on the left, a typical French Quarter town house with heavily shuttered windows and peeling plaster walls. She went over to the green door on the far side and rang the bell. When no one answered, she rang the bell again.

"You looking for somebody?" one of the musicians on the corner called out as he flipped his long hair behind his back.

"Is this the building owned by a woman named Avi?"

"Why you want to know?" he asked as he came over to where she was standing.

Ibby held out the picture of her mother and showed it to him. "Have you seen this woman?"

He took it from her, then shook his head and handed it back.

"Are you sure?"

"Who is she?" the man asked.

Ibby didn't want to sound desperate. "A friend."

The man called to his buddies. "Dudes, come on over here and take a look at this."

One of the other fellows, with a long beard, came over. "Yeah, man?"

He took the picture from Ibby and showed them. "You seen this chick?"

The two men shook their heads. "No, man," the bearded one said. "Not one of us."

"Do you live here?" Ibby pointed to the building.

The bearded man put his hands into his jeans pocket, and gave her a funny grin. She could tell he was high on something.

"Can I take a look around?" Ibby took the photo back from the man with the glasses.

He shrugged. "You can go in. The door's not locked. But no one's there."

Ibby pushed the heavy green door open and walked cautiously down a dark and dank carriageway.

"Hello—anybody home?" she called out.

When no one answered, Ibby went to the end of the carriageway. It opened onto a brick courtyard where several iron tables and chairs were haphazardly scattered about. Someone had been here recently because there were empty plates and cups left on some of the tables. At the far end of the courtyard, along a brick wall that must have been twenty feet high, a fountain of a lion spewed water. The smell of stale incense lingered in the air. On the upper galleries, sheets and clothing hung from the railings. The place had an eerie feeling. It looked as if everyone had left in a hurry.

"Hello! I'm looking for Vidrine Crump!" she hollered.

The man in the wire-rimmed glasses appeared behind her.

"You scared me," she said. "I didn't hear you come in."

Alone with the stranger, she became nervous and fled down the carriageway and back onto the street. It had begun to rain, a hard rain coming down in sheets. She stood underneath the gallery to the building, wondering what she should do, when water began dripping onto her head from a hole on the flooring above.

The man in the wire-rimmed glasses came out and stood next to her. "Why are you looking for that woman?"

She wiped the rain from her face. "She's my mother."

"Is she lost?" he asked.

She glanced at him sideways, unsure how to answer. "No, *I* am." Then she trudged off down the street, muttering to herself as rain pounded her face, "This was a stupid idea."

By the time she got to the stop on Canal Street, one of the buses was just leaving. Drenched and filled with disappointment, she decided to walk home. As she made her way down Tchoupitoulas Street near the edge of the river, she took the picture of her mother from her purse. She stared at it for a moment, then tore it up and tossed it into the gutter. She wiped the rain from her face as she watched the pieces float away like a shattered memory, until they eventually disappeared down the storm drain.

Chapter Twenty-Nine

Doll was in the kitchen with Queenie when the doorbell rang. Queenie looked up from the sink. "You expecting somebody?"

"No, Mama. Probably just Omar the Pie Man, or maybe one of them other street vendors who come by every week trying to sell us something. I'll go see."

When Doll answered the door, she found a woman sitting on the front steps, her back toward the door. Doll stepped out onto the porch and shut the door behind her. "Can I help you?"

A warm breeze passed across the lawn. The woman wrapped a tattered shawl around her shoulders as if she were chilly.

Doll tapped her on the back. "You need something?"

The woman glanced up. Doll could tell from the haggard face and bulging eyes that she was sick.

"Fannie here?"

The voice was weak and raspy, but there was something familiar about it. Doll couldn't quite put her finger on it.

"You know Miss Fannie?" Doll asked.

"You might say that."

The woman's loose linen dress was faded, and her toes had worn holes clear through the top of her sneakers. For the life of her, Doll couldn't figure out who this woman was, or how she would know Fannie.

"You want something to drink?" Doll asked, thinking perhaps the woman was a vagabond.

She shook her head. "Ibby here?"

Doll took a step back. There was only one person who would ask such a question. She tried to think of a quick answer. "Why no, she ain't here. Miss Fannie . . . she done . . . sent Ibby off to camp for the summer."

Vidrine began to cough, a deep wet cough that lasted for several seconds. She peered up at Doll. "That's good. I don't want her to see me like this."

Doll went down the steps. The woman was so thin, her head looked as if it might topple off her spindly neck. Her hair was sparse and wispy, and several of her teeth were missing. She looked nothing like the Vidrine Doll had once known.

"I'm dying, Doll," Vidrine said flatly. "I don't have much longer to live."

"What you want? Money?" Doll knew Miss Vidrine must be mighty desperate if she was asking Miss Fannie for money.

Vidrine buried her face in the crook of her arm.

"You wait right here," Doll said.

"Listen." Vidrine reached up and grabbed Doll's arm. "I didn't mean for it to turn out this way. I meant to come back for Ibby. You've got to believe me. But then I got sick. I just need enough to get by for a few more months, that's all. Just a few more months."

The way Miss Vidrine was looking at her, she couldn't help feeling sorry for the woman. "Where you living?"

Vidrine began to shake. "Wherever I can find a bed."

"You homeless? That why Mr. Rainold ain't been able to find you?"

Vidrine covered her face with her hands.

"You stay right here. Don't move. You hear me? Don't move."

Doll ran inside, down the hall, and into Fannie's bedroom, where she closed the door and locked it. She paced up and down trying to decide what to do. Should she ask Vidrine in? Should she let her stay until Miss Ibby came back? What would Miss Fannie do if she found Vidrine sitting in the house when she returned? Doll tussled with these questions for several minutes, then put her hand on her hip and looked up at the ceiling.

"Please forgive me, Lawd, but I don't see no other way. You know something better, you better tell me right now. Show me the way." She waited for a sign, anything, to let her know she was doing the right thing. "So unless you got something to say, this is the way it's gone be." When all she heard was the whirring of the overhead fan, she said, "Well, all right then."

She opened the door to one of the massive armoires. The two upper shelves were filled with shoeboxes, but she'd learned long ago that these boxes didn't contain shoes. Like many who had lived through the Depression, Fannie didn't trust banks, preferring instead to stuff her mattress, cut holes in the floor, and hide cash wherever it suited her, sometimes even in places she'd forgotten about. These shoeboxes were just one of her many hiding places.

Doll took down a shoebox and counted out ten hundred-dollar bills, wondering how much Vidrine would need to live out the rest of her days in some semblance of comfort. She counted out another five hundred just for good measure, then stuffed the wad of cash into the pocket of her apron and headed back into the hall.

Queenie saw her coming out of Fannie's bedroom. "Doll, what you doing in Miss Fannie's room?"

Doll waved her off. "Just getting some cash to pay Omar the Pie Man." She hurried toward the door. When she got outside, Vidrine was gone. Doll panicked, then heard rustling in the azalea bushes below the front steps.

"Miss Vidrine, that you?" Doll hurried down the steps.

She found two eyes peeping out from the bushes.

"I fell off the steps," Vidrine whispered.

"You about scared the living daylights out of me." Doll helped Vidrine up, brushed her off, and tried to hand her the money.

Vidrine stared at it but didn't take it. "Does Fannie know?"

"No, and let's keep it that way," Doll said. "Now go on, take it."

Vidrine stashed the cash under her clothing. "How is my baby girl?"

Her eyes were so pitiful, it almost made Doll want to cry. "Miss Ibby has turned into a fine young lady. You'd be right proud of her."

"Fannie taking good care of her?" she asked.

"Yes, Miss Vidrine," Doll said. "I can promise you that. She's taking real good care of Miss Ibby. Real good care."

Vidrine dropped her head. "When the time comes, tell Ibby I loved her. Will you do that for me?"

"When the time comes, I'll tell her." Doll's words caught in her throat.

Vidrine pulled her wedding ring off her finger. "Here. Give her this. It's all I have. Tell her I'm sorry." She pushed herself up and started down the brick walkway toward the street.

Doll put the ring into the pocket of her uniform. "Peace be with you, you hear?"

Vidrine shuffled down the sidewalk like an old woman. As she disappeared around the corner, Doll wondered when was the last time she'd eaten.

"Vidrine, wait!" Doll cried out, wishing she'd made a basket of food for Vidrine to take along with her.

But Vidrine just kept walking as if she didn't hear.

For a brief second, Doll wondered if she'd done the right thing. *It's what Miss Vidrine wanted,* she reassured herself as a crack of thunder rattled the air.

"Too late for that, Lawd." She shook her head. "Now, I know I said a lot of nasty things about Miss Vidrine over the years, and I'm sorry for that. Sure am. But what's done is done."

She went up to her sewing room, closed the door, and sat down behind her sewing machine. She picked up the doll she was making Ibby for her birthday and looked it in the eyes: "I sure hope I done the right thing." When she felt for the ring in her pocket, it wasn't there. "Lawd, what I done with it?" She emptied her pockets. "Well, I'll be," Doll said as she stuck her finger through a hole in one of her pockets.

She ran down the stairs and out the front door and began searching the front steps for the ring.

"Got to be out here somewhere." Doll squinted, the rain blurring her vision. She scrambled around on her hands and knees for several minutes and was about to give up when she saw the ring sticking up sideways through a crack in one of the bricks. "Thank you, Jesus." She stuffed the ring in her bra for safekeeping and was about to get up when Queenie appeared at the front door.

"What in the devil's name is going on? Why you crawling around out in the rain like that?"

Doll scrambled to her feet and brushed off her wet uniform. "I slipped on the steps."

"Uh-huh. Where the pies? Didn't you say you were buying pies from Omar?" She pointed down the street. "And lookey there. Here come Miss Ibby. She all wet, too."

Ibby stopped at the gate. "Doll, why are you standing there in the rain?"

"Well, Miss Ibby," Doll said, "I could ask you the same thing."

Chapter Thirty

When the day of her party arrived, Ibby sat in Doll's sewing room all morning as Doll fussed with her hair, pinning and unpinning a hairpiece to her head.

"Why do I have to wear one of these? Can't you just tease and spray my hair like everybody else?"

"Needs to be just right," Doll said.

"But I feel so silly," Ibby said, looking at herself in the handheld mirror.

"You gone look beautiful—now hold still. After I finish with you, I got to go take care of Miss Fannie, and believe me, that's gone take up the rest of the day."

A branch of the oak tree rubbed against the window, making a sound like fingernails on a chalkboard.

Doll winced. "Daddy was supposed to trim that tree for the party. Guess he didn't make it to the branches up top. Hope he cleared the front walkway, or the guests ain't gone be able to get in the front door. I don't know why Miss Fannie won't hire a tree man to come shape up that tree. It's like she's afraid to mess with it."

"Why's that?" Ibby asked.

"I don't know. She's always been that way about that tree, like it means something to her. It was here when she arrived, and I guess she wants it to be here when she's gone." Doll patted the hairpiece on Ibby's head. "Okay, I got it looking right pretty. Don't go messing up what I just done, you hear me? Now I got to go see about Miss Fannie."

When it finally came time for the party guests to arrive, Ibby and Fannie stood in the front parlor—Ibby in her floor-length dotted swiss dress and an orchid corsage, Fannie in a knee-length robin's-egg-blue peau de soie with a corsage of pink roses—waiting to receive their guests. The scent of Fannie's Oriental Rose perfume filled the room. Doll had spent all afternoon making Fannie look presentable. She'd dyed Fannie's hair and had given her a perm, done her nails, and even put on false eyelashes.

"Doll did a nice job on your dress. I hope you told her so," Fannie said.

"She did a nice job on you, too," Ibby shot back, still mad at Fannie for making her wear an old-fashioned long dress.

The grandfather clock in the hall chimed, a reminder that eight o'clock had now come and gone. It was an hour past the party time, and still no guests.

Crow was busy rearranging the bottles on the makeshift bar that had been set up in the front parlor. Birdelia was in the kitchen rewarming the hors d'oeuvres for a second time as Doll set another platter of food on the dining-room table. Through the front window, Ibby could see T-Bone and two musician buddies of his sitting in the rockers on the front porch.

Birdelia came into the room and held a silver tray out to Ibby. "Cheese puff?"

"No, thanks." Ibby swatted at a paper lantern above her head.

It was the first time she'd ever seen Birdelia in a maid's uniform. She knew Birdelia hated wearing it, but Doll had given her no choice.

Birdelia narrowed her eyes. "Don't get used to it."

Crow was straightening the glasses on the bar. "Queenie borrowed this here tuxedo from Mr. Lionel, the undertaker." He tugged on the lapel. "Don't fit quite right."

"You look just fine, Poppy." Birdelia patted her grandfather on the back. She put the tray of cheese puffs down on the bar and yanked on her apron. "Mama's uniform don't fit me quite right neither."

Crow said, "Birdelia, why don't you go ask T-Bone if they need a drink of water before the guests arrive?"

"I just did that not fifteen minutes ago, Poppy," Birdelia protested.

"I'll go," Ibby offered. She started toward the front door.

Fannie grabbed Ibby's arm with her gloved hand. "Be patient, dear. You never want to be the first to arrive or the last to leave. It's fashionable to be late."

"Except to a funeral. It's not fashionable to be late to a funeral," Crow chimed in.

Queenie came into the dining room to check on the food. "Lawd, this rate, I'm gone have to take it all back into the kitchen and warm it up again."

"The guests will be here shortly," Fannie said, taking a quick glance at her watch.

Everyone's attention was drawn to a noise that sounded like the howling of the wind.

"It supposed to rain tonight?" Queenie asked.

"No," Doll said, "that's the oak tree in the front yard scraping against the house. Always scares me when I hear it 'cause it sounds like an old woman crying."

"Crow, didn't I ask you to trim that tree back for the party?" Fannie asked.

"I did, Miss Fannie. Cut off a big limb that was blocking the front walk, but that's a big tree. Couldn't do nothing about some of them other branches leaning against the house."

There was a shuffling on the front porch as the first guests arrived. Sister Gertrude burst through the front door, her robes swinging with every step. She embraced Fannie in a hug that seemed out of character.

"Fannie dear, I'm so happy to see you." She gave Fannie a kiss on the cheek. "Am I late?"

"No, Gertie dear. You're right on time. Come on in." Fannie gestured toward Ibby. "You know my granddaughter."

"One of our best students." Sister Gertrude patted Ibby lightly on the shoulder.

"I'll catch up with you as soon as the rest of the guests arrive," Fannie said before turning her attention to a man that came in right behind Sister Gertrude. "Why, hello, Kennedy. Been a long time. I see you've risen in the ranks. You're a commander now. It's about time."

He kissed Fannie's hand. "Thank you. So nice to see you." Then he turned to Ibby. "I believe we've met."

Ibby shook his hand. "Yes, sir. Thank you for coming."

"Kennedy, dear, would you mind escorting Sister Gertrude to the bar?" Fannie asked.

"My pleasure." He held his elbow out for Sister Gertrude.

Emile Rainold came next, followed by several of the neighbors, including the Jeffreyses.

"How do, Miss Fannie. So nice of you to invite me."

Ibby turned to find Annabelle Friedrichs and her mother, Honey, dressed in matching pink taffeta frocks. Mr. Friedrichs wasn't with them.

Annabelle cordially stuck out her hand and forced a smile. "Thank you for having me, Ibby."

Ibby shook her hand and was busy watching Annabelle sashay off into the crowd when she heard Winnie's voice.

"Miss Fannie, may I introduce my parents, Myrtis and Winkie Waguespack, and my three brothers, Wiley, Whitfield, and Werner."

"Fannie." Myrtis Waguespack shook Fannie's hand, then turned to Ibby and smiled ever so sweetly. "Why, Ibby Bell, don't you look a picture! Such a pretty yellow dress. Bless your heart, where did you find such a thing?"

Myrtis Waguespack's remark seemed less like a compliment than a veiled insult. Ibby could tell by the look on Fannie's face that she was not pleased by it either.

"Doll made it for her," Fannie replied.

"My, aren't we lucky to have somebody like Doll to do our sewing for us," Myrtis Waguespack said.

Fannie returned the favor by eyeing Myrtis's green-and-blue-plaid dress, which made her round torso look like an overstuffed chair. "Isn't that one of your mother's dresses? Yes—I believe I remember seeing her in it at Ida Brewbacker's funeral a couple of years ago."

Myrtis Waguespack smiled, but her eyes were simmering. "Why no, you must be mistaken, Fannie dear. I had it made for Winnie's party, but thank you for noticing."

Wiley Waguespack stepped forward and nudged his mother out of the way. "Ibby, nice to see you again."

Ibby's eyes met Wiley's as she shook his hand. She had danced with him at Winnie's party last week. His cheeks carried the familiar Waguespack ruddiness, which was not very attractive on Winnie but was boyishly charming on her brother. Ibby couldn't take her eyes off him.

"I think that's the last of the guests. Let's go join the party," Fannie said.

Ibby lingered by the front door.

"Ibby dear, are you expecting someone else?" Fannie asked.

Ibby was still harboring the notion that her mother might show up. It was foolish, she knew.

She gave a small shake of her head. "No, Fannie. There's no one else."

Fannie went in to join the party, but Ibby hesitated, gazing through the glass in the front door as she pulled off her white gloves and tossed them onto the table in the front hall.

Doll came over with a tray. "What you doing standing here in the hall all alone?"

"No reason." Ibby shrugged, taking one last glance at the door.

"Miss Ibby, you waiting for your mama to show up?" Doll asked. "Get that thought right on out of your head and get on in there and chase after that boy you got your eye on." She nudged Ibby with her elbow.

"What boy?" Ibby said.

"You know darn well which one. I seen the way you looked at that Wiley fella when he came in. Now go on."

Ibby noticed Sister Gertrude standing next to the bar sipping on an old-fashioned and talking animatedly with Fannie. She never did understand how the two could be friends. She wandered into the dining room and dipped a fried oyster into the bowl of cocktail sauce. She spotted Wiley Waguespack chatting with one of her classmates, Marcelle de Marigny, across the table. Ibby couldn't hear what Marcelle was saying, but the ruddiness in Wiley's cheeks had deepened. He glanced up for a moment but took no notice of Ibby.

Winnie came up and stood beside Ibby. "I see Marcelle is putting the moves on my brother."

"He's so handsome," Ibby remarked.

"Well, you might as well forget about my brother."

"Why, is he seeing someone?"

Winnie looked at her with exasperation. "Wiley told me he thought you were cute, but it would never work out."

"Why not?"

"Because my brothers are only allowed to date good Catholic girls, that's why."

Ibby dropped the oyster back onto the platter, not caring if anyone noticed. "Will you excuse me?"

Ibby was trying hard to quell the urge to slap Winnie Waguespack as she wandered through the crowd. She spotted Emile Rainold entertaining a short bald man in conversation. Mr. Rainold was perspiring profusely, occasionally wiping his brow with the back of his hand. Across the way, Honey Friedrichs was flirting with their next-door neighbor Mr. Jeffreys. Ibby noticed Mr. Jeffreys's diminutive wife, Inez, standing on the other side of the dining room, watching her husband's antics.

Ibby headed over to the bar.

"What'll it be, Miss Ibby?" Crow was perspiring as well. He patted his cheek with a cloth. "Champagne? Maybe a Sazerac?"

"Just a Shirley Temple."

People in New Orleans were used to drinking more than communion wine by the time they were teenagers, but Ibby didn't much care for alcohol. As she turned to go, she bumped into T-Bone, spilling her drink all over his starched white shirt.

She picked up a cocktail napkin and tried to wipe his shirt. "I'm so sorry."

He grabbed her hand. "It's okay, Miss Ibby. Don't worry about it."

The warmth of his hand made Ibby look up.

"You look right pretty this evening, Miss Ibby. Right pretty."

Across the way, Fannie was giving Ibby a disapproving look.

"Miss Ibby, you all right?" T-Bone asked.

Ibby smiled at her grandmother, then reached over and gave T-Bone a big kiss on the cheek.

Fannie came charging over. "Ibby darling, why don't you go mingle with some of the other guests?"

"I'm fine right here."

Fannie grabbed her arm and pulled her away, whispering in her ear, "Don't embarrass me in front of my friends, young lady, or there will be consequences."

Ibby yanked her arm away and stormed into the kitchen, fuming. She undid her corsage and hurled it across the room. It landed beside the open back door.

Queenie came in carrying a tray. "What you doing hiding in the kitchen? That don't look like no party face. Something wrong?"

Ibby shook her head.

"We gone run out of food soon if those people keep eating like they is. You'd think they hadn't eaten in a week. You seen Birdelia? Where that girl gone off to?" Queenie muttered as she carried the tray into the dining room.

Ibby was about to go back into the party when she heard a rustling in the backyard. At first she thought it was just the low grunts of the bullfrogs. Then she heard it again. It sounded like somebody whispering. She turned off the kitchen light, not wanting to be seen, and looked out the window.

A single light attached to the garage cast a thin yellow line across the yard. Someone was standing in the shadows, smoking a cigarette. When he stepped forward, Ibby saw that it was T-Bone. Then someone else giggled, and an arm that was so white it glowed in the dark reached over and took the cigarette from his mouth. Ibby could just make out Annabelle's profile as she put her elbow on T-Bone's shoulder and took a drag from his cigarette.

Ibby was about to march out and give Annabelle a piece of her mind when she heard another voice.

"Why don't you go back on inside, Miss Annabelle?" Birdelia tugged on Annabelle's arm, trying to pull her away from T-Bone.

Annabelle yanked her arm away. "Don't touch me."

Somewhere in the dark, a deep voice emerged. "Hey, brother, I been looking for you."

The man was dressed in black trousers and a black T-shirt. His bushy Afro caught the light from the garage as he strode up the driveway.

"Purnell, what the fuck you doing here, man?" T-Bone said.

Purnell came over and slapped T-Bone on the back. "Ain't you glad to see me? Who's the white bitch hanging all over you?"

"Shut your mouth, Purnell," Birdelia said.

Purnell grabbed Birdelia by the shoulder and gave her a hug. "That any way to talk to your uncle, little bird? Last time I saw you, you came up to my shoulders. Now look at you, all growed up."

"That's on account you ain't been around, Uncle. You'd rather hang out with them troublemakers."

"That's not true," Purnell said. "Can't get a job, that's all."

Ibby jerked around when the kitchen door opened. There was a bump, then a crash as a metal tray dropped to the floor.

"For God's sake, Miss Ibby, what you doing standing there in the dark?" Doll flipped on the light switch.

The voices in the backyard caught Doll's attention. She went over to the window and stood next to Ibby.

"I'm in a tight spot. I ain't leaving until I get me some cash," Purnell said to T-Bone.

"I ain't got any on me," T-Bone said.

"Oh, Lawd," Doll said. "That's my brother Purnell. I got to get rid of him before Queenie finds out he's here."

She opened the screened door and let it bang shut behind her.

"Miss Annabelle, you get on back inside now, you hear me?" Doll pointed toward the house.

"Why should I?"

Doll looked as if she was going to grab Annabelle by the neck and drag her inside herself. "You want me to go fetch your mama?"

"I'm going." Annabelle dropped the cigarette and started toward the house.

"No, unh-unh, Miss Annabelle. You go on up the driveway and go in the front door."

After Annabelle left, Doll turned to Purnell. "You know better than to come around here when we at work."

"I'm in trouble. Understand what I'm saying?" Purnell said.

"This ain't the place."

"I ain't got no choice, sister."

Doll shoved him. "I got nothing for you. Now, go on. Get out a here."

Purnell leaned in defiantly. "Want me to march in there, tell all them white folks about you?"

"What you talking about?"

"You know. Think I never figured it out?"

Doll glared at Purnell. "You don't know nothing. Now here, take this." She took a few bills from her bra and counted them out. "Now go, before Mama sees you."

"It ain't enough," Purnell said, holding out his hand.

"It's all I got."

He shook his head angrily. Ibby thought he was going to get into a fistfight with Doll, but he turned and ran down the driveway, disappearing into the night as fast as he'd come.

T-Bone and Birdelia came in through the back door just as Queenie barreled into the kitchen carrying an empty chafing dish. She set the dish down and yanked Birdelia's arm. "Come on over here and help me fill this tray. Where's that daughter of mine?"

Doll came in the back door, perspiring heavily.

"What you doing out back, Doll?" Queenie asked.

"Had to get rid of something, that's all," Doll said.

As Doll sat down at the kitchen table, Ibby noticed her hands were shaking as she straightened her hairpiece.

"Doll, something you want to tell me?" Queenie asked.

"No, Mama."

"You sure?" Queenie eyed her. "Why you sweating? You never sweat."

"Just a hot night, Mama, that's all."

Queenie turned to T-Bone. "Crow ain't feeding Miss Fannie bourbon, is he?"

He shook his head. "Miss Fannie ain't the one you need to be worrying about. You seen that nun? She's out there pounding them old-fashioneds."

"The last thing we want to do is overserve a nun. Don't want no trouble tonight." Queenie shook her head. "T-Bone, get on in there and make sure that don't happen. Do something to liven up the party."

"What you want me to do?" he asked.

"I don't know"—Queenie handed a tray to Birdelia—"but think of something quick. The last time I looked, Mr. Waguespack was doing a slow waltz with Sister Gertrude as Fannie sang a rendition of 'You Know What It Means to Miss New Orleans.'"

Birdelia followed T-Bone out of the kitchen.

Doll drummed her fingers on the table. "You know, Mama, they is something strange about that nun. She ain't no normal run-a-the-mill nun."

"Everybody acting all crazy tonight. Just like you. You ain't yourself this evening. You sure they ain't something you want to tell me?"

"No, Mama."

"Miss Ibby, why you still in here?" She waved her hand. "Miss Fannie didn't go to all this trouble for you to be sitting here in the kitchen." Her head shot up when some music started playing. "T-Bone bring a piano player with him?"

"Not that I recollect," Doll said.

"Then who's that playing Professor Longhair?"

Ibby and Doll began snapping their fingers to the sound of "Big Chief," a tune that in New Orleans had become synonymous with having a good time. Whenever it was played, the locals tended to get up and dance.

Doll peeked through the door. "Mama, you got to come see this. You ain't gone believe it."

The three of them stuck their heads through the door. Birdelia was standing at one end of the dining room table with a stack of linen napkins in her hands, passing them out to the party guests, who were fashioning them into do-rags by tying the four corners into knots and placing them on their heads. When Ibby had first seen this, at a party a few years back, she thought everybody had had too much to drink— they danced around with do-rags on their heads, waving napkins in their hands. Now she was just as likely to join right in and dance along with them.

"Look at Mr. Rainold! I didn't know he could play the piano!" Queenie mused.

Mr. Rainold had taken off his jacket, his red suspenders dangling by his sides, as he stood, banging away at the piano. T-Bone was leading a line of napkin-headed people around the room, his trombone swinging up and down to the rhythm as Sister Gertrude brought up the rear, doing a little jig.

"Well, I'll be," Queenie said, watching Crow clap his hands and whistle.

Doll pulled Ibby into the dining room. As soon as Fannie saw her, she grabbed Ibby's hand and dragged her into the second line. They danced around a good half an hour, until Queenie came into the dining room carrying the birthday cake. The crowd gathered around the table and sang "Happy Birthday" as Queenie lit the candles. Fannie raised a glass.

"To my lovely granddaughter on her sixteenth birthday."

Ibby paused a moment, holding her breath, hoping Fannie wasn't going to surprise her with another birthday doll.

"Well, what are you waiting on, dear?" Fannie said.

Ibby breathed a sigh of relief and blew out the candles.

It isn't such a bad party after all, Ibby was thinking as Queenie cut the cake.

After Ibby said her goodbyes to the last guest, she stood in the hall and gazed absentmindedly through the glass in the front door.

Doll came up and stood next to her. "I can tell what you're thinking."

"I'm not thinking anything."

"Yes, you is," Doll said. "I can see it in your eyes. You're disappointed your mama didn't show up."

Ibby hated how Doll could always see right through her. "No, I'm not."

"Then how come you got that poor-pitiful-me look on your face when you should have a that-was-a-right-fine-party look?"

"I couldn't care less if my mother came or not," Ibby said.

"That ain't true, but Miss Ibby, no use crying over spilled milk. Miss Fannie went out of her way to throw this party for you, sent out fancy invitations, had the house painted, fixed up the yard. She's never done that for anyone before. You should be happy."

Ibby didn't want to listen to Doll anymore, even though she knew she was right. She went upstairs to her room.

A little while later, Doll came up to find her. "Here, I brought you something."

Doll handed Ibby the life-size doll she'd made her for her birthday, dressed in an exact replica of the dress she had worn this evening, down to the corsage and white gloves.

Ibby flung the doll onto the floor.

"Listen"—Doll wagged a finger—"you lucky she didn't give it to you in front of all those people. If she had her way, that's what she would have done, but I talked her out of it."

"I hate those dolls!"

"You gone hurt my feelings."

"Why does Fannie keep giving me dolls? I'm too old for dolls. They're weird."

Doll picked the doll up from the floor and brushed the yarn hair to the side. "These dolls are Fannie's way of showing she loves you. One day you'll understand."

"Why can't I just have a normal life like everybody else?" Ibby said.

"Normal? What's normal? You think everybody at that party tonight got a normal life? We all got something we don't like, that we want to change." Doll pointed a finger. "Miss Ibby, I'm gone tell you something you may not want to hear. It's about time you grew up. They ain't such thing as normal, and I ought to know. Your grandmother loves you. And if you can see it in your heart to let her in, she'll more than make up for your mama not being here for you. Understand?"

Ibby sat up and wiped her nose with the back of her hand. "You think I'm a brat?"

"I think you're a sixteen-year-old that's mixed up like any sixteen-year-old. Which brings me to another thing. You can't go kissing no black boys in front of Miss Fannie, even if it is T-Bone, you understand me? It just ain't right."

"Why can't I kiss T-Bone if I want to?"

"Well, for one thing, he's family. And for another, white girls shouldn't be kissing black boys. You need to find a nice white boy to kiss."

"But I like T-Bone," Ibby said.

"Miss Ibby, how can I make you understand?"

"He told me I was pretty."

Doll shook her head. "Miss Ibby, lots of boys gone tell you you're pretty. The first time someone told me I was pretty, nine months later I had Birdelia. We don't want nothing like that to happen to you. Now you go on and get some sleep." When Doll came over to kiss Ibby good night, her foot hit something under the bed.

"What's this?" She reached down. "Miss Fannie's photo album. I thought I told you to hide that thing."

"I did. Under the bed," Ibby said.

She sat next to Ibby on the bed and started flipping through the pages.

"What are you doing?" Ibby asked.

"There's been something on my mind all night. Where's that ad with Miss Fannie, the one that has the other lady with the alligator?"

"Toward the back," Ibby said.

"Here it is." Doll unfolded it and smoothed it out. "Uh-huh— thought so."

"What?" Ibby asked.

"Something about that other woman look familiar?"

"No, not really."

Doll pointed at a photo. "Look at Gertie the Gator Girl."

Ibby stared at the tall broad-shouldered woman with her foot on top of the alligator. "Yeah, so?"

"Look again, real close. Something about her mouth."

Ibby still didn't understand what Doll was getting at.

"Miss Fannie never did say how she knew Sister Gertrude. Now I know why."

Ibby's mouth fell open. "That's Sister Gertrude?" Then it hit her. "Fannie told me Sister Gertrude taught her how to dance. Now I know what she meant!"

"They say the Lawd works in mysterious ways," Doll said. "And this sure is one of them."

Chapter Thirty-One

Later that week Ibby was in the kitchen watching Birdelia practice some dance moves out on the back porch when Queenie set a box on the table in front of her.

"What's that?" Ibby asked.

"Miss Fannie ordered stationery so you can write thank-you notes to everybody that came to the party," Queenie said.

"But there were over a hundred people there! That could take me all summer!" Ibby protested.

"I believe that's the point. Give you something to do so you stay out a trouble. Besides, you can thank your friend Winnie Waguespack for giving her the idea. She the one that sent you that thank-you note after her party."

"Why don't you just tell Fannie I wrote them and be done with it? Be our little secret," Ibby suggested.

Queenie shook her head. "That won't do. Miss Fannie say she want to see them when you finished."

Ibby opened the box to find engraved monogram note cards.

"Look at that—your initials are LAB, for Liberty Alice Bell. Like one of them Labrador hunting dogs," Queenie chuckled.

Ibby closed the lid. "Don't remind me. Annabelle Friedrichs

discovered that my first day of school, when she saw the monogram on the collar of my uniform. She's been barking at me in the hall ever since."

Birdelia stuck her head through the back door. "Tell Mama I be back in a little while."

"Where you off to?" Queenie wiped her hands on her apron.

"I might go over to Audubon Park," Birdelia said.

"Now listen here," Queenie fussed at her. "T-Bone just got that part-time job over at the Audubon Stables. Don't go messing it up for him while he's at work."

"Can I come?" Ibby asked.

"If you want." Birdelia shrugged.

"What about your thank-yous, Miss Ibby?" Queenie asked.

"I can do those later." Ibby followed Birdelia out the back door. "Or never."

Queenie opened the screened door and called out after them, "You hear what I say, Birdelia? Don't go messing around with T-Bone while he's at work."

"Yes'm." Birdelia gave a backhanded wave and kept walking.

Birdelia headed toward Magazine Street, a few blocks from Fannie's house toward the river. When they got to the stables, they went around back, where they found T-Bone hosing down one of the horses.

"Why you all here?" T-Bone asked.

Birdelia reached up and grabbed a cigarette from his shirt pocket. "Just came to see how you doing."

"Why don't y'all go on up by the river, near the Butterfly? I'll meet you there in about twenty minutes, when I get off."

"Why you whispering?" Birdelia asked as she lit the cigarette.

A high-pitched voice called out from inside the barn, "Why isn't my horse saddled yet?"

Annabelle Friedrichs sauntered out of the stables, dressed in tight black riding pants that barely contained her fat rear end.

"Well, who have we here?" Annabelle eyed Birdelia savagely before approaching Ibby. "You got a horse here?"

"I'm thinking about getting one," Ibby shot back. "I wanted to check out the stables before I decided."

It was a lie of course, but Ibby was determined not to let Annabelle get the best of her.

"Well, you can't keep it here—the stables are full," she said smugly before turning toward T-Bone. "Hurry up and saddle my horse. I don't have all day."

"Yes, Miss Annabelle," T-Bone said as he walked into the barn.

"Why don't you go and help get my horse ready?" Annabelle said to Birdelia.

"I don't work here," Birdelia said.

"She's with me," Ibby said defiantly.

Annabelle tapped the side of her leg with her riding stick. "Oh, I forgot. Ibby Bell always was a nigger lover."

T-Bone must have heard Annabelle's comment because he came out of the barn looking so angry, Ibby thought he might smack Annabelle. Instead, he led her horse out calmly and handed her the reins.

"Here you go, miss."

"Aren't you going to help me up on the saddle?"

T-Bone gave Annabelle a lift up. After she trotted off, he headed back inside the barn without a word.

Birdelia turned to Ibby. "My grandma has a saying: 'Ugly is as ugly does.' That Annabelle one big fat ugly."

They walked to the back of the park toward the river, where they passed the zoo and the public swimming pool with the padlocked gates. When they crossed over the levee, they came upon a big open field. At the far end, near the river, was a concession stand that looked like a butterfly, with wings jutting out on either side. Birdelia stopped to buy a snowball.

"You want one?" She licked the red syrup off the side of the paper cup.

"No thanks," Ibby said. She was still thinking about the way Annabelle had spoken to T-Bone. It had left a sour taste in her mouth.

Birdelia led Ibby to some steps that went down to the batture of the river. They sat on large boulders the Army Corps of Engineers had placed around the river's edge to keep erosion at bay. Beyond the rocks was a small beach of river mud littered with garbage where pigeons were scavenging. The water lapped against the rocks as a tugboat pushing a grain barge let out a whistle as it passed under the Mississippi River Bridge, scaring up the pelicans perched in the rafters.

After a while, T-Bone came down to the batture to join them. He lit a cigarette.

"I'm sorry about the way Annabelle acted just now," Ibby said.

T-Bone gave her a small sideways glance. "Used to it."

Everyone sat in their own thoughts, watching the river. Ibby could tell T-Bone was angry, even if he tried to pretend he wasn't. Birdelia stood up on the boulder and began throwing pebbles at the pigeons. When they scattered, she skimmed a stone across the water, where it skipped several times before disappearing beneath the surface.

"We got company." Birdelia pointed behind T-Bone.

Three colored boys about T-Bone's age approached. One of them had on a jacket with the hood pulled up over his head, even though it was at least ninety degrees outside.

"Hey, man," the boy said to T-Bone as the two other boys hovered behind him.

"What you want, Peanut?" T-Bone said.

Peanut narrowed his eyes. "Say, what you doin' with that cracker?"

T-Bone shook his head. "She ain't with me, man. That's Birdelia's friend."

Birdelia whispered to Ibby, "They nervous 'cause they not used to being around no white girl, that's all. To them, all white folks is trouble. Just don't say nothing, or they might pick a fight with T-Bone."

The boy pulled a plastic bag from his jacket pocket. "Got me some bitching weed. Twenty for the lid."

T-Bone shook his head.

"Hey, man, got to sell this shit. You don't want a whole lid, how about half?" Peanut pulled a joint from his pocket and handed it to T-Bone. "Try it."

"How I know it's the same shit that's in the bag?" T-Bone asked.

Peanut took out a pack of rolling papers from his pocket. He handed the bag to one of his companions, who held it open for him while he pulled out some weed. He was about to roll a joint when they heard a whistle. Ibby looked up to find a policeman standing on the retaining wall, pointing down at them with a billy club.

"You, down there in the jacket—what's that in your hand?" the policeman yelled.

The boy dropped the bag as if it were on fire. "Nothing."

Ibby felt a tug on her sleeve. Everyone began to run.

"I know her," Ibby heard someone say.

It was that voice again.

Annabelle Friedrichs was sitting high up on her horse, looking over the edge, pointing down at Ibby with her riding stick.

Ibby ran as fast as her feet would carry her, up over the seawall, past the railroad tracks, through the park, but somewhere along the way, she lost Birdelia. At Prytania Street, she stopped and bent over, trying to get rid of the stitch in her side. She glanced around, out of breath. When she was sure no one was chasing her, she walked the rest of the way.

By the time Ibby got to Fannie's, Birdelia was standing by the back door as if she were afraid to go in. Crow was standing just inside the door. Ibby could see Doll in the kitchen with her arm around Queenie's shoulder.

"What happened?" Ibby whispered to Birdelia.

"My uncle, Purnell. Poppy says he's been shot."

Fannie came into the kitchen and placed a hand on Crow's shoulder and handed him an envelope. "This should take care of it. Let me know if there's anything else I can do."

"Thank you kindly, Miss Fannie," he said, wiping a tear from the corner of his eye.

Doll tried to rouse Queenie from the stool. "Come on now, Mama—we got to go to the hospital."

Crow went over to Queenie and slid his arm around her middle.

Doll tried to lift her up by her arms. "Come on, Mama."

Birdelia went in and grabbed her grandmother's hand and tugged at it. "Come on, Mee-maw, we got to go."

"My baby, my baby, my baby," was all Queenie was saying, over and over.

T-Bone appeared at the back door, sweating. "What's going on?"

"Come on over here and help Mama get to the car," Doll said.

Birdelia whispered to T-Bone, "Purnell."

That was all Birdelia had to say.

Chapter Thirty-Two

After the Trouts left, Ibby stood by the kitchen door, listening to Fannie on the phone in the hall.

"I'd like to place an order for delivery on Elysian Fields Avenue," she said, puffing on a cigarette. "No, not in the Marigny—closer to the lake. . . . What do you mean, you don't deliver to that neighborhood?" Fannie slammed the phone down, fuming. Her hand remained on the receiver, as if she were trying to decide what to do.

She picked it up again. "Leah, this is Fannie Bell. I need some food sent over to the Trout family. . . . That's right, Queenie and Crow. . . . What happened? Their boy Purnell was shot. . . . No, they just left to go over to the hospital, don't know the arrangements yet. I need your help in telling me what I should send over. . . . What's the usual?" She repeated the order. "Fried chicken, gumbo, fried catfish, bread pudding, and sweet potato pie. What about booze? . . . You'll take care of that? Whatever you think, you know better than me. . . . Wonderful. Just let me know how much it is, and I'll send the cash over later. . . . My number? Twinbrook seven four three five one. Bye-bye now." Fannie hung up, stormed into her bedroom, and slammed the door.

Ibby remained in the kitchen, waiting to see if Fannie was going to come out of her room, when she smelled something burning. Queenie had been in such a state earlier that she'd left the burner on under the pot on the stove. As Ibby turned the burner off and put the spoon in the sink, it dawned on her that she couldn't remember being in the kitchen when Queenie wasn't there.

"Ibby darling, are you in the kitchen? Come on out here," Fannie called from the dining room.

Fannie was sitting at the table. "Listen, honey, Queenie and Doll won't be around for a few days, so we'll just have to make do. Purnell was"—she paused—"such a nice kid before he got mixed up with that crowd. He used to come around here when he was a teenager, do odd jobs, tend the lawn."

"How'd he get shot?" Ibby asked.

"They didn't say—I'm sure Kennedy will fill me in later. But I expect it had something to do with his Black Panther friends. Such a tragedy." She tapped her finger on the table thoughtfully. "Kids get in trouble sometimes—no matter how much you love them."

"Purnell . . . is he dead?" Ibby asked.

"Crow said Purnell was shot in the head, something about a scuffle downtown with the police. I'm not holding out much hope for his survival, dear. I expect there'll be a wake as soon as the body is released to the funeral home."

"What's a wake?" Ibby asked.

"Oh, sometimes I forget you're not from around here. It's an old custom—they lay the body out so people can come and pay their last respects."

"Where everybody can see it?" Ibby was aghast.

"Out in the open on full display, dressed in their Sunday finest." Fannie pointed a finger at Ibby. "Listen to me. When I die, promise me you won't let them do that to me, put me in an open casket to be gawked at. I want a closed-coffin funeral—remember that." She paused to light a cigarette. "The one thing the Negroes really know how to do is throw a funeral. Goes on for days, with lots of food and drinking and carrying on. Then they have another party, where there's dancing and singing. And then they throw yet another party after the funeral, to give the departed a good send-off."

"I've never been to a funeral," Ibby replied. "I didn't know it could be like that."

"That's right. Your mama saw to that, didn't she? Saw to it that your daddy was cremated. Never was a funeral. Which reminds me"—she pointed at Ibby again—"don't let them go cremating me when I die. The departed should have proper burials. Otherwise their souls wander around the earth all agitated. And do you know why else they have funerals?"

Ibby shook her head, afraid to interrupt her tirade.

"They have funerals so the living can say goodbye for the last time, so every Tom, Dick, and Harry on the street doesn't stop to say 'I'm so sorry about so-and-so' for the umpteenth time. It's worse when you go and cremate somebody, because there's not even a grave to visit. Then suppose the worker at the crematorium got the dead bodies all out of order—then what? How do you know you have the right ashes? You know what I mean? How would you know?"

Ibby twirled her hair, upset by what Fannie was saying. She still thought of her daddy as her daddy, not as just some ashes in a jar.

Fannie said, "I'm sorry. I got a little carried away—funerals always do that to me."

Ibby sat up in her chair. "Are we going to the funeral?"

"Of course! They're family." Fannie got up from the table. "You can wear the Indian-looking dress Doll made for you."

After Fannie left, Ibby went into her father's room to find the urn. When she opened the armoire, it wasn't in its usual spot between the sneakers and the loafers. Ibby searched under the neatly stacked shirts and pushed the hanging clothes aside. After a while, she sat back on her heels. The urn was nowhere to be found.

Ibby took one last look around the room. She hadn't realized how much comfort the urn had given her, just knowing it was safe in the armoire. Now that her father was missing, she felt a part of her was missing, too. Why would someone move it?

The house was noticeably quiet except for the sound of the oak tree in the front yard scraping against the house. It was an eerie sound, like fingernails on a chalkboard. Ibby listened. She felt sure that the old tree was trying to tell her something.

Chapter Thirty-Three

The screened door creaked as Doll held it open for Crow, T-Bone, and two neighbors who were carrying Purnell's body into the house. All the furniture in the front room had been removed, save for the heavy Naugahyde sofa, to make room for the makeshift waking table, consisting of two sawhorses topped with a piece of plywood draped with a cloth.

"If you don't mind, we be taking our leave now," one of the men said after they'd settled Purnell onto the waking table.

"We got a houseful of food," Crow said, "thanks to all of you, and Miss Fannie was kind enough to send over three whole cases of Old Crow. Come by later, take a drink."

"Be honored," the man said as he tipped his hat, and the other man followed him out the door.

Doll and T-Bone stood by their father. They were all staring down at Purnell, who was dressed in his finest suit. He looked as if he were asleep, his arms crossed over his chest, his eyes closed. Doll thought she could even detect a slight smile across his lips. She was amazed at how well the undertakers had been able to disguise the bullet hole to his head.

"The undertakers done a right fine job on Purnell," Crow said as he touched Purnell's hand with such tenderness it brought tears to Doll's eyes.

Doll put her arms around her father's shoulders. "Yep, Daddy. They done a mighty fine job."

"Purnell looks like he could get up and walk right out of here at any moment. Wake right up, and walk right out. Like nothing ever happened," T-Bone added.

"Sure do. Sure do." Crow nodded. "How's your mama doing?" He looked at Doll with those dark eyes rimmed in yellow that had always made her heart melt.

"She's taking a rest, lying on her bed with a pillow over her face. Been that way awhile."

"She taking this mighty hard. Third boy to pass on. Don't get no easier," Crow said.

"Nope, don't get no easier," Doll repeated.

At a knock on the door, Crow looked up. "Not even sundown yet, and we already got our first visitor. Come on, T-Bone. You gone tend the bar."

"Birdelia!" Doll screamed. "I need you!"

Birdelia came down the hall and stood in front of her mother. "No need to yell. I'm right here, Mama."

"Sorry, baby. I didn't see you. Better start putting the food out. We already got visitors." She waved her hand toward the kitchen and went over to answer the door.

"Am I the first one here?" a pudgy woman carrying a tray asked. "I brought you some deviled eggs."

"Yes, you is, Leola, but you always the first one to come." *And the last one to leave, too,* Doll muttered under her breath.

"I am not," Leola protested.

"Yes, you is, and you know it, but it don't matter none. Come on in." She took the tray of deviled eggs from Leola.

Leola followed Doll to the kitchen. "Birdelia, find a place for Leola's eggs, then prop the front door open with one of them plastic chairs on the front porch. People can let themselves in. Sure they find the bar soon enough. I'm gone go back and check on Mama."

"I'll help Birdelia," Leola said, shooing Doll away with her hand. "You go on back and tend to your mama. Good thing I came when I did."

"Uh-huh." Doll headed toward Queenie's room at the back of the house. When she opened the door, her mother wasn't in the bed.

"Mama?"

There was no answer.

She called out again, "Mama?"

The door to the bathroom was ajar. When she crossed the room, she spotted her mother sprawled on the floor on the other side of the bed.

"Mama, what are you doing?" Doll knelt down beside her. "Why you on the floor?"

Queenie was staring up at the ceiling.

"I know you can hear me, Mama. No use playing possum." She grabbed Queenie's arm and pulled her up into a sitting position. "What you doing lying on the floor like that?"

Queenie sighed. "Fell out a bed. Didn't have the strength to get up."

"Now come on. Get back in bed. Leola is already here. Expect all the other folks be by shortly." She took her mother's hands and pulled her up, then settled her on the bed, tucking the covers around her.

"Purnell here?" Queenie asked.

Her mother's eyes held so much sadness that Doll had trouble keeping her composure. "Yes, Mama."

"How he look?"

"Just fine," Doll said. "Undertakers done a fine job on him."

"I want to go see." Queenie threw back the covers.

"You got plenty of time for that. You just rest awhile," Doll said, patting her shoulder.

Queenie slumped back down on the bed and threw her arm over her forehead.

"You want visitors?" Doll asked.

Queenie turned her head and looked at Doll. "I want to talk to you first."

Doll sat on the bed next to her. "About what? I already got all the food set on platters. Birdelia's putting it out for the guests, and Daddy and T-Bone, they out back setting up the bar."

"That's not what I mean." Queenie took Doll's hand.

"What you mean then?"

"You sorry?" Queenie asked.

"Mama, them pills the doctor gave you, I believe they making you all funny."

"No, Doll. It ain't the pills. I mean, you sorry you my daughter? You ever sorry you here?"

Queenie had never spoken to her like this, but Doll knew her mother never did take death well. The loss of Purnell was on her mind, stirring up thoughts of her other two sons that had departed this world too soon.

Doll tried to soothe her by stroking her cheek. "Now, why would I be sorry?"

"Things could have been different," Queenie said.

"Different? How? You the best mama I know. I ain't going nowhere." Doll squeezed her mother's hand.

Queenie squeezed back. "I just wanted to make sure, baby, that's all. Just wanted to make sure."

Chapter Thirty-Four

A funeral was held for Purnell Trout at the True Love Baptist Church a few days later. When Fannie and Ibby arrived, the funeral procession was about a block away from the church. The grand marshal, dressed in a black tuxedo and a peaked hat, was leading the procession, taking slow, measured steps. A group of men in black pants and white shirts with bow ties marched behind him, playing "Just a Closer Walk with Thee." Ibby spotted T-Bone alongside a trumpet player, just behind a man beating a large drum with "Excelsior Brass Band" painted in gold on the side. T-Bone's arm moved as if it were an extension of his instrument, his cheeks puffing out as he blew into the trombone with his eyes closed and his head bent low.

Following closely behind was a group of men wearing pastel suits and sashes embroidered with "The Duke of Wellington's Walking Club." Crow was leading the group in a cotton-candy-pink suit set off by a sash edged with pink and blue satin roses and a pink bowler hat. He looked proud as he waved a fan decorated with pink and black ostrich feathers.

Doll was following them, her arm around Queenie's shoulders, and Birdelia walked alongside, holding Queenie's hand. Behind them, two white stallions in heavy black harnesses pulled a magnificent black carriage on wooden wheels. As it rolled by, Ibby noticed the side of the carriage was inset with a large oval plate-glass window, the coffin on full display just inside.

The church was standing room only by the time they got in the door. The sickeningly sweet smell of lilies filled the air as the band members spread out along the altar behind the minister, the open casket sitting on a gurney in the middle of the aisle just in front of them.

The church was stuffy. The woman next to Ibby was fanning herself furiously. Just as the door to the church closed and the Reverend Jeremiah was about to begin the service, Doll turned and scanned the audience. She put her hand up.

"One moment, Reverend."

He glanced up from his Bible as Doll made her way up the aisle.

When she got to the back, she called over the crowd, "Miss Fannie! Miss Ibby! You come with me. Family sits up front."

"Don't mind us," Fannie said, trying to wave her away.

The whole church turned to see what was happening.

"Come on, Miss Fannie," Doll insisted.

"Oh, all right." Fannie sheepishly scooted past the people along the back wall.

Ibby followed Fannie down the aisle as the congregation whispered among themselves. As soon as they took their seats, the Reverend Jeremiah cleared his throat, and the murmur began to subside. The church became so quiet that Ibby could hear Fannie breathing next to her.

"Thank you for coming, Miss Fannie," Reverend Jeremiah said.

Fannie gave a brief nod, keeping her gaze on her hands folded in her lap.

From her vantage point in the front row, Ibby had a close-up view of the body in the casket. She tried to look away but couldn't help but notice a metal saucer perched on Purnell's chest.

"What is that for?" Ibby whispered to Fannie.

Fannie bent over close to her ear. "In the old days, it was a custom to put a saucer filled with salt on the chest of a corpse to keep the body from purging."

"Purging?"

"After people die, sometimes the body fluids come out."

"Come out where?"

Fannie gave her a sideways glance. "Wherever they can, dear."

Ibby's attention was soon drawn to Reverend Jeremiah's magical voice.

"Brother Purnell's time in this hard cruel world is over," he began. "No longer will he be sitting in the back of the plane, flying coach. No, brothers and sisters, Brother Purnell, he's flying first-class now, swaggering up to the pearly gates in all his glory."

"Amen," the congregation said.

"Brother Purnell had a short life that did not do justice to all that he was, all that he stood for. He was a proud soul, not one to back down easily in the face of adversity. I draw your attention to the Second Corinthians, chapter eleven, verse nineteen. It says, 'For ye suffer fools gladly, seeing ye yourselves are wise.' A fitting eulogy for our Brother Purnell, don't you think? As we all know, Purnell Trout was not one to suffer fools gladly. What I want to say to you, my brothers and sisters, is that we are all fools, in our own ways. You know what I'm saying? But I tell you now, that it is in this very folly, this naked truth, that we find the basis of our affection, and even respect, for one another—"

"Respect!" someone shouted.

Ibby looked over to find Queenie rocking back and forth with her eyes closed, moaning.

"Goodbye, Purnell," she mumbled. Then every once in a while, she'd cry out, "My baby!"

Ibby fanned herself with her hand, just as the Reverend Jeremiah opined about the scourge of murders that had overtaken the city and how needless and unnecessary it all was. Ibby looked up, drawn by the preacher's fiery tone. T-Bone was sitting just behind him, and his eyes met hers. She didn't know how long he had been staring at her. She smiled back, lowering her head so no one would notice that she was blushing.

As the preacher raised his hands, the sleeves of his robe flapped like angel wings. "I ask you God Almighty to take this boy into your arms."

With that, Queenie got up, walked over to the casket, and began sprinkling white powder all over the body, before taking her seat again.

"Why did she do that?" Ibby whispered to Fannie.

Fannie leaned in. "I believe that's baking powder. She wants to make sure Purnell rises up to Judgment Day."

When the Reverend Jeremiah finished his sermon, T-Bone stood and played a solo on his trombone. The congregation clapped and sang along to "What a Friend We Have in Jesus."

Queenie stood once again and went over to the casket. When the reverend nodded, she bent over and kissed Purnell on the lips.

"Goodbye, my baby," she said as she touched his hand.

Then she began wailing so loudly that Reverend Jeremiah came over and put his arm around her. Doll and Birdelia went and stood beside her. Then the whole congregation filtered into the aisles, waiting in line to view the casket.

Fannie nudged Ibby. "Follow Birdelia."

Doll leaned over and kissed Purnell on the cheek. Birdelia did the same.

Ibby looked back at Fannie with alarm. "Am I supposed to kiss him?"

"Just touch his hand and move on," Fannie said.

Ibby held her breath, closed her eyes. She reached into the casket, feeling for Purnell's jacket because she didn't want to touch his hand, but instead of fabric, her hand fell on something hard. She opened her eyes to find her fingers on his nose. Horrified, she hurried up the aisle, her heart beating fast.

After the last of the congregation paid their respects, the pallbearers lifted the casket and carried it out of the church. Once outside, the band started to play "When the Saints Go Marching In." The pallbearers raised the casket into the air and began shaking it to the beat of the music.

"What are they doing?" Ibby asked.

"They're giving Purnell one last dance," Fannie said. "We all deserve one last dance, don't you think, darling?"

A dark cloud made its way across the sky as the pallbearers put the casket in the waiting carriage. A light sprinkle fell around them, but people didn't seem to mind. They danced in the rain behind the carriage that was rolling slowly toward the cemetery, waving white handkerchiefs.

Ibby was about to follow along, but Fannie held her back.

"Aren't we going to the cemetery?" she asked.

"No, dear. This is one time I think we should just let them be."

Chapter Thirty-Five

When Mr. Henry came by the next day, Fannie placed a sizable wager that the National League would win the All-Star Game. They were busy watching the game that afternoon when Ibby heard the back door open.

When she got to the kitchen, she found Queenie putting her purse away in a drawer and Doll picking up a broom from the utility closet.

"What are y'all doing here? I thought you'd take some time off after . . ." Ibby wasn't sure how to finish the sentence.

Queenie shook her head. "Life ain't no cakewalk, baby."

Ibby went over and hugged Queenie. "I'm sorry."

"I know, but we got to move on. You got to dance even when there ain't no music." Queenie paused. "*Especially* when there ain't no music. You know what I'm saying? Besides, we just come by this afternoon to make sure you all doing okay. We'll be back tomorrow for good."

"Willie Mays gets an unearned run!" Fannie screamed from the front room.

"She must be in there watching the All-Star Game," Doll said. "She never misses that."

Queenie opened the icebox. "Mr. Henry been by with the groceries, I see."

Her words were cut short by the sound of the tree scraping against the house.

"I thought that tree looked like it was leaning more than usual when we walked up the driveway just now," Doll said.

"It's been making a lot of noise the last few days," Ibby said. "I said something to Fannie, but she said it had been that way ever since Hurricane Betsy and not to worry about it."

Doll nodded. "Sure, that hurricane's when that tree started to lean, back in 1965, but it's been getting worse every year since."

Queenie looked up at the ceiling. "Listen. Don't it sound different somehow?"

Doll turned an ear toward it. "You right, Mama. That old tree, I think it about had it. That's what it's trying to say."

"It's been saying that for a long time," Queenie said. "I got other things I got to tend to than listening to that old tree, like figuring out what we got in the icebox so I can make dinner. Saw some eggplant and tomatoes in the yard. What else we got?" She stuck her head into the icebox.

"I'll be up in the sewing room if you need me." Doll left the kitchen.

Ibby went back in the front parlor to watch the game with Fannie. After a little while, Queenie brought them a snack.

"When did you get here?" Fannie asked.

"A little while ago," Queenie said. "Just came around to make you some dinner. We be back tomorrow, same as usual."

When she turned to go, Fannie said, "Queenie?"

"Yes, Miss Fannie?" She had one hand on the kitchen door.

"Glad you're back."

"Why, thank you, Miss Fannie. Glad to be back," she said as the door swung closed behind her.

The sound of the tree scraping the house was getting so loud, Fannie had to turn the volume up on the television.

"Damn tree," Fannie said. "Remind me to tell Crow to trim it next week, will you, Ibby?"

"Hank Aaron up to bat," the announcer said.

"That's my boy." Fannie leaned in closer to the TV.

Doll came running down the stairs, screaming, "This it! This it! This it!"

"What is she going on about?" Fannie turned up the volume on the TV to drown out Doll.

Ibby followed Doll into the kitchen where she found her waving her hands around.

"This is it, Mama!" Doll said.

Queenie looked up at the ceiling. "That noise. It ain't stopping."

The moaning became louder and more drawn out until it gave way to sets of pops that sounded like champagne bottles being opened, then a loud squeal that was so shrill Ibby had to put her hands over her ears.

"Jesus, Mary, and Joseph!" Doll hollered.

In the next second, glass shattered and wood split as the giant tree came crashing down.

"Where's Miss Fannie at?" Queenie's voice was panicky. "She didn't follow you in here?"

"No. She's still up front," Ibby said.

The three of them looked at one another, afraid of what they might find when they opened the door.

The only sound in the house now was the blare from the announcer's voice on the television: "Tony Oliva just hit one off the left-field fence. . . . Will he be able to pull off a home run today?"

When they peeked into the front room, they could see the back of Fannie's head. She was still sitting on the couch but was pinned on either side by two branches that had forced their way through the front window.

"Think she's okay?" Queenie whispered. "She's awful quiet."

The three of them tiptoed into the room to find Fannie peering from behind the tree limbs like a caged bird. Ibby put her hand over her mouth, trying not to laugh, but the way Fannie kept peeping from behind the branches, Ibby couldn't help it—she burst out laughing.

"Miss Fannie, you done got yourself in a pickle." Queenie slapped her knee and bent over, giggling.

"Sure enough," Doll snorted. "Don't know how you gone get out of this one."

"Glad y'all think this is so funny." Fannie glared, although she was trying hard not to laugh herself. "Anybody going to do something, or you all plan to keep me in here all day?"

"I don't know. What ya think, Mama? Maybe we should let her stew in there awhile."

Fannie switched the channels back and forth on the television. "At least it didn't hurt the TV."

"Thank God," Queenie said between laughs. "Don't know what we would a done then."

Ibby's pocketbook was on the hall table. She retrieved her Polaroid camera from it, then came back into the room. "Fannie, look this way."

Fannie put up her hand as Ibby snapped a photo. "Stop!"

"Queenie and Doll, get over there by Fannie so I can take a picture."

Queenie got as close as she could and made a clown face while Doll pointed at Fannie. Fannie's mouth was wide open, and she was saying, "No, please don't do that," as Ibby took the picture.

"Do something quick! I need to whiz like a racehorse," Fannie said.

"I'll get you a pot," Queenie chuckled.

Ibby went over and stuck her head out the front door. The old tree looked like a sleeping giant that had eased itself to the ground and rolled toward the house for a final rest.

"Doll, I hate to tell you this," Ibby called out, "but some of the limbs may have pushed themselves into your sewing room."

Doll came out onto the porch. A good portion of the tree was blocking the driveway and spilling over into the neighbors' yard, and a hole the size of a small swimming pool gaped where the tree had uprooted itself.

Doll pointed at the house next door. "Mr. Jeffreys, he gone be mighty mad when he come home and find he can't get in his driveway. He's been after Miss Fannie to cut that tree down for years."

"Quit worrying about the tree," Fannie yelled, "or you're going to have another mess to clean up!"

"Really, Doll. What are we going to do?" Ibby asked. "She's trapped. She's going to pee in her pants if we don't do something soon."

"Got a saw in the shed. I can probably cut her out of there until we get a tree man here." Doll's face grew serious. "Look where that branch is sitting next to Fannie. If you hadn't come into the kitchen, that branch, it might have landed right on top of you, Miss Ibby. Just glad everybody's okay. I'm gone go see about the damage upstairs."

Ibby glanced over at the front window where the tree branches had forced their way inside like octopus tentacles. Suddenly it didn't seem so funny anymore.

"Will somebody hurry up?" Fannie said.

"Calm down, Miss Fannie. We figure out something," Queenie said, still chuckling. "Someday."

"All right. You've had your laugh." Fannie sank down into the couch and crossed her arms.

Doll came running back down the stairs. "Lawd!" she cried. "That tree done made a mess of my sewing room. Big limb came through the window just missing the sewing machine."

"Is that all you're worried about? How about trying to get me out of here?" Fannie squawked.

A few minutes later Doll came back with a small handsaw. "Daddy's coming over with some plywood to board up them front windows. But he can't do nothing until some of them branches are cut back from the house," she said as she began to saw one of the branches.

"This rate, it's going to be Christmas before you get me out of here," Fannie complained.

Doll held the saw up. "You want to try?"

"I'm gone go see if Crow can track down someone to come haul this tree off." Queenie went back to the kitchen.

After a good twenty minutes of caterwauling from Fannie, Doll was finally able to cut a path wide enough for her to crawl through. The second she was free, she made a beeline to her bedroom.

Crow pulled up to the house in a borrowed pickup truck with sheets of plywood in the back. Birdelia and T-Bone were with him. Crow got out and began to survey the damage, shaking his head, as T-Bone came up beside him. Then the three of them started down the left-hand side of the house and came around the back.

Ibby followed Doll into the kitchen to greet them.

"Did you get ahold of anybody?" Queenie asked Crow as he came in the back door.

He scratched his head. "I phoned over to Roosevelt Jefferson. He got that tree-trimming business, you know."

"What he say?"

"He gone come over take a look this afternoon, soon as he finish up another job."

"We got lots to do before the sun goes down," Queenie said. "Got to get boards up on them windows—otherwise skeeters gone be buzzing around like they own the place."

"Understand." Crow nodded.

Queenie beckoned Birdelia and T-Bone inside. "Y'all come on in. Birdelia, you go on upstairs, see if you can help Doll clean up the mess in her sewing room. Crow, T-Bone, y'all follow me into the front room."

"What about me?" Ibby said.

"Just try and stay out of the way, baby," Queenie said.

Ibby went up to her room and opened the window. Mr. Roosevelt and his crew had arrived with a large truck carrying heavy equipment. They were standing around the hole in the ground left from the up-rooted tree, talking to Crow. The root ball was so big it reached far above Crow's head. The hole left by the tree was much larger than she'd imagined, maybe eight feet wide and eight feet deep.

As Mr. Roosevelt's men began to sever the outer branches with chainsaws, Ibby leaned out the window to get a better look. Fannie had come out onto the front porch and was pacing back and forth with a strange look on her face.

Ibby didn't know why, but she felt sorry for the old tree, the way it was being hacked up. She thought back to Balfour and his accident. If that tree hadn't been there, the balsa plane might not have gotten caught up in it and Balfour wouldn't have crawled out on the gutter to get it. If he'd lived, her daddy wouldn't have been sent off to boarding school, and Fannie wouldn't have had a nervous breakdown. Could one tree do all that?

Fannie had stopped pacing and her arms were dangling by her sides. Ibby wondered if Fannie was thinking the same thing.

Mr. Roosevelt's crew worked until sunset, but they'd only been able to clear away the branches from the inside of the house so that Crow and T-Bone could board up the windows for the evening. Fannie stayed on the porch, even after Mr. Roosevelt's men left.

"Come on now, Miss Fannie," Queenie said. "They gone. It's dark. I got some supper for you on the table."

But Fannie refused to come inside. She sat on the swing on the corner of the front porch until Queenie brought out a plate of food. Queenie sat on the swing with her, feeding her a bite of fried chicken every so often. Everyone inside held their breath, wondering if that swing could bear the weight of both of them.

"What's gotten into her?" Ibby asked from just inside the door.

"Don't know, baby," Doll said.

Now Doll was fidgeting too. Everyone seemed to be on edge ever since that tree came crashing down.

Crow and T-Bone packed their tools into the truck.

"We ready to go," Crow said.

"Just a minute." Queenie waved him off. "Doll, come over here and help me get Miss Fannie in the house. Miss Ibby, might need your help too."

Fannie's hand began to shake uncontrollably as they lifted her from the swing.

Ibby helped Doll get her to her room. Queenie came in behind them as Doll stretched Fannie out on the bed. As Queenie took off Fannie's shoes, the look on Fannie's face never changed.

She looked as if she'd seen a ghost.

The next morning, as soon as the sun was up, Fannie was up, too, pacing on the front porch in her housedress and slippers. Queenie had to coax her inside to get dressed, but once Mr. Roosevelt arrived, she was back on the porch, watching.

Ibby and Queenie stood in the doorway for a while, watching, too.

"What is it about that tree that has her so uptight?" Ibby asked.

"Who knows?" Queenie said offhandedly.

"How old do you think that tree was anyway?"

"Why you want to know?"

"Just curious."

"Old enough," Queenie said under her breath. She appeared irritated by the question.

Fannie stayed out there most of the morning, watching Mr. Roosevelt and his men saw branches from the tree and drag them over to the grinder.

Queenie came out at one point and said, "Miss Fannie, Wimbledon about to come on. Don't you want to come in and watch it?"

Fannie shook her head. That's when Ibby knew something was wrong. Fannie never missed Wimbledon. Ibby sat with Fannie on the porch swing for a while, trying to engage her in conversation, but Fannie never spoke a word. She just sat there, watching the tree. After a while, Ibby gave up and went upstairs. She stopped in her father's room to look for the urn. When she opened the armoire, it still wasn't there.

Ibby went across the hall to Doll's sewing room, where she found Birdelia dancing around to an Aretha Franklin song playing on the radio. Doll was standing out on the upstairs balcony, watching the goings-on in the front yard.

Doll came inside. "You need something, Miss Ibby?"

"Daddy's urn isn't in the armoire. Do you know what happened to it?"

"Oh Lawd, Miss Ibby. I forgot, you know, with everything that's been going on. A few weeks back, Miss Fannie asked where that urn was, so I brought it down for her and set it on the dining room table, thinking she just wanted to look at it for a spell. Then when I came back downstairs a little while later, Miss Fannie was gone. That urn, it was gone, too."

"Oh," Ibby said. "I just thought you'd moved it."

"No, baby. I didn't move it. Figured Miss Fannie had taken the urn out for a joyride in that new car of hers, but when she came back, she didn't have the urn with her. When I asked her where it was, she said next to Balfour."

"What did she mean, 'next to Balfour'?" Ibby asked.

"You know, in the cemetery."

Ibby looked at the floor. "I guess she wanted Daddy to have a proper burial. You know how she's always talking about proper burials. I just wish she would have told me."

"Well, yeah, that would have been the best thing, but you know Miss Fannie. She got her own way of doing things."

"That's for sure," Birdelia piped in.

Doll nodded over at Birdelia. "Listen, girls, why don't you go catch yourselves a movie over at the Prytania Theatre? No use hanging around here."

Birdelia waved her hand. "Good idea. Come on, Miss Ibby."

"You run on downstairs, Birdelia. There's something I want to talk to Miss Ibby about, alone."

As soon as Birdelia left, Doll shut the door. She had a strange look on her face.

"Come on over here, Miss Ibby." Doll sat on the settee across from her sewing machine and pulled a yellow piece of paper from her pocket. "This telegram came for you this morning. I been holding on to it until the right time, but Miss Ibby, there ain't never a right time." She handed it to Ibby.

Ibby took it from her and sat next to her on the settee. It was a telegram from an attorney in California. Ibby read it aloud. " 'This is to inform you, as next of kin, that Vidrine Crump Bell' "—Ibby paused—" 'has passed away of natural causes. As per her last request, her body will be cremated and her ashes spread into the Pacific Ocean.' "

Ibby's hand dropped to her lap and the telegram slipped to the floor. She felt as if someone had punched her in the stomach. Over the last four years, she'd spent hours thinking of what she might say to her mother if she came back. She'd never expected it to end like this. No last words. No goodbyes. No *I'm sorry*.

"I know you're upset," Doll said, touching her hand.

"I hated my mother for leaving me here."

"I thought you liked it here."

"That's not it. I hated my mother for not caring enough to come back for me." She put her head in her hands.

Doll slipped her arm around Ibby's shoulders. "Oh, baby. I don't think it was like that. I think your mother just lost her way. That's all. I know she loved you."

"And how do you know that?" Ibby said flatly.

" 'Cause she told me so herself," Doll said.

Ibby looked at Doll. "What? When would she have told you?"

Doll drew in a deep breath. "Miss Vidrine came by the house a few weeks ago."

Ibby jumped up. "Why didn't you tell me? My mother came back, and you didn't tell me?"

"Listen to me. Your mama came by to tell you she was sorry."

"I bet," Ibby said, trying hard to hold back tears.

"I think she meant it, Miss Ibby. She say she didn't mean for it to happen this way. She didn't mean to get sick. She thought you'd be better off here, with Miss Fannie. She was destitute, Miss Ibby. She had no place to go."

"Then why didn't she come here? Why didn't she ask Fannie if she could stay here?"

"'Cause I think she was too proud. I think she wanted you to remember her the way she was. She asked me to give you this." Doll pulled the ring from her pocket.

Ibby wiped her cheek with the back of her hand and took the ring from Doll. "It's her wedding ring. The one Daddy gave her."

"She told me to be sure and tell you she loved you."

Ibby slipped the ring onto her finger and toyed with it. "Did she really say that, or are you just making that up to make me feel better?"

"Your mama asked me not to say anything until she passed. It's been on my mind ever since she came by, a few days before your party."

"So she *was* here." Ibby twisted the ring on her finger.

"Yes, Miss Ibby."

"Does Fannie know?"

"No, baby. I was afraid if I let on to Miss Fannie, she might go riding around trying to find Miss Vidrine. I didn't tell no one, not even Queenie."

"I went looking for my mother, you know. That day I came home in the rain, I had gone looking for her."

"I figured as much," Doll said.

"She didn't want me to find her."

"No, Miss Ibby. I feel for sure she wanted to see you, but she was very sickly. I don't think she wanted you to see her that way."

"I just wanted to see her one last time."

"Miss Ibby, I'm sorry if I done wrong, but I handled it the best way I knew how."

Ibby wiped another tear from her cheek. "Don't say anything to Fannie. I don't think she could handle the news right now. That tree had her all worked up for some reason. I'll tell her in my own good time."

"If that's the way you want it." Doll grabbed Ibby's hand. "I know it's a shock."

"I don't want to talk about it anymore. Not now. Not ever." Ibby yanked her hand away and hurried toward the door.

She found Birdelia standing in the driveway, waiting for her.

"What my mama want with you?"

"Nothing," Ibby sniffled.

"You mad about something?"

"No."

"You look mad," Birdelia said.

"Forget about it."

"What my mama say got you so upset?" Birdelia asked. "You been crying?"

Ibby ignored her questions. "Let's go."

When they got to the end of the driveway, they could see Fannie sitting idly on the porch swing with her feet dangling and her head hung low, as if she were thinking about something that had happened a long time ago.

T-Bone was out in the yard, helping his father clean up after the tree men. He put down his rake and came over to speak to them.

"I got a gig over at the Union Hall on Tchoupitoulas tomorrow night. Why don't you and Birdelia come catch me play?"

Ibby didn't answer. She was looking past him, at Fannie.

Please don't leave me, Fannie. You're all the family I have, now that Mama's gone.

"Miss Ibby, did you hear me?" T-Bone asked.

Birdelia poked Ibby. "Ain't you gone answer T-Bone?"

Ibby drew her eyes away from her grandmother and looked at T-Bone. "I'm sorry. I've just got something on my mind. I'd love to hear you play tomorrow night."

"Awright then." T-Bone lifted his hand in a kind of backward wave and sauntered off.

When they got back from the movie, Mr. Roosevelt and his men were wrapping up for the day. From the looks of it, they'd gotten only about half the tree.

Fannie was back to pacing on the porch. Queenie was waddling along next to her, but she wasn't consoling Fannie, as she'd done the day before, and the day before that.

This time Queenie had a worrisome look on her face too.

That night Ibby had trouble falling asleep. She couldn't get her mother out of her mind. She remembered what Doll had told her not too long ago, that it hurt to love sometimes. Ibby wondered if there was ever a time when love didn't hurt.

She leaned over and opened the window. The smell of sawdust hung in the air as a passing cloud draped the tree in an eerie shadow, making the roots look like bony fingers reaching up from the depths of the earth. There was something sad about the tree, the way it was sprawled on its side with its outer branches cut off. Ibby rubbed her arms, thinking about her mother, feeling alone and exposed, just like the tree down below.

She heard a rustling noise. She didn't think much of it at first—probably just a wandering raccoon scurrying down the alley on the left side of the house. Then she heard it again, a scuffle below the window. She turned the light off in her room and peered down, trying to figure out where the noise was coming from. She could just make out some sort of shadow hovering near the edge of the hole left by the tree. Was it an animal? Whatever it was seemed to be looking for a way to get down into the hole.

"Who's there?" Ibby called out.

There was no answer.

"Anyone there?" she said again.

She hurried down the stairs and out the back door, hoping to catch whatever it was that might be down there, but when she got to the front of the house, all she saw was a stray cat skidding across the yard.

Perhaps I'm just spooked by what Doll told me today, about my mother, Ibby thought.

When she peeked over the edge of the hole, she felt the earth move beneath her feet. She jumped back. *I'm a fool,* Ibby thought. *There's no one here.*

Ibby made her way to the back of the house and went inside. When she started up the stairs, she was startled by a noise coming from the landing. She froze. Was there someone in the house? She was trying to decide if she should run next door for help when she heard a small voice.

"Let me in."

Ibby was surprised to find Fannie on the landing in her bare feet and white nightie, trying to open the door at the top of the stairs. She kept twisting the knob and pushing her shoulder against the door, repeating the same words.

"Little Mama. Little Mama."

From the look in Fannie's eyes, Ibby thought she might be sleep-walking.

"What's wrong, Fannie?" Ibby came a little closer.

"The room. It's locked." Fannie pointed at the door.

"I know."

"Open it."

"I can't. I don't have the key." She put her hand on her grandmother's back, trying to calm her.

Fannie tussled with the knob. "Open it."

"I told you, Fannie. I don't have the key."

Fannie tried the knob once more, then looked over at Ibby with exasperation. "Little Mama is in there."

"Who's Little Mama?"

Fannie shook her head.

"Come on, Fannie, let's go back down to your room."

"No!" she cried. "I need to get Little Mama out!"

Her outburst startled Ibby, but she tried to remain calm for fear she might upset Fannie more. As it was, Fannie was wringing her hands and looked as if she were about to cry.

Ibby gently coaxed Fannie away from the door, trying to think of a way to get her back down the stairs. "Let's come back tomorrow, okay? I think Little Mama is asleep. We don't want to disturb Little Mama when she's asleep, do we?" She kept talking as she led Fannie down the stairs, Fannie's dirty feet leaving marks on each step as they went along.

After Ibby managed to get Fannie settled in her bed, she closed the door and took a deep breath. Had something happened in that room? And who was Little Mama? No one had ever mentioned her.

She went back to the top of the stairs, to the locked room that Fannie had been trying to get into. All the rooms on the second floor were accounted for except this one. She shook her head. There was so much about her family she still didn't know.

After four years of living in this house, it was still holding secrets from her.

Chapter Thirty-Six

The next evening, after Mr. Roosevelt and his men left, Ibby went up to her room to get ready for her rendezvous with Birdelia to watch T-Bone play at Union Hall. She slipped on a skirt and a top, and at the last minute, she added an extra dab of Wild Orchid No. 7 perfume. She tried to sneak past Fannie, who was watching the Steeplechase horse races on the television. She'd almost made it to the kitchen when she heard Fannie call after her.

"You going somewhere, young lady?"

"Oh, um, yes ma'am. Just out for a little while."

"With whom?"

Ibby knew Fannie probably wouldn't approve of her going out to meet T-Bone at a dance club. She hesitated. "With some friends," she said.

"What friends?"

"You, know, just some friends from school. And I might meet up with Birdelia."

"Where are you going?"

"Over to Union Hall to hear some music."

Fannie peered over her reading glasses. "What do you have on?"

Crap, Ibby thought. *She's going to make me go upstairs and change my clothes.* "Just a skirt," she replied.

"You call that a skirt? Where's the rest of the fabric? It's so short, it looks as if your rear end might show if you bend over."

"It's the style, Fannie. Everyone's wearing them."

"Is that what young women wear these days?" She looked Ibby up and down.

Fannie removed her glasses, and gazed at Ibby with a blank expression. "Looks nice," she finally said.

"Can I go?" Ibby fingered her suede shoulder bag nervously.

"Oh, all right. Don't be late," Fannie said.

ↄ⃝ↄ⃝ↄ⃝

Union Hall was an old storage warehouse adjacent to the wharves on the Mississippi River. It was nothing more than a big empty space with a stage at one end and a bar at the other but it was always crowded. When Birdelia and Ibby arrived, they had to stand in line to get in.

After a fifteen-minute wait, they paid the entrance fee and made their way through the crowd toward the bar, as two large ceiling fans buzzed overhead. There was no air conditioning, and everyone was sweating, but no one seemed to mind.

Ibby didn't protest when Birdelia handed her a Cuba libre. She held the plastic cup up in the air, trying not to spill it, as they jockeyed their way toward the stage. When they were about twenty feet away, Birdelia gave up.

"This the best we can do!" she yelled over the roar of the crowd.

They spent the next hour sipping drinks, being jostled around, and sweating. It was close to ten-thirty before a heavyset black man in a T-shirt and blue jeans came up to the microphone.

"How y'all doing?" he said to the audience.

People in the audience raised their hands and whistled.

"Thank y'all for coming out tonight. You ready to get down?"

The audience went ballistic. "Yes! Yes! Yes!" they chanted.

It was so loud, Ibby tried to cover an ear with her free hand.

"That won't do you any good." The young man next to her raised his cup and smiled.

It was Wiley Waguespack, Winnie's older brother, the one she had a crush on until Winnie told her he was only allowed to date Catholic girls.

"Where's Marcelle?" Ibby asked. "Aren't you dating Marcelle?"

"What?" he asked, cupping his hand to his ear.

"Never mind," she said. She didn't really want to know anyway.

Then the band came on stage and started playing a new sound called funkadelic and everyone danced in place. Near the back of the stage, T-Bone was swinging his trombone in a practiced rhythm with the rest of the brass section. Clapping and swaying with the people around her, Ibby tried to ignore the fact that Wiley had put his arm around her shoulders.

When some of the members of the band began to dance like James Brown, Ibby exclaimed, "I know how to do that!"

She wobbled her knees and shuffled her feet around the way T-Bone had shown her.

Wiley stepped back and watched. "How'd you learn to dance like *that?*"

Birdelia turned to look. "You must got some black in you some-where 'cause I ain't never seen no white girl dance like that."

Ibby was disappointed when the band stopped playing. She checked her watch. It was one in the morning.

People were filtering out the front door, but Birdelia pointed the other way, toward the stage. "Let's go find T-Bone."

Wiley tugged on Ibby's arm. "I'm heading over to Bruno's Tavern. Want to come along?"

A part of Ibby wanted to go, but she knew Wiley and she could never be a couple, not according to Winnie. So what was the point? Besides, she'd come with Birdelia, and she didn't want to disappoint T-Bone.

"No, I can't. Thanks for asking, though," she said.

She could see Wiley's confused face when she headed in the other direction with Birdelia. She smiled to herself. Turning Wiley down had given her a certain sense of satisfaction.

When they got up to the stage, T-Bone jumped down to greet them.

Ibby tucked her sweat-soaked hair behind her ears. "You were fantastic."

He grinned. "Thank you kindly, Miss Ibby. Say listen, I'm gone head over to the Ebony Lounge to watch the chicken drop. You want to come along?"

Birdelia shook her head. "I got to get the car back. Mama don't know I took it."

"Miss Ibby can come with me. We'll swing by, pick you up," he said as he placed his trombone in a leather case and snapped it shut.

"Naw. You go ahead," Birdelia said.

Ibby whispered to Birdelia, "I'm not going without you."

"Why? He ain't gonna bite," Birdelia said loud enough for T-Bone to hear.

Ibby was embarrassed. "That's not what I meant."

Her pulse quickened when T-Bone came and stood next to her. His T-shirt was soaked through, leaving a V-shaped spot in the middle of his chest.

Birdelia cocked her head. "Okay, then. Better hurry. Chicken drop gone start in twenty minutes."

As T-Bone was helping Ibby into his black Camaro, she saw Wiley Waguespack drive by and give her a double take. She gave Wiley a big wave, which caused him to almost swerve into another car.

As T-Bone started the car, Ibby asked, "What exactly is a chicken drop?"

"Oh, it's just a silly betting game they invented over in Tremé," he explained. "They throw a hen in a cage with a bunch of numbers painted in circles on the floor of the coop. If the chicken poops on your number, you win."

When they drove up to the Trout residence, all the lights were off and the street was dark. Ibby didn't see Birdelia sitting on the stoop until she jumped up and ran over to the car. T-Bone drove a few blocks before stopping in front of a white stucco one-story building with a metal awning. There were hordes of people of all ages milling about on the sidewalk.

T-Bone dropped Birdelia and Ibby off by the front door. "Y'all go on in while I park."

Ibby and Birdelia went inside the lounge, where music from a jukebox sifted through the smoke-filled room. When Birdelia held up three fingers at the bar, an older woman wearing a flowered dress and a white apron handed her three plastic cups.

Ibby followed Birdelia over to a table in the corner.

T-Bone came in shortly. "Placed your bets yet?"

"We waitin' on you." Birdelia slid one of the cups toward T-Bone.

He picked it up. "It's almost time. Let's go out back."

A side door led to an outdoor courtyard, where the main attraction was a cage made of chicken wire perched on wooden legs. A stout man in a T-shirt and suspenders with a cigar dangling from his mouth was collecting money from patrons eager to place bets. T-Bone handed Ibby and Birdelia a slip of paper.

"Just put your name and a number on the betting slip," he said. "Don't worry about the fee. My treat."

"Five minutes!" the man called out.

When all the bets were in, the man with the cigar plucked a fat hen from a pen in the corner of the yard and put it inside the cage.

"Chicken, do your shit!" he shouted loud enough for everyone in the courtyard to hear.

The bird sat in the same spot for several minutes despite people sticking their fingers through the wire mesh trying to prod it. It cocked its head a few times, then moved three steps and sat down again. Each time the chicken moved, there was hollering and jeering. This went on for a good twenty minutes until finally the chicken scrambled over to the corner of the cage and pooped.

"Number four! Right on the edge!" the man yelled through his stubby cigar.

"Did you win?" Ibby asked T-Bone.

"Naw. I ain't never won. Just for fun," he said.

When they went back inside, a white girl about Ibby's age was sitting at the bar, leaning on her elbow as she took a drag from a cigarette.

The girl was watching Ibby in the mirror behind the bar. She turned around. "Why, Ibby Bell. That you?"

"What are you doing here, Annabelle?" Ibby asked.

Annabelle smiled in a sickly way that let Ibby know she was drunk out of her mind. She almost fell off the stool when she pointed at T-Bone. "You with that stableboy? And that little nigger girl you always hang out with." Annabelle put her hand over her mouth, realizing her faux pas at using the word *nigger* in a black bar. She lowered her eyes toward T-Bone's crotch, then looked back up toward his face. "You know what they say."

T-Bone took a step back. "Miss Annabelle, this ain't a good place for you. You want us to take you home?"

"With you?" She closed one of her eyes and tried to wink.

"You with anyone?" he asked, looking around.

"No, man," a man smoking a joint at a table nearby said to T-Bone. "That skank drove up, parked out front, and came in all by herself about an hour ago."

"Why she here?"

He squinted in her direction. "Why you think, brother? She been here before, lots a times."

"You messing with me, Shorty?" T-Bone said.

"No, man. You want some, you stick around." Shorty cocked his head in the direction of the door. "All you got to do is take her out to her car. She do it right in the backseat. She don't care."

Annabelle grabbed T-Bone by the shirt and pulled him toward her. "What was your name again, stableboy?"

He tried to move away, but she was clenching his arm.

"Let's go." Birdelia tugged on T-Bone's sleeve. "I don't want nothing to do with that piece a white trash. Come on, T-Bone. She's nothing but trouble."

Annabelle pointed at T-Bone. "You'll be back."

When they were about halfway down the block, Ibby heard a shriek. Annabelle was laughing hysterically as she fumbled with her keys, trying to open the door to her car.

Then another man came up from behind and helped her into the car and slipped into the backseat beside her.

Chapter Thirty-Seven

T-Bone didn't say a word as they drove along Louisiana Avenue and Birdelia snoozed in the backseat.

"That ain't the first time," T-Bone said after a while, breaking the uneasy silence.

"What do you mean?" Ibby asked.

"That Miss Annabelle. It ain't the first time she done something like that." He gave her a quick glance. "She come up to all the guys at the Audubon Stables flaunting her chubby white ass. She wasn't picky, do it right there in the barn. Then up by the river, behind the trees down in the batture—saw her there once or twice too."

Ibby looked away, not sure she really wanted to know if Annabelle's escapades included him.

T-Bone shook his head. "I know what you're thinking, but I never did nothing."

She kept her gaze on the window. "I wasn't thinking that at all."

"Miss Ibby?" He touched her hand.

When Ibby turned around, he was leaning toward her. She thought he was about to kiss her, so she leaned in and closed her eyes.

"You know I like you, but—" T-Bone started to say.

Ibby opened her eyes to find T-Bone sitting about as far away from her as he could, leaning against the door.

"But you're black and I'm white," she finished for him, "and I'm only supposed to kiss white boys. At least that's what Doll told me."

"She said that?"

"Yes, after I kissed you at my party. I got a lecture."

"She gave me a lecture too. Said we're like—"

"Family. I know," Ibby said.

They sat there for a moment, not quite knowing what else to say.

"Miss Ibby, there was something else I was trying to tell you just now. . . . The band I played with tonight is going on a tour of Europe, and they asked me to go with them."

"I'm really happy for you." After a few moments, she said, "T-Bone?"

"Yes, Miss Ibby?"

She wanted to say *I still like you*, but she knew that would be selfish on her part, so she said, "Don't forget to send me a postcard."

By now it was three in the morning. The roads were deserted. As T-Bone turned the car onto Prytania Street, Ibby suddenly felt exhausted. It had been a long, trying day. All she wanted to do was crawl into bed. Ibby hoped Fannie was asleep because she was probably going to be in trouble for coming home so late.

Birdelia was just waking up when they pulled up in front of Fannie's house. She stretched her arms and looked around.

"What's Poppy's Cadillac doing in front of Fannie's house?" She pointed to the car parked in front of them.

"Can't be his car—you took it home not too long ago. Weren't everybody asleep?"

Birdelia put her nose up against the glass, trying to get a better look. "That's it. Recognize the dent in the back bumper."

No lights were on in Fannie's house, the only illumination coming from a single streetlamp that cast a paltry haze over the street.

"Sure is quiet," Birdelia said as she got out of the car.

T-Bone glanced over his shoulder at the old Cadillac. "Something's not right. I better walk you to the door, make sure everything's okay."

"I'll come too. Not sitting out here all by my lonesome," Birdelia chimed in.

As they started up the front walk, a flash of light spooked them. All three stopped short.

"What was that?" Birdelia whispered anxiously.

"Came from the tree," T-Bone whispered back.

"What you mean?" Birdelia grabbed his shirt and held on.

Then there was another flash. This time it was pointed at them.

"What you doing here, boy?" came Crow's voice, his head just visible above the hole in the ground. He was shining a flashlight at T-Bone.

"Daddy, what's going on?" T-Bone asked.

Another head popped up. "Birdelia, why you all here?"

"Doll?" Ibby inched closer. "That you?"

"Oh Lawd, Miss Ibby. What y'all doing out this time a night?" Doll said.

"Who's there?" came another hushed voice from below.

Doll looked down. "Shhhh, Mama—you gone wake Miss Fannie."

"*Queenie's* down there?" Ibby asked as Crow disappeared back into the hole, taking the flashlight with him, leaving them once again in the shadows.

"Shhhh," Doll said again. "Why y'all up?"

"Been to the chicken drop," Birdelia said. "What you doing in that hole?"

"I found it," Crow said.

"You remember where you put it?" Queenie asked.

"Yes, woman. I found part of it. Lookey here."

"Found what?" T-Bone put his hands on his hips.

Doll was standing on a ladder peeking out from the hole as Queenie and Crow searched with the flashlight for something down below.

"Long story, brother," Doll said before turning her head. "Mama, you get on out and let T-Bone come down. He got better eyes."

Soon Queenie's head appeared. "Help your mama out, boy."

T-Bone took Queenie's arm and led her out, then backed down the ladder and disappeared into the hole.

"Birdelia, you skinny, go on down there," Queenie said, "see if you can lend a hand, and take this garbage bag down with you."

"What the heck is going on?" Ibby peeped over the edge.

Queenie took Ibby's arm and led her to the front steps, away from all the commotion. "Come have a seat next to me."

As Ibby sat, she could just make out Queenie's profile in the dark. She was brushing off her dress. When she finished, she took Ibby's hand in hers.

"I didn't think Miss Fannie knew, but the way she's been pacing on this porch makes me think she must have seen me and Crow out here that night all those years ago." Queenie rocked herself as she always did when she was thinking about something that upset her. "For a long time now, you been wanting to know about that room upstairs, the one at the top of the stairs. Well, child, I'll tell you about that night. It weren't too long after Master Balfour died and your father got sent off to boarding school. Miss Fannie, she'd only been home a couple of weeks after going to the hospital with a nervous breakdown. She was still fragile. I kept an eye on her, especially when Mr. Norwood would go off on his stints on the river. When I look back on it, I shouldn't have gone off to the market that day. Things might have been different."

ℰℐⓈℰℕ

When no one was around, Fannie liked to listen to music. She'd go upstairs, open the windows, and turn up the phonograph until music filled the room. Occasionally a neighbor complained, but most of them had gotten used to the sounds of Glenn Miller or Tommy Dorsey in the late afternoon. On this particular day, Fannie was standing in the middle of her and Norwood's bedroom in her bare feet, listening to "In the Mood" by Glenn Miller. She turned the phonograph up as loud as it would go, so loud the glass in the windows rattled, and danced around waving a silk scarf, letting it float around her. Then she'd stop and go the other way, spinning slowly with her eyes closed until she grew dizzy. It was her way of chasing away the loneliness when Norwood was away on the river. She'd been up in their room for several hours now, pretending she was with him in front of a big stage in New York. She'd never been to New York, but he'd promised he'd take her there one day.

She was so wrapped up in her dreams that it took her several minutes to notice there was someone at the door to the bedroom. It was one of Queenie's cousins, named Muddy, who came around every so often looking for money.

"You have no business up here, Muddy. You know better." She waved him away, annoyed that she'd been disturbed in the middle of a song.

Muddy was a large man, over six and a half feet tall, pushing three hundred pounds. His face was void of expression, as if he hadn't understood what Fannie was saying. He was a bit slow. She tried to explain so he'd understand.

"Queenie's not here, Muddy. She's off at the market. Now go on. You can wait downstairs in the kitchen." She then turned her back and went back to dancing. When she opened her eyes a few moments later, Muddy was standing a few feet away from her. "What are you doing? I told you to go on downstairs. Now do as I say." This time there was anger in her voice. She didn't like people getting that close to her, much less an uninvited guest in her bedroom. "Did you hear me?"

Muddy stood there as if he wanted to ask her something but was afraid.

"You want money? That's what you want?" she asked. "Here. I have some right here."

She opened the drawer to the table next to the bed, where she kept cash and a small pistol. She counted out ten dollars and tried to hand it to him. He looked down at the money. Fannie thought he was trying to decide what to do. Maybe he thought it wasn't enough.

"Here, go on. Take it and get on out of here like I told you." She tried to put the money in his hand.

He swatted it away and shook his head. He took a step closer.

"Just what do you think you're doing?" She felt a tinge of panic rise up in her, but she still thought he just didn't understand. "Take the money and go!" she demanded.

The next thing she knew, he had pushed her to the floor and pulled up her dress. She tried to fight him. She clawed at his face, but he was strong. He slapped her across the cheek, startling her. She began to cry. He pushed her down. She felt his big belly on her chest as he thrust himself inside her. She tried to scream but nothing came out except a tear that trickled down the side of her face. There was nothing she could do but listen to the music and the sound of Muddy's guttural moans.

When he finished, he rolled over and fell fast asleep. She pushed him aside and crawled out from beneath his leg. She reached into the open drawer by the bed and pulled out her pistol. She stood over the sleeping man and pointed the gun at him.

"How dare you," she hissed.

She shot him five times, then once more in the face for good measure. Then she slumped down on the floor next to him with the gun still tightly gripped in her hands, the music that once made her so happy now drowning out her cries as blood seeped from beneath the body and inched close to where she was sitting. She didn't move. She didn't move even when she heard someone come into the room.

"Lawd, Miss Fannie, what have you done?" Queenie bent down next to Fannie and coaxed the pistol from her hands. "I got word that Muddy had gotten out of the asylum a few days ago. I'm sorry, Miss Fannie. I'm sorry I weren't here when he came by. He usually no trouble. . . ." She rambled on as she helped Fannie up. "Come have a seat over here on the bed. Let me get you cleaned up. Then I figure out what to do with Muddy."

Fannie vaguely heard her talking, but she was in a fog. Nothing seemed real. She let Queenie help her onto the bed. She stared up at the ceiling. The music was still playing, but her tears had dried up, as if there were none left to be had.

Queenie came over to the bed with a damp washcloth and began to wipe her face. "Lawd, Miss Fannie, they is blood all over your dress. We got to get you out of it before Mr. Norwood comes home. When he coming back from the river?"

"Tomorrow night," Fannie answered in a faint voice that didn't even sound like hers.

"You in shock, Miss Fannie. You just lay there nice and calm while I clean you up."

Fannie grabbed Queenie's hand. "He mustn't know. He must never know! It would kill him."

Fannie knew her life would be over if Norwood ever found out that a colored man had raped her. He would never forgive her for what had happened. She would be tainted forever in his eyes.

Queenie's small eyes quivered as she patted Fannie on the shoulder. "Now, don't you worry, Queenie gone take care of everything. You understand?"

Fannie closed her eyes. She could hear Queenie on the phone in the hall.

"Crow, get on over here," Queenie said. "Don't need no lip. I'll explain when you get here. Just get here as soon as you can. Understand?"

She came back into the room and put her hands on her hips. "You sure as hell done shot him dead." She closed the windows and turned the music down. "No one will know what happened to him, lessen you say anything. Muddy always did have a habit of wandering away from that nuthouse across the lake. Them folks will just think he wandered off somewhere for good. Understand what I'm saying, Miss Fannie? Crow coming over now. We gone take care of him."

Queenie scuttled about, trying to clean up the mess. She ran up and down the stairs more times than Fannie could count, bringing up towels to sop up the blood. Crow came into the room just as she was finishing up.

Crow took off his straw hat and scratched his head. "God Almighty."

"We worry about God later," Queenie snapped. "We got to get Muddy out of here before somebody sees him."

"How? He must weigh close to three hundred pounds," Crow said, scratching his head again.

"We gone roll him up in this here blanket and drag him down the steps. Then we gone put him in the trunk of the car and take him away where no one will find him. Soon as it get dark, we bring him down."

"See you got it all figured out," he said.

"Just do what I say," she fussed.

Crow shook his head and went down the stairs. Fannie could hear a car being backed into the driveway. Queenie rolled the body up in a blanket. When Crow came back into the room, they dragged the body down the stairs, Muddy's head making a loud thump each time it hit one of the steps. When they got him downstairs, Fannie could hear them arguing about what to do next.

"I don't think we gone be able to lift him in the car—he too heavy," Crow said.

"What else we gone do? Can't leave him here. We got to try. If that don't work, we come up with something else."

"Like what?"

"I don't know. Now come on, go out the back way."

Fannie heard the back door open and close. Then the house became quiet.

Fannie wasn't sure how long she lay there, listening to the creaking of the windows and the whoosh of the ceiling fan overhead. After a while, when the light in the room had dimmed and darkness set in, she got up and looked out the back window. Crow and Queenie were trying to lift the bundle into the trunk of the car, but no matter how much they tried, it kept falling back to the ground. They bickered about what to do for a few minutes.

Then Crow went into the garage and came back out with a wheelbarrow. Queenie tipped it forward as he rolled the body onto it. Then they disappeared around the corner, pushing the wheelbarrow up the alley toward the front of the house.

Fannie went across the hall into the spare bedroom that overlooked the front yard. Queenie had turned out all the lights in the house. There was no moon, and the front yard was so dark she had trouble seeing below. Even on a clear night, it was hard to see down into the yard, much of it obscured by the oak tree and the thick bamboo that lined the alley on the side of the house.

Fannie was peering into the shadows when Crow emerged, pushing the wheelbarrow, as Queenie walked beside him, carrying a shovel. They stopped beside a large hollow in the oak tree where the boys used to play castle when they were young, the massive size of the trunk obscuring their hideout from the street. Queenie handed Crow the shovel, and he began to dig. He must have shoveled dirt away from the roots of the tree for a good half hour. When he seemed satisfied, he pushed the wheelbarrow closer and tipped it into the hollow. The body tumbled into the ground. Queenie pulled the wheelbarrow away as Crow shoveled dirt back around the base of the tree. When he finished, Queenie jumped up and down on the ground, making sure the dirt was packed in. She nodded to Crow as she rubbed her hands together, and then they disappeared down the alley.

A little while later, Queenie came back upstairs to Fannie's bed. "Let's get you a nice bath, get you out of them clothes."

Fannie slipped off her dress and handed it to Queenie. There was blood on her slip.

Queenie shook her head. "Why Muddy done that to you?"

Fannie closed her eyes. She'd been trying not to think about that part.

"Don't you worry no more about Muddy," Queenie said. "You hear me? We done took care of it."

The next day, Queenie scrubbed and scrubbed the floor in the bedroom trying to get rid of the stain on the floor. No matter what she tried, she couldn't get rid of it. The blood had embedded itself into the grain of the wood.

"What are we going to do?" Fannie asked. "Norwood should be back by dinnertime. He'll notice that stain."

"We gone cover it up. I'll fetch the Oriental rug from the library downstairs and bring it up here."

"Won't he wonder why we've done that?" Fannie asked.

"I never knew a man that paid no mind to decorating, lessen it's something that gets in his way," Queenie said.

That evening Queenie prepared Norwood's favorite dinner, and Fannie did her best to act as if nothing had happened. Norwood appeared at the front door around six looking tan and fit from all the time he'd spent on the river. Fannie greeted him with a big kiss on the mouth.

"Been gone a week, and you act like I been gone a year," he said.

"Just missed you, that's all." She grabbed his hand and pulled him into the house.

"Crow plant some new flowers around the base of that old oak?" Norwood nodded toward the front yard. "Never known him to do that before. Looks nice."

Fannie steered his attention away from the tree. "Queenie made your favorite dinner, crawfish étouffée and stuffed mirliton. It's on the table waiting."

Queenie came down the hall to greet Norwood. "Welcome home, Mr. Norwood."

He gave her a sideways glance. "Thank you, Queenie. Something going on?"

"What you mean, Mr. Norwood?" she said, following him into the dining room.

"You all fussing over me like I been away at the war or something," he said as he took a seat at the table.

Fannie sat across from him. "Queenie, bring Norwood a tall glass so he can pour himself a drink."

Norwood picked up the whiskey bottle and looked at the label. "Mount Vernon? You know that's my favorite. What's the occasion? You pregnant again?"

Fannie felt the blood drain from her face. "No, of course not. Why would you say something like that?"

"My favorite dinner? The whiskey? You've never acted this way when I've come back from the river before."

Fannie shrugged. "Just missed you, that's all, darling."

After dinner, Norwood retired to the library, where he liked to read the newspaper and have a few drinks before bedtime. Fannie remained at the dinner table smoking a cigarette and reading a *LIFE* magazine as Queenie cleared the plates.

"Fannie, where's the carpet that used to be in here?" Norwood called out from the library.

Queenie and Fannie exchanged sharp glances before Norwood appeared in the dining room.

"Why, Mr. Norwood, I moved it up to your bedroom," Queenie said. "Fannie always say that bare floor up there was hard on her feet."

"If you say so." He shrugged and went back to the library.

"I thought you said he wouldn't notice," Fannie said in a hushed voice.

A little while later Norwood yelled from upstairs. "Fannie, would you come here a moment?"

She looked at Queenie, her eyes wide with fear.

"Go on, Miss Fannie. It'll be okay. Just don't say nothing," Queenie said.

"What if he notices the bruises on my legs?" Fannie asked. "Why do you think I got him that whiskey? I hoped he'd get drunk and fall asleep in the library tonight."

"Fannie?" Norwood called from the top of the stairs. "Where's the pistol that's usually in the drawer by the side of the bed?"

"What'd you do with it?" Fannie whispered.

"Got rid of it. Didn't think he'd notice. That pistol ain't been touched in years."

Fannie pushed herself away from the table. Her hands were beginning to shake.

"Stay calm, Miss Fannie."

When Fannie reached the bedroom, Norwood was standing by the side of the bed, rifling around in the drawer. The corner of the Oriental rug was askew, leaving a portion of the bloodstain visible. Fannie rushed forward and tried to kick the carpet back into place.

"I got rid of that old thing years ago," she said. "It made me nervous sitting in the drawer, loaded like it was. Could have hurt somebody."

Norwood gave her a peculiar look. "Every time I leave for a stint up the river, I check to see if that pistol is there. It was in the drawer when I left on Monday," he said. "Fannie, what's going on?"

She became flustered when she noticed the bloodstain was still visible. She burst into tears.

He sat on the edge of the bed. "What is it, honey? Whatever it is, you can tell me."

She didn't know what to do. He pulled her over to the bed. He put his arm around her shoulder. She sat on the edge of the bed next to him, but no matter how much she tried, she couldn't take her eyes off the bloodstain on the floor. She felt panic welling up inside her.

"Fannie?" he said, pointing at the floor. "What is that?"

She began to shake uncontrollably. She tried to get up and run from the room, but he caught her. He put his arm around her waist, then pulled the edge of the rug back.

"It looks like blood. Did you hurt yourself?"

She tried to push him away, but he was holding her so tightly she thought she might pass out.

"Fannie," he said in a stern voice, "tell me what happened."

Queenie appeared in the doorway. "Weren't her fault, Mr. Norwood. Muddy come around when I weren't here. Miss Fannie used the gun on him. He gone for good. Don't need to worry yourself about him no more."

He held Fannie by the shoulders and stared into her eyes. "Did he take advantage of you, Fannie?"

Her head wobbled. When she didn't answer, he tightened his grip on her shoulders.

"Answer me, baby. Did he rape you?" He shook her and began to weep.

Fannie couldn't look at him.

He glanced over at Queenie, looking for an answer.

"I'm sorry, Mr. Norwood," was all Queenie could say.

He pushed Fannie down onto the bed and ran out of the room.

Queenie bounded down the stairs after him. "Mr. Norwood, Mr. Norwood! Don't go!" she pleaded.

The whole house shook from the force of the front door slamming. Fannie could hear him backing the car out of the driveway. The bottom edge of the bumper hit the street and scraped as he put the car in gear and took off down the street, the tires screeching against the asphalt.

Fannie waited all the next day for him, and the next. On the fourth day, there was a knock at the door.

Queenie came up to her room. "Miss Fannie, I'm sorry to disturb you, but they is a Coast Guard officer at the front door with your friend Kennedy. They say they need to talk to you."

Fannie wiped a tear from her eye with a handkerchief. "Ask them what they want," she said through a sniffle.

"The Coast Guard man, he say he needs to talk to you . . . in person." Queenie came over to the bed to help her up.

When they got to the bottom of the stairs, the man asked Fannie to come into the front parlor and have a seat on the couch. He sat down next to her as Kennedy stood close by. Fannie noticed Kennedy was avoiding her eyes.

"Mrs. Bell, your husband, Norwood, has gone missing."

"I'm aware of that," Fannie said. "He left a couple of days ago, and I haven't seen him since."

"No, ma'am, what I'm trying to tell you is that one of the crew on the *Pelican II* said Mr. Norwood spent the last couple of days on the tug. The crew said he seemed upset, had been drinking. Captain Bell was a steady fella, from what I understand."

"I can vouch for that," Kennedy chimed in.

"What I'm trying to say, ma'am, is that it would take a lot to upset him. I'm told by his crew that he wasn't a big drinker, but they said he'd been drinking for days on end, ever since he got on the boat. Any idea what it was about?"

Fannie toyed with the handkerchief in her hands. "Why no, I have no idea."

"They said he slipped and fell off the boat yesterday afternoon while he was feeding the pelicans. He wasn't wearing a life vest. The wake from a passing ship evidently threw him off balance. The boys say they never saw him resurface."

Fannie kept her gaze on the floor, but her hands were shaking. "I see."

Kennedy added, "The Coast Guard has been scouring the river all night looking for your husband. At this point, Fannie dear, I'm not keeping my hopes up."

The look on his face confirmed her worst fears.

"I didn't mean to be so blunt, ma'am," the Coast Guard officer went on. "It's just that I suspect if we ever do find your husband . . ."

"I know what you're trying to say," she said, wringing the handkerchief.

"I'm sorry." The man got up to leave.

Kennedy came over to her. "I'll let you know if I hear anything."

"Thank you, Kennedy." She tried to smile. "I can always count on you."

Queenie showed them to the door.

Several weeks later, when news reached them that the Coast Guard had called off the search, Queenie moved all the furniture from Fannie's bedroom down to the library.

Fannie never set foot in that room again.

✣✣✣

"So you see, Miss Ibby, I think Fannie must have seen me and Crow bury Muddy that night," Queenie said. "Why you think she never wanted that tree cut down? She was afraid somebody gone find Muddy down in that hole. Some secrets should stay buried."

Ibby thought back to that day in the cemetery with Fannie. "Fannie told me Granddaddy Norwood went out with the pelicans. I had no idea what she meant, but now I think I understand."

"Never did find Mr. Norwood. Only a plaque out there at the cemetery."

"Queenie?"

"Yes, baby?"

"The other night I found Fannie upstairs trying to get into the room at the top of the stairs. She kept saying 'Little Mama.' What did she mean by that?"

Queenie looked over her shoulder at Ibby. "I'm sorry, baby. I said all I can say for one night. Now help me up. They must have found what they looking for by now."

The sun was just coming up as the Trouts pulled away from the house. Mr. Roosevelt arrived a few hours later to finish up the rest of the tree.

Oddly, Fannie didn't once come out to the porch to watch.

Chapter Thirty-Eight

All was quiet at the house the next afternoon until Crow appeared at the back door clutching his hat.

Ibby had never seen Crow look so distraught, not even the day he came to tell them that Purnell had been shot.

"What's wrong, Daddy?" Doll held the door open for him.

"Sit down, Queenie," he said as he came in. "It's bad."

"What could be so bad, Daddy?" Doll asked.

He dropped his head. "It's T-Bone. They come by the house just now and arrest him, take him away to jail."

Queenie scrambled to her feet. "What? What for?"

Crow glanced up. His hands were shaking. "For the rape of Miss Annabelle Friedrichs."

Queenie let out a wail so loud that Ibby thought the back windows might shatter. Fannie poked her head into the kitchen to see what was going on.

Queenie padded over to Fannie and draped her hands on her shoulders. "T-Bone, he just been arrested. You got to call your friend in the police department and get him out. Please, Miss Fannie. He didn't do nothing. They made a mistake."

"Calm down and tell me what happened." Fannie helped Queenie into a chair.

Queenie put her head in her hands. "You got to help him!"

Fannie touched her shoulder. "I can't help unless you tell me what's happened."

"They arrested T-Bone for rape," Doll said.

"They say he raped Miss Annabelle Friedrichs," Crow said.

"When?" Fannie asked.

"Last night," Crow said.

Fannie looked from person to person, waiting for an explanation. After a while, Doll broke the silence. "T-Bone didn't do it."

"How do you know for sure?" Fannie asked.

"Birdelia can speak for him. She was with him last night."

Fannie shook her head. "Doll, you know that won't help. We got an underage white girl accusing a black boy of rape. The police won't care what another colored girl has got to say in the matter."

"But there were other witnesses," Doll offered. "Don't that count?"

Fannie shook her head. "It's Annabelle Friedrichs's word against his."

Doll kept eyeing Ibby, trying to get her to speak up. She knew she should tell Fannie what happened, but she was afraid if she told Fannie the truth, she'd get in trouble. When Queenie slumped down and let out a whimper, Ibby knew she had no choice.

"He didn't do it," Ibby piped up.

"How would you know?" Fannie said.

"Because I was with T-Bone last night, too," she said.

Fannie squinted at her. "What do you mean?"

"Birdelia and I went over to see T-Bone play at Union Hall," Ibby said. "We left there about one-thirty in the morning, then went to see the chicken drop over at the Ebony Lounge."

"The police, they say it happened about three in the morning, according to Miss Annabelle's account," Crow chimed in.

Ibby shook her head. "She's lying. T-Bone was still with Birdelia and me."

"Why would she make it up?" Fannie asked.

Ibby spoke. "She was at the Ebony Lounge when we were there.

She tried to flirt with T-Bone, but she was so drunk, she could barely stand up. When we left, we saw her getting into her car. Someone got into the car with her, but it wasn't T-Bone."

"But why T-Bone? Why not name the boy she was with?" Fannie asked.

"T-Bone's been working at the stables over there in Audubon Park, where Miss Annabelle keeps a horse," Doll offered. "She knows him from there. Maybe she got mixed up, thought she was with him, when it were somebody else."

"T-Bone couldn't have done it," Ibby said. "She's just saying it to get back at me."

"Back at you? That's one heck of a way to get back at *you* by charging someone else with rape just for spite. I hate to tell you, Queenie, but I don't think I can do anything for T-Bone with that kind of charge against him, no matter how many phone calls I make. It's a white girl's word against a black boy. And to make it worse, she's not even eighteen. This is serious. I don't know what I can do except post the bail. Unless—" Fannie stopped short.

"Unless what, Miss Fannie?" Queenie was wringing her hands. "Unless what?"

"Unless we can get her to drop the charges," Fannie said finally. "That's the only way."

"It'd be a cold day in hell before Miss Annabelle gone admit she's wrong," Doll said. "She just ain't that kind of person."

"Yes, but that's all we have to go on right now." Fannie picked her car keys off the hook on the wall near the back door.

"Where you going?" Queenie asked.

"To pay Annabelle a visit," she said.

Ibby hopped up from the stool. "I'm coming with you."

"Fine. Let me make a quick phone call first. I think I'll ask Kennedy to meet us there, in case she does change her mind."

As they were heading out the door, Doll caught Ibby's arm. She grabbed her close and hugged her, then whispered, "Have strength in adversity, Miss Ibby. God will show you the right course. Remember that."

Ibby sat in the front seat of the car, studying her grandmother's profile as they drove along. She was thinking about everything Queenie had told her the night before, and it made her realize how someone's life can change in an instant. If Queenie had been at the house the day Muddy came around, he would have gotten his money and left, and Norwood might not have gone off on his boat. She thought about her father, falling and hitting that rock. If it hadn't been raining that day, would he still be alive? Then she thought about T-Bone, how his life was about to change just because he happened to be at the Ebony Lounge last night when Annabelle Friedrichs was there.

Fannie glanced over and caught Ibby staring at her. "What is it, Ibby? Is there something you want to tell me? Because I don't want any surprises when we get there."

"No, ma'am, just thinking."

"About what, dear?"

"About life, I guess."

Ibby was wondering, was it possible to change a person's fate? As they pulled up to the Friedrichses' apartment on Magazine Street, she figured she was about to find out.

Kennedy was already there, leaning up against his squad car, waiting for them. "Good day, Miss Fannie." He tipped his cap.

"Good day to you, Kennedy," she said. "Thanks for meeting me here."

"I understand you may have information that contradicts the statement Miss Friedrichs gave at the station this morning," he said.

"Between you and me, Kennedy, I'd like to forget about this whole mess," Fannie said as she untied the scarf from her head and stuffed it into her pocketbook.

"How do you propose to do that?" he asked.

"By getting little Miss Friedrichs to see the error of her ways and drop any charges she may be planning to make against T-Bone," Fannie said as they walked up the front walk.

Kennedy didn't look very optimistic.

"Would you mind staying just outside the door, in case we need you?" Fannie asked.

"Sure thing." He stood off to the side as she rang the bell.

The door opened just a crack. When Honey Friedrichs saw Fannie, she tried to slam the door, but Fannie stuck her foot against the jamb.

"What do you want?" Honey demanded.

"I want to talk to Annabelle." Fannie now had her hand on the door, fighting with Honey, as she tried to open it.

"Go away. She has nothing to say to you." Honey tried to kick Fannie's foot from the threshold.

"I have evidence that she doesn't quite have her facts straight. Before we go to the police and charge her with perjury, I thought she'd like to hear what we have to say. Otherwise we'll be heading down to the police station with Commander Kennedy here."

Fannie nodded in his direction. He stepped forward so Honey could see him.

"What kind of information?" Honey asked, still trying to wrestle the door from Fannie.

"If you let Ibby and me in, I'll tell you," Fannie said.

Honey opened the door just enough to let them in.

Honey Friedrichs hadn't aged well. Her face was puffy and her nose red from too much alcohol, and her hair looked as if it hadn't seen a comb in quite some time. Annabelle was sprawled on the couch with a blanket pulled up to her chest. She had a black eye and there were bruises on her neck.

"What are they doing here?" Annabelle shrieked.

"They want to talk to you," her mother said.

"I don't have anything to say. Tell them to leave!" Annabelle demanded, pointing to the door.

"If you don't talk to them, they say they're going down to the police station to give a statement," Honey said.

"Well, let them." Annabelle turned her head.

"Annabelle, I have reason to believe that T-Bone Trout wasn't with you last night," Fannie said in a surprisingly soothing voice. "Or any other night for that matter."

"How would you know? He raped me, then beat me up and left me to die." She glared at Fannie with such ferocity that Ibby thought she might leap up and tackle Fannie to the ground.

"No, he didn't, Annabelle," Fannie said calmly.

"Yes, he did!" she screamed.

Honey put her hand on Annabelle's shoulder.

"Get off me!" She yanked her mother's hand away.

"You're lying," Ibby said.

When Annabelle's head swiveled around, her eyes were wild. "How dare you!" She pointed at Ibby. "Get out! Mama, send them away!"

"You weren't with T-Bone last night. I was."

"You slut!" Annabelle hissed.

"Call me what you want," Ibby said. "But he wasn't with you. He was with me, and Birdelia, the whole night. We have witnesses who can testify that it's true."

"I don't care what you say. You're just covering up for him. It's my word against his." Annabelle's face tightened.

"Annabelle, do you know what they do to people who make false charges?" Fannie gave her a stern look.

"I don't have to talk to them. Mama, make them leave. Why'd you let them in in the first place?" She pushed her mother away from the couch.

Fannie went on. "Let me tell you how it will go down if you don't drop the charges. They'll put you up on the witness stand—"

"So?" Annabelle interrupted.

"And they'll hear about how you were having sex in the stables," Ibby chimed in.

"What?" Honey's head shot around.

"Don't listen to her, Mama. She's making it up." Annabelle glared at Ibby.

"Then they'll hear from several more eyewitnesses as to how you liked to tie your horse up down by the batture and have sex under the willow trees." Ibby kept her eyes on Annabelle as she spoke.

"That's not true! She's lying." Annabelle wagged her finger wildly at Ibby.

"Then several more witnesses will testify that Monday night wasn't the first time you had been to the Ebony Lounge. They'll testify that you'd been there on several occasions. And each time, you had sex with men in the backseat of your car, which you had a habit of parking right out front."

"Annabelle!" Honey cried.

"Shut up, Mama."

"I saw you get in your car that night," Ibby said. "But it wasn't with T-Bone, because T-Bone was standing right next to me, with Birdelia on the other side of him. We saw a man get into your car. So did Shorty. So did the bartender at the Ebony Lounge. So did the officer who was on duty that night, who was standing just outside the door to the Ebony Lounge, the same officer who happens to be standing just outside your door right now."

Kennedy coughed into his hand.

Annabelle sat upright. Her mouth flew open.

"Then, if that's not enough for you, the lawyers will start on Miss Honey here." Ibby tilted her head. "They'll say how the apple doesn't fall far from the tree. They'll outline her affair with Mr. Jeffreys down the street." Ibby was spitting out her words.

"Calm down." Fannie grabbed Ibby's arm.

She yanked it away. "They'll show that's why your father left your mother. They'll go into the rest of your mother's sexual exploits, just to prove that her daughter is just like she is."

Honey Friedrichs put her hands on her hips. "Annabelle Friedrichs, you tell me the truth. That boy do this, or were you just whoring around again?" She bent over until her face was just a few inches from Annabelle's. "Answer me, or I swear to God I'll beat the living daylights out of you."

"Annabelle," Fannie said calmly, "all you have to do is drop the charges against T-Bone. Seems like a sweet deal to me. If I were you, I'd take it. Otherwise, we'll see you in court."

Annabelle was looking from her mother to Ibby, her mouth agape.

"Well?" Fannie tapped her foot. "I don't have all day."

"Okay," Annabelle said quietly.

"What did you say?" Honey asked.

Annabelle threw the blanket down. "Okay! I said okay!"

"Say it out loud. Say T-Bone didn't rape you," Ibby said.

Annabelle made a face.

"Say it, for the record," Ibby said.

"He didn't do it."

"Just to make clear. You will be going down to the station and signing a piece of paper stipulating that all accusations against T-Bone have been dropped. Is that correct?" Fannie said.

Annabelle stood. "Yes."

"Now, why don't you go down to the station with Commander Kennedy, and we'll be on our way. You heard all that, didn't you, Peter?" Fannie called.

Kennedy stuck his head in through the door. "Yes, ma'am."

"Why'd you do it, Ibby? Why didn't you just let it be?" Annabelle whined.

"I couldn't let you ruin his life," Ibby said.

"Why? He's just a—" Annabelle cried.

Ibby wagged a finger at Annabelle. "Don't go there. T-Bone Trout has more class in his little pinky than you'll ever have."

Annabelle lunged at her, but Honey held her back.

Ibby felt Fannie's grip on her shoulder. "Time to go."

Kennedy escorted Annabelle and Honey to his squad car. As soon as he drove off, Fannie started her car.

"I'm mighty proud of what you did in there, Ibby. It took a lot of courage. I'm just curious, though. Was that all true?" Fannie asked.

Ibby looked the other way, out the car window. The sun was sitting low in the sky, hovering over the horizon as if it didn't want to let go. She gave her grandmother a half smile. "Most of it."

Fannie patted her on the knee and gave her a wry smile back. "That's my girl."

Ibby remembered what Fannie had said in the cemetery not long ago. She said you had to live the life given to you. *Maybe that's true,* Ibby thought as she watched the last vestiges of the day fade away.

But sometimes it's possible to give life back.

Part Three

1972

Chapter Thirty-Nine

It was late May, and Ibby was studying for her last exam, hunched over her desk as the window unit blasted cold air her way, riffling the pages of her history book. She'd stayed up most of the night cramming and was having trouble concentrating. She picked up the postcard she used as a bookmark and was about stick it into the book so she could get some coffee when she turned it over. The edges of the card were frayed, and the writing on the other side had almost completely faded. It was a postcard from T-Bone, one he'd sent from Germany when he'd first left to tour with a band in Europe four years ago. He'd been there ever since.

Ibby looked at her watch. It was almost five o'clock. She still had a lot of studying to do. When she'd enrolled at Tulane University two years earlier, she'd moved out of Fannie's house and into an apartment across town with the promise that she'd spend every Sunday evening with Fannie. She hadn't missed a Sunday supper in two years. She was so far behind in her studying that she was seriously thinking about calling Fannie to cancel when the phone rang.

"Miss Ibby?" Doll said.

"I know I'm late," Ibby replied.

"I think you should come around," Doll said.

"I don't think I'm going to be able to make it tonight, Doll. I've got my European history exam tomorrow, and I'm just not ready for it yet. I'm afraid I'm going to have to skip supper." She was feeling guilty. She knew Queenie had already prepared a big meal in anticipation of her weekly visit.

"No, Miss Ibby, I think you need to come," Doll repeated.

Ibby held the phone out from her ear, wondering what had her all riled up. "I'm sorry but I'm really behind in my studies."

"Miss Ibby, I need you to come on by *now*."

"Is something wrong?" she asked.

There was no answer—Doll had hung up. Ibby held on to the phone receiver, thinking what an odd conversation they'd just had.

She got up from her desk and stood by the window, watching the other students that had already finished their exams heading over to Bruno's Tavern. She wished she was one of them. She thought about what Doll had just said. Perhaps a break might do her some good. And Queenie's courtbouillon, fried okra, and bread pudding would be just what she needed to get her through the long night of studying ahead. She slipped on her clogs and headed for the door.

When she arrived at Fannie's house, Doll was standing on the front porch, obviously upset about something. Ibby noticed Fannie's car wasn't in the driveway.

"Come on in, Miss Ibby," Doll said.

Queenie was in the front hall, wringing her hands. "We didn't know what else to do, Miss Ibby, so we call you."

"Where's Fannie?" Ibby followed Queenie into the dining room, where two places were set for the evening meal.

"Miss Fannie, she went out for a drive, but she ain't come back," Doll said.

The grandfather clock in the hall chimed six times.

"Maybe she forgot the time," Ibby offered. "She could just be late. You know how she gets sometimes when she drives around in that car."

"Miss Fannie, she left the house early this afternoon. She never goes out for more than an hour or two," Queenie said. "We kept waiting around, thinking she'd be back, but she been gone a good five hours now."

"Besides," Doll added, "she knows you come around for supper about this time. She'd never miss that."

"Do you know where she went?" Ibby asked.

"She never tells us. But I know sometimes she goes out to visit the family in the cemetery," Doll said.

"What do you want me to do, drive around and look for her?" Ibby asked.

Queenie heaved up her chest. "Yes, Miss Ibby. That might be a good idea."

"All right then, I'll go out to the cemetery, see if she's there."

"Come on, Mama. Let's get back to the kitchen." Doll took her mother's arm. "Maybe she show up soon, then you can quit your worrying."

Queenie swatted her arm. "Like you ain't worried."

Ibby was sure Fannie would turn up sooner or later, she always did, but by the time she reached the cemetery, the gates were locked for the evening. She drove to the racetrack, to the perfume shop, anywhere she thought Fannie might be, but after an hour she gave up. When she returned to the house, Fannie's car was still not in the driveway.

Queenie and Doll were both waiting on the front porch this time.

"Well?" Queenie asked.

Ibby shook her head. "She hasn't called?"

"No, Miss Ibby. Where could she be?" Queenie's eyes began to well up.

Ibby put her arm around her shoulders. "Let's go in the kitchen and figure it out."

They all sat down at the kitchen table.

"Has anyone called the police?" Ibby asked.

"We didn't want to do nothing until you got back, in case you found her," Doll said.

"Do you have Commander Kennedy's phone number?" Ibby asked.

"It's in that little book Miss Fannie keeps by the telephone." Doll pointed toward the hall.

Ibby dialed the number. "May I speak to Commander Kennedy?"

"Speaking."

"Kennedy, this is Ibby Bell."

"You caught me just as I was leaving. What can I do for you? How is Fannie?"

"Well, actually, that's why I'm calling. She seems to have gone missing. She left the house this afternoon and hasn't returned. We're getting a little worried. You haven't heard of any accidents or anything, have you?"

"Let me check." Ibby could hear him scoot away from his desk. He came back on the phone a few minutes later. "I don't see any that would correlate. Do you want me to file a report?"

Ibby hesitated. "No, I'm sure she'll turn up. You know how she is."

"I'll call if I hear anything."

Ibby put down the receiver and went back into the kitchen. She sat back down at the table, trying to appear chipper.

"What he say?" Queenie asked.

"He said there weren't any reports of accidents, but he said he'll call if he has any news," she said.

Queenie set a plate in front of Ibby. "Best go on and eat. Getting pert near eight o'clock."

Ibby picked up a fork and chewed on a piece of okra. "Tell you what. I'll get my books and study here in case Fannie shows up. Why don't you all take some supper and go on home? I'll call if I hear anything."

Queenie and Doll looked at each other.

Ibby could tell this wasn't sitting too well with them. "No use everybody sitting around here panicking. Besides, how am I going to study with you two fretting?" she said.

"Miss Ibby's right. Come on, Mama," Doll said.

"I'm gone leave Miss Fannie a plate in the oven, case she do come back," Queenie said.

After they left, Ibby finished her supper, then drove to her apartment to get her books. She half-expected to find Fannie sitting in the dining room smoking a cigarette when she returned. But when she pulled up to the house, it was dark.

Ibby went in and sat at the kitchen table. She opened her textbook, trying to get in a bit more studying, but the house was so quiet it was making her nervous. Every five minutes or so, she'd get up and look out the back window. When it got to be midnight, there was no doubt in her mind that Fannie was in trouble. Sometime during the night, she dozed off on the lumpy couch in the front parlor.

She was awakened by the sound of the back door slamming at six-thirty the next morning. Queenie came into the kitchen grumbling because the oven had been left on all night, the plate of food she'd left for Miss Fannie still in it.

"Like to have burned the whole house down," Queenie was saying as Ibby came into the kitchen.

"Ain't a good sign, Mama. Means Miss Fannie ain't here," Doll said.

"Morning," Ibby said groggily.

"You stay up all night, Miss Ibby?"

"Most of it." Ibby yawned.

"No phone calls?" Queenie asked.

Ibby shook her head.

"Lawd Almighty." Queenie fell back down onto a stool.

"I really hate to leave, but I have an exam at eight. I'll come straight back when I'm finished." She saw the way Doll was looking at her. "Maybe I should skip it. I'll see if I can get in touch with the professor."

"No, no. We here in case she come home. You go on. Hope we have good news when you get back," Queenie said.

Ibby had trouble concentrating on the exam. All she could think about was Fannie. It had been almost twenty-four hours and no news. She put down her pencil and rubbed her eyes. This was a dumb idea. She handed in her exam early and left. When she got back to Prytania Street, there was a car in the driveway, but it wasn't Fannie's.

As she opened the back door, she heard voices in the dining room. Queenie and Doll were sitting at the table with Emile Rainold.

Queenie came barreling over. "Oh Miss Ibby! Miss Ibby!"

She hugged Ibby so hard she almost knocked the wind out of her. Ibby had never seen her so distraught.

Please let Fannie be all right, Ibby was praying as she took a seat at the table.

Emile reached over and put his hand on hers. "I'm afraid I have some bad news. The police found a car in Lake Pontchartrain this morning."

Her arms fell to her sides when the gist of what he was saying slowly sank in.

Mr. Rainold paused before continuing. "There is no way of knowing for sure, but they believe Fannie may have stepped on the gas instead of the brake, accidentally plunging the car into the lake. I'm so sorry."

Ibby imagined her grandmother looking at her watch, realizing that it was time to go home and have supper, and then hitting the gas pedal hard, the way she always did when she backed out of the driveway, only this time the car would lunge forward, hurdling over the seawall and into the water.

"Miss Ibby?" Doll said. "You okay?"

"I'm sorry." Ibby sighed. "I was just thinking about Fannie, out there . . . all alone." Her voice trailed off and she hung her head. *Why couldn't I have been there to help her?*

"She may have had a heart attack," Mr. Rainold said after a while. "There was no sign of struggle."

"Where is she now?" Ibby asked, her voice almost a whisper.

"Bultman's Funeral Home is taking care of the arrangements. She's evidently built a sizable tomb for the family out at the cemetery."

"Yes, I know all about that," she said.

"As per her wishes," he said, "there is to be a small service at the Holy Trinity Episcopal Church, then the burial for family only out at the cemetery."

Mr. Rainold must have noticed the puzzlement in her face. Ibby had never heard Fannie mention any kind of religious affiliation.

"Fannie gave quite a bit of money to the Holy Trinity Church over the years," he added.

No one said anything for quite some time.

"I expect the earliest the funeral can take place is Thursday. This is such a shock to all of us," he said. "Ibby, you know I was a great admirer of your grandmother's. She was quite a woman."

When no one spoke, he picked up his briefcase and stood up.

As soon as he left, Ibby's head fell into her hands and she began to sob.

Queenie came over and put her arm around Ibby. "It gone be all right, Miss Ibby."

She sank her face into Queenie's chest. Queenie rocked her as if she were a baby. She could hear Doll sniffling close by.

"Well, you knew she weren't just gone die in her sleep," Doll said after a while.

Queenie looked over at her. "Ain't that the truth. No, not our Miss Fannie."

Doll and Queenie always did know how to make Ibby laugh, even in the worst of times.

৩౮౷౮

The next morning Mr. Rainold came back with some papers for Ibby to sign.

"Bultman's Funeral Home has placed the obituary in the newspaper. Fannie wrote it herself years ago." He handed a copy to her.

Ibby glanced at it. The obituary was so lengthy it must have taken Fannie years to write. It included things Ibby hadn't known about Fannie, such as that she had a baby sister who had died when she was only three and that she'd missed a beloved dog named Max she'd found as a stray when she was eleven. Then it listed about fifty charities she'd given money to over the years. "I had no idea," Ibby said after a while. "Fannie never mentioned these things."

Emile Rainold nodded. "She was a very mysterious but generous woman."

"And where did this picture come from?" Ibby asked. "I've never seen it."

"She had a photographer take it several years ago. It's quite becoming, don't you think?" he said. "She was a handsome woman."

Queenie came in to serve coffee.

"It says she was sixty. Did she write that?" Ibby asked, squinting over at Mr. Rainold.

"No, she had left that blank," he said. "I had to fill in some of the final details. She didn't have a birth certificate, so I had to rely on her word."

"That be about right," Queenie said. "I think she was barely eighteen when she and Mr. Norwood moved into this here house."

"The services are planned for Thursday morning at ten-thirty," Mr. Rainold added.

"That gone give me only two days to cook. How many you think gone come by after the funeral? Couple hundred?" Queenie asked.

"A couple of hundred?" Ibby gawked. "I thought you said she planned a small funeral."

"Small to Miss Fannie ain't the same thing as small to you and me," Queenie said.

"I think Queenie's right. Fannie knew a lot of people in a lot of different circles," Mr. Rainold said.

"I better get started." Queenie rushed off toward the kitchen.

"Ibby," he said in a low voice. "Are you up to going over the will? We can wait if you like."

She took in a breath. "We've got to do it sooner or later so let's get it over with."

"There's not much to it, really," he said.

As Mr. Rainold read Fannie's last will and testament, his words were all a jumble, floating over her head. She felt as if a bulldozer had run over her, then backed up to make sure she was squished flat. Nothing was registering.

"It's fairly straightforward," Mr. Rainold went on. "Fannie wished for Queenie and Doll to take some memento from the house, anything they like."

She fidgeted with the edges of her shirt. "Okay."

"She took the liberty of paying off the remainder of your college tuition at Tulane, as well as Birdelia's at Southern University," he added. "So at least you don't have to worry about that." He put the document down on the table. "There isn't much else left in the estate, except for this house, which she willed to you." He pointed at various objects. "Now I see she has some things of value, such as those Drysdale paintings on the wall and all that Newcomb pottery in the china cabinet, which you could probably sell at auction." He peered at her over his reading glasses. "And there's about five thousand dollars in a bank account. But she never did keep much cash in the bank."

"She never trusted banks after the Depression," she said. "That much I know."

He touched her hand. "I know this is all happening so fast. I'll let you think on it. You don't have to do anything about it now. I just wanted you to know where things stood."

He got up and let himself out.

Ibby sat at the table for a good long while after he left. She thought about what Fannie had said after Purnell died. She said people should have proper funerals so everyone could say their last goodbyes. Fannie had spent so much of her life worrying about where she was going to be buried. In an odd way, it seemed strange that she wasn't here to witness her own send-off.

Ibby could hear Queenie banging around in the kitchen. Whatever it was Queenie was cooking was making her hungry.

"Now, Miss Ibby, don't you fret," Queenie said as Ibby came into the kitchen. "We gone take care of everything. I done this so many times I could put on a funeral in my sleep."

Ibby forced a smile. "Thank you, Queenie. I don't know what I'd do without you."

"Now listen, baby. This is what's gone happen. By the time we get back from the burial, people gone be lined up at the door waiting to get in the house so they can get their fill of food and drink. They gone hang around all afternoon, and some into the night, before they take their leave. And they gone all tell you how much they adored Miss Fannie, whether they liked her or not." Queenie gave out a light chuckle.

Ibby didn't laugh.

"Come on, Miss Ibby. Got to carry on."

Ibby looked up at her. "I just don't feel like it right now."

"I know you're sad, but that ain't the way Miss Fannie would have wanted it. She had a good life, all in all, and she loved you. That's what you need to keep in your heart. Remember the good times. Like when that tree came through the window and Miss Fannie was trapped like a caged bird. Remember that? Remember how she looked?"

That brought a smile to Ibby's face.

"That's what I like to see." Queenie patted Ibby on the back. "Now listen, I gone do all the cooking. Doll can whip up a nice black funeral dress for you. Crow can bartend. That's about all there is to it." She shook her head. "We sure gone miss that old lady."

Ibby smiled again. Queenie always did refer to Fannie as "that old lady" even though Fannie was younger than Queenie.

Doll came into the kitchen. "Miss Ibby, Mr. Rainold told me to pick out Miss Fannie's burial clothes. You care?"

"Why don't you pick out a nice dress," Ibby said as the doorbell rang.

"Oh, and another thing," Queenie said as Doll hurried past them to answer the door. "I expect that doorbell gone be ringing every few minutes. The second word gets out that Miss Fannie has passed, people gone start dropping off food."

Doll came into the kitchen holding a brown paper bag. "Mr. Rainold done sent a honey-glazed ham over. Right good-sized one, from the looks of it."

Ibby wiped a tear from her cheek. "Before I forget. Mr. Rainold said that Fannie wanted you each to have something from the house, so take whatever you like."

Queenie pointed toward the front parlor. "Miss Fannie, she been real kind to us over the years. Real generous. But if you don't mind, I know Crow be delighted to take that big TV off your hands."

"It's yours," Ibby said. "Doll, what about you?"

Doll wrinkled her nose in a thinking sort of way. "I believe I'd like to have me that bust of Miss Fannie that's in the upstairs hall."

Queenie scrunched up her face as if it were the most ridiculous thing she'd ever heard. "What you want that ugly thing for? They a reason she put that upstairs, you know, so nobody have to look at it."

"Can't explain it, Mama. Just kind of growed on me over the years. Less, a course, you want it, Miss Ibby."

Ibby waved her hand. "You're welcome to it."

"Where you gone put that thing? Not in my living room!" Queenie balked. "Nosiree, not in my house."

"Don't worry, Mama, I find a good place for it," Doll said.

"It better be a place out a my sight," Queenie said. "That all I ask. It give me a heart attack just thinking about it."

❧❦❧

On Thursday morning, a limousine showed up to take them to the church. When they arrived, there was a waiting line to get into the front door.

"Lawd, look at all them people," Queenie said as the limo turned the corner. "Think the whole city done showed up."

"So much for a small funeral," Doll added.

They were escorted through a side door to a private chapel to wait for the service.

"Look at that," Ibby said, pointing to a sign over the door. "The Frances Bell Chapel. Fannie donated a chapel to the church. I wonder why she never told anybody about it."

It was a beautiful little chapel with stained-glass windows and embroidered cushions on the pews.

"I bet they is a lot she never told nobody about," Queenie said. "Could have lived to be a hundred, and we still wouldn't know what she was all about."

At precisely ten-thirty, a deacon led them into the church filled with music being played by a harpist and instructed them to sit in the front row. Fannie's closed casket, decorated with a mound of white lilies, rested on a cloth-draped gurney at the bottom of steps that led up to the altar.

"I wish T-Bone could have been here," Ibby whispered to Queenie. "That's the one thing missing. Fannie would have loved for him to play at her funeral."

"I know, baby. He would have liked that, but there was just no way to get him back in time," Queenie said.

As the preacher came down the aisle carrying a cross atop a wooden pole, a soloist in the choir balcony began to sing "Amazing Grace." When she finished, the preacher took his place behind the pulpit.

"Please stand." He raised his arms. "We are here to honor the passing of a very great lady. . . ."

The rest of his words were a blur, but the first ones stuck with Ibby. *We are here to honor a very great lady.*

After a sermon, the preacher said, "Fannie's granddaughter, Ibby, has asked Saphronia Trout to say a few words. Saphronia?"

Queenie scooted out of the pew and made her way up the steps. The preacher stepped aside, and Queenie came up and stood behind the pulpit.

"Hello, everybody." She poked at the microphone, testing it to make sure it was on. "Miss Ibby asked me to say a few words about her grandmother, but I don't know if just a few would be enough to say what I want to say about Miss Fannie."

Queenie's remark caused a buzz of laughter to erupt in the church.

"Miss Fannie, she were like no other lady I ever met," Queenie went on. "I worked for her for over forty years, which is why Miss Ibby asked me to say something about her. I knew her longer than just about anybody here, with a few exceptions." She nodded at Kennedy and Sister Gertrude. "But I think we can all agree, Fannie lived her life the way she wanted to. She didn't worry about what other people thought. That's because she didn't need to. She was a giving-back kind of person, and each person she touched"—she pointed at the audience—"and you know who you are, will always remember it. That's why just about everybody in this church is here, she touched all of you in some way."

Ibby wept softly as she listened.

When Queenie finished, she came and sat in the pew next to Ibby. She patted Ibby on the knee. Ibby grabbed her hand and squeezed it.

Then the organist started playing "Flee as a Bird," whereupon hundreds of white doves were let out of cages as the casket was wheeled out of the church. It was a beautiful gesture, Ibby thought as she watched the birds circle around overhead, then dart through the front doors over the heads of people leaving the church.

"Well, you knew she had to do *something* crazy," Queenie said as they got in the waiting limousine.

After the service, they went to the cemetery, where Fannie was buried in the magnificent marble tomb she'd had built for herself. After the final words were said, Queenie threw in some baking powder for good measure, to make sure she rose up on Judgment Day and not the other way around.

By the time the limo pulled into the driveway at the house, people were lined up all the way down the block.

"Lawd, look at them all." Queenie got out of the car and fussed at Crow. "Hurry up, old man. We got work to do."

Pretty soon, there was a dull roar in the house.

Ibby didn't feel much like talking so she made her way back to the kitchen. Queenie came in carrying an empty tray.

"What you doing in here, having your own pity party? You get on out there and greet them folks. They came 'cause of Miss Fannie," Queenie said as she loaded up another tray with mushrooms. "You hear me? This ain't about you."

Queenie tugged at Ibby's arm until she got up from the table, then she pushed Ibby into the dining room. There were so many people hovering around the table, picking at the food, that you would have thought no one had eaten for weeks. Ibby tried to squeeze past them, but a woman Ibby didn't recognize tapped her on the shoulder and spoke to her as she stuffed boudin balls in her mouth.

"I'm so sorry about your grandmother," she said. "She was such a fine lady."

"Thank you," Ibby said, brushing past her.

Mr. Jeffreys, Commander Kennedy, the Reverend Jeremiah, Sister Gertrude, Mr. Henry, Mr. Pierce—they were all there. The neighbors on Prytania Street came, as did their maids at the special invitation of Queenie. The mayor made an appearance. Even Lucy the duck lady rolled around on her skates, relegated to the front yard because Queenie wouldn't let her in the house with her ducks.

When Ibby felt she'd spoken to everyone, she excused herself and went upstairs.

The stained-glass window looked naked without the bust of Fannie holding court in front of it. Ibby went over to the door just across from the stairs, that one that had remained locked all these years. To her surprise, when she tried the knob, it turned. She opened the door to find a bare room with a large brown stain on the floor not far from the window. Ibby decided to leave the door open.

She wandered over to the next door, to her father's old room, and opened the door. She rubbed her hands over her arms. It had been eight years since her father died. It seemed a lifetime ago. So many things had changed since then. She let her hand linger on the knob before heading over to Balfour's room. When she tried the handle, it was also unlocked. The room appeared to have been left untouched since the day Balfour died. There were bubblegum wrappers crumpled up on the table beside the bed, and a pair of shorts lying on the floor. Except for the spiderweb hanging from the ceiling fan, it looked as if Balfour had just gone down the hall to take a bath. She felt the room was still waiting for him, so she left the door open.

"You're all free now," she said.

Chapter Forty

Doll and Queenie were in the kitchen cleaning up after everyone left.

Queenie was at the sink washing dishes. "Let me ask you something, Doll. Miss Fannie, she say anything to you before she left in her car that day? You know, anything peculiar like?"

Doll dried the dishes as Queenie handed them to her. "Well, she say she thought I ought to open my own business, a dressmaking shop, but it weren't the first time she brought that up. Why, Mama, she say something to you?"

"She said it about time I retire," Queenie said. "Retire. Can you imagine?"

"Well, you are getting up in years, Mama. You almost seventy. And you been working since you were eleven years old."

"What that got to do with it? How was I gone retire with Miss Fannie around?" Queenie leaned on the counter. "You think she drove off into the lake on purpose?"

Doll quit drying the dish she was holding and stared at the ground.

"You know something you ain't telling me?"

Doll nodded.

"Spit it out." Queenie wiped her hands on her apron.

"Mama, sit down," Doll said.

"Just tell me."

"No, Mama. Come sit. You're not gone believe."

She sat down at the table and Doll came and sat next to her. "Doll, you got that look in your eyes. She say something to you that day?"

Doll pulled Fannie's pearls from her pocket and held them in the palm of her hand.

"What you doing with those? I thought they were lost when Miss Fannie went into the lake."

"No, Mama. She done give them to me that morning."

"Why she do that?"

"She called me into her room while she was getting dressed. Said she wanted to talk to me."

☙ ⊙⊙ ❧

The day started like any other. Miss Fannie was in her room getting dressed before Mr. Henry came by to take her bets. Doll was passing in the hall when Miss Fannie called out to her.

"Doll, that you?"

"Yes, Miss Fannie."

"Come in here a moment, will you?"

Doll stopped, wondering why Miss Fannie was being so polite. She usually just yelled Doll's name out as loud as she could so Doll would come running.

Doll stuck her head in the door. "You need something?"

Fannie was at her dressing table, staring at herself in the mirror. She motioned for Doll to come over.

"What you want?" Doll stood just inside the door. She wasn't in the mood to listen to any of Fannie's foolishness this morning.

"I just want to talk to you," Fannie said.

"Well, hurry up 'cause I got lots of things to do."

"Please, Doll. Come over here."

Doll's eyes grew wide. Miss Fannie never said "please."

Fannie was holding her pearls.

"You need me to help you put your pearls on? That it?" Doll asked.

"You know how much these pearls mean to me," Fannie was saying.

"'Course I do. Mr. Norwood give them to you on your wedding day. Not a day you ain't had them on since."

Doll was afraid Fannie was about to launch into the story of how Mr. Norwood had given her the pearls. But Fannie just sat there, staring at the string of pearls in her hand.

"Miss Fannie, something wrong? You thinking about Mr. Norwood?"

Fannie looked up at her with steely eyes. There was something funny about those eyes today.

"No, Doll, I was thinking about you," she said.

"Me? Why you thinking about me?"

"Kneel down."

"What? Why?" Doll thought it was an odd request, even coming from Miss Fannie.

"I want to talk to you face-to-face," Fannie said.

"Well, okay, but you could stand up, you know," Doll said as she dropped to her knees.

"I know how much you've always admired these pearls," Fannie said.

"Well, yeah. So?"

"Give me your hand."

Miss Fannie is acting mighty strange this morning, Doll thought as she held out her palm.

Fannie placed the pearls in her hand. "I want you to have them."

"What? No!" She tried to give them back. "You love them pearls."

"That's why I want you to have them." Fannie closed Doll's fingers around them and placed her hand on top of hers. "Because I love you."

"Miss Fannie, you just feeling all sentimental this morning," Doll said, trying to put the pearls back on the dresser.

Fannie waved her off. "Doll, I mean it. I've been thinking about it for a long time. I want you to have them."

"Well, okay." She stuck them in her pocket, sure Miss Fannie was going to change her mind later in the day. "I'll just keep them for you until you want them back."

"You do that," Fannie said as she put on some lipstick. "And I want you to start thinking about that dress shop you've been wanting to open. Now is as good a time as any, don't you think?"

ᏣᎶᏬᏬ

Queenie shook her head. "Why didn't you say nothing?"

"What I'm gone say, Mama? If I had told you, you would have thought the same thing I did, that she was just having one of her moments and was gone ask for them pearls back when she returned."

"And she never came back," Queenie mumbled.

"No, she didn't," Doll said, looking down at the pearls in her hand.

Queenie stood up and kissed her on the head. "I'm glad she gave them to you. You deserve them."

"Yeah, but Mama, what's Miss Ibby gone say? Miss Fannie should have given them to her."

"We'll let her know when the time is right. But not today. Just keep it to yourself until we can figure out how to tell her."

"Think I should just give them to her, pretend Miss Fannie never gave them to me?" Doll asked.

"No, baby. Miss Fannie wanted you to have them. Miss Ibby will understand, once we tell her."

"Okay, if you say so." Doll put the pearls back in her pocket.

"When the time comes, we'll tell her," Queenie said. "I just got to figure out when that might be."

Chapter Forty-One

Ibby was sound asleep at her apartment when the phone rang the next morning.

"Mama wants you to come by our house," Doll said. "And she wants you to bring one of them dolls."

"What? Why?" Ibby asked.

"She just do. Don't matter which one," Doll said.

"Okay, but I have to go over to Fannie's house to pick one up. They're up in my room where I left them when I moved out."

"No hurry, just come when you can," Doll said.

When Ibby pulled up in front of the house on Prytania Street, the weathervane on the roof was spinning around so fast the horse looked as if it were chasing its own tail.

"Well, I guess you're free too," Ibby said as she got out of the car.

She went in through the front door and stood in the hall. It was strange being in this house, all alone, the only sound coming from the swaying of the pendulum of the grandfather clock. The dining room table where Fannie usually sat in the mornings was empty, not even a place setting. Ibby caught her reflection in the gold-leaf mirror over the fireplace, just the way she had that first day when her mother dropped her off. She'd been a scared little girl who thought her life was ending. She was staring back as a grown woman now who knew that her life hadn't ended that day—it had just started.

Ibby went upstairs to her old room. She hadn't been up here in two years, not since she'd moved out to go to college. Her record player was still sitting on the dresser, an album still in it. There had always been a funny smell to the room. Doll called it "that old house smell" that lingered no matter how much she tried to disguise it with Pine-Sol or room fresheners.

Ibby went into the turret room, where all the dolls Fannie had given her were sitting on the bed, leaning against the wall, staring back at her with unblinking eyes. There were seven of them, one for each birthday up until she started college. Ibby couldn't imagine what Queenie wanted with the dolls. Maybe she was just feeling sentimental about Fannie this morning and wanted something else to remember her by.

When Ibby got to the Trouts' home, Birdelia was waiting for her on the porch. She ushered Ibby inside with a sleepy half-smile. Crow was having coffee at a small dinette table.

"Morning, Miss Ibby," he said wearily as he got up to greet her.

Ibby motioned for him to sit back down. "How is everybody?"

"All tuckered out," he said. "But in one piece. That's what counts."

"Look, Miss Ibby." Birdelia pointed at something on a table next to Fannie's old television that had found a home near the far wall. "You like it?"

Ibby let out a small laugh when she realized she was looking at the bust of Fannie, adorned with a felt fedora and Mardi Gras beads.

Doll came toward them, dressed in a pair of slacks and a sleeveless green turtleneck. "Don't tell Mama. She ain't noticed."

"Not yet, but she gonna soon enough," Birdelia chuckled.

"Mama's back in her room lying down. She still a little worn out from yesterday."

"I can come back," Ibby offered.

"No, no. She has something she wants to say." Doll motioned for Ibby to follow her. When they got to the back of the house, Doll stuck her head in the door. "Mama, Miss Ibby's here."

Queenie waved Ibby inside. "Come over here, baby. Please excuse me for not getting up."

The room smelled of lilac and mothballs. Queenie was still in her nightgown, her gray hair hanging loosely around her neck. Ibby cautiously sat on the edge of the bed, holding the doll that she'd asked her to bring.

"I remember that first time you came to visit Miss Fannie. You were a shy little thing. Had that Captain Kangaroo haircut, just like your grandmother. Remember?"

"Of course I remember. I was terrified," Ibby said. "Mama had convinced me that Fannie was a witch."

"Fannie was many things, but a witch wasn't one of them," Queenie chuckled. Then she grew serious. "Speaking of your mama. Listen, child, I know your mama passed a few years ago. I'm sorry."

"Doll told you?"

"Sure she did. Miss Fannie knew, too. Mr. Rainold told her not too long after you found out. But Miss Fannie, she never said nothing on account you told Doll not to say anything. Maybe that's why she never told you."

"Told me what?"

"About all them birthday dolls, baby. Didn't you ever wonder why she kept giving you dolls for your birthday?"

"Well, yeah, I thought it was odd, but after I got to know Fannie, it didn't seem so strange anymore."

"Believe she stopped giving you them dolls when you turned eighteen. There was a reason for that."

"I don't understand," Ibby said.

"Miss Fannie wanted to make sure them dolls were kept in a safe place, up in that little attic room of yours, until the right time come."

She shook her head. "She hoped you'd live in that house after she was gone, you know." A pained look came across her face.

Ibby put her hand on Queenie's shoulder. "What's wrong? Are you worried that if I don't move back into the house, you won't have a job?"

Queenie crinkled up her forehead. "Oh, no, Miss Ibby. That ain't it at all. My back's just aching a little. I'm old. Maybe it's time for me to retire. Been working in that house for close to fifty years, you know."

"Are you worried about the money if you retire?"

"Oh, no, baby. It ain't about money. Miss Fannie, she took real good care of us. She took care of you, too, in her own way."

"'In her own way'—that's a good way of putting it."

Queenie shook her head. "No, baby, you don't understand. After your daddy passed, Miss Fannie was afraid Miss Vidrine might have plans to move into the house and take over. That was one thing she swore she'd never let happen. So the day you arrived, she came up with a plan to make sure your mama wouldn't get her hands on any of your inheritance." Queenie opened the drawer to her bedside table and pulled out a pair of scissors. "Now, hand me that doll."

She lifted up the doll's dress, put the sharp end of the scissors into the fabric, and jerked down until the doll split open.

Ibby gasped. "What are you doing?"

"Where you think all your grandmother's money disappear to?" She pushed her hand inside the doll and began to pull out wads of cash. "She hid everything in here, up until you turned of age. That way no one could take it away from you."

Ibby's mouth fell open. "They always did have an odd smell about them. It was the money!"

"We held our breath all those years, afraid you gone figure it out, but after a while, when you quit paying attention to them dolls, we didn't worry about it no more. So like I said, Miss Fannie done took real good care of you."

"Who came up with the idea of making dolls?"

"Miss Fannie never did trust banks. You know that. She hid most of her money in the walls, or in boxes in her closet, or anywhere else she could think of. She knew Doll could sew something right pretty for you. So she had her make them dolls."

"How much is there?"

"My recollection? Pert near a hundred thousand dollars each doll," Queenie said. "And that don't even count the jewelry and stock certificates she got tucked in here." She pulled an envelope from the doll and handed it to Ibby. "Miss Fannie invested in the oil business early on. Believe those stock certificates for Esso worth a fortune."

"I want you to keep some of it." Ibby pushed the pile of money her way. "It's only fair."

Queenie pushed it back. "That's your inheritance, Miss Ibby. We done just fine by Miss Fannie. Bought us this house. Gave Crow that car. Doll's been talking about opening her own dress shop for years— she even got a spot picked out over on St. Claude Avenue. Miss Fannie gave her the money to do that a long time ago, she just never got around to it. And Birdelia, she's in college. First one in the Trout family to earn a college degree! Imagine that! And T-Bone? He's off doing what he always wanted to do, playing music all over the world. No, Miss Ibby. We don't need that money."

Ibby wiped a tear from her cheek.

"No need for tears, Miss Ibby. But there is one more thing. Miss Fannie made me swear not to tell you as long as she was alive. Well, she ain't here no more, God bless her soul, and it's about time you knew the truth. Remember the night you found us in that hole in the front yard looking for them bones?"

"Of course I do. You told me the story of Muddy."

Queenie squeezed her hand. "That weren't the end of the story, baby." Queenie went on. "You remember how I told you Miss Fannie locked herself in her room after Mr. Norwood fell into the river? I came to the house every day after that, talked to her through the bedroom door, left meals for her. And every day I'd come back to find the empty tray outside her door. This went on for a long time, baby. Months. Until one day I heard screams coming from Miss Fannie's room. The neighbors, they probably thought she was just having one of her spells. But I could tell this was different."

❦❧❦

The first thing Queenie smelled when she opened the back door was the metallic scent of blood. She rushed down the hall to Fannie's bedroom door and banged on it. When there was no answer, Queenie tried the handle. To her surprise, it was unlocked. When she opened the door, she found Fannie in bed, lying on her back. Even with the sheets pulled up, there was no missing that big belly.

"Lawd, Miss Fannie. Why you never say nothing?"

When Queenie threw the covers back, she found Fannie covered in blood. She suspected the reason Fannie was in so much pain was that the baby was breech. She knew she needed to do something quickly or she was going to lose both Fannie and the baby. She hurried to the bathroom, grabbed some towels, and soaked a washcloth in some warm water.

When she came back into the room, she placed the folded washcloth on Fannie's forehead. "Here, Miss Fannie. Hold this on your forehead. Make you feel better."

Fannie grabbed it and threw it onto the floor.

"Listen to me, Miss Fannie. I'm gone have to turn this baby before it'll come out. Understand?"

Queenie had her hand on Fannie's stomach, feeling for the head. When she found it, she nudged the baby around by pressing on Fannie's stomach on either side of her belly. Fannie let out another scream. She was sweating profusely.

"Give me some time, Lawd," Queenie said. "Give me some time."

After twenty minutes or so, Queenie felt she had the baby turned. She wiped Fannie's forehead and spoke to her gently. "Now Miss Fannie, when I say so, you got to push down hard. We gone get this baby out. Okay now, push."

Fannie's face scrunched up in the worst grimace Queenie had ever seen on a human being.

"That's it, Miss Fannie. One more like that, think we gone have a baby. One more push now. Give it all you got."

This time when Fannie bore down, the baby came sliding out and let out a wail.

"I got it, Miss Fannie. Oh, she a beautiful baby girl. The most beautiful baby girl I ever seen."

Fannie fell back onto the pillows.

Queenie rushed to the bathroom. After she cleaned the baby up, she wrapped the child in a towel and set the baby on her knees. She had never seen a child with eyes like that, one brown and one a bluish gray.

"Let me see her!" Fannie called out.

Queenie fretted. *How I gone tell her? What I'm gone do?*

"Queenie, is something wrong with the baby?"

"No, Miss Fannie. Just gone clean her up a little." Queenie was stalling, trying to figure out what to say.

When Queenie looked into those eyes of that baby, she knew what she had to do. She swaddled the baby and brought it over to Fannie, who held it in the crook of her arm.

"Miss Fannie, she a beautiful little girl. Looks just like a little king cake baby, with perfect little arms and legs, just a little china doll." Queenie stroked the baby's face with the back of her finger. She was afraid of what Miss Fannie might do now that she had seen the baby.

Fannie closed her eyes.

"Now, I know what you're thinking, Miss Fannie. You thinking you can't keep no colored baby. But I have an idea. Just listen to what I have to say. Just listen."

Fannie put her arm over her face. Queenie had no idea what Fannie was thinking. All she knew was she had to save this baby.

Queenie began to talk, not knowing if Fannie was even listening. "Miss Fannie, this is what I'm gone do. I'm gone take this child and raise her like my own. Take her home and say she mine. Folks, they won't know the difference. I'm so fat, no one ever knows when I'm with child until my babies show up anyway. Be the same for this child. Miss Fannie, I always wanted a baby girl. Now I got one. This way I can bring her around every day. You can watch her grow up. What you say, Miss Fannie?"

Fannie was lying there, staring at the ceiling. She was so still, Queenie was afraid she might have up and died from the shock of it all.

Fannie looked at Queenie. "You would do that?" It came out just above a whisper.

"Sure, Miss Fannie. It'll work out just fine for both of us that way."

"What about Crow?"

"Don't you worry none about Crow. He's gone be tickled to have a baby girl. You'll see."

Fannie stared at Queenie for a good five minutes. "So, what are you going to name her?"

A huge sense of relief passed over Queenie when she heard that. She picked up the baby and bounced her up and down in her arms. "Well, think I'll name her Viola, after my mama."

"Viola," Fannie said, managing a smile. "That's a nice name."

"But look at that pudgy little face. Just like a little doll. Think I'm gone call her Dollbaby. What you think, Miss Fannie?"

Chapter Forty-Two

Doll had been listening by the door. There it was, the secret of her life, all out in the open. Doll had never heard her mother tell the story like this. In fact, this was probably the first time the whole story had ever been told. Doll smiled to herself. *Mama never told me I had a pudgy face.*

It was like the knife she'd had in her back all these years was gone, tossed away.

There was no remorse. No fear. Only a sense of relief.

Doll felt for the letter in her pocket, the one Mr. Rainold had given to her after the funeral. She pulled it out and examined the writing on the envelope. It was addressed to Viola Trout and was written with a fountain pen in swirly letters, smudged on one side, where Fannie had let her finger slide across the wet ink. It was Fannie's handwriting, no doubt. Doll ran her finger over the letters, trying to imagine Fannie writing her name on it. She hadn't had the gumption to open it. She wasn't sure she wanted to know what was inside.

Doll slipped her finger under the flap and took out the letter. Her hands were trembling as she read it.

My dear daughter:
There, I just said in writing what I wish I'd had the courage to say to you a long time ago. What I have to tell

you will never make up for all the lost years, all the times
I wish I could have held you in my arms to tell you how
much I love you. Not that it would have mattered. You
likely never would have let me. And why should you?
Queenie loved you so much. She was about the best
mother a child could have. But I loved you just the same.
I can only hope that in your heart, you've kept a small
place for me.

What I want you to know is that I'm proud of you,
proud as any mother could be. I know how it must
have hurt you making those beautiful dolls for my
granddaughter, Ibby. I know you thought there
should have been one for Birdelia. After all, she's my
granddaughter too. I wasn't so shallow not to realize
that. So that first year, back in 1964, when you made
that first doll, I opened up a safe-deposit box at the bank
in your name. In it, you will find your inheritance. Do
with it what you want. Open up that dress shop you always
talked about. And remember me every once in a while.

All my love,
Fannie

Doll turned the envelope upside down. A small key fell into her
hand.

For the first time, Doll realized that Queenie had been right. She'd
been living in a fool's garden all these years. No one had kept her in
this house against her will.

Doll whispered, "Of course I loved you back, Miss Fannie. Why
you think I stayed?"

Doll put the letter back into her pocket and wiped her eyes once
more before leaning on the doorjamb. She was waiting to hear Miss
Ibby's reaction to her mother's story.

❧❀❧

"Why'd you do it?" Ibby asked.

Queenie shook her head. "At the time, I didn't see no other way. The way I looked at it, I got the daughter I always wanted. Miss Fannie, she got to watch Doll grow up. I did it for all of us."

"I wish Fannie had told me."

"She wanted to, baby. I could see it in her eyes. But she thought if you knew, you might never come back. She didn't think you'd understand."

"Did my father know?" Ibby asked.

"No, baby. No one knew except Miss Fannie . . . and Crow."

"Does Doll know?"

Doll held her breath, waiting to hear her mother's answer.

Queenie tightened her face. "Sure she do, but I regret the day I ever told her. Miss Fannie and I sat her down, when she were about twelve years old. After we told her, I saw how it pained her to know. It was one thing for Miss Fannie and me to share the secret. But Lawd, I never took into account that the burden of the truth would end up on Doll's shoulders after we told her. It was awful to watch, knowing I had put her in that position. At the time, I thought she was lucky to have two mamas that loved her. I realize now that my decision to keep her may have been a cruel one. I hope she doesn't hate me for it." Queenie pointed a finger at Ibby. "And I know deep down she must have loved Miss Fannie, too, 'cause why else would she want that bust? Who else would want such an ugly thing? Ain't that right, Doll?"

Doll got up and sheepishly opened the door.

"How long you been out there?" Queenie asked.

"Long enough," Doll said.

"Come on over here." Queenie held out her arms.

Doll gave her mother a hug and sat on the bed.

"How much you hear?" Queenie asked.

"All of it," she said in a low voice.

"You okay?" Queenie asked.

"Why didn't you ever tell me the story, the way you just told it to Miss Ibby?" Doll asked. "It may have helped me understand."

"'Cause, baby. I didn't think you wanted to talk about it. I thought you hated me for what I did."

"No, Mama. I loved you for it. It were a mighty brave thing to do." Doll took her mother's hand. "Remember the day Miss Ibby first came to the house and you told me I was a seeker? Someone who was looking for something I was never gone find? Mama, you were wrong, 'cause I did find it." She squeezed her mother's hand. "What I was looking for was right here all along. I love you, Mama."

"I love you, too, baby," Queenie said.

"Before I forget, Miss Ibby, I got something else for you." Doll took Fannie's pearls from her pocket. "Miss Fannie gave these to me the morning she left."

Ibby took them from Doll. "I thought they were lost."

"I think you should have them," Doll said.

Ibby handed them back. "No, Doll. She gave them to you. She wanted her daughter to have them."

"Miss Ibby's right, Doll. Put them on," Queenie said.

Ibby helped fasten the pearls around Doll's neck.

"How I look?" Doll asked.

"You look grand," Ibby said.

"You see, Miss Ibby, we always have been your family. And we always gone be your family, whether you like it or not." Queenie leaned over and nudged Doll. "So, what you want Miss Ibby to call you? Auntie? Taunt? Tee-tee Viola? Mamou?"

Doll waved her hand in the air, in just the same way Fannie used to. "No, Mama. Dollbaby will do just fine."

Chapter Forty-Three

After Ibby left Queenie's house, she went for a drive out by Lake Pontchartrain and parked near the spot where Fannie's car had plunged over the seawall a few days earlier. She put down the top of her Volkswagen Beetle and rested her head on the back of the seat, enjoying the clear day as pelicans dipped down in the lake, searching for fish fluttering in schools near the surface of the dark, glassy water. A small airplane flew by overhead, leaving a thin trail of smoke across the sky. It was hard to believe that Fannie had been doing the same thing just a few days ago, right here, in this same spot.

She reached into her pocket and took out the photograph of Fannie, the one she'd taken when the tree came crashing through the front window and pinned her on the sofa like a caged animal. In the picture, Queenie was standing behind Fannie, pointing at her and making a face. Fannie was grimacing with her arms folded across her chest. It made Ibby laugh every time she looked at it.

She held the photo up in the air in a sort of tribute to Fannie and thought back to the day she'd met her. At first, she didn't quite know what to make of her, but in the end, Fannie had proven to be like a majestic ship moored eternally to the same spot—unsinkable, unmoving, and totally misunderstood. Ibby had come to grips with the woman who was her grandmother, and with the two other women in that house on Prytania Street who irrevocably shaped and nurtured Fannie past the ghosts she left behind. If Ibby had known then what she knew now, perhaps things could have been different, but as Queenie would tell her, that's just the way it was, and just the way it should be.

Doll had told her that you can't choose the day or time when you will fully bloom. It happens on its own time, when you least expect it. Like today, when Ibby had thought she was alone in the world. Then Queenie told her the story of Dollbaby.

A breeze from the lake caused the photo to slip from her fingers. A pelican swooped down and caught it in its bill, looking back briefly before gliding out over the lake. Fannie had once remarked that Norwood had gone out with the pelicans. In a way, it seemed fitting that Fannie had, too, and that they were now together for eternity.

Ibby looked out into the lake and thought about something else Fannie used to say.

It went something like this.

Whenever there's a loss, there's bound to be a gain somewhere else. You just have to know where to look for it.

And she knew, at least this time, Fannie had been right.